ALSO BY BONNIE STANARD

Kedzie, Saint Helena Island Slave

Master of Westfall Plantation

SONNY

COLD SLAVE CRADLE

Slave property was such a token of aristocracy and riches that many persons made presents of little slaves to favorite children, godchildren, grandchildren, to newborns, and in rare instances the unborn were devised to the unborn. —*Slave Trading in the Old South by Frederic Bancroft*

BONNIE STANARD

FAIRVIEW PUBLISHING
2013

COPYRIGHT 2013 BONNIE STANARD

All rights reserved.
No part of this publication may be reproduced or transmitted in
any form or by any means, electronic or mechanical,
including photocopy, recording, or any information storage and retrieval
system, without permission in writing from the author.

Book cover and interior design produced by
STANARD DESIGN PARTNERS
of Cincinnati, Ohio
www.stanarddesign.com

ISBN - 978-0-9860019-3-2
Library of Congress Control Number: 2013941328

PUBLISHED BY FAIRVIEW PUBLISHING

FOR

Ginny Padgett

ACKNOWLEDGEMENTS

It would be hard to overstate the influence of my family and friends on whatever I accomplish. From my teachers at Pelion School I came to realize that knowledge enlightens a person to possibilities. The older I get, the more I think those possibilities are infinite, and only by studying what is already known can we begin to imagine them.

I was born to the conflicts of the Southern character. My mother, who grew up in a self-sufficient farm family with passionate but nondenominational religious beliefs, had no prejudices regarding ethnic groups. The lot of them begrudged authority, and the women were unconventional. My father, from a strong Baptist family with a residual loyalty to the Confederacy, was a poor man's Tilmon Goodwyn. He believed in keeping the black man, as well as women, "in their place." He, as well as my mother, was fiercely attached to us children.

My parents' attitudes are reflected in me and my siblings. Perhaps because of our differences, my Rawls family provides an ongoing dichotomy about what it means to be Southern. My surviving brothers and sister, Danny, David, and Nila, never cease to interest and sometimes amaze me.

Little did I know in February 1971 when I married Douglas Stanard that I had undertaken an adventure that would transform me, and by that I mean bring about an upgrade. I can't imagine the person I'd be today without Doug's influence, but I seriously doubt I'd be publishing *Sonny, Cold Slave Cradle*.

I have discovered that life is full of miracles, so much so that we fail to notice them. Three obvious miracles came to me in the form of Jason, Matthew, and Davis Stanard. Could I have written the story of *Sonny* had I not known the kind of love a parent has for a child?

My primary source of information about the Southern slave's way of life was the narratives recorded by the Federal Writers Project in 1937-38. These memories of former slaves are available on the internet at http://memory.loc.gov/ammem/snhtml/snhome.html. Various published collections of these narratives, too numerous to mention here, have provided background for this novel.

Several books that I kept on hand and frequently consulted are: John Vlach's *Back of the Big House*; Charles Joyner's *Down by the Riverside*; Frederic Bancroft's *Slave Trading in the Old South*; Theodore Rosengarten's *Tombee, Portrait of a Cotton Planter*; Eugene Genovese's *Roll, Jordan, Roll*; and Willie Lee Rose's *A Documentary History of Slavery in North America*. Information about recipes and cooking came in large measure from *The Carolina Housewife* by Sarah Rutledge.

I am indebted to my editor Stephen Bauer of Hollow Tree Literary Services. He has saved me from many a muddle. Stanard Design Partners of Cincinnati, Ohio has managed to make my story more appealing with their professional cover and lay-out design. My thanks to Diane Land for proofreading and to members of the Columbia II chapter of the SC Writers Workshop for their helpful critiques.

The map on the following two pages shows the south-most coastline of South Carolina and the location of St. Helena Island. The Island appears at the seam between the pages below St. Helena Sound. Going westward from the island, you'll find Beaufort, marked with a star. The map locates it on Port Royal Island but it was considered the mainland by the slaves. Because of the many islands surrounding St. Helena, a slave would need a boat to get to the mainland. That is to say, escape was not just perilous, but virtually impossible.

Charleston and the Charleston Harbor appear at the upper right of the map. As you can tell, travel from the island to Charleston by land involved crossing numerous waterways going inland before a coach could turn north toward the city. In 1857-58, few if any bridges existed, and travelers depended on ferries. The railroad constructed about this time connected Charleston and Savannah, bypassing Beaufort.

Today St. Helena Island retains much of its natural beauty. Descendants of slaves, who make up most of the inhabitants, celebrate their Gullah heritage. There are few reminders of the island's slave history. Of the numerous plantations that once flourished there, few houses remain, the most prominent being Coffin Point Plantation; Seaside Plantation (Edgar Fripp); and Tombee. None of these is open to the public. There are no obvious traces of what was once the town of St. Helenaville.

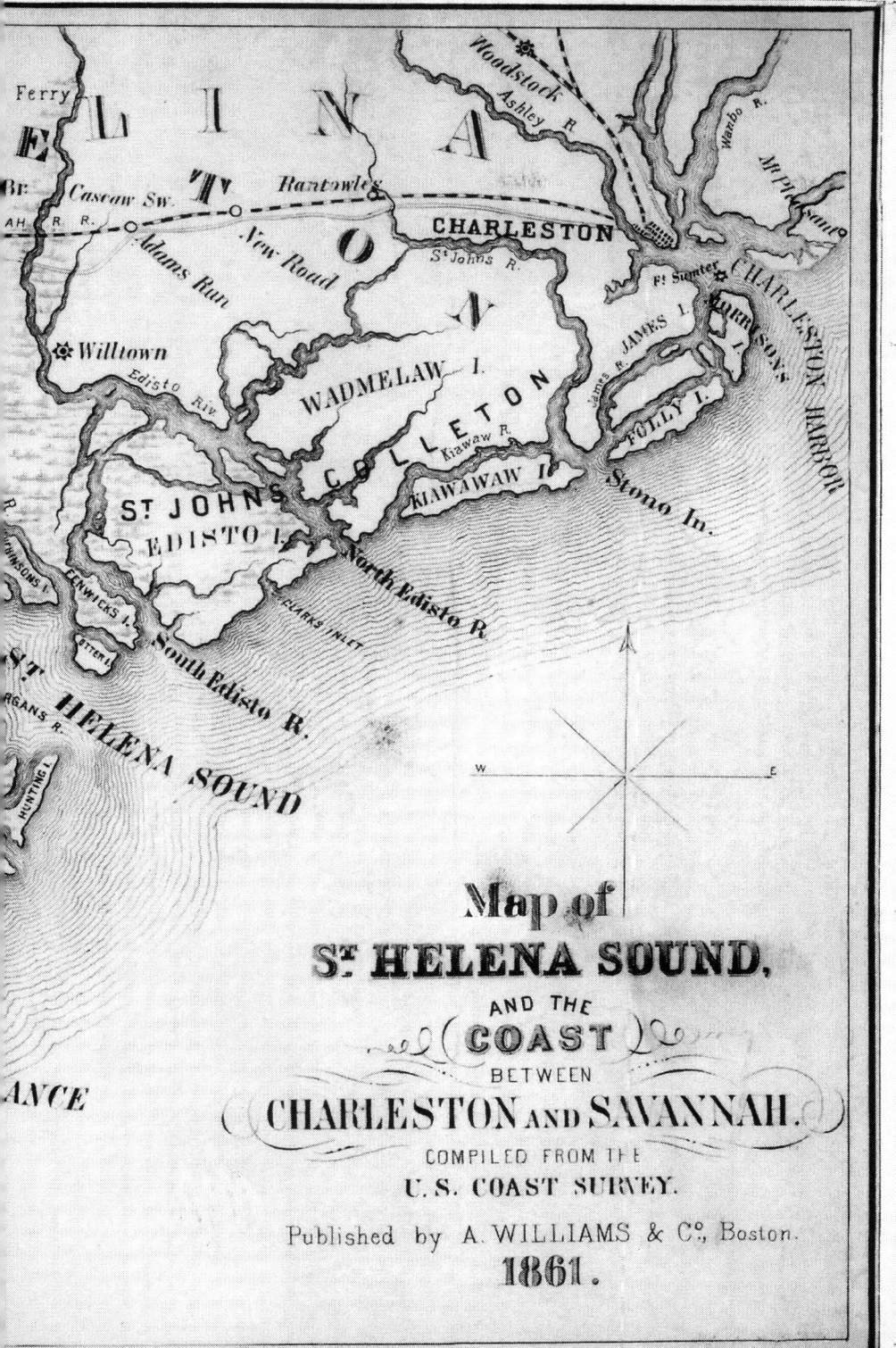

TABLE OF CONTENTS

SONNY, COLD SLAVE CRADLE

PART I	A SORROWFUL WOMAN WILL BEAR A BOY-CHILD	15
PART II	POOR MILK FOR A SUCKLING BABY	132
PART III	AN ODDS-ON PAPPY	206
PART IV	A QUALITY CARRIAGE TO DEAD GONE	262

PART I
A SORROWFUL WOMAN WILL BEAR A BOY-CHILD

CHAPTER 1

PIANO AWAITS A BIRTH

AUGUST 1857

Wink needed Iverson's help. When he couldn't wait any longer he hustled over to the quarters where Lovey's screaming curses had turned to regular wails. Hardly a person was about the street except the children, who sat wide-eyed on the ground near the sick house until Flurry shooed them away.

"You seen Iverson?" Wink said to Flurry, who suckled the babies.

"He be in wid Mammy Livy and Lovey." Flurry herded the younguns toward the chillun house. Mammy Livy usually tended the babies and children too young to work in the fields, but she had her hands full. A shriek blistered the air. The older children paused and turned toward them.

"Go on, you chillun!" Flurry shouted.

"Lovey's baby coming head foremost?" said Wink.

"Eh! Eh! Baig'um fuh sump'n'!" came from the cabin. Lovey's yowl turned African though she spoke better white talk than most anybody in the quarters.

"Not coming a-tall and she been working on it since daylight."

Wink knew. Anybody with ears knew. The children whispered and skittered or froze, depending on how loud Lovey cried. The hands had taken their dinner in silence and had left for the field mumbling in sympathy. "Ki! Hebby cumplain." "Wus'den'ebbuh." "Tummuch fuh tittuh."

"Go in there and tell Iverson we got to unload Massuh's piano," said Wink.

"Tell him yourself. I'se wore out wid her birthing," said Flurry.

"Iffen you is wore out, I reckon by now Lovey is half dead," said Wink.

"Dat's where she wants to be, by all accounts," said Flurry. She picked up a fearful little boy who was crying. Another one chimed in. "Shhhhh! Now don't carry on. Dis yelling business is going to stop any time now." But the children only added to the noise.

Wink dreaded the thought of entering the room with Lovey. He paused at the door, which was open to the sun's warmth, and stuck his head inside. "Iverson! You in here?"

"Dishyuh ebbuhlastin' hu't!...Ooommunpt!" Lovey's moan was working up to a climax.

Iverson came to the door and handed Wink an empty water bucket. "Git some water."

Wink argued. "We got to get Missy's piano unloaded! Massuh be here directly." He held the bucket. The smell of blood was making him sick.

"Iffen this baby don't come directly, won't be no baby." Iverson's fear showed in his eyes.

"Let your mammy handle it. She been catching babies ever since I was borned." On the rare occasion when Wink had kept the master waiting, he had spent enough time in the field digging grass afterwards to convince him that nothing, not even birthing, should cause a delay.

"Mammy needs help. Lovey done scared half to death and as weak as a kitten."

A stabbing moan drew Iverson back into the room. As Wink followed him, he saw that Lovey was lying down, a bad sign, for mostly women sat between two chairs to birth babies. An iron pot, along with a kettle, sat in the fire and put off steam, adding heat to the room. Mammy was sweating. Iverson wiped his shiny face.

"Mammy, tell Iverson you can take charge of this here birthing," Wink said above the wailing.

"Dis girl is bleeding too much." A pile of wet and bloodstained bedclothes was piled in the corner. Lovey had bled the month before, when she'd used a fire poker to try to get rid of the baby.

Mamba said she drank up her supply of turpentine a couple of weeks ago for the same reason. And yesterday, Anner claimed Lovey had jumped out of a tree, though Limbo said Mooey had pushed her.

Mammy Livy poured what water remained in the kettle into a pan and cleaned the blood off Lovey's saddle parts. Wink should have turned his head, but he couldn't help but stare at Lovey's trembling body. "Give dat girl some brandy."

Blood trickled from Lovey's mouth where she'd bitten her tongue. When Mammy tried to put a stick wrapped in cloth between her teeth, she screamed. Iverson said, "Lovey, just squeeze down on dis baby. He'll come on out."

Lovey gave forth a gasping hysterical cry. Wink went to the well for water, went to the kitchen for brandy, and took a dram himself. When he returned, he filled the kettle and handed Mammy the brandy. Lovey's cry was growing weaker. "Ummmmph! Jedus gimme mussy!"

Somehow Mammy had both hands inside Lovey's cooch. "Push down," she said to Iverson, who had his hands on Lovey's girth. Wink couldn't stand the sound of her choking and panting.

He wandered the street, hoping to catch a field hand not in the field. Farley, the black overseer, crossed to the white people's well, drew a bucket of water, and drank. He could get away with that while the master and his family lived in the village, but they'd be moving back to Westfall as soon as the crickets stopped chirping of a night.

Wink hailed Farley. "I needs the key to the big house."

"What for?"

"The massuh sent Missy's piano."

"He moving back?" said Farley, whose high and mighty tone slipped to one of disbelief. The master had never returned his family to the swampy lands of the plantation while the heat still made the marshes fume with the dangerous vapors that brought on summer fevers.

"Nah. Dis be a new piano. Reckon Missy be needing finer music," Wink said. Moving day would come soon enough if it waited another month. Hauling the household goods from the village to Westfall was a back-breaking job that usually took a couple of days.

"Finer music?" Farley grumbled. "She be needing more'n dat piano." He marched off to his cabin and returned with the key.

"I needs help hauling the piano in the house," said Wink.

"Git Iverson. I got hands to tend to." As Farley stalked off, he said over his shoulder, "And don't put dat key on my porch. Put it in my hand when you finish."

Wink turned back to the quarters to wait for Iverson.

Mooey walked by, a kid goat in her arms, which she petted with obvious affection. She was so skinny a stranger might mistake her for a shirttail girl in spite of the banyan she wore. Wink still thought of her as a little girl chasing chickens in the back lot.

Some people suspected Mooey had been caught by a haint. Flurry said a hag had a hold of Mooey's tongue, and that's why she could only make noises like a forsaken calf. In particular, people got worried when Mooey hurled out sounds in the middle of the night that set the dogs to bawling. On temperate nights when the moon was full, she'd stay in a tree until Auntie Nell hunted her down. When people in the cabins saw a light bouncing around the woods, they whispered, "Dat be a haint keeping company wid Mooey," and closed their doors and shutters.

Mooey ignored people when they spoke to her, which offended white folks and aggravated Farley and got her into a heap of trouble. The slaves faulted witchcraft, and the whites said she was simpleminded. But Wink had discovered she couldn't hear good.

But whatever her shortcomings with people, Mooey communicated well with animals. She kept her kid goat in her cabin. Children were scared to touch her, for there was no telling what kind of creatures she kept in her clothes. For a while she had a pet squirrel. Then she stored a frog in her pocket.

When Wink found out about her frog, he hit on a game of chance, a race between her frog and his, his being any frog he could capture. In the back lot, he and Mooey put the two frogs in the center of a circle drawn in the sand, and Wink took bets from the hands on which frog would reach the line first. So many frogs began to show up in his cabin he quit the matches and tried to show Mooey he didn't want any more frogs, but it took a while.

One time the overseer got riled because Mooey ate some of the watermelon she was supposed to feed the hogs. Wink ate too, but because of Mooey's condition, he never had to worry about her snitching on him. The longer Farley had shoved her and shouted, the deeper she dug her fist into her apron pocket. This infuriated him. "What you got in dat pocket?" But Mooey just shuffled her feet and twisted her fist. He yanked her hand out of her pocket and with it came a small snake that slithered up his arm. Scared the overseer so bad he peed in his pants. That could have been the reason he told the others that Mooey put the snake in her mouth and ate it. But Wink knew better. Mooey gave snakes to the hogs to eat.

She liked to give treats to the horses as well. Of a night as everybody settled down, Mooey occasionally came to the stables. For a while she tried to give the horses worms and lizards. Wink showed her that they liked tender young corn cobs, but Mooey chewed on the best cobs and didn't leave much for the horse.

Because of her noises and behavior, some people were afraid of her; of those who weren't, some mistreated her or cursed her when she didn't act natural. But Wink never ran her from the stables. That she was mute seemed less believable to the slaves than that she was possessed of a hoodoo spirit.

She lived with Auntie Nell, who treated her like a daughter and prepared her food. Though Mooey kept mostly to herself, when misfortune occurred, blame often drifted in her direction, and sooner or later somebody would accuse her of witchcraft. That Auntie Nell was widely respected as an elder went a long way in protecting Mooey.

In the distance, Lovey's whimpers sounded like she was fighting for breath. Then, a sudden silence. When Wink returned to the sick house, Iverson handed him an empty bucket. "Git some more water."

On a cot was a bloody, slimy infant boy. Mammy was smacking him on the back. Wink shot an indignant spit of tobacco at a nearby chicken and went to the well. By the time he got back, the baby was crying. Lovey was choking in sobs. Iverson was washing his hands.

"Come on!" Wink grabbed his elbow and ushered him toward the front yard where the wagon waited at the portico.

Iverson wiped his face with his rag.

"Lovey had a hard time of it," said Wink. As they crossed the yard, a procession of ducks honked and flapped out of their path.

"It was worser than usual. She come on wid pains so fast we didn't have time to find a rusty ax till it done got bad."

A rusty ax under the cot hadn't much helped Wink's former wife when she was having Louisa, but he didn't challenge Iverson. "Her baby look to be a sound little feller?" He adjusted the boards he had fixed as a ramp to the back of the wagon.

"Anybody come through what he come through gots to be strong. Onliest trouble, he be a yellow baby."

"Dat so? Reckon that be what caused Lovey to act up," said Wink. Lovey had been a house servant, but when she got in the family way, the master sent her from the big house back to field work.

Wink climbed into the flatbed with the piano. The two of them pushed and shoved and worked the upright down the ramp. In getting it up the long range of steps, Wink relied on Iverson's muscles, for he was among the strongest slaves on the plantation. Once it was on the portico, the two of them sat on the steps and rested.

"Your mammy better at catching babies than Doctor Drayton," Wink said.

"Yessuh. But she be bout wore out."

"Is you her oldest youngun?" Wink had an interest in Mammy Livy because of her first husband. He had been sold off the plantation when Mammy didn't come with any children. After he left, Iverson was born, the son of another man. Whatever brothers and sisters he had were no longer at Westfall.

"I'se the oldest, but Mammy was old when she had me. Musta been thirty or more." He waved his rag at gnats in his face. "There was five of us lived long enough to git out of shirttails."

Because Iverson sighed heavily, Wink didn't ask any more questions. He stood up and slapped the piano. "Let's finish dis business," he said.

CHAPTER 2

THE FOAL

SEPTEMBER 1857

 Mooey perched in the bullbay tree, a huge evergreen growing in front of the big house, and watched. Her eyes recorded pictures that became memories, which she used to understand happenings. The stableman and several other hands hauled a shiny cabinet with carved doors from the wagon parked in the yard to the portico. Among the things already on the portico were shiny wood pieces of household goods including a bureau, washstand, and carved elbow chairs. When everything had been unloaded, the stableman turned the wagon around the bullbay, and the hands, except for one who stayed behind, ran and climbed into the back as they headed down the carriageway.

 Mooey waited. The boy left tending the household goods sat on the steps for a while before lying on the floor. Rarely did field hands approach the big house. As a girl, she had been forced off the porch and switched. In spite of that, Mooey climbed down and sneaked up the steps. The boy was asleep.

 Several crates of goods rested with the furniture. She dug into one and pulled out a silver teapot, tray, and goblets. In another, she admired scarfs with colorful threads sewn to look like flowers, ribbons, and leaves. An ache to own a thing of such beauty overtook her. She nudged through the many cloths and removed the smallest one decorated with a picture of a vine with grapes stitched in colors of green, blue, and yellow. She stuffed it into her apron pocket.

With the palm of her hand, she stroked the smooth grain of the furniture without snagging as much as one splinter. She sat in one of the chairs, delighted by the cushioned seat. The boy stirred. When he turned, he rolled so near the edge of the porch he awoke and caught himself. Mooey slipped quickly down the steps and ran.

In the back yard, the woman who ruled over the cow lot, pig sty, and chicken coop grabbed her arm and led her to the barn where they filled a bucket with ear corn. They toted it to the field fenced in for the hogs. Mooey followed the Lot Boss and did whatever she did. As they crossed the field, her feet trailed the woman as they stepped over earthen mounds and pits where the hogs had rooted up what was left of the yams. The sandy soil warmed Mooey's feet and filled the spaces between her toes. If she happened upon a yam or a piece of one, she saved it for Auntie.

Wind sweeping across the open land carried scents that made Mooey aware of hog muck, horses, dry straw, the ocean. She had seen the ocean but once, an adventure that remained clear to her. Her mother had been alive then. If she gave herself over to the pictures in her head, she could see her mother's eyes and the continuous concern in them. Until the afternoon when her eyes closed for good. An afternoon like many others when the heat invaded her body. Mooey guarded herself from pictures of her mother's sweats and the terrible shivers, so powerful they jolted her off the cot. Her mother no longer able to work the field or cook supper.

When the Lot Boss stuck corn under the nose of a brood sow and led it to the smaller pen, Mooey did the same thing. Separated from the other hogs, the sows were able to eat extra rations without being disturbed. Mooey had learned that a shove from the Lot Boss meant she had somehow messed up. On those occasions, she watched her more closely in order to do the same thing she did in the same way.

Every day more household goods arrived at the big house in the stableman's wagon. He and several helpers hauled the many tables, sideboards, candleholders, crates and boxes to the portico and from there into the house. At night, Mooey sneaked up the steps and gazed in the dark windows. The rooms she had known all summer as empty were turning into colorful places with things worth looking at.

As soon as the stableman and his crew returned the pots, pans, and kitchen goods, the cook returned and moved into her quarter, a room built onto the kitchen house. The kitchen door, which had been closed and locked most of the summer, was opened, and it stayed open except at night. The cook scrubbed the room and built a fire, one that burned continuously. Once again, the smell of beef roast and hog bacon drifted about the yard and reminded Mooey that she wanted something better than ash cake to eat.

When the master's carriage rolled into the yard, Mooey knew the white missus and her children had returned. With them installed in the big house, it was no longer safe for Mooey to peek in the windows or sit on the portico. No sooner had they unloaded their trunks than the two boys chased each other under the steps. They lassoed the dogs and threw pebbles at the guinea hens. As evening came on, the missus and daughter sat on the portico. With them so nearby, Mooey didn't feel like resting in the bullbay tree. Even if the leaves were sizable and thick enough to hide a bear, Mooey could smell the white people.

One morning, as Mooey headed to the cow lot, she was distracted by an unusual sensation. A slight itch, like a fuzzy worm crawling on her skin. She had learned to pay attention to spirits, those things that in some way tweaked her bodily and more often than not gave her warnings. She believed they lived in trees, the sky, the ground, or just the air itself. The sky spirit impressed Mooey as the strongest by virture of its harsh flashes that told of coming rain. As she diverted from her path, the crawling sensation got stronger the nearer she came to the stables.

She stuck her head inside and tiptoed into the passage between the stalls. Even the ground spirit began to signal her feet. At the largest stall, she paused and slowly pulled open the gate. Inside lay a mare surging with breath. The leg and hoof of a foal poked from its rear end. The stableman looked up with worried eyes, which worried Mooey, for he was a person she could amuse with the least effort. He handed her an empty bucket and motioned her to the well.

When she came back with water, he washed out a bloody rag and wrapped it around the poked out leg. The mare's breathing wafted steady streams of air over Mooey. When the mare's belly shuddered, the stableman pulled on the leg.

While Mooey watched, too engrossed to notice the ground spirit's warning, a thud came to the back of her head. The Lot Boss shoved her toward the outside gate and kept shoving until Mooey was in the cow lot. One of the milkers stood with a full bucket, which Mooey took. With it, she headed to the kitchen.

When the buckets of milk had all been carried there, she hurried back to the stables. A newborn foal lay on the hay. When she stroked its fuzzy hair, it gave her a look fresh as first light of morning. So flat lay the baby's hair on the bulging ribs its every breath appeared enormous. Mooey snuggled its nose and rubbed its ears. It swayed back and forth and jerked its legs together as if trying to get up.

The stableman brought the mother from a nearby stall, but at the gate, the mare pulled back on the lines and had to be coaxed inside with a handful of oats.

The foal's dewy eyes strained toward its mother and held its face up as if expecting an affectionate nudge. Instead, the mare stamped the floor and bit the foal's nose, bringing blood. Mooey rose to her knees and slapped the mare's muzzle as the foal laid its head on the hay.

The mother reared on her hind legs. Mooey flinched. The size and heft of a horse had never looked so mighty, so high, so close. She cowered over the foal, expecting the hoofs to crush both of them. The stableman yanked on the halter lines hard enough to draw the horse aside, and when the mare came down, her forefeet trampled the floor beside Mooey and the foal.

Though the mother horse deserved no kindly treatment, the stableman rubbed her neck as he led her out. When he returned, he shooed Mooey from the stall.

She reluctantly left the foal, for it needed a mother's care. Mooey knew about that, for her own mother had chased away children who had hurt her as a child. Once when several boys had forced dirt down Mooey's throat, tears came to her mother's eyes. After she had cleaned Mooey up, they went to the cabin of one of the boys. Her mother raised revolution with the grown-ups and hit the urchin with a stick and drove him down the street. That had put an end to the dirt in her mouth.

Because the stableman took kindly to Mooey, she sensed that he would look after the foal and protect it from the mother.

In the kitchen she helped the cook strain the fresh milk into clean crocks after which she toted them to the springhouse. The path, narrowed by the summer's growth of myrtle and yaupon bushes, swished against her banyan.

Her footsteps hastened when a picture darted into her head of the foal, miserably alone and frightened without its mother. Mooey still missed her mother, especially when her brother was around. He had been as mean as anybody when they were growing up. Once he and his friends had tied Mooey to a tree and left her there during a rainstorm. When her mother found out, she had run after them with a fire poker. Her brother had hid for a couple of days. When he finally came home, she gave him a switching.

After her mother died, Mooey learned how to run fast and climb higher in a tree than any of the boys. If she saw mischief in the eyes of her companions, it was the way she escaped.

Mooey hurried back to the stable. The foal jerked about helplessly trying to gain its feet. She scratched its ears and back. She tugged at the soft yellow hoofs, finding them mushy to the touch. The legs wrestled nervously. The stableman came to the stall, watched the foal's clumsy-footed efforts, and propped up the hind legs. Mooey held up the forelegs, but as soon as they relaxed, the foal collapsed.

The stableman pointed and motioned with urgency, and it didn't take Mooey a minute to figure out she needed to slip away. She cut behind the stables and circled to the nearby barnyard. The Lot Boss slammed the feed bucket into Mooey's arms, turned her toward the barn, and gave her a shove. Mooey couldn't picture what she was supposed to do. The bucket meant food, but was it for the chickens? The hogs? The ducks? The cows?

At the barn, she wandered until she came upon the corn bin where she dug for feed and came up with about a handful, hardly enough to cover the bottom of the bucket. The stableman had showed her how to funnel dried kernels into the grinder and turn the crank to make cracked corn. He had rescued Mooey at times when the Lot Boss swatted her, which had happened regularly when she first started to work with the animals.

When she had enough feed in her bucket, she noticed several chickens clucking about the barn. They followed her trail of cracked corn to the chicken yard. The foal's situation bothered her so much she dumped the entire contents of the bucket into a single feeder, but as she headed toward the stables, the big white master, who had power over all the people and buildings, rode into the yard. He and the stableman went inside the horse barn. Mooey didn't dare enter while the master was around.

The cows were bristling about the lot, which showed Mooey that she was supposed to take them into the pasture. It was a task she usually enjoyed on sunny days, not only for the clarity of the heavens but for the smell of pine, cedar, and grasses. Sunlight showered the pastureland and dazzled the leaves. She led the bossiest cow into the same area as the previous day and used the same stake to tether her.

By the time she returned to the barns, the stableman was dragging the foal on the ground. Mooey watched, her heart pounding. He hoisted the body into the back of the wagon and climbed on the seat. Before he could snap the lines on the horse, she scrambled into the back and sat with the baby horse. It didn't move and she understood why when she saw the blood on the hair of its head.

Mooey had noticed that trees didn't have blood but animals and people did. And it looked the same for everybody, though she could hardly figure how such a dark thick liquid could be in a person with white skin. The negros drained the blood from animals they ate and used it to make broths and puddings. When she first bled into her bloomers, she worried that her spirit was quitting her body. The terror passed when Auntie showed her rags and girdled her with them. Eventually, a long-ago picture of her mother washing bloody rags and drying them by the fire came to her, and she realized her mother had bled.

The foal's death caused tears to stream onto her cheeks. She had trusted the stableman to protect the baby horse and instead he had ended its innocent life, and to what purpose? Then she remembered the animal's failed attempts to stand. But that wasn't the animal's fault. It had tried with all its heart and then some more.

The stableman drove them to the public road before he turned and looked at the back of the wagon. The sympathy in his eyes puzzled her. If he felt sorry for the foal, why had he killed it? Her opinion of him changed. Despite his good humor, he had muddy water for body spirit instead of blood. They traveled some distance before he pulled the horse to a stop.

Mooey hated the way his shoulders slumped. Whatever his misery, he deserved no sympathy. He tugged the body off the wagon, and as he dragged it into the thick undergrowth beside the road, Mooey followed. He halted and dropped the corpse at the foot of an ancient cedar tree, rotted in the trunk. After a pause, he headed back to the wagon.

When Mooey comprehended that he wasn't going to bury the foal, she chased after him, for in her mind was the picture of the buzzards pecking at the foal's skin. She grabbed a handful of his shirt and motioned shoveling the ground to make a hole.

He shrugged, shook his head, and stepped up to the wagon seat.

Mooey ran and stood in front of the horse and seized its halter.

The stableman came down off the wagon, grabbed her up, and threw her over his shoulder. Mooey twisted and tried to squirm from his grip, but his fingers held her all the tighter. As soon as he dumped her into the wagon, she clambered out. He waved her back toward the wagon.

She motioned in the direction where he'd left the body and pointed her finger at him. He had no right to take the foal's life without giving it a better chance. She wanted him to know that the foal had as much right to respect, even if dead, as any other being. Mooey squatted and beat her hands on her head. He picked her up again and sat with her on the tailgate with his arm wrapped around her until she calmed down.

Tidal waves of the stableman's breath rolled over Mooey with a strong smell of tobacco. She sat still until his arm relaxed. He stepped to the ground and went after his hat, which she had knocked off. With it in his hand, he stood at the edge of the woods and looked in the direction of the cedar tree as if he might go back and bury the foal. But he didn't move. Mooey looked into the woods.

The horse shifted nervously. The stableman hustled back to the wagon, putting on his hat.

Mooey worried. Perhaps the foal's spirit had beckoned him. She jumped down and ran into the woods toward the baby horse. Just as she saw the coarse black bristles and the blood-smeared snout of the wild boar chewing on the foal's neck, the animal saw her. From behind her, the stableman grabbed her arm and jerked her so hard she stumbled. They scrambled toward the wagon, the boar chasing them.

The stableman lashed the horse, which darted forward so abruptly Mooey hit the wagon bed hard. The boar roared into the rear wheel and knocked them sideways. She grabbed the side rail to keep from tumbling out the back. The wagon shuddered and rolled with a bump as the horse galloped forward.

Their escape left Mooey feeling sad, a lonely sadness. When they arrived back at the carriage house, the stableman motioned her to follow him, but she wouldn't. If he hadn't killed the foal, she would have been excited by his attention. She trudged toward the quarters, brooding over the picture in her head of the ferocious hog with its snout grubbing into the body of the poor baby foal.

CHAPTER 3

FISHING

SEPTEMBER 1857

In the heat of the afternoon, after the hands had returned to the field to pick cotton, Wink hitched up the flatbed wagon. He'd been tasked with porting Master Goodwyn's mended bateau to the creek where Goodwyn and Jervy, the neighboring master, were going fishing. Several weeks earlier, he'd used coal tar to patch the bottom of the boat, which was just stable enough for two fishermen and himself. With the tar well-dried, he had touched up the paint, mostly gray with a blue stripe.

With Iverson's help, Wink hoisted the master's bateau onto the flatbed wagon. He climbed up to the wagon seat and, with Iverson beside him, flailed the straps and called, "Giddiup, girl! Let's trot!" They passed water oaks and pitch pines. The grate of the wheels into grit was broken by the brisk clop-clop of the horse's hoofs and an occasional jangle of the harness rings.

The horse swished its tail at flies. Wink gave it a slap with the line to urge a faster gait. Iverson shifted on his seat. "They sell Bibles in the village?"

That Iverson would ask about wares didn't surprise Wink, for he occasionally traded in St. Helenaville for the slaves. However, a book was about as legal as a pistol. "What you want wid a Bible?"

Iverson gazed ahead where the shaded wagon-track road burrowed through a tunnel of aged live oaks. Sunlight sprinkled here and yon through the leaves. "The Bible has miracles."

"When you learn to read?" Wink pushed back his leather hat to scratch his forehead, which, because of a receding hairline, extended to the height of his head.

"I heard tell of a man over in Walterboro what took a Bible wid him fishing. He got into the worst kind of storm and his boat turned over and he held on to his Bible. They say the water washed him up on the shore."

Wink spat tobacco juice over the side. "I seen books on the main, but not at Salina's store." Wink spoke quietly even though the only other listeners were gnats, dragonflies, beetles and yellow jackets. It was so still the trees seemed to be napping.

The mere fact that Iverson would ask such a question showed he wasn't one of the Massuh's guineas like some people thought. Because he was the best field hand on the plantation, people resented him. But Iverson had a dignity Wink respected, even if he didn't follow the man's religion. "You got specie?" The horse reared as buzzards flapped up from a dead fox in the road. Wink's callused palms and forefingers tugged on the lines.

"I got money." Iverson dug into his pocket and produced several coins. "How much is this?"

Wink gave him a sideways glance, as if Iverson was some kind of thief. "Where you git that?"

Iverson reared back and looked at him. "Massuh done paid me good for the wagon I made his boy. And I got a goat coming on. Going to sell it too."

Wink looked at the money. "That be about six bits."

"Enough to buy a Bible?"

"More'n enough." Wink spat again. "Why don't you git a free one? Ask Preacher Chaffee."

"I don't want hisn."

Wink slapped the horse into a canter. "One Bible's good as another, ain't it?"

"I want a nigger Bible."

"What's the difference?"

"Don't take no second sight to know Reverend Chaffee preaches white religion."

"What makes you think he ain't speaking from the Bible?"

"When he says, 'Slaves, obey your masters,' how you know it's in the Bible?"

"I don't pay no mind to the man."

"I can't sleep at night thinking God done took my younguns away from me and give them to Massuh Goodwyn."

"That what Reverend Chaffee says?"

"Might as well. What's I supposed to do iffen Massuh sells off my boy to some trader? I supposed to let my boy go? Like it be the right thing to do?" Iverson took a breath. "That be Reverend Chaffee's god."

"How you know Brother Milton reads the Bible?" Wink had more than one suspicion that the traveling black preacher made up his religion to suit the occasion, not unlike the white preacher.

"The man can sit in my cabin and read out chapter and verse on any page I ask. Iffen he can't read, he's got the whole book in his head."

Brother Milton was overdue for a visit to Westfall. Though a slave on the mainland, he made the trip as often as his master and Master Goodwyn allowed. The last time he'd come, so many slaves from nearby plantations visited that Iverson collected money to buy a shoat to barbecue. The shout lasted from Saturday until Sunday afternoon, and people right and left crossed over, but Wink never got the calling. After Brother Milton left, people acted happy, said things like "God struck me dead!" "My chains fell off."

"I ask you, if there ain't a heaven, what's colored folks got to look forward to?" An unfamiliar weariness entered Iverson's voice. Wink had heard that Iverson needed religion like Limbo needed whiskey.

At the landing, the master and Jervy sat on a board bench. Wink and Iverson quickly launched the boat, stocked with reels, rods, bait, and other gear. The two white men sat on either end of the boat, and Wink took the center bench as they cast off on the slow-moving tide.

Lazy shadows stretched across the creek. Where the sunlight slipped through bushes it illuminated swarms of gnats. Wink dipped the sharp-edged, flat paddle into the water, propelling the boat into the stream with hardly a ripple. On shore behind them, Iverson minded the horses and wagon.

Wink's spare shoulders strained as he tugged the paddle into the depths, urging the boat with the tide from Haigh Creek to its merger with the Cowen where the master wanted to fish.

Jervy sat on the bench and adjusted his pole from time to time. "Hank Johnson in Beaufort does it," he murmured.

"But a sterile nigra's not going to breed," said the master.

Wink got the gist of the conversation. The name "Hank Johnson" stuck inside his head like a knot. Wink didn't know the word sterile, but when he figured it out, his head thrummed. The master's particulars about breeding added another reason to worry. Wink tilted his better ear to the speaker.

"You only go to such extreme measures on the incorrigible ones. And you're probably better off not getting young from them." Jervy leaned over and cupped water in his hand. "More mud. It must've rained up Gibbs Island." Wink had noticed the mud the minute he saw the creek, but Jervy's talk had turned more than creek water muddy. That the man so easily passed judgment on who should and shouldn't bear young inflamed Wink's headache.

When Master Goodwyn pulled a wriggling fish into the boat, Wink worked the hook loose from the jaw with pliers, then trailed tin-nosed twine into the mouth and out the gills, and made a noose. He fanned gnats from his eyes and tossed the fish over the side, now secured by line to the boat, all the time listening to the white men, though he kept his face a mask of passive disinterest. He had heard of Jervy's procedure.

"Can you get as much work out of an altered nigra?" Master Goodwyn said. Wink glanced at his master as he tied a different lure on the line. Goodwyn had the shrewd eyes of a gambler who could win at poker with a pair of deuces.

"I made a mistake with the first one. Sent him to the fields the next day. We brought him in, but he bled to death."

Wink knew the negro Jervy spoke of. Though it had been two years, Wink remembered it like yesterday. The intelligence of such an injury committed against a slave had spread in Westfall's quarters and aroused talk of vengeance, but nothing came of it. The injustice of the man's death still weighed on Wink, like guilt, as if he hadn't lived up to his duty as a human being. The victim had been a high-spirited man, always talking about going back to Africa. He'd once sneaked into Westfall's stables when he tried to run away, and Wink let him hide overnight. Wink's head was going numb with talk of men like they were bulls or hogs.

Jervy carelessly shifted on the seat, and Wink moved to offset the rocking it created. The wind changed and with it came a chill that made him shiver.

"The only difference you'll notice is you don't get lip," said Jervy.

The masters' conversation so sickened Wink that he willfully thought of the only woman he'd ever liked better than his horses, thoughts that flooded his groin with desire. He'd hardly noticed that his attachment to Puddin had grown beyond mere fondness until the day when one of the field hands said his wick got wet looking at her. That started a fight, much to Wink's confusion, for he prided himself on having enough sense to stay out of scraps. His longing for Puddin took on a physicality that became urgent. He felt like giving her more loving than she'd tolerate.

When Jervy landed a bass, Wink strung the fish onto twine, his fingers steady in spite of his agitation. What little pleasure slaves found in life was basic and primarily physical. Times when he'd been on the mainland he'd promised himself he'd run, yet knowing in his heart he wouldn't leave—poor as it was, Westfall was his home. But this talk he was hearing changed things. He'd rather die in the woods than have a white man cut him.

Jervy's line snagged on a waterlogged root. Wink backpaddled until it freed up. He sacked Jervy's cooter and trailed it in the water and calmed himself by focusing on a raw shrimp he mashed onto Jervy's hook. What he wanted was to get away from these white men and their talk. He hardly heard their haggling over the terms of a hireling.

The flood tide reached its crest, and as it ebbed, a raw breeze came from behind and lapped under Wink's shirt. He dug the paddle so deep his hand went underwater as he drove the boat toward the stand of palmetto trees marking Caper's Creek Landing, where Iverson waited. Wink could survive mean horses, poor quarters, and scarce rations, but the master was not going to mess with his body parts. A powerful anger had lodged in his throat, and it had no place to go but down. A draft of whiskey went a long way in turning bad things into just things, but Wink had used up the supply he'd bought off a buckra in the village. The extra jar he'd saved for Limbo was still hidden in the stables, waiting for Limbo to come up with enough money. The way Wink felt, Limbo wasn't ever going to see his whiskey.

CHAPTER 4

MOOEY'S CABIN

AUGUST – SEPTEMBER 1857

As darkness descended on the cow lot, Mooey carried the last bucket of milk to the kitchen house. She had been toting milk long enough that she was able to picture exactly how many trips to the kitchen she made every night and every morning. The cows had given an additional bucket that afternoon, one more than on previous evenings. She suspected the crumple-horned cow. Mooey had given her a handful of cooked peas she had sneaked from Auntie's pot, not that this was something she had ever done before. Their pot went empty too soon too many times for Mooey to feed an animal. But the crumple-horned cow was her friend.

The cook, whose eyes took in Mooey and held her, placed a big crock on the table beside the bucket. Mooey nervously held a loosely woven cloth over the top while the cook poured a stream of milk through the cloth into the crock. If Mooey stretched the gauze too tight she could picture the milk spilling over the sides. Too much slack and she knew the milk puddled and the cloth sagged into the crock. When she made mistakes, a glance from the cook could bother Mooey as bad as a swat on the head, which was what she got often enough from the Lot Boss.

When the crocks had been filled, the cook hooked one to each end of a yoke and helped Mooey hoist it to her shoulders. She plodded along the path to the creek. Shadows of night emerged from the ground. Were her feet not sure of the path, she would have tripped on knotty roots. She sensed that ground spirits from deep in the earth were called to the surface by roots and became trees, flowers, shrubs, weeds, or briars, depending on whether the spirit was strong or weak, good or bad.

She tilted first one and then the other crock on to one of the watery shelves of the springhouse built in the creek. After the second crock had been secured, she returned to the kitchen.

The cook patted Mooey on the back and gave her a biscuit. Mooey felt the delight that arose in her throat and spread her lips in a smile. She pranced out the door with her prize. The glee that tickled her throat in rhythmic waves was how she'd first realized her power to make people notice her. However, the way they'd bent away from her, contorted their faces, or moved their lips, or thrashed with their hands had frightened her, and she had run to the woods, where she felt safe. There, she touched her lips and practiced moving them like other people, but no matter how much she exercised her mouth, people shook their heads and grimaced, and either stared at her or ignored her. With her fingers on her throat, she discovered she could make a wiggly movement down there, something so mysterious her head filled with images of wiggles, throats, and the movement of people's lips.

This wiggle was obviously connected to her lips, but she didn't know how, and it seemed unrelated to swallowing. Or taking breath. It served no obvious purpose. Mooey reasoned out the mysterious movement as a spirit dwelling in her throat. This spirit was like the wind. Sometimes it was quiet. Sometimes it just tickled her throat like a breeze. But it became powerful and stormy at sharp moments when she was either very happy or very sad, when people either excited her or hurt her. When so aroused, it wiggled in her throat and cast spells on people and made them behave in strange ways. At the same time, it was a helpful spirit, for most of the time it made people go away, which Mooey preferred, especially when somebody hurt her or when something bad happened.

On her way across the lot, she saw it was dark enough so she could go anywhere in the yard she wanted, even to the front of the big house where the white people lived. The master's dogs, a worry to those people unwilling to befriend them, rarely bothered Mooey. She had used food scraps to get acquainted with not just the pack leader but every dog until eventually they wagged their tails at her.

As she sneaked to the bullbay tree, she paused at the portico. A lamp light glowed inside the window. She didn't dare tiptoe up the steps and plop into one of the big white chairs with pillows. Nothing gave her more of a sense of importance than overlooking the yard from the height of a cushioned chair on the portico. Even the yard seemed at her command from such a landing.

As a child she had been hauled off the portico, but she went back anyway until she got a switching. At times she sat there of a night when everybody was asleep and felt uppity in spite of her head rag and threadbare banyan. She felt so smart she might just refuse to feed the hogs. Or gather eggs. Or bring in the cows. But when she came down the many steps to the yard, she didn't feel smart any more. Once she'd taken a chair cushion back to her shanty, but Auntie's horror at seeing it frightened Mooey and she returned it to the portico.

Auntie let Mooey know when she made mistakes. Because of her care and the food she made for their meals, Mooey had come to depend on her. For a while after her mother died, Mooey had lived with Mammy, who tended the babies and children while the mothers and fathers worked the fields. But Mammy couldn't make the children behave, and Mooey got into trouble every day for fighting. Things got better when she moved in with Auntie.

Mooey grabbed a bullbay limb and pulled herself up inside to a deeper dark where thick leaves creased the moonlight. The tree's low growing branches made it one of the easiest to climb. She collected as many leaves as fit into the hamper she made of her apron tail. Nobody would notice them missing, not even the black man she knew as Early because he arose first of a morning and roused the slaves to their work. He had power over the others and lashed them to keep them early with everything. His arms gesticulated, his steps shook the ground, the brim of his hat clouded his eyes. She avoided him.

As she entered the street at the quarters, her kid goat pranced toward her, straining the tether. Mooey untied the rawhide knot, and the kid bounded after her to her cabin. Upon pushing open the door, Mooey became so confused she turned around and ran out, dropping her leaves. She slowed to get her footing in the moon's pale shadows and made her way to a particular live oak that grew on the wooded side of the gardens where the slaves grew vegetables.

Trees helped Mooey figure things out or at least get over puzzlements. Of the numerous oaks about Westfall, not many of the big ones lent themselves to climbing. She knew every one that did. As she straddled a branch, she quieted the throat spirit, which shuddered nervously.

Though Auntie had been in the cabin when Mooey had entered, things weren't right. The place smelled like evil spirits had moved in. The water bucket had been moved from its wall shelf and replaced by a basket. On the extra cot sat a woman of such lovely looks Mooey identified her as "Lovey." She belonged in another cabin. Lately, she had birthed a baby, a matter of some interest to Mooey, who had a suspicion that women got babies from men. This woman held her chin so high she behaved like a white person, which Mooey admired in a distant way. At the same time, her way of acting gave Mooey to suspect she wasn't kind hearted. On the floor had been a big basket with a blanket that twitched.

Mooey's breath trembled. A sense of dread overtook her when she suspected she'd have to share the cabin with the woman. Even after people got to know Mooey, some of them had sharp feet or blunt hips or fists like snake bites. It usually meant pain.

Perhaps the woman Lovey had been a vision or a passing spirit, like the one that came to the moss of the live oaks in warm weather. That spirit was very old, but it could pinch a whelp on Mooey's skin that caused an infernal itch. It had undoubtedly got into her hair, for she had been feeling something like ants crawling on her scalp. The itch was about to drive her crazy.

A sudden stirring caused a magic downfall of leaves that blew over her like solid rain. She took out her fine linen scarf embroidered with grapes and wiped her runny nose. Lovey could have been visiting Auntie. Maybe by now she had returned to her shanty.

Upon climbing down, Mooey crouched and sneaked within view of her cabin door. The friendly kid goat dawdled nearby, cropping the tops off garden plants. Mooey pulled its mouth away from a leaf, for Auntie had become angry about its chewing in the garden.

Auntie came out of their cabin, stood in the light of the open door, and turned in all directions, her lips and mouth disturbing her face. Mooey, who yearned to be safe, leapt from where she squatted, picked up the kid goat, and ran to her Auntie.

In the candlelight of the cabin Lovey took aim at the kid as soon as they entered the room. With eyes alive with emotion, she pointed and spouted.

Mooey kept herself close to Auntie until she felt safe enough to perch on her own cot with the kid goat, which usually slept in their cabin. The orange peelings that scented the shucks in her tick did little to relieve the stinky new smell. Mooey sniffed in different directions until she became sure the basket was giving forth a reek like the hut in the woods where everybody went to dooky.

Lovey's gyrations grew so bold that Auntie stood before Mooey, making motions that meant the kid couldn't stay. Apparently the basket on the floor had something to do with Auntie's taking Lovey's side of the argument. When Auntie reached for the goat, Mooey kissed it goodbye and allowed her to take it back to its tether.

Lovey pushed aside several cups and put her vials and looking glass on the mantle like the place belonged to her. Hardly had Auntie returned when in came a woman who ignored them to talk to Lovey. The two gestured cheerily causing much disturbance, which so upset Mooey she refused the supper of ash cake and cabbage and climbed into her cot. She pulled her thin blanket over her head, peeked through a hole, and watched until the woman left and Lovey lay down on the cot.

After a time, a stillness settled into the very joints of the timbers. Mooey crept out of her cot and dragged the basket near the window. By the light of the moon she took a look inside. There lay a baby of perfect features, a little round head covered with woolly black hair, thick eyelashes, a little nub of a nose, an upper lip that pointed into his lower lip. He slept peacefully as if he didn't know his smell. She hardly dared to touch him for fear he'd change in some way. Her lips, near his nose, warmed in the glow of his sweet breath. She smiled at him. He was sunny even in sleep, and "Sunny" became the way she captured images of him. Such a little creature seemed to have a big spirit. With her hand on his chest she felt a calmness she had rarely known.

The following morning, Mooey arose and went for hot water to the big iron pot with the fire where she had to wait behind others for her turn. Back in the shanty, she and Auntie sat on their cots, drank herb tea, and ate ash cakes while Lovey slept. At one and the same time, Auntie and the other field hands started out of the quarters and toward their daily work. After they left, Lovey rushed out the door, leaving Sunny in the basket on the floor.

Mooey looked into the basket, expecting to see the peaceful little creature she'd seen the night before, but his mouth opened in a twitchy way, and his twisted face pained Mooey. She touched his neck and detected an angry throat spirit. She couldn't leave him alone in the cabin where the dogs or chickens might get at him, but she didn't know what to do. So she sat beside the basket and patted Sunny on the chest and stomach.

Eventually the woman with big breasts who suckled the babies came in the door with a whoosh. She made the air feel like a storm was coming up. From the woman's quirky head and bulgy lips Mooey came to understand that she, not Mooey, had charge of the baby. She pushed Mooey out the door.

In back of her many visual memories, Mooey saw the peacock. The image wouldn't go away until she figured out the peacock hadn't been fed in too long a time. Mooey headed for its pen. But a rush of cold air hit her in the face, and she changed direction and went directly to the cow lot. The Lot Boss stood by her stool, pail in one hand, and gestured at Mooey with such ferocity the cows awaiting milking stirred about the lot nervously.

A yellow fly, enfeebled by the colder nights, looped lazily around Mooey's head and landed on her arm. While she swatted it away, the Lot Boss, with a scrunched up face, motioned her toward the barn. Mooey's frets about the peacock being hungry scattered like dust in a wind when the woman stomped toward her. She ran for the barn, grabbed an armful of hay, and spread it in several troughs.

Across the lot, the gentle brown cow with crumpled horns looked on with eyes glossy with fear. Mooey felt protective toward her, for this cow left the lot last of a morning and entered behind the others of an evening. In an effort to soothe her, Mooey took her a handful of oats.

The Lot Boss lit into Mooey with another round of powerful gesturing.

Mooey returned to the barn loft and hauled out more hay, which she put in the troughs of the cows being milked. If the Lot Boss had more hair in her eyebrows, her forehead would disappear altogether. Naturally Mooey felt the weight of those eyebrows all morning.

At the end of the day, she finished hauling milk to the spring and returned to the cabin, eager to see the baby, but neither he nor the mother was there. After supper in came Lovey with the basket and three other young women. Mooey squeezed into her cot not only to rest but to avoid their company. Even after Auntie lay in her cot and pulled up her cloth, they frisked about the room, coming and going, drinking the brew Mooey knew to cause brutish doings, if not fights. Her Auntie raised up on her elbow at them, but they paid her no mind. What seemed like an eternity passed and the visitors left. Lovey blew out the candle and collapsed on her cot like a fallen log.

In the night, Mooey woke up scratching her head until her scalp bled. The itching tortured her in spite of the washing she had given her wool with lye soap. In her restlessness, she became aware of other movement in the room and slipped over to the basket where Sunny squirmed and kicked. She touched his face. His throat spirit spread to the little lips, which opened wide in shivers. He squirmed and kicked off his cover. As her finger trailed across his cheek, his lips latched on to it and sucked eagerly. She rubbed her cheek on his and kissed his forehead. When his little lips abandoned her finger and opened wide, Mooey felt the treadle of movement in his throat. He seemed to work so hard, his entire little body striving with great effort, his arms and legs jabbing to no avail.

Mooey felt his hunger in her stomach and, as she had seen Auntie do, dipped a small rag in molasses and touched it to his lips. His tongue and lips eagerly sucked the entire rag into his mouth. His face turned red. His breath went solid in his little chest. Mooey's terror drummed from her throat to her lips as the spirit spiraled out of her. Sunny struggled, his face turning black. Auntie raised up, took one look, and stuck her finger down his throat. When she pulled the rag out, Sunny's chest surged with breath.

Mooey cried because of her mistake, which had stopped his breath. She could hardly bear the vision that progressed forward to what would have happened without Auntie.

Through her tears, she saw Sunny alone in his basket, sucking on his fist. Lovey, who had hardly moved as her son had struggled to breathe, rolled over, made a face like she had a bellyache, and settled back down. Poor baby. Mooey picked him up and rocked him in her arms. Auntie looked on as if she didn't trust Sonny to Mooey's care. She showed Mooey the rag and shook her head, but it wasn't necessary. Mooey knew her mistake. After a time Auntie lay back in her cot.

As Mooey cuddled Sunny in her arms, he sucked on her finger. The big-breasted woman was needed, but Mooey was too flustered to go outside and fetch her. On a previous night, she'd found the woman in the cot with Mooey's brother, and he had hit her with a fire poker.

Mooey held Sunny close so she could feel his breathing. Such a pretty little baby, so at the mercy of people and many of them unkind. She wanted to make him bigger and stronger, but he was new and he had to live for a while to get past the danger of being small-sized and easily ignored, slighted, and considered worthless.

Because Sunny's bright smiles cheered Mooey, his foul smell bothered her less. While the others slept of a night, she picked up the sleeping baby and placed him in the cot beside her where she could hug and snuggle him. The woman with breasts, who was kindly but sharp, came to feed him. In the early morning before day, he yawned and stretched and woke Mooey. He twisted his little butt and kicked his feet. In the cot's warmth, she caressed his fingers and toes, his nose and ears. She loved his woolly hair and tiny fingernails. She kissed the bottoms of his feet. She put her cheek to his lips and felt his little puffs of breath. Before she knew it, he was sucking on her cheek.

Shadows flickered on the walls. Before Auntie aroused, Mooey placed Sunny back in the basket. It was time to get a light for the candle. Mooey stretched and reached for her linsey woolsey dress.

Mooey was hardly accustomed to Sunny and Lovey living in their cabin when Early arrived one morning with another slave, a familiar man who had the best-kept cabin in the quarters. In a gourd in his quarter grew the only ivy vine Mooey had ever seen. Because of it, he became "Ivy." The two men inspected one wall, pointed here and yon, and stirred up the dirt floor.

Mooey headed to the cow lot, but she could feel something like gnats flying inside her head, a feeling she associated with worrying. To settle herself she rubbed the neck of the crumple-horned cow. Then she was able to get to her tasks.

Mooey could usually tell dinnertime by the position of the sun in the sky, but on cloudy days, dinnertime was when the field hands came to the quarters. She was hungry before the stableman drove in a wagonload of hands. As she walked to the shanty, a heron flew over and squirted a dooky that fell and sheeted the hem of her banyan and her toes — it was either an evil spirit or a good spirit warning of evil. She rubbed sand on her dress to clean off the guano and dug her toes in the ground. She paused at her cabin door, wary of possible danger, and peeked inside. Several planks lay on the floor. The slave Ivy stooped over the frame of a cot he was building. Auntie gave her a worried look and went outside with the empty water bucket.

Ivy caused Mooey no fear for he was kindly to all creatures. He fed the kid goat extra nibbles. When he killed a setting marsh hen with a scythe while cutting marsh grass, he placed the eggs under a banty hen, which mothered the hatchlings. His children kept the babies for pets.

His wife, who worked in the fields with him, gave Mooey ash cake if she dallied about their door long enough. They were so kindly she visited in their shanty to enjoy its beauty when nobody was there.

Though their place was like everybody else's in size and shape, they had made it different, beginning at the door where gardenia bushes grew on either side of a doormat made of shucks. The door opened and shut without dragging the ground.

Inside, a rug of plaited hemp made the floor feel more like wood than packed dirt. Bright colored cloth covered the plank walls. The place usually smelled of bacon or peas. Occasionally Mooey helped herself to brined fish from a keg. Sometimes it was shrimp. Several grooved and polished chairs matched the table near a fireplace fitted out for cooking with iron rods of differing heights. From them hung more cooking pots than in other cabins.

A loft big enough for two cots had been added with a ladder to get up there. Hanging from the loft and draping to the floor was a burlap curtain that hid the two cots built under the loft. Mooey liked best of all the cots hidden behind the curtain, which was woven with colorful ribbons. On the walls were pictures, mostly of flowers, but there was one of a bearded white man looking at the sun.

Auntie returned with water. She and Ivy motioned to each other companionably. Several people stuck their heads inside, and the room filled with nods and waves. When Ivy left, their cabin had another cot. Mooey's throat worked itself into motion even as she tried to tone it down. Auntie stopped spooning up collards and sat on Mooey's cot and patted her back, but Mooey felt that the throat spirit was about to take over her entire body. She ran to her tree where she could calm the dreadful shivers affecting her.

The few strings of moss Mooey had left on the branches swayed lightly when a breeze, haunted with the smell of mud flats, lumbered by. Mooey felt better. She was hungry. She returned to the cabin and ate what Auntie gave her. The hands returned to the field, and Mooey headed for the chicken yard. There was no telling who she'd see in the new cot when she returned to the shanty at the end of the day.

With a basket in hand, Mooey gathered eggs. The dorking hen could be counted on to lay hers behind the tool shed. Mooey collected those first, for the dogs sometimes got to them before she did. She searched about the chicken yard where several hens laid their eggs under bushes. She picked up several banty hen eggs. They were so small the cook never asked about them and Mooey gave them to Auntie. Inside the coop she went from nest to nest, pictures of her cabin and the new cot trailing through her mind. Somebody else moving in. She'd have to give up another part of her place to a stranger.

After delivering the eggs to the kitchen, Mooey watched as the stableman drove the wagon into the back lot. As much as she now distrusted him, she missed his jocularity. What she needed was a cheerful greeting from somebody. As much as he deserved her rejection, she decided to put an end to it.

She sneaked to the barn on purpose to make herself known to him. He hauled bags from the wagon into the barn. She approached the dark bay horse hitched to the wagon. It raised its head and fluttered its lips. Mooey rubbed its nose. The horse tried to kiss her lips, but she turned a cheek.

Because the stableman took no notice of her, she climbed into the wagon while he unloaded a sack and hauled it into the barn. She rolled a heavy sack to the back gate. He returned, paused, and let fly brown spit that punctured the ground. That he could be so heartless and so genial mystified Mooey.

From the time she began to help with the livestock, he had amused himself and her with his trickery. On the first day she fed the milking cows, he had waved her over to the stables. After his considerable gestures only confounded her, he had closed her eyes and opened her mouth and insisted that she hold the pose. Eventually a sweet sugary ball had touched her tongue. The fresh flavor spread into her throat and nose and lingered until the candy melted.

His return to the plantation usually meant something good, and she had eagerly closed her eyes and opened her mouth until the time he put chew tobacco on her tongue. It had burned her mouth and brought tears to her eyes. She had spit it out to his great amusement.

When he finally noticed her, he leaned on the side of the wagon and beckoned her closer. A dimple creased his cheek giving him a mischievous look. His eyes gave over to merriment. He signaled her to shut her eyes.

Mooey approached cautiously, eyes wide open, and extended her palm. His lips spread into a jubilant smile as he pulled something from his pocket, which he concealed in his fist. His palms rubbed together as if he washed his hands. Mooey watched carefully, and though she couldn't see the favor, her mouth watered for a sweet. He extended his two fists for her to choose one. His eyes twinkled. His lips curled playfully, dimple beaming.

Mooey studied his fists. His look and gestures gave hints to first one and then the other. She could hardly stand the suspense as she fingered one. He opened an empty fist. Then he showed her the round red candy she hadn't guessed. He put it back into his pocket. As she sulked off the wagon, he motioned her to help with a bag, but she ignored him.

She kicked a dried poot and went after the cows. While driving them in, she felt in her apron pocket and found the candy. How did that get in there? She put it into her mouth. The sugary taste put her into a better mood.

After the milking tasks were done and the crocks stored in the springhouse, Mooey went by the bullbay and collected its sturdy leaves in her apron. When she entered her cabin, she gasped and dropped her leaves. The girl she loved like a sister sat on the new cot. Mooey regarded her as "Lacy," not only because of her fine qualtiy but because she had lace dresses. Lacy had been gone for so long she was almost grown up. A big smile. They hugged and carried on something awful, dancing around the room. After a spell, their cuddling turned into wrestling until Auntie made a stop-it face. After releasing Lacy, Mooey could hardly settle down enough to pick up her leaves. In her excitement, she accidentally pulled out one of the ribbons in her hair, which Auntie wove back into place.

After supper, Mooey plopped on her cot and studied her friend. She was wearing a fancy dress, made of fine material only white people wore, and it fit like a grown-up's. As Lacy sashayed out to get a light for the candle, Mooey pictured herself wearing the pretty blue dress.

With Auntie's help, Mooey had begun a panel for the window and was stringing together bullbay leaves using twine and a big wood needle. When she finished a row of leaves, she added it to what was already hanging. As the bottom grew longer, it kept people from looking inside when the shutters were open.

In the cordial way in which Lacy and Auntie acted toward each other, Mooey noticed Lacy had lost a certain gaiety. Her friend's more modest movements seemed to indicate a change, one that made Mooey lonely.

Lovey entered, carrying Sunny, followed by a couple of other women, and the room was astir with bad air until the visitors left. In the darkness, the baby's basket shuddered. Lacy rustled in her cot. Finally a calm descended, and the moonlight felt easy in the window.

Whether Lacy was the same person or had grown into a different one, Mooey believed the two of them would still be friends. When she decided that, she could relax, and baby Sunny's solemn sleep tempted Mooey to join him.

CHAPTER 5

SUNDAY AT THE QUARTERS

NOVEMBER 1857

By November when every field of cotton had been picked several times with several more times to go, mild days were giving way to wintery chills. Wink, unlike the field hands, worked every day of the week. Not only did he look after Westfall's horses, but he was at the master's call to run errands or drive, whether to the village or the main. Field hands could laze around on Sundays, but Wink had to find what rest he could.

On their day off, some hands slept but some kept busy about the quarters. Most women washed the family's clothes in the creek or in Iverson's iron wash pot. They cooked ash cakes, yams, and big pots of collards or cabbage, enough to last the greater part of the week. The men tended winter gardens, cut greens, and dug potatoes. They sawed wood and found kindling or went hunting or fishing.

Wink, who lived alone since his wife had been sold, grew no vegetables. In fact, he had no garden plot like most families. His cabin, a room connected to the stables by a wall, was removed from the other slaves. Most of them lived in a settlement of cabins built in two rows and separated by what they called the street. At the approach to the quarters was the overseer's house, a double-room structure built of planked boards. Wink only cooked when he couldn't cadge food from the kitchen house or the quarters. Most people willingly shared their family's food with him because he hauled manure from the stables to fertilize their vegetable plants.

Having no wife posed no problem with respect to washing clothes. He paid Mamba to do that.

Sundays, either Wink or the master drove the family to church, but on this particular day the master came to the stables and, as was his wont on occasion, curried Gideon and trimmed his mane before saddling up.

"Missus be going to church?" said Wink.

"No. No need for the carriage." Master Goodwyn flung himself in the saddle and rode away, saying he'd be at Riverben, Master Jervy's place. Wink had noticed the neighboring plantation house had added a new piazza of first class quality. He had a suspicion Master Goodwyn had noticed that Jervy's overhaul put Westfall's big house in the shade. It was unlikely that either owner noticed that the slave quarters of both places, by comparison to the manses, looked like hutches for animals.

Wink returned to his cabin and pushed the coals to the back of the fireplace to smolder, for it was still warm enough in the day to do without a fire. Come nightime, he'd stoke the embers to flames and warm up his place, for winter had rooted in the deep of night. He took a short nap and woke up to a mid-morning sun.

Before heading out the door, he felt in his pocket for the small pouch containing money due Limbo for the pelts Wink had sold in the village for him. The peddler had paid less than usual, and Wink wondered if Limbo would think he was being cheated. Most slaves wouldn't know the difference between a three-cent piece and a double eagle, but Limbo had been trading pelts long enough to know.

He was barely out the door when he met Anner, who looked after the master's children in the big house. He hoped she wasn't bringing a message requiring him. Lately she'd been delivering little more than her opinion, usually complaints about the master's no-manners boy. Everybody knew she had the easiest task on the plantation, but most anybody would take to the fields to avoid the company of the white boys.

"Wink, I got something for you." She held her hand in her apron pocket and smiled as if she knew a secret.

"Something to eat?"

"No, but you going to like it."

"Chew tobacco?"

"No." She projected her upper lip as if his guess disgusted her.

He closed the door behind him. "Yes, mam, Missis Anner, what you got in your pocket?" Wink liked to tease her; her serious nature begged for it. He strolled toward the quarters.

Anner accompanied him. "You starting to act like your mules. Don't call me missis no more." The white brocade kerchief she wore on her hair matched the whites of her eyes. The white shawl she pulled around her shoulders made the dark of her neck and face look all the blacker. "What you in a hurry for?" She stopped walking.

"Going hunting." He turned and faced her.

"I'm going to give this to Claude iffen you don't have no time to talk to me."

"I don't ask no odds of you, Anner." Whatever it was, Wink knew her favors weren't free.

"You just too busy for me, I see that right now!" She whipped her shawl to herself.

Oh, hell. Now he'd riled her, and there was no telling what she'd do. He leaned toward her. "Sweetie, I gots to get in after a rabbit or I be short on food supply. When you going to bring me some a that cake what falls on the massuh's floor?"

"He'd feed cake to the dogs before he'd give any to us," she said, a vexatious glaze to her black eyes.

"His dogs already eating bettern me." The stringy piece of dried beef Wink had eaten for breakfast had already deserted his stomach, and the sun was nowhere near the middle of the sky and eating time.

"You know I'd give you my ham and biscuit if I could." She moved closer to him.

Wink could only imagine the kind of good victuals she ate in the kitchen of the big house. "What I wants now is a ashcake. I reckon I'll see what I can find." He walked away, easy-like, hoping he wasn't leaving her in a pucker.

"I'm going to save what I got. I'm going to give it to you when you is in a better humor."

Wink strode the street, unusually noisy for a Sunday and stressed with a baby's cry. At the chillun house he poked his head in the open doorway. Mammy Livy stood at the table dipping clabber into a piggin.

On Sunday, with the hands at home, the children and babies stayed with their mother or parents. Only the one baby shrieked as he lay on the cot, his mouth and chin a-tremble, his fists clenched.

"What's wrong wid that baby?" Wink said above the noise.

"He's colicky. Bout to drive me crazy as a loon." Mammy sat in a chair and drank the clabber.

"Whose baby is it?"

"Lovey's," said Mammy. "And colicky wid good reason, I reckon."

Wink whistled in the baby's face. The shrieks paused, and when it looked like another cry was coming, Wink whistled again. This calmed the baby for a few minutes after which he launched another shriek. His body gave a violent lurch.

Wink had to get out of there before that baby put him bad out of heart.

He wandered in the quarters and peeked in saggy doors in case some fire was unattended. Flurry came out her door, carrying a basket of stinky baby napkins. Even if he could steal an ashcake from her, he wouldn't do it, for her children needed them.

Wink pushed open the door to Thor's cabin. "Git up, you lazy coots!" Nobody liked to sleep late better than Thor and Limbo, who lived together. Their cabin, except for the kettle in the dying fire and a well-worn table, had a grim and unused look. Greasy plank walls, wardrobe without doors, the smell of animal pelts. Dried spills matted their blankets. No rug in sight or kegs or tallow candles. A pot rested on the hearth away from the smoking embers. Four rickety chairs, used for card games, were pushed into the corners, one turned on its side.

Most shanties had provisions of a sort, kegs of molasses and vinegar, crocks of cornmeal, baskets of root vegetables. Most had iron pots about the fire or on swinging racks. Some shanties had baskets with rags, seashells, or dried herbs. Many a woman managed to steal or trade for pieces of crockery they kept on the mantelpiece or in cupboards. Some had wall pictures, tin buckets, jars, bottles, and such they bought from gypsies.

"Come on! I seen a rabbit practically in the street!" Wink urged Thor up.

He threw back Limbo's blanket and tucked the money pouch into his pocket. "This is what you got for the pelts." Wink said loud enough for Thor to hear in case Limbo was still asleep.

Thor pulled on his shoes and coat, sipped on a cup of tea, and the two of them headed to the woods. "Claude awake?" said Thor.

"Naw. Drink still working on him from last night," said Wink, who'd been unable to wake Claude.

"He be wore out from throwing bones so late," mumbled Thor.

Wink, who had lost over a dollar playing craps, was all the poorer for the hooch he had shared with the others, most especially Claude.

Thor, the only slave allowed to take out the master's rabbit hounds, was the son of a man owned by Morgan, who operated the ferry across the Beaufort River. As they departed the quarters, Claude shambled after them and called, "Hold up!" Limbo followed Claude. Under a ceiling of pines, oaks, and palmettos, the hunters trailed Thor who followed Peaches and Taz, the hounds. They checked their boxes, two of which had trapped rabbits.

They studied the sandy ground for tracks. Plentiful scat littered the trails, but they passed over piles that were white or crumbly, knowing they were old. When the scat looked like small brown berries, Wink picked one up and rolled it in his fingers, feeling for moisture. Thor pinched another in two and showed them the dark color to the core, which meant a recent dropping.

As they inched into the undergrowth of bushes and bare vines, the dogs dashed ahead, barking and yelping. Suddenly a rabbit bolted from a rotting stump, and the dogs gave chase. The hunters fanned out and ran over ditches, around bushes, and between trees, heedless of the rips in their clothes. Because rabbits ran in circles, the group split in opposite directions to form a ring.

The animal was fast on its feet, but quick to tire. When the dogs chased it into a hollow log, Wink covered one end and Thor the other. Before the rabbit could get a second wind, the men beat the log and shouted until it hopped out and Thor grabbed a hind leg.

They came in from hunting with four rabbits and delivered one, which was due the master, to the kitchen house. Claude took one. Wink and Limbo skinned and gutted the remaining two while Thor went inside and rekindled the fire. They brought in the cleaned carcasses, and Limbo eased onto his cot while Wink cut up the rabbits and added them to the iron pot on the fire. They threw in turnips and onions Gussie gave them.

Lovey arrived with carrots, which she scrubbed and added to the pot. Nobody objected, not that they would, for Thor had taken an interest in her, though some people avoided her like the measles. Since she'd moved back to the quarters, her attitude had changed. Once a high-flying person with a mellow laugh, her humor had a spiteful edge. She'd become bossy. That the baby turned out to be yellow started rumors and speculations, most of which held that the baby probably belonged to the master. Should that be the case, most people agreed that Lovey's future depended on Missus Goodwyn's sway over her husband.

There were others less convinced about the father. Some people disliked Lovey's biggity ways and said the baby was the offspring of loose embraces, likely a traveling peddler or gypsy.

Lovey tried sitting on one of the chairs, but when it wobbled, she sat on the side of Thor's cot. Limbo, lying on his, said to her, "Why don't you git that roommate of yours to a frolic sometime?"

"Auntie Nell don't do much dancing," said Lovey as the men chuckled.

"You knows I mean Kedzie."

"That gal's shore worth looking at," said Thor.

"Your sister come closer to getting anything out of Kedzie," Lovey said to Limbo. "Why don't you ask her?" Thor, lying behind her, brushed his hand over her back.

"Mooey's so dumb she can't shoo chickens." Limbo pulled a deck of cards out from under his bunk.

"She don't take no notice of Farley and gets away wid it. Ain't another soul on the place can do dat," said Thor, who climbed a ladder to the makeshift loft of pine slabs lying on cross beams.

"She's got dirt in her ears." Several of Limbo's cards flipped to the floor. "And iffen you look past the dirt, ain't nothing in her head but cotton."

"Hand me my pelts," said Thor, reaching down toward Lovey.

"I holds her in high opinion. She done scared off every black buck what tried to throw her." Lovey handed the pelts up to Thor.

As Thor laid them out on boards where other pelts were drying, Wink could only wonder why his friend hadn't sold his. "She's smart enough to make massuh think she's dumb," said Wink. Limbo treated his sister bad as white people treated negros. If Mooey had a mean bone in her body, she'd have rapped a fire poker over his head by now. Instead, when Limbo knocked her around, she climbed a tree.

"What you niggers talking bout? Mooey never cooked a ash cake in her life," said Limbo. "When Mammy was sick, who you think cooked for her? Washed her clothes? Shore as hell wasn't Mooey."

Thor climbed down and sat on his cot.

"Farley don't cook nor wash clothes. Dat make him stupid?" said Wink.

"He's got Flurry. Mooey don't have nobody." Limbo put down his cards and stood to warm at the fire.

"She's got Auntie Nell," said Lovey.

"And a good thing she do, cause she don't get no help from you," Wink said to Limbo.

Limbo carelessly shrugged his shoulder. "Lovey, iffen you gets Kedzie to a hoedown, I'll give you my deck of cards." Limbo stirred the stew.

"Kedzie gots a mind about her." Wink had noticed how she had grown up when he brought her back to Westfall from the village where she'd lived so long some people hardly remembered her. "And she be well favored, shore nuff."

"She'll find the misery in that." Lovey stood, took the stirring spoon from Limbo, and tasted the broth.

"What you mean?" Limbo said.

"She'll find out soon enough." Lovey went out the door.

While the stew cooked, Wink went to the stables to see to the horses. He had been working on Lad's habit of head flicking. He rode back and forth beside the pasture fence, talking all the while. "Come on, boy. One step, two step, do-si-do." He placed his flat palm on the horse's crest to call attention to the habit.

Anner waved at him from across the pasture and broke into a run toward him. Lad snorted and pulled up. Wink tightened the lines. When Anner came within earshot, he said in a firm but low voice, "Don't come running up to dis horse lessen you wants a hoof in the face."

Anner stopped in her tracks.

Wink backed Lad up, dismounted, fondled the horse's ears, and dropped the lines. He approached Anner, who hadn't moved. Her eyes were squeezed shut. In her hand was a calling card, which he took. "The horse be behind me. You can open your eyes," he said.

"A visitor come, and Missus says for you to fetch Massuh from Riverben."

"Yessum!" Wink said as if he took orders from her. He smiled in a mocking manner.

"When you knows me better, you won't think dat be so funny."

Wink laughed. "Yessum, Missis Anner! I be on my way directly!"

"You is provoking me a purpose!" She withdrew from her bosom a jar shaped like a barrel with staves and rings. "So I reckon I'll give this marmalade to Claude," she said.

Wink's eyes flashed. The sight of marmalade sweetened his tongue. "Honey, is I ever treated you mean?"

"You ain't been treating me like your honey, that's for certain." She extended the jar to him.

"Where you git dis pretty jar of sweets?" It might have enough marmalade for a week of ash cakes. Wink rubbed the paper label on the pot and wished he could read the words.

She smiled. "I been bad, but Billy don't notice." She turned back toward the big house.

Wink walked the jar to his cabin and hid it in a basket under groundnuts. It was too fancy to be an ordinary kitchen jar of marmalade.

When Wink remounted, Lad took off in a gallop as if he'd been waiting for a chance to stretch his legs. Whatever errand Wink ran, he rarely took a direct route. He went aside, around, and beyond, always watching for signs of possum, coon, deer, or runaways. The previous week he'd seen hazy smoke above treetops in an area he knew to be wooded. He suspected gypsies had hollowed out enough brush to make a clearing for a camp. At Riverben he discovered his master had ridden to the Sandmire Field.

On his way there, Wink took a trace that crossed a brook. Lad balked at crossing. The horse seemed worried by the backwash around a fallen tree. "That's just the water drawing breath." After a bit, Wink's sweet-talk turned to commands and Lad went through.

At Sandmire, Wink pulled up a short distance from where his master sat astride Gideon, talking with Master Jervy. When his master motioned Wink nearer with a tilt of his head, Wink delivered the card and returned to Westfall.

The longer the stew cooked, the meatier the smell and the more callers who came by Thor's cabin to check on it. Claude came in and sat on the hearth. He plucked strings and twisted screws on his banjo, putting his ear close to the higher and lower tones. As soon as he played a song, even more people just happened by. When the stew was done, Wink dished up as much as he could get into a bowl, for he knew there'd be no seconds. When he headed for his quarter, Thor followed.

If there was such a thing as family to Wink, it was Thor and Claude and Billy the butler, not one of whom was related to him. It had been over ten years since his mother died from a headache. Years before that, she had been sold to a rice planter up in

Georgetown. By the time Wink got the message that she was sick and made the trip to see her, she was so far gone she didn't answer him. People caring for her said it was a jinn. Said a conjurer told her to blow her nose to get rid of it. Said she blowed and blowed and a purple lizard came out, but she died anyway.

He and Thor ate their stew in silence. Wink held his bowl in one hand, scooped spoonfuls into his mouth, and spit out a bone now and then. One of the master's hound dogs sniffed the floor and cleaned up the bones. A wind stirred up and whiffled around the corners of the cabin.

Wink's dream of the previous night lingered like a hum he couldn't get out of his head. In it, he had been able to write a letter—the words he spoke came out of his mouth as solid spit and stuck to paper in lines just like real script. A person he knew in his dream but didn't upon waking took the letter and read it aloud, but the words were different, not at all what he had said.

Thor sat quietly and slurped at the side of his bowl. He and Limbo were known as grubbers, for they relied on the charity of others to get meals. Neither of them cooked anything unless somebody helped them.

Wink hadn't been tagged a grubber because he lived apart from the other slaves. Between the wild game he brought in and the rations he traded, he managed to eat most of the time. If he became desperate, he wheedled a meal from Gussie. Lately he had been calling on Puddin about meal time.

"You recollect Jervy's nigger what bled to death five or more years gone?" Wink hadn't been able to forget the conversation he'd overheard while the master was fishing. "I'se telling you, Massuh was talking about cutting us like horses!"

Thor wiped his nose with the back of his hand. "We oughta cut off his rocks," he said. "Me and you and Limbo. Next time he comes in the quarters. You hold him down and I'll slice them off."

Wink swallowed and said, "You won't slice off nothing wid Farley's bullet in your head."

"That shit-faced old tomcat! He try to put his hand on me, he's going to lose some breath. I'll go to hell before I take a cut."

*

A bald sun glared with frigid light. Wink pulled down his felt hat and tugged at his coat collar. Gusts of cold wind blew away what had been a temperate day. As he crossed the yard, he tucked in his chin and walked past Farley's house. Until Farley occupied it, the house had belonged to the white overseer, a man who had stolen hams from the smoke house and blamed it on the slaves. Claude had been whipped as well as a couple others. The smell of collard greens rushed from the open door as Flurry came out of it. She was the wet nurse, and she used her bosoms with pride, not only to suckle babies but to attract men.

"Flurry, one of your chilluns is sick." Wink had taken a bucket of clabber to the chillun house where the little girl lay on a cot while other children chased about in boisterous play.

"I been giving her lightwood tea."

"She needs a good scrubbing more'n tea," said Wink. Flurry's children had more boils, worms, dysentery, and fevers than any others, and Wink believed it was because Flurry didn't keep her children clean. They stank of urine and feces and wore their clothes until the cloth got stiff with dirt.

"What you know about tending chillun?" Flurry said.

Though she didn't have book learning, she knew people and how to inflict wounds with words. Wink walked on by. He didn't know about tending children because he didn't have any, and therein was an injury.

Once in the stables and at work, Wink clucked and called another horse from the pasture and looked into yet another mouth. He had noticed whole oats in stable muck, a sign that one of the horses wasn't chewing properly, possibly because of sharp teeth. He paused at the sound of a woman's cry, Anner crying, not loud, for her thin voice could produce only so much sound.

He walked through the stable's passage from the paddock to the yard side. In the distance at the whipping tree, Anner stood in her lowell shimmy, shriveled and angry, as Farley repeated, "Take it all off. Dat be the massuh's word."

"But I'm not no field hand!"

"I don't reckon he wants them pretty clothes messed up." Farley spit on a chicken pecking near his brogan.

Anner cast accusatory glances about the yard as if holding any onlooker accountable for her situation. With the hands back in the field, only Mammy Livy and Flurry and the children peeked from the corner of a cabin. Wink quickly withdrew under the shelter of the stable. With the gate latched, he kept out of Anner's sight, for she wouldn't forgive him for looking at her getting the whip.

Rarely was a house slave given a flogging. Wink could only wonder what Anner had done. Had she been caught stealing cake or biscuits? He wondered if he was a first-class turd for pestering her for food from the kitchen house.

Anner took off her shimmy, neatly folded it, and stacked it on top of her shoes and dress. She wrapped her arms across her bare breasts.

"Iffen you don't take off them drawers, I'se gonna." Farley snapped his whip against the whipping tree. As she stepped out of her drawers, he pushed her against the tree. She moaned as he tied her thin arms around the trunk. Wink could see even from that distance that Anner was trembling. In spite of the situation, the sight of her bare buttocks made him aware of how long it had been since he'd been with a woman. He suspicioned that she could be his for the taking, and if they had been in his cot at that minute, he'd have taken every inch of her.

The master arrived, and when he nodded, Farley stood back and flicked the lash on the flawless skin of Anner's back, skin so smooth Wink flinched at such uncalled-for injury. She bucked and shrieked. Wink winced. Another flash of the leather whip, and she hiccupped. "Pray, Massuh!" Her cries pained Wink. The whip whistled. Her body jerked into the bark of the tree before the leather sizzled on her skin. Red whelps oozed blood that splattered as Farley laid on another lick. If Wink could pray, he'd beg for the wherewithal to rescue her.

When several lashes came near her head, Master Goodwyn said, "Keep away from her face."

Wink despised the master's pathetic concern over her face. All the negros knew of his aversion to visible scars. It had hardly been a year since he'd sold a slave whose face had been cut in a fight. When Anner drooped to her knees, Farley splashed a bucket of salt water on her and she yelped.

"Tell Mamba to keep an eye on her," the master said as Farley hauled her over his shoulder and took her toward the sick house. By suppertime most of the slaves had heard about Anner's lashing, but nobody seemed to know what disservice she'd done.

After several days, no real reason for Anner's lashing came to light in spite of considerable speculation. Wink's conscience bothered him. He could only hope Anner hadn't been whipped for snitching the marmalade for him. He waited until dark to visit the sick house, built apart from the quarters and near a live oak with a branch that touched the roof. Auntie Nell, as one of the oldest slaves, often sat with the sick. The negros believed that people who had lived longer had tougher skin and were less likely to catch a disease should a fever turn into typhoid, cholera, or scarlet fever.

Anner lay on her stomach and faced Nitsy, her sister, who sat on a stool at the far side of the cot and talked to her. Wink slipped inside the door and warmed at the fire with Auntie Nell.

Nitsy said, "You gonna move back in the quarters?"

"I be cold as a wagon tire before I pick up a grubbing hoe." Anner carried on about how much she hated field work.

"Why'd Anner get the strop?" Wink said quietly to Auntie, who sat eating turnips from a bowl.

"I hear-say she be slacking off. Not doing her task," said Auntie.

Wink stared at the fire. What Auntie said lifted a load off his mind. He relaxed and listened to the lull of the voices.

"See where your uppity ways gots you." Nitsy pulled back the blanket to look at the scabs on Anner's welts.

"I ain't uppity. I just don't want to live wid no useless tom cat," Anner said.

The smell of cooked turnips made Wink hungry, and he was about to leave, but Anner had insulted Nitsy's man Claude. Wink, who liked Claude, leaned forward his good ear, for there was no telling what he might hear.

"Claude gots a roving eye. But leastways his eye be all that roves." Nitsy placed the blanket back on Anner's back.

"Den he got a eye on his whanger," said Anner.

Wink looked at Auntie Nell, who scooped broth from the bottom of her bowl. Obviously Claude needed defending, but Wink didn't speak up.

"I got eyes enough to see you is trifling wid me." Nitsy spoke so loudly Auntie Nell shushed them.

As Nitsy left in a huff, Anner said, "Who dat?" and turned her face to the fireplace.

Wink saw her swollen lip. "You going to stay in dat bed all winter?"

"I was wondering if you was ever going to show up."

"Farley done made hash outa your back." Wink walked as close as he wanted to get.

"I just about died and you don't show up for three days." Anner's eyes filled with tears.

"I done seen Auntie Nell been taking good care of you." As Wink said this, Auntie went out the door and he was alone with Anner. He touched her cheek. She was crying. Now he'd done messed up with her. Wink could hardly stand to see anybody cry. He kissed her cheek and nibbled her ear. "Honey, you going to feel better. Now, none of dat crying ..."

"I done got a double handful of trouble and you don't even send word."

"Here I is, Baby. Is this any way to treat me when I come to see you?"

Anner sniffled, turned, and sat up. She kissed Wink full mouth.

There could be no doubt that she was better. Wink could only respond in kind to her bodily command of him, but he didn't settle easily into her touch. An entanglement with Anner could only mean trouble. Besides, he had his eye on Puddin though she had not encouraged his attention.

Anner flinched at his hand on her back. "That no-account Billy!" she said. "He's a rip-jack."

"What did Billy do?"

"He's the reason I got in this mess."

"Billy?" Wink could hardly imagine Billy hurting a fly.

"He told the Massuh I wasn't doing my task. He brought this on me." Anner sighed. Her hand stole into his shirt. "I had plenty time to think about it and I'm going to fix his flint."

Wink considered himself obligated to console Anner, even if it meant unsanctified bodily contact. He felt like warning Billy but of what? Anner's conniving? That was nothing new. Billy dealt with it morning, noon, and night.

* * *

Mooey had daily tasks, whatever the day—tote milk, gather eggs, feed the stock, put out and bring in the cows. However, this was not true for everyone. A day arrived regularly when the hands were allowed to remain at the cabins rather than head out to the fields. Mooey wasn't allowed to stay with them, and she didn't understand why. On such days, the lively bustle in the quarters distracted her from her tasks, and she was likely to spill milk or forget to feed the ducks or guineas.

During one morning when the field hands slept late and lazed about the cabins, Mooey begrudged tending the chickens, hogs, and cows. At dinnertime, she quit looking for the hog that had gotten out of the pen. As she crossed the yard, she noticed Auntie washing clothes at the iron pot everybody used. Several other women stood about, waiting a turn.

That the cabin door leaned open wasn't unusual, for Auntie sometimes failed to completely close it. Nonetheless Mooey hesitated outside, for an itchy fear hummed into her head. Her confusion increased on peeking past the door. The only person inside was the big-breasted woman's daughter, who didn't belong there. Everything was wrong sided. Except for one tick draped on a chair near the hearth, the rest were missing from the cots. The one remaining blanket looked wet and was spread over a cot rack. The fire had burned down to glowing embers. Mooey gasped to see that Sunny's hair had been cut so short his head looked naked. With no clothes and no cover, he flailed his arms and kicked his legs as if he needed help. Children had stripped him naked before. Mooey had puzzled over this until she saw the children wrinkle their noses and throw his stinky napkin into the fire.

The young girl looked up in surprise and darted out the door, taking with her a fancy dress Mooey had seen but once before. Mooey wanted to run after the girl and retrieve the dress, but Sunny looked cold. His brow frowned. She pushed rags under him to soften the basket and keep away the cold floor, but he continued to shiver. As soon as she draped a cloth over him, he peed on it. He stopped wiggling and stared at her as if he couldn't figure out why he was getting wet. Mooey smiled at him and replaced the wet cloth with an old banyan she grabbed from the rag basket. She took off her apron and wrapped him and the banyan into it.

Whatever the cause of the upheaval in the cabin, Mooey couldn't fix it, so she sat with Sunny. Somebody so little shouldn't be so alone. Her heart took a failing when she noticed how his mother shunned him. Mooey rubbed the little nubs left on his head. He twisted his arms out of the cloths, reached up, and brushed her arm. She held his little cold hand, kissed his fingers. The brilliant gleam in his eyes told her that he trusted her and liked her. She rubbed her nose to his. His face, a picture of constant and lively eagerness, entertained Mooey.

When Auntie came in carrying a bucket of steaming water, Mooey watched to see if she took notice of the missing dress. Auntie merely put the bucket on the hearth and stoked the fire. Mooey left for the big-breasted woman's cabin but was waylaid on seeing Lacy in the shanty of the woman whose kindly spirit showed as yellow lights in her eyes. Mooey fixed the woman in her mind as "Magic," not only because of her air of mystery but she made potions and healing bags for sick people. In her cabin were shelves of small gourds, all of them filled with earthy powders, teas, and seeds. Mooey helped Magic by collecting things like beetles, snake skins, roots, and bark. For the smells alone Mooey often visited her shanty to take pleasure in sensing mint, grass, mud, weeds, hog fat, and such.

Magic was tending Lacy's hair with a tight comb. Mooey, who couldn't gather enough visions to find a way to notify her friend about the dress, abandoned the effort and continued to the suckling woman's cabin. Several children played with oak galls near the hearth. Mooey looked under cots, in baskets, behind a wardrobe, and in pots. She squeezed, shook, and kneaded ticks and blankets but didn't find the dress. As she climbed a chair to see into overhead boards lying like a loft, the young girl came inside. She pushed the chair and Mooey fell. The children, who had played with hardly a notice of Mooey, stopped and looked. When the young girl kicked Mooey, she grabbed her foot and flipped her to the ground. Mooey skedaddled back to her cabin.

Ever more disorder. In the center of the room was the big tub everybody used at one time or another to wash themselves. Auntie poured cold and hot water into it and took charge of Sunny. She inspected his scalp, which made him angry. Mooey patted Sunny on the head, but Auntie waved her away. Matters got worse when Auntie sat him in the tub. Sunny jabbed his arms, kicked, and squirmed. From the shape of his mouth it was obvious a powerful spirit was riled. Magic arrived and while Auntie held Sunny, she inspected his scalp with such intensity Mooey divined that they were treating the itch. When they finished giving the baby a scrubbing like he'd never had, they put him back in his basket.

Auntie added warm water to the tub and gestured to Mooey to remove her clothes and get in. She quickly submitted to their care, for she was willing to do anything to stop the itch that had kept her awake nights.

The door spun open allowing a gasp of cold air. Early, the negro boss man, stepped inside and wagged his head at Mooey, who scrunched down in the water, for she knew she wasn't supposed to be dallying with the others. He would have dragged her out of the tub but for Auntie, who talked up to him. In the end, Mooey continued to wash up instead of going with him to the lots.

Auntie lathered soap into Mooey's scalp and poured on rinse water. After Mooey dried her head with a clean cloth, she sat on a stool by the fire while Auntie dragged tiny tines through her hair, inspecting as she went. Every now and then she swept a nit off the comb and showed it to Mooey before mashing it on the hearth. Mooey's head, already sore, felt every hair like an ache. After Mooey's scrubbing, Auntie took a turn in the tub.

While Mooey rocked Sunny by the fire, Auntie and Magic brought in the remaining ticks and blankets they'd washed and hung them on a rope they strung before the fire. They spread their cleaned clothes over chairs and cots. At milking time, when Early didn't return to lash Mooey back to the cow lot, her mind saw somebody else taking her tasks. That somebody became the Lot Boss, which gave Mooey an ache. She could almost feel a blow like the ones the woman had landed on top of her head in the past. She could make Mooey's eyes go swimmy.

The later it got the more Auntie fussed over the ticks, still too damp to use. It began to look like the lot of them would have to sleep on the floor. Auntie's old bones could hardly rest even when sleeping on a cot. As Mooey dressed and was leaving for the cotton house, Lacy came in, but it was getting dark and Mooey didn't wait around to see if she missed her dress.

Mooey tried the outbuilding's door, hoping Early had forgotten to lock it. But it was fastened shut. Like other storage barns, it had open spaces just below the roof, which Mooey reached by climbing a corner where mismatched boards provided toe holds. She tugged aside a loose board to enlarge a hole and climbed inside.

When she returned to the cabin with first one and then another bag of cotton, Auntie smiled big and pretty, even though she had lost a front tooth several days before. They ate supper from the pot on the fire without Lacy. The big-breasted woman came by to suckle Sunny and jostled about the place before moving a blanket to make room to sit on a chair. She stuck out a peevish lip. By the time she left, it was full dark, and Lacy still hadn't come in for supper.

Auntie made makeshift ticks from the sacks of cotton, but, for both of them, their feet ran over the end. It was only after they lay down that Lacy entered. She paced nervously about the room shifting ticks, cloths, and fidgeting with ragbags and baskets. Her nose looked dark around the edges and her eyes red, like she had been crying. She sank on the floor as if her strength had deserted her. Even the shadowy light from the fire seemed to tremble. Mooey fretted about Lacy's dress, but she didn't have what she needed to explain about the breasted woman's girl. It wasn't the first time Mooey felt a gap between parts of herself.

Sunny's mother came in and bustled about angrily before settling on a blanket on the floor. Many fuming spirits wrestled in their cabin, and though Mooey yearned to move Sunny onto her cotton pallet, she didn't dare.

CHAPTER 6

TRIP TO BEAUFORT

DECEMBER 1857

Many days Wink drove wagonloads of cotton from the fields to the gin house in the light of the moon when field hands worked late picking what remained of the cotton. The month of December came in with weather so mild that for a couple of days everybody forgot winter was just around the corner.

After the night of the first freeze, the field hands put on their shoes and Wink his wool stockings, a sign that summer had indeed passed. Wink dragged out his extra blanket and, along with the other men, chopped or sawed a supply of firewood. People closed their cabin shutters and stoked their fires, even during the day.

After cleaning the master's carriage, greasing the axles, and oiling the wood, Wink installed glazed panes in the windows to protect against winter winds. Though the sun was shining, a blanket of clouds appeared on the horizon. The sudden but brief downpours were all but past, replaced by what might be days of drizzle when the hands hoped enough field work had been done that they could gin cotton or shuck corn in a shelter. Those times when the master's son had to stay inside tortured Anner and she tortured Wink. Sometimes she brought the boy to the stable to sit on horses in their stalls while they were feeding.

This time she had come alone, but the boy was obviously on her mind. "He done broke the door on the Massuh's gun cabinet."

"That boy dragged one of the dogs in the house!" "Dis morning he hid so long Missus railed me out."

Wink looked through the toolbox for a knife and a rasp. "I speck you better off getting railed at than having to slog to a wet field in raw-bone weather," he said.

Besides being nurse to the master's children, Anner also ran errands, which brought her to the stables when either the master or mistress wanted Wink to hitch up the carriage. He had noticed that her delivery of these messages took so long that he'd have the horses hitched up by the time she returned to the big house.

Wink held no grudge against Anner, though she had been chosen nurse at the big house ahead of his wife Raynell, who had done her best to get the job. That wasn't to say Raynell hadn't held a grudge. Up until she left Westfall, she claimed Anner had told lies about her—especially concerning the death of a particular hog. Whether or not Anner had actually said Raynell fed lye to the hog, the rumor spread, and Farley had called into question Raynell's involvement though nobody got a licking.

Not long after, Anner became the white children's nurse and Raynell and her daughter were sold to Habersham plantation. For a time, Wink had visited them, but it got to the point that he no longer wanted to make the effort. She didn't seem to care if he came, and he usually returned from the visits feeling empty.

Anner had taken over from Dina, Kedzie's mother, who had been sent to the master's mother, Missus Lambeth, in Charleston after the Goodwyn baby died. And Wink did know for a fact that Anner had spread word that Dina had bewitched the Goodwyn baby, even though other people had thought so too.

Anner leaned on the stall, her arms resting on the top, to deliver a message. "Massuh says to hitch up the carriage early in the morning. Missus and Missy be going to the main."

"Yessum. He done told me." Wink, inside the stall, cut off dead hoof with his knife as the horse chewed on a turnip he had given it. The trip couldn't come soon enough. His supply of whiskey had dwindled to barely a pint, and Claude had already spoken for that. Wink was getting into the habit of buying whiskey to sell. The only reliable source on the island was the boarding house near the ferry landing, but they charged more than most negros could pay. To supply cheaper liquor to them, he'd connected with a Beaufort man of mixed blood who sold brooms, bells, soap, and the occasional pig from a cart parked behind the First Presbyterian Church.

"I ask you, how can I mind the table and them boys at the same time?" Anner had been returned to service in the dining room, a subject she could talk about for hours.

Wink was figuring with some relief that he had enough specie to buy the whiskey he needed. With Christmas in the offing, he could sell twice what he could buy. However, to do that, he needed not only more money but a secret way to haul in his supply, a hiding place on the carriage that wouldn't arouse the master's suspicion.

"I said to the Missus, 'You wants me to shut the front door whensoever I see it's been left open?'" Anner patrolled the open gateway, looked toward the big house, and came back.

Wink realized he hadn't been paying enough attention to her and stopped thinking about the trip to Beaufort.

"She said, 'The door been left open?' I showed her how the door was cracked. Course she don't know I opened it." Anner smiled contentedly. "Billy be charged wid the front door. He's so bigheaded about letting in Massuh's high-toned friends."

Wink nodded his head as if he agreed. What in God's name was this woman talking about?

"Wink, don't Puddin give you meat bones from the massuh's kitchen?"

"What you want wid meat bones?" Wink took whatever bones Puddin gave him. He couldn't coax the dogs out of the yard with just a whistle when people came visiting.

"You got more'n you going to use ... give me some."

Wink scraped out what remained of dead frog from a hoof. "I needs my bones." If he had been talking to Puddin, his conversation would have taken a dirty-mouth tone and he'd be dodging her wood spoon. When she got fired up at him, it gave him greater enthusiasm for her.

Anner wheedled. "I got a present in my pocket."

"Let me see." Wink put down the horse's hoof and walked the animal around the stable.

Anner produced a cigar.

"Bring me a sack. I'll give you some."

Anner gave him a mysterious smile. "Massuh's going to mess in his drawers when he sees the dogs in the house. And he be going after Billy." She swallowed so much mirth she mumbled, "Billy's going to pay up for putting me on the whipping tree."

Wink removed the horse's halter. He wished he had paid more attention to Anner. He couldn't make heads nor tails of what she was saying, but the cigar smelled real good.

*

In the early hours before daylight, frost covered the outbuildings and yard. It was so cold Wink put on extra wool socks. He ventured out of his small shanty, which shared a wall with the stables. His place smelled of hay. This had bothered his wife so much she'd slept in the quarters on nights when the smell was strong, but he had grown to like it. In winter he stacked fodder against the common wall on the stable side, which made his place warmer.

His footsteps came down brittle on the frozen ground. From the quarters came the clang of pots and the squeak of door hinges. Smoke churned from the chimneys and drifted downward spreading the scent of cinders. Thin sheets of light streaked from around closed shutters. Wink pulled his hat to his ears and glanced across the yard as a light flashed, and Farley came out his door, picked up firewood, and returned inside. It was the sort of day a body dreaded leaving the warmth of his hearth. Wink shifted his lantern from one hand to the other in order to warm the one not in his pocket.

In the stables, the wintry chill threw a quiet on the horses, mules, and oxen. Skittles climbed to her feet as Wink came into her stall. "Shore-nuff! Dis be cold!" The oil lantern he attached to the hook on the wall gave a solitary light. The bridle's metal rings sprinkled an icy jingle on the silence. He enclosed the cold bit in his palms and blew his warm breath on it. "Wooeee! Warm up here afore my hand be freezed!" The bit wasn't warm enough for Skittles who pulled back and snorted her disapproval. Wink put his face against the horse's and rubbed her nose. "Now what's got in my girl dis morning?" He talked, nuzzled her, and rubbed the bit. She took it in her mouth when he tried again.

In the chill of Tootie's dark stall, Wink's breath warmed similar jabber as he put on the bridle, pulling her ears through the straps. Skittles and Tootie, the team the master preferred with the carriage, walked close together as they went to the carriage house. They blew clouds of smoke, stamped, and shivered in the spacious air of the yard.

Wink kept up a stream of conversation. "Dis be one cold-ass morning, girls. Yessuh. So cold you can lean on your piss." Tootie snorted in agreement. If there was a mother hen among the horses, it was Tootie. Her nose had nudged many a wayward filly or angry gelding.

Wink opened the carriage door and gave the interior a quick look. Chickens and cats, if not rats, had been known to take up residence inside. The leather walls glistened with oils he had applied to keep them clean and supple. The previous summer he'd replaced the many leather-covered cushion pins that had come amiss, which had fallen out or more likely been taken by the master's children. Wink had chased them away more than once.

After he harnessed the horses to the carriage, he walked them toward the big house.

The kitchen windows glowed with light from the fire Puddin had going. As the cook, she was usually up well before the big house and to bed at night after most everybody went to sleep. Wink stopped and went inside. She was bending to the flames, turning side meat sizzling in an iron pan.

Puddin's penetrating eyes, big black orbs, softened when people enjoyed the food she prepared. Her lips seldom smiled, but their natural pose was pleasant, as if she had good thoughts. She was a person of strong beliefs and claimed food was a kind of medicine to the spirit—if it was bad, life wasn't good, but if good, nothing could be too bad.

Wink liked her rounded hips and the way she communicated with them. He came up behind her, grabbed around her waist, and quickly bumped her in the behind with his crotch. "You gots time for my hammer?"

She swung at him with the long-handled fork in her hand. Her eyes were darts of pure excitement.

He ducked and gave her wide berth.

"You bout the worst I ever seed." Her brown face glistened with sweat from the roaring fire.

"Now you is a wild flower and you knows it." He would have grabbed her waist but she raised her fork again. Wink relaxed and stuck the sole of his boot toward the fire.

"Where you going so early in the morning?" She took a biscuit from the oven, split it open, and put in a piece of meat from the pan. She handed it to him.

"A mite of coffee shore taste good on a morning like this." Wink took in the good smell before biting into the biscuit.

Puddin poured some in a cup. Coffee was one of the rarified things only allowed the whites, but the master didn't miss a smattering now and again.

"Missus going to town. Missy Margarita going too." Wink tasted the coffee. A warm glow traveled from his throat to his stomach to his soul. He had one foot in God's kingdom.

"This be the Missuses' dinner. Yours be in the sack on top." She handed him a basket covered with cloth. Her thick-bodied nose benefitted from a well formed crest. Her eyelids and lashes played with her gazes.

He drained the last drop from the cup, fine old crockery she kept just for him. "I be back tomorrow." Wink wanted to believe she deliberately teased only him. "I knows you be terrible lonesome what wid me off on the main."

Her glance at him lingered long enough to fire up his expectation.

"I spect so," she said with a look that tickled Wink because her pretense gave him hope that she might some day mean it.

She turned to the meat sputtering in the spider.

The sound of Tootie's whinny called him to the yard, and he drove the carriage to the front of the big house. Since Billy didn't wave from the door, he shook the reins loudly. "Tootie, call these white folks out." The horse neighed.

Wink wrapped his blanket tighter and stuck his nose into it. Leather gloves kept the raw cold from his hands, which he rubbed together. His open seat offered no protection from the weather.

Billy ran down the steps and handed him the foot warmer. "They be down directly." Wink placed the warmer in the floor of the carriage.

In time, he aroused and chimed the reins again and said to his horses, "Iffen they don't come on, we going to miss the ferry." Skittles cranked her ears. Tootie shook her head harness as if jingling for the mistress. Since the ferry only left for the mainland on an incoming high tide, its departure time varied about an hour every day. Wink, who could read numbers and tell time, kept close watch on the tide schedule, but he could better control the tides than the white women. As far as he was concerned, they didn't have much brain power, for their heads were small, a fact they disguised by fluffing up their hair.

Even if they were late Wink waited on the carriage; he'd learned his lesson. Once he'd quickly run to the door when the mistress was so late they were going to miss the ferry, and a goose spooked the horses, which took off down the carriageway. It was an hour before Wink could get the carriage back to the house. He killed the goose, for it also chased the negro children, and put it into one of Puddin's baskets. Before he could sell it off the plantation, the meat started to rot and he threw it into Station Creek. She got mad at him about the basket, but he couldn't return it after all that rancid mess.

As soon as the master came down the steps with his wife and daughter, Wink jumped to the ground. The master helped them inside and pulled up their blanket and closed the door. Mistress Goodwyn laid her head back on the small needlepoint pillow she'd brought, but her daughter gazed about eagerly and waved farewell to her father.

Wink whistled and called, "Giddiup, ladies! Let's go to town!" The horses heaved forward and the carriage took to the road. He kept them at a spirited canter along the macadam road and over plank bridges, the lanterns swaying with the pitch of the cab.

He checked the pocket watch his master had given him and urged the horses faster. The early morning horizon emerged through the trees, just starting to stand apart from the wall of darkness. Ice-glazed water in the ditches beside the road gave off a tinny shine.

They arrived just as the island ferry was casting off. As they approached, Wink whistled loudly through his teeth, and Morgan, the ferry captain, stopped soon enough to rope the bulwark and pull back to the wharf.

With the team secured by lines to the flat, they cast off to the whispering of the river's waters. Morgan and his slave Caleb—and more importantly the force of the incoming tide—propelled the pole boat toward the distant mainland.

Skittles and Tootie stood balanced and calm. They seemed to listen to the chantey Caleb sang. Wink stroked Skittles's mane and took in clean breaths of cold air. His trim moustache grew heavy with ice. He anchored a chud in his cheek and dug a turnip out of his pocket. Skittles licked at it and swiped Wink's cheek while he sliced off two pieces with his pocket knife. Both horses munched their treats.

As they disembarked at the quay near Carteret Street, the carriage rolled loudly onto cobblestones. Close-set houses were shuttered against the cold. Light flickered from the lamps inside, rimming the shutters. The few pedestrians on the road were bundled up and hurrying along.

Wink delivered his mistresses to Cordy's Mercantile Store and parked the carriage on the street where he and the horses waited. He could almost feel the warmth of the potbellied stove he could see through the glazed front windows. Two men in the store frequently stood in its range, circled, and departed.

After some time a clerk dashed out the front door and to the carriage. "Mistress Goodwyn wants a package of material from the cab," he called up to Wink on the seat.

Wink, who hunkered under his blanket, said, "Must be inside wid the rest of their things."

"Come down here and find it," said the young man, rubbing his hands on his arms.

"The door is open." Wink hardly looked at the boy.

"You lazy greaser!" The young clerk opened the door and leaned inside. As he plundered about the blanket, Wink gently ruffled the lines, and the horses took a couple of steps forward. The open carriage door knocked the clerk down in the street. "You black bastard! Your mistress is going to hear about this!" He got up and retrieved the package he'd come after, then ran across the street, leaving the door open.

In time, the mistress and her daughter appeared in the doorway, followed by the clerk carrying a box. As they approached the carriage, Wink climbed down. He took from the boy the box containing oranges and other fare and stored it in the boot. The clerk returned with another box with almonds, raisins, and fruit. As Wink reached for it, the man dropped it on the cobblestones spilling everything. "Your man is as clumsy as an oaf!" he said to the mistress before bidding them good day and returning to the store.

Wink picked up pineapples and bagged goods and replaced them in the box, which he stored under his seat.

It was dinner time, and Wink parked the carriage at a clearing on the Beaufort River while the mistresses sat in the cab and ate the food Puddin had packed for them.

When he dropped the women at the dressmaker's, Wink got permission to water the horses, an excuse for him to do his trading. He made his way to the cart vendor behind the Presbyterian Church. To his dismay, the man had only one jug of whiskey left to sell. Wink wrapped it in a croker sack, secured it under his carriage seat, and headed for the Victoria Hotel doorman, the best source for not just gossip but intelligence of any sort. On the way, he struck a light for his cigar, knowing it would attract the attention if not envy of the negros about town.

"Boss, you know iffen Raynell Goodwyn still be at the Habersham house?" Wink occasionally asked about his former wife, not that he was interested in her, but Raynell's daughter would be about eight years old by now.

"Habersham..." The man's neatly cropped white beard and tailored suit gave him distinction. He turned inside the door and motioned over a younger man. "Wasn't that a Raynell what died wid the baby?"

Wink felt no surprise or sadness. Their marriage had been a disappointment to both himself and her. If she had died, she had taken his secret with her. They had had no children though he had put out for her enough to fill the yard with younguns. It had bothered him. The bother turned to a serious worry when she got a baby girl by a field hand, which confirmed that the fault fell not to her but to him.

"No suh. Dat woman was Nezzie Pringle." The younger man, in fitted waistcoat and well-made leather shoes, stood outside but watched inside through the door window.

They wrangled over whether it was Raynell or Nezzie, contradicted each other, and provided no dependable information. A bell sounded and the younger man skittered back inside.

The doorman was more helpful when Wink asked about whiskey, though the details of how Wink could meet this supplier bogged down. At last, Wink told the doorman where he'd be the rest of the afternoon should the man be in the environs.

In the alley between West and Charles Streets, Wink waited with the horses and carriage for the missus and her daughter. Several other drivers with carriages parked nearby, likewise awaiting mistresses or masters, some likely in taverns on New Republic Street.

Occasionally a horse dropped steaming turds on the cobblestones, publicizing familiar and earthy odors. The blanket kept Wink warm enough, but the wind, chilled by the river, bit into his knees and toes. He considered getting down from the carriage seat, stretching his legs, and stomping life into his feet, but thinking about it didn't spark any action. It was easier to situate like Skittles and Tootie, both standing stonelike.

Skittles occasionally turned her head and looked at Wink as if to say, "How much longer we going to stand here?" The sun had given way to clouds, which feathered together and cast a dreariness on the afternoon. A nearby horse blew its nose. Skittles's coat shivered.

"Hey Sambo, you looking cold up there."

Wink looked over his shoulder at a white man wearing boots with a cowhide patch sewn over the toe. Wink fingered the paper coupon in his coat pocket that his master had signed, ready to produce it on command. Hardly a week had passed since the Master paid to get Thor from the patrollers. Thor had made the mistake of wandering over the Island causeway while hunting rabbits, and the patrollers had caught him without a pass.

"Yessuh," Wink said, keeping his nose down.

The man's hand extended a bottle containing what looked like water. "This'll warm you up. Best whiskey in the parish."

Wink wondered if this man knew the doorman. At the same time, he wasn't stupid enough to trust a white man offering him something to drink. He took the whiskey and touched his tongue to the bottle, pretending to pull a long draft when in fact he barely tasted it. "Dat be mighty generous a you." Something like nerves warmed his arms. His muscles tensed. He forgot about the cold.

The white man took a drink from the bottle. "Just looking for business," he said, his face a stubble of beard with scars, one of which ran from his cheek into his lower eyelid. He tipped up the bottle for another drink and offered again.

Wink took the bottle. "Dis tastes bout as good as what I gits from the doorman at the Victoria Hotel." Whatever the man's purpose, the fact that he would share a bottle with a negro meant he wasn't the usual threat.

"Yessir. He do know good hooch. His guinea was just by my place." The man tamped the cob in the neck of the bottle. "There's more where this come from, if you interested."

Wink sized up the white and said, "How much it cost, a bottle like dat?" A foggy mist began to prickle his nostrils. He rubbed his nose on his sleeve.

"I don't sell one like this. I sell by the cask. At least three gallons a draw," the man said quietly and looked about as if nearby drivers might have moved closer. He put the bottle inside his coat and motioned Wink over to a nearby building.

Whiskey by the cask. Wink shed his blanket, stepped down from the carriage, and followed to the stoop at the back door of the office of "Travis & Maes, Partners-at-Law."

"I can let you have this here sample for a half dime." The man pulled out the bottle and, without offering Wink any, took another drink.

The man took Wink's money and handed over the bottle. Wink's Adam's apple galloped with the rush of liquid. He gave a whoosh to catch his breath. The liquor was as good as any. However, when he heard how much a cask cost, he wished he hadn't lost so much money to Claude in a poker game. "I don't have enough money wid me, but I knows a nigger do." Wink figured he could get his hands on some cash, maybe from Claude or Limbo, if he still had money from the pelts.

"When can you have it?"

"Yessuh. I'se from St. Helena way, and I be in Beaufort ever so often wid the massuh."

"You from St. Helena Island?" The white man pointed his ruddy finger at Wink.

"Yessuh. The massuh, he gots a big plantation." Wink avoided naming names.

"How you going to git a cask from here to the island?" The man's breath smelled like tobacco dirt.

"Dat's the easy part. See the carriage seat? Dat storage chest under it be big enough." Wink nodded in the direction of the carriage. "Yessuh. A cask be bout right. What wid my money in St. Helena, I'se going to need some time. How you reckon that out?" Wink wanted to ask the man where he lived so he could return when he had the money, but such a forward question might spook him.

The man pulled up his collar against the cold and looked at Wink. "Tell you what. When you git your money figured out, come to the Bayside Leather Shop and ask for Artis."

"Dat be on Bay Street?" said Wink.

The man gave him directions, pulled the brim of his hat to his eyes, and was gone.

CHAPTER 7

INFLAMMATORY FEVER

DECEMBER 1857

After a time, Wink moved the carriage from the alley into the street and parked near the door to the dress shop. A hawker led a horse down the cobblestone street calling, "Prime filly, nine hundred and worth every dollar! Three-year-old! High blooded!" The dappled gray's smooth gait bode well for a good riding horse. Its big eyes betrayed anger or fear. As they passed by, Wink clucked at it, and the horse reared, strained its lead, and looked at him as if expecting a rescue. He'd seen the filly earlier at the wheelwright's place. What Wink wouldn't give for nine hundred dollars.

His mistress and Margarita emerged from the dressmaker's shop and paused on the street to talk with a man Wink recognized. Every coachman from Charleston to Savannah knew Reverend DeMere, who was usually in trouble with the sheriff—if not in jail—for defending slaves in one way or another. The extent of conversation between them was more than casual, which aroused Wink's curiosity. It was unlikely that his mistress befriended him because of his reputation.

"Margarita, we must go!" Mistress Goodwyn was saying.

"If I don't see you again, dear, God's blessings on you." The reverend waved to them as they resumed their walk to the carriage.

They rumbled past white houses so big five or six slave families could live in one with room to spare. Where the shutters hadn't yet been closed, veiled windows glared at the street. On Federal Street he slowed down as they neared the Fortier mansion where they would stay the night.

A barking dog raced beside the horses. Skittles shied. Wink called, "Whoa, there. Calm yourself!" The dog snapped at Skittles's hock causing her to rear up. Wink gripped the lines, leaned forward, and said, "Whoa, whoa!" The skin of his palms measured the pinch of the horses' bits. Skittles neighed in a high pitch and stamped. Wink's arms, shoulders, and hands grappled with the riotous lines, pulling right and holding firm. When he was younger, he'd cursed at such a dog, which only added to the horses' terror. The cur kept up the yapping. Wink took the lines in one hand, reached for his demijohn, and threw water on the dog. The animal bolted backwards, halted, and shook its fur before slinking away.

"Uuh-huuuh, girlies! Come on down, baby-cakes. Dat trash is crawling back in some hole." Wink's voice coaxed the horses into a normal pace. He took a drink of the water, sheeted with ice.

At the Fortier mansion overlooking the marshes, Wink pulled the horses to a stop on the carriageway of crushed oyster shells. "Whoa, ladies! Whoa, now!" Before Wink could help his mistresses from the carriage, a doorman in a frock coat with brass buttons opened the cab door. An elderly lady hardly able to control her hoops came onto the piazza where she fussed over the mistress like hifalutin white folks did. The lady's son, who owned a plantation up near Coffin's Point, had more slaves than Masters Goodwyn and Jervy combined.

Wink unhitched Skittles and Tootie and gave them water before walking them several blocks to the public stables. He curried their coats and put them in a small paddock. From the boy working at the stables, he was able buy a jar of whiskey. Back at the Fortier house, he stashed it under the driver's seat with the jug and covered both with a sack of apples he'd bought for Iverson. After inspecting the wheels and giving the entire carriage a good look, he headed to the rear of the big house and found the cabin where the servants slept empty. Since the household slaves had spent the day cooking and serving their mistress, the fire had dusted down. He brought in kindling and blew on the coals until they flamed up.

A maid brought Wink a bit of lamb and a muffin of batter bread. So pleasurable was the smell of the meat he hardly wanted anything, even eating it, to interfere with his enjoyment. He nibbled at first one side then the other. When the piggin was empty, he licked the bottom of the few remaining specks.

The soft cotton of the tick felt so good he hardly stirred when the household servants came in loud as a battering ocean in a storm. They sat around the fire and talked. Wink pulled his blanket over his head, but it didn't keep out their racket.

In the night the wind rattled the roof shingles and blew open a shutter. One of the men got up and pulled it shut and latched it. The next morning, fast moving clouds curdled the sky. The wind swept high and low as Wink walked to the kitchen and ate breakfast while the cook went after wood for the fire. Puddin never let so many ashes pile up in her hearth.

With little to do but wait for the ferry's departure at ebb tide, Wink got permission from the mistress to walk to the mercantile street for a plug of tobacco. He already had one in his pocket, but she was none the wiser. He searched out the leather shop where the white man Artis and his whiskey could be found. But for the carved wood stirrups over the door, the narrow building looked like every other shop on Bay Street.

It was with some difficulty that he kept his hat on in the wind as he called at the stables for the horses on his way back to the Fortier mansion. Before he hitched Skittles and Tootie to the carriage, he knocked at the back door and asked for Mistress Goodwyn. "Missus, you wants me to drive to the ferry to see iffen they going to the island in this weather?"

"No, we're almost ready. We'll be out directly."

Wink waited with the carriage at the front steps. It was some time before the women emerged from the house. In the turbulence they held down their skirts and didn't linger over saying farewell. Even the horses didn't like the rustling of the trees. Skittles swished her tail and pawed. Since he hadn't brought blinders with him, he tied his handkerchief over Skittles's eyes and walked her and Tootie out the carriageway and into the street, murmuring and crooning to them. "Just baby steps, miladies! Pretty shoes ... Easy does it!" Once on the cobblestones, the horses settled enough for Wink to recover his handkerchief and climb on his seat.

At the wharf, the waves spurted onto the bank and rocked the ferry. Morgan's man, Caleb, in spite of his sturdy build, lurched like a drunkard. Skittles was blowing, working herself to a frenzy. Wink took a nip from the botttle in his pocket and spit some into Skittles's mouth.

He spoke at the window loudly enough to be heard above the roar. "Missus, iffen I bees you, I be leaving the carriage and horses at the stable here. And borrow Morgan's sulky on the island to get us to Westfall."

Mistress Goodwyn said, "I don't want to borrow a rig. The ferry will be stable once we're aboard."

"Yessum," Wink said. That was a bad decision and he knew it. Any idiot could see the crossing was going to be rough if not chancy. Should the winds increase enough to tip the ferry, the weight of the carriage could send the horses to the bottom of the river.

Caleb helped a man lead an ox on the flat and secured the animal with a tether. Morgan motioned for Wink to lead the horses on board. A dread sank into Wink's heart. Even if the mistress was a foolish woman without much common sense, he reluctantly followed her orders but not without resentment. Skittles balked and wouldn't move until he tied his handkerchief over her eyes. Tootie nudged her partner and snorted sympathetically. Only when he offered them nubbins from his pocket did they settle enough that the ferry could cast off. Wink's hand never left Skittles as he talked to both horses, mumbling an old Christmas song "... fiddle and dance away, tis holiday." He chewed on a tough nugget of sap until it was soft and he could stick it on her nose, which provided some distraction.

Rain, though not plentiful, came down forcefully. His coat was getting wet. Water washed over the brim of his hat.

After three hours of struggling with a shifting wind, the ferry got mired as they approached Ladies Island. Wink and Caleb jumped into the bog to try to prize them free. Wink could hardly move as he sank to his hips in mud. He and Caleb pushed against the ferry and shoved it with all their might.

The wind suddenly changed direction and aided their effort. The ferry rocked free. Caleb was hauled on board, but the mud held Wink down. The men struggled to pull him up as the flat washed further from him. Just as Wink thought he was lost, Caleb extended a pole and shouted for him to grab hold. Wink wrapped himself around it and after tense moments of shouting, tugging, heaving, and twisting, the mud slipped away.

Morgan and Caleb poled vigorously until a faint light came into view. A ferryman at the dock awaited them and secured their lines to the landing post. Wink had lost his hat. Rain whipped his face. His clothes soaked his skin, and mud covered his brogans.

Skittles and Tootie bounded off the ferry with such exertion they almost toppled the carriage. As soon as the wheels rolled steadily, Wink drank the rest of the sample whiskey to calm his shaking.

The wind came and went in gusts. The rain slowed to a drizzle, but the entire causeway had turned into a waterway. Wink stopped at a plank bridge to test the soundness of the foundation pillars. On deciding it would hold for them to pass, he led the horses across. As he mounted back to the seat, his shoe, as wet inside as out, slipped and he caught himself, but as he settled on the bench, violent shivers overtook him.

They pulled up to Westfall's steps late. The master met them, followed by Billy with an umbrella. With some satisfaction, Wink heard the master upbraid the mistress for traveling in such weather. At least the man recognized the risk his wife had inflicted on Wink and the horses, even if his concern was merely for his property. As soon as the ladies were safely on the portico, Wink drove the horses to the carriage house, stumbled to the stable, and lay on a pile of hay.

"Wink?" Puddin's voice sounded far away. "Good Lawd. You is a mess. The Massuh is going to leave dis man to die." Wink didn't feel like he was dying, but what he heard worried him. Maybe this was farewell to Puddin. He hated to leave. Nobody else would take care of the horses like he did. Tootie's long, loud neigh drifted away.

He became aware of Iverson picking him up and carrying him across the yard, into a warm room, and laying him in a cot. He could tell they were taking off his clothes, but for the first time in his life, he didn't care about their seeing his skinny legs or stark ribs.

The warmth of a wet wash rag glowed against his skin, and the comfort gave him a peaceful feeling, like the world was suddenly friendly. He knew the hand washing him to be Puddin's. He wanted to wake up and tell her that she was the best woman who ever lived. But on second thought, her touch felt so good he didn't want to risk an end to it. He swallowed liquids put into his mouth with the medicine horn and went to sleep trying not to.

The room was dark and too warm to be Wink's shanty. A roaring heat arose inside his belly and he sat up. His head pounded. "Dammit to hell!" His tongue dried up. His eyeballs ached. Sweat poured into them turning an ache into a brilliant pain. He wiped his eyes, which inflamed the pain.

In trying to get the blanket off, he became entangled in it. "Hell-fired mess."

Puddin arose from the foot of the cot. "Put yourself back in this cot!" She nudged his shoulders to urge him back.

"Let go! I can't sleep in here." He shrugged her off.

"You not in any shape to go anywhere." She put her palm to his forehead.

"Baby, I gotta get outa here." Wink hardly understood himself, but he felt like he had to be back in his cabin. Something about the room made his chest fold up and squeezed his breathing. He remembered the feeling from his childhood. "God-a-mighty! Don't get in my way!"

Puddin disappeared.

In trying to stand up, he fell and was surprised to find himself on a wood plank floor. Where was he?

At first he suspected the warmth that flooded him meant heaven, but that didn't last long. Of a sudden he couldn't hold himself down on the cot. The racket in his body tore him up. He was losing a fight with the devil. The way his head hurt a hatchet could have landed on it. Just when he thought his blood had frozen, he began to sweat. The devil's poker stabbed him in the eyes. He couldn't swallow. Dying was so damned hard. His body roared with pain. He wanted to get rid of it, even if the devil took it.

From somewhere beyond the noise of his torture, he recognized Mamba's voice. Good. He wanted to tell her to hide his whiskey from the master. No, he wanted to tell her he needed his whiskey. He needed a dram. No, a cup. Just give him all the liquor he had.

Wink was moved to a board and carried out of the room. Maybe he was lying on the cooling board where they put all the dead people. Maybe they concluded he was dead. The sound of Iverson praying at his side lulled him. Was he dead?

His ears woke up to Mamba's voice. She was talking to somebody about a poultice. He was on a cot. Every muscle in his body ached. Mamba stood nearby, a cup and spoon in her hands. "Here, take this." She extended the spoon to his lips. He swallowed what tasted like turpentine.

The next time he opened his eyes, Puddin put a spoon to his mouth. It was brandy. He felt better. At least she understood what he needed.

In a lucid moment he realized Puddin's attentions. He didn't want her to see him like this.

Voices came and went. Sunlight turned to dark. Children shouted in the distance. Auntie Nell stuck a spoonful of soup in his face, but he didn't want it.

He felt a warm puff of air in his face. It tickled his nose. Another puff. Sometimes he felt like he floated in warm water. The puff came as breath from somebody hovering over him. Wink opened his eyes to a face close to his. By the light of the fire, he realized it was Mooey. A smile lit up her face, and she showed him a biscuit. A weird sense of unreality came upon him, and he couldn't tell if he was awake. When the piece of bread touched his lip, he spit it out. Mooey picked it up and ate it. Another lump came to his mouth. He chewed and swallowed it. Persimmon bread. He wondered where she'd gotten it. She ate a crumb and gave him one until the bread was gone. He closed his eyes and as he drifted away, felt the soft brush of her lips on his cheek.

The white doctor leaned over and listened to Wink's chest. Where was Mamba? Wink coughed. The doctor stared into Wink's eyes and ears, listened to his chest, and pronounced it inflammatory fever. When Wink realized the towel and basin were for blood letting, he bolted up. The doctor pushed him back into the cot and said to Mamba, "Hold his arm steady."

"God dammit! Don't you cut on me, you cussed reptile!"

Mamba called Auntie Nell over to help hold him down.

"This white devil is going to kill me!" Wink was so loud that Flurry stuck her head in the door.

"Come here and help," said Mamba.

"Get that knife away from me!" Wink said. The white doctor would kill him if he wasn't already dead. He tried to twist away from the man, but somebody held him down.

"How much blood you letting out?" said Mamba.

"Enough to restore the balance of bodily fluids." The doctor brought up a basin.

When Wink saw the knife going for his arm, he let fly with every curse word he ever knew. The sorry-ass doctor cut a hole so big blood was shooting everywhere. Wink found the strength to knock somebody off his arm. "Git that son-of-a-bitch away from me!"

They took the basin away. Mamba put a patch on the cut and wrapped up his arm while the doctor packed his satchel. "Give him plenty tea, as much as he'll take," said the doctor as he situated his hat and left.

Wink dozed when he could, but at night the fever got worse and his head hurt so bad he had to sit up. He awoke to take whatever Mamba gave him, but he refused the white doctor's medicines, which Auntie Nell tried to give him.

One morning after Wink had spent a restless night, Iverson came to the sick house with possum stew his wife Gussie had made. "Is Wink on the mend?" he said to Auntie Nell, sitting before the fire.

She coughed and hacked and spit into the fire. "Last night it sounded like he was on his way, but I don't know if it was up or down."

"Is he awake?"

"Not that you'd know it."

When Iverson shook him, Wink burst loose with curses. Iverson put the bowl on the hearth and said to Auntie, "I best leave this wid you."

When Wink came to himself, he spit out the stew and swore at Auntie Nell for trying to poison him. Mamba made him tea from a hog's hoof that she had parched in ashes and pounded to a powder. He half-heartedly cursed at her and told her to feed it to the pigs.

Food didn't interest him. It wasn't that he disliked what was brought, he just didn't care. When he realized Auntie Nell's presence, he should have worried. She sat with dying people. The master came in but Wink didn't open his eyes. Not that he avoided the master. He just didn't care.

Auntie Nell put the medicine horn in his mouth, and he swallowed whatever she gave him and slept. Puddin brought him chicken broth and loaf bread.

"What took you so long?" He sat up as best he could and ate.

"Everbody says you been raising merry Cain." Puddin sat in a chair beside his cot.

"Dat's cause you been ignoring me." Wink said. That Puddin had stripped and cleaned him the night he fell ill made him uncomfortably conscious of an intimacy he hadn't shared. Anybody else wouldn't have bothered him. "You seen the devil I is when I'se flat-out helpless to do his calling."

"I seed your devil." Puddin stood to leave. "And it be scary enough widout any calling."

"Now, baby, you don't see me at my best." Wink sank backward and lay on the cot.

"I wouldn't truck wid your best nor your worst."

"You knows my worst. I'se going to show you my best, when I be perter." Wink's voice trailed off and his eyes went shut. His lips moved with other things he had to say, but he couldn't carry on.

When Mamba came by and tucked something under Wink's tick, he aroused from sleep and said, "What you doing?"

"I fixed up this mojo bag. There's a full moon and you is weak to spirits."

"What makes you think I need mojo?" said Wink. There was no telling what communication Mamba had had with spirits.

"Puddin done worried about you. The shape you in, a hag might ride you to death."

It pleased him that Puddin worried for his sake.

Shortly thereafter, he awoke to the polished smile of the white preacher. "Mister Wink, Puddin asked me to come by and say a prayer with you."

Maybe Wink was dreaming. He closed his eyes, but he could smell the white man's soap.

"Merciful Lord ..."

What the hell was Puddin doing asking this white man to his bedside? The singsong voice lulled him into a soothing daze and when the voice finally ended, so did the daze. "Preacher Chaffee, dat do make me feel better." He smiled to himself. Puddin was playing with him. He had to get off the cot or she would have every preacher and two-headed doctor on the island in the sick house with him.

When Wink finally moved back to his quarter, his fire had long gone out. Puddin brought hot coals and built one for him. She brought food but he couldn't persuade her to sit and eat with him. In an effort to impress her with his recovery, he stood too quickly and in falling against his table, cut his face. Puddin helped him back to his cot and wiped the blood from his eyebrow and handed him a rag. "You lay yourself down and hold this on the cut. And stay there till I gets back."

She returned with the kitchen brandy and was cleaning his wound with it when Wink reached for the bottle. "Darling, you is putting dat in the wrongest place." As soon as she gave it to him, he took a big gulp.

She grabbed the bottle back. "You is mischief in spite of the devil."

"My head feels a whole lot better now." Wink lay back and allowed her to wrap a rag on his cut.

Mamba came to his shanty every day with quantities of feverroot tea to give him strength. "Iffen I had herbs to work up good sense, I'd sprinkle it in Missus's tea. Dat woman near bout got you killed."

"It'd take more'n herbs to give dat woman good sense." Wink was gratified that Mamba stuck up for him. So did Limbo, who came by and said, "Massuh having a helluva time wid one of his gins. Can't nobody get it to work worth shit since Missus put you in de river."

When Wink felt up to it, he went to the stable and helped the hired liveryman who had taken his place. Before he was steady on his feet and while he was still coughing up catarrh, the liveryman left and Wink resumed his tasks. The master sent him to the village for the mail. Sent him to borrow a sewing machine. Sent him to fetch Missy Margarita from the ferry.

CHAPTER 8

SHOUT MEETING

DECEMBER 1857

Wink returned from the main with crates the steamer had unloaded on the wharf. The master's goods were marked with the word a nearby white read out as London. Though he had heard of London, Wink wanted to ask about its whereabouts, but the man would only converse so much.

At Westfall, he unloaded the crates to the portico and unhitched the horses. He still felt the effect of the fever he'd survived, but before he could rest, he visited the quarters and went to Mamba's place to deliver the news he had from Caleb at the ferry.

She stood behind Polly's chair, combing her daughter's hair and plaiting it in small cornrows. "How you doing, Wink?" Without a headrag, Mamba's short thick hair revealed the fine proportions of her head. More than weariness seemed to weigh down her ample shoulders.

"Fair to midlin, I reckon."

Thor stuck his head in the door long enough to say, "Wink, we getting up a card game. Come down to my place."

Wink responded with a quick shrug. What he wanted was to lie down and rest up.

"What you looking sorrowful about?" Wink wondered if Mamba already knew.

Polly stopped playing with the ribbon in her lap and turned her face up to her mother. "Mammy, what's the matter?"

"I been thinking bout asking Massuh for a pass to visit Mammy." She looked at Wink. "You hear anything lately?"

"Can I go wid you?" Polly smiled and bounced in her chair.

"No, baby. It be too far. All the way off the island and past Beaufort. Long ways," Mamba said.

Wink felt like apologizing for what he had to say. "Your mammy's down in the cot. Don't hardly eat much." He waited about in case Mamba needed somebody.

"Last night I dreamt Mammy was lying in the cot and when I pulled back the blanket, her body was covered wid hair."

Polly's eyes grew round. "She got a jinn?"

"No. That means she is changing." Mamba's eyes clouded. She wiped her nose with a handkerchief she took from her apron pocket.

Polly turned around. "I'll ask Massuh for a pass for you."

Mamba sat and smiled kindly at Polly, who climbed on her lap. Mamba tugged her daughter closer.

Wink didn't offer encouragement. Caleb had also said the doctor hadn't treated the elderly woman because she wasn't likely to get well.

"I'se going to make a poultice for Mammy. You'll take it wid you next time?" Mamba looked into the fire.

Wink had delivered numerous things over the years, from duck feathers to conch shells, but never a poultice. "Be glad to. Dat's bound to make your mammy feel better." As Wink left, Mamba held her daughter and stared into the flames.

One date and then another had been set for Brother Milton's shouting at Westfall. Wink brought news and took news. At last the pastor was coming and everybody knew it. "Wink, iffen you sees Brother Milton on the road, you be sure to give him a ride," Iverson had said several days in advance.

By noon on the Saturday of the meeting, Wink and Thor were sitting in the sun, washing mud off the oysters they'd dug from the tidal marsh, when Wink noticed the geese honking and scurrying under the big house. Brother Milton's arrival gave rise to an uproar of barking, clucking, and squawking. Iverson took charge of the visitor, who could hardly get to his cabin for the people crowding around him.

Wink and Thor built a fire in a backlot pit and fitted over it the iron grate that Wink owned but he hardly claimed for everybody used it. They scattered their oysters on the grate and covered them with a wet burlap sack. As soon as the shells loosened, Wink and Thor had to fight off people of all sizes to get oysters for themselves.

When Wink went to his cabin, thinking to lie down for a rest, he opened the door to find Anner, already on his cot. She sat up. "Massuh wants you to hitch up the buggy."

"How long you been here?" Wink wondered if she had plundered his cabin and found his whiskey.

"Not long. I'se just resting my feets." She wiggled a foot.

"Billy send you?" Wink began to worry about a delay in getting his orders. He wondered if the master had been waiting.

"Billy ... that nigger owes me a grudge, and I'm about ready to even the score." She stood and straightened her dress. "I tell you, I bout got them dogs in the house already."

"What dogs?"

Anner twitched toward him and smiled. "Is you funning wid me? What dogs is herebouts but the Massuh's?" She touched his neck, straightening his shirt.

Wink had the uneasy feeling he'd never figure out this woman, but the way she smiled, it didn't seem to matter. "You know where the massuh's going?" He felt gamy, for it had been a long time since a woman had touched his body with intentions.

"He's going to take back dat fancy sewing machine Missus borrowed." She drew him to the cot with a racy gleam in her eye. "I'se the one waiting for you, not the Massuh." She pulled him to her as she lay back. "You my kind a man, Wink."

Wink ached for the touch of a woman's bare skin. The fierce pleasure that arose from such comfort helped him forget the privation and shame of slavery. His body filled with appreciation and his lips fully expressed it. He unbuttoned her dress. When her hand went inside his shirt and spread his skin with chills, his body drove him closer to her, so close his bare chest felt the warm rush of her breasts like molten silk. Her nipples rubbed into his skin.

Footsteps sounded outside.

"Wink!"

It was the master. Wink buttoned his shirt, helped Anner from the cot, and opened the door while Anner stood behind it out of sight.

"Yessuh! You wants the buggy?" Wink stepped outside and walked as best he could behind the master.

"Let's try Puff with the buggy. Bring it to the front and come inside for the sewing machine."

By the time Wink returned at sundown, a bonfire flamed up and popped fiery embers into the air in the back lot. Brother Milton was sermonizing the slaves, who either sat on blankets spread on the ground within range of the heat or stood about in the shadows. Because the master objected to African talk, only a smattering of the localisms came out in the brother's sermonizing, simple slips, like *yent, mek, talk'um,* or *we'self.*

Wink unhitched Puff and stored the buggy in the carriage house before feeding and watering the horses and mule. From the yard came the chatter of the negros and the thundering voice of Brother Milton. Wink reckoned any man could change, and some of them, such as Brother Milton, had done so in spectacular fashion.

It was widely believed that, as a younger man, the Brother had stood as stud for his master and that more women than a body could count had borne his numerous children. It was a fact that the Brother's expression played over the features of many a youngster in Prince William's Parish. The stableman at the roadhouse in Jacksonboro had his square jaw, and a girl at the Fortier mansion in Beaufort had his high cheeks, and the former errand boy at Salina's store had his prominent temple bones.

Wink resented the Brother's claim to godliness, but in truth what he resented was the power of the man's spunk. Wink's features couldn't be found in the face of any child living on either the island or mainland and never would. The fact that he was unable to sire sons or daughters was known only to himself and his former wife, and he carefully guarded the secret, for the story of Mammy Livy's first husband was well known to older folks in the quarters. She'd had a husband for years without bringing a baby, and old man Pyatt got outdone about it and sold her husband. Though the baby girl born during Wink's marriage had been sired by a field hand, Wink had taken full credit.

As Wink latched the stall gate on the last of the horses, he went to the yard and stood in the far shadows with Thor, Claude, and some of the other men. Under the endless expanse of heaven and in the presence of unknown stars, Wink took a deep breath.

One of the older men tipped back a bottle and whispered, "It be writ, de grinder cease because they be few."

"What the hell you mumbling bout?" said Claude, who had been complaining about having to listen to the Brother when he could have played his banjo for a shindig.

"Losing his teeth," said Thor, and they stifled their merriment.

Limbo skirted the shadows, taking nips from a bottle. He pushed Mooey off a barrel and took the seat for himself. "Go on back to the quarters!" he said, loud enough that several people shushed him.

"Behave yourself," muttered Wink. He and Thor pushed Limbo off the barrel, but Mooey had already skipped away.

Limbo sidled up to Wink and asked if he had any more hooch. Claude and several field hands had asked the same question, but Wink didn't want to become known at Westfall for trading liquor. "I see about it when this here preaching is done."

As Wink and Thor stood together, Lovey eased up behind Thor and leaned into his back. Another song began, with Puddin leading the melody. What Wink wouldn't do to have her lean into his backside. Her voice glowed. It inspired Wink with reverence. Puddin's song could make the Bible a truth that he could believe. Even the trees whispered overhead like kindly spirits worshiping her song.

Brother Milton ended by appealing to the stars with open arms. "Wait on the Lord, brothers and sisters! Just hold on till we cross over!" The slaves returned to their shanties, their voices spirited.

Wink wanted to walk Puddin to her quarter but Kedzie went with her. He headed for his place with the whiskey business on his mind. Limbo caught up and walked with him.

"You got specie?" said Wink. It wasn't unusual for Limbo to hanker after more whiskey than he could pay for.

"Massuh owes me for a basket of oysters. I'll settle up when I get dat." Limbo wore his wool in a frizz, which on a fuller man would have looked head-heavy.

"I'se not carrying no accounts."

"But I spect I'll get more'n enough for a pint. I'll turn over the whole lot."

"I have a notion I needs somebody to trade hooch wid the field hands, somebody what works and lives in the quarters," said Wink, who had been mulling over a way to distance himself from trading.

Limbo slowed his steps and said, "I knows every nigger what ever took a dram. I can trade hooch under Farley's nose."

"Trouble is, can you stay sober? Can you figure specie?" Wink didn't go into the question of whether Limbo would drink up the merchandise instead of selling it.

"I can come close on both counts."

They reached Wink's shanty. He opened the door and went inside, followed by Limbo, whose excitement sounded in his voice. "I knows most specie bills, the big ones from the little ones." He sat on the stool and held his hands to the embers.

Wink tossed a log on the coals. "We can work dat out." Wink was prepared to teach Limbo to recognize the specie they needed. In any case, their buyers didn't know the difference between a two-bit piece and a dollar note. "We'll give it a shot. On one condition." He sat on his cot and looked Limbo over. "On one condition ... you never tell nobody where you gets your hooch."

Limbo gazed up. "Why come?"

"Cause dat's the way we going to do the trading. Iffen, after we get this working, a nigger comes to my door instead of your door for hooch, you and me not going to do business."

Limbo shrugged. "Iffen this is business, what's I going to put in my pocket?"

"I'll give you two gills of whiskey for every three-gallon cask you sell."

Limbo smiled. "Dat suits me!" He bounded to his feet. Before he left, Wink gave him several coins and explained the amount of whiskey each would buy. He told him to study them until he had them in his head.

It was a start. Now what Wink needed was a supply of whiskey.

CHAPTER 9

THE DEVIL'S DRAYMAN

DECEMBER 1857

For some years past, the master and his family had traveled to a relative's plantation for a week or more to celebrate Christmas. Wink had driven the family from St. Helena Island as far as Georgia and Virginia. Things were different this year. Every Goodwyn in the family was descending on Westfall to celebrate the holiday.

Wink's hope of bringing in a supply of whiskey drifted away in the midst of the many demands of the white family. Though he went to the mainland, more often than not the master's presence was inescapable. They returned with household supplies such as brandy, ale, opium, quinine, and white sugar. But nothing for Wink.

A week before Christmas, Master Goodwyn came to the carriage house while Wink was at work shining the plate handles of the doors and rubbing the other metallic parts of the carriage. He gave Wink directions about where to move the carts, wagons, and buggy to make room for the carriages of their visitors.

Wink's tasks multiplied every time the master appeared. He had to make space in the stables for the additional horses. With help from several field hands, he built fences to divide the paddock into sections that would allow him to separate the horses. He went to nearby plantations for extra provender and stocked up on fodder, oats, corn, and hay.

At times he was ordered to the big house to help Billy. They pulled out trundle beds and placed extensions on the big table, which became so long it barely fit into the dining room.

On his way back to the stables, he walked by the gin house and paused for his usual spit and hawk socializing. Kedzie, who was packing cotton, glanced about with red, puffy eyes. "Now, who done put you in a bad humor?"

She wouldn't look at him.

"She be wanting to see her mammy," said Auntie Nell as she packed cotton into the sack.

"Massuh don't give you no pass?" Wink said to Kedzie, who sniffled and wiped her nose on the clean cotton. Wink had asked for a pass to visit his former wife and her daughter, but as he expected the master had refused on account of all the carrying-on expected over Christmas. Rarely did he or the household servants get passes anywhere.

"Massuh give her one, but she don't have no ticket to get to Charleston," Auntie said.

"I reckon Massuh thinks I can walk." Kedzie stuffed the cotton tighter into the sack with her foot. "Where am I supposed to get the money?"

"Wink, iffen you loan her enough for a ticket, I'll give you the quilt I been working on," said Auntie.

"Granny, you needs that for your rheumatism," said Kedzie.

"Mamba's going to git eel skin. She says to wrap my leg in it to take away the pain." Auntie picked out a few strands of yellow fiber from a wad of cotton. "Somebody done a poor job of cleaning dis cotton."

Wink took specie from his pocket and counted out the amount for a ticket on the steamer. "Here. You can pay me back whensoever you gits the money."

As Kedzie took the money, her eyes blazed. "Wink! You is the best friend!" She jumped over and gave him a hug.

As it turned out, Wink gave Kedzie a ride to the village when he went to fetch the Goodwyn boy, who attended boarding school there. On the causeway, they picked up and dropped off other slaves going for visits with relatives.

Back at Westfall, Wink went with Billy to the cellar to bring up the master's sea turtle. They placed the large barrel on the kitchen stoop. Once word spread that the master promised a firkin of scuppernong wine to the person catching the turtle with its head out of the shell, so many people passed by the kitchen Wink didn't feel free to make his usual visits to Puddin. Even the children kept watch and screamed at the sight of the head, which caused it to disappear as quickly as it appeared. Puddin shooed them away, and the watch turned serious. In no time, Polly raced to Wink with the urgent message that the head was out. Wink hurried to the kitchen stoop, sidled up to the barrel, grabbed the gig from the nailhook, and gigged the head at the neck. Servants and children dropped what they were doing to watch Puddin whack the head off with the butcher knife. "The turtle done lost his head!" went up as a cheer. The event turned into full-blown jubilation, and the firkin of wine passed from hand to hand.

Wink made trips with the wagon to pick up tables and chairs the master borrowed from an uncle who also lived on the island. Wink and Iverson hauled in a cedar tree, which Billy helped them put up in the front parlor.

Wink dressed in his new livery with brass buttons and took soot from the chimney, wet it, and brushed his boots. Looking his best, he stood in the kitchen door and waited for Puddin, who tended pots at the fire, to notice him. Strong whiffs of frying onion and boiling meat drifted from the steaming pots. White potatoes with milk and onions sputtered in the spider. Gussie sat at the hearth and plucked a turkey, throwing the coarse feathers into the fireplace and bagging the downy ones.

Polly stopped turning the grinder handle that pulverized cloves and said, "Look at Wink! Wid the shiny buttons." Mamba looked up from grating cinnamon and smiled.

Puddin, who was fussing over yams she'd just pulled from the fire, turned around. Her face lit up. "My-oh ... You is dressed up to beat the band." She gave out a whistle. A seductive look crossed her face, which made more than his buttons shine.

When the first carriage of relatives came to a stop at the steps, Wink waited for the coachman to unload his people and their trunks before pulling the horses to the stables and helping him unhitch the team. Iverson, taken from the field to help at the big house, showed the coachman to a cot in the quarters. For several days, carriages continued to arrive. The master and mistress greeted each visitor with hugs, kisses, and laughter while the visiting coachmen off-loaded the trunks.

With the addition of the visiting coachmen and footmen, the quarters turned into nightly frolics. Claude played banjo, Lettie the quill, and Nitsy the bones. A visiting coachman brought his fiddle, which he played in fine style. Tubs turned into drums and spoons kept time. Mamba sang, as did Flurry, Matilda, and others.

Wink, who sold out of whiskey, made a deal with a Riverben slave and, though he paid a high price for it, he sold it for even more. He was in a good mood when he ambled toward the kitchen, Puddin on his mind. His mood changed when he saw the fiddle player at the door, making as if he needed a tow sack. "Nah, this one's not big enough." He handed it back to Puddin and when she brought another one, he said, "Now, sweetie, this one's too big."

"I don't have time to worry wid you," Puddin said.

Wink stepped up to the stoop. "I got a tow sack. Come wid me!" He motioned the fiddle player to follow him, but the man kept on yammering with Puddin. "I knows that. Listen here, we going to have a big time in the quarters tonight. Everbody says you can lay a hoodoo on a man wid your singing. I wants to hear you."

Wink, walking away, didn't hear Puddin's answer, but she went to the quarters after supper. Cold though the night air, a fire of music excited the cabins. Claude hardly paused from playing the banjo long enough to drink his share of the whiskey he had bought from Limbo. Children pranced in the street. Everybody swayed to and fro, making up new moves for the pigeon and shuffle toe. The fiddle player taught Puddin a new song and, when they sang together, she inspired everybody to sing. The fiddler watched her, and Wink watched him. When Puddin smiled at the man, Wink's head clouded up with worry.

On the day before Christmas Eve, the hands returned to the gin house after dinner and sang songs peppered with laughter. They dallied at ginning and packing cotton, and Farley shouted threats that went astray in the midst of their bawdy behavior. He could hardly keep them in the gin house, much less get work out of them. He allowed them to knock off work earlier than usual.

Wink watched as a plain wagon driven by a stranger, obviously not a Goodwyn, rolled from the carriageway into the yard. The white man pulled his horse to a stop, tied the lines to the hitching post, and walked to the back door. With roundabout and trousers of coarse corduroy, he was either lost, looking for work, or on an errand.

Too many times, trouble had arrived at Westfall as a stranger. Trouble in the person of a slave trader. Wink's first thought was that Lovey had been sold. When the master moved her out of the big house, some people had speculated that it was just a matter of time before he'd put her in his pocket. She grew big with child, and the baby of mixed blood was born. Because nobody dared rail against the master, women blamed Lovey and men resented her.

In unguarded moments, Wink cursed the negros. The master had misued the woman, and even her own people turned their back on her. Iverson, at least, made no excuses for the master. Though the woman needed a defender, Wink could only look on dispassionately. Whatever he did, he could not thwart the master's will, and any effort on his part might well send him to the block.

Back of the big house, the stranger rapped on the door. Billy came out on the porch dressed in a black vest and shiny cravat. When conversing with whites, he always looked like he was about to say something, as if he had an answer whatever the question. After a short exchange, Billy returned to the house, and the stranger sat on the back steps and waited, presumably for the master, who had ridden down to the Sandmire Field with his cousins.

Wink devised an excuse to go to the kitchen, which was no more than five rods from the back porch. He watched Puddin for a few minutes and asked her an inconsequential question before leaving by way of greeting the buckra on the steps. "Who you come here for?" he said in spite of knowing how inappropriate the question.

"Don't worry, Boss. I'm not come fer you."

"You after my wife Lovey?" said Wink. The man, whose small rheumy eyes gave away no secrets, had no way of knowing Wink had no wife.

He pulled a pipe from his coat pocket and packed it with tobacco without a sign of an answer. Maybe it wasn't Lovey.

In the evening when Wink went to the well for a bucket of water, he waited his turn while Flurry drew water. Farley walked up and dipped water from her bucket and drank. "The Massuh done sold somebody," said Flurry, who entertained the slaves with her exaggerations, but Wink watched Farley's answer.

"Who said that?" said Farley.

"What that man doing here if he don't come for somebody?" She looked in the well and adjusted her shawl tighter to her shoulders.

"You got so smart you know the massuh's business?" Farley hung the gourd dipper on a hook.

"Who he's getting?" said Flurry.

"You got a regular talent for churning up the niggers wid your fool talk." Farley turned but paused before departing. "Keep your trifling nonsense to yourself. And go git Mooey and bring her to my house."

"What you want wid Mooey?" said Flurry.

"Maybe I want her to kiss my black ass! Go on, and keep them flappy lips shut."

"If it be kissing you want ..."

"God amighty, woman! Is there any way to get you to shut up?" Farley stalked toward his house.

Flurry turned to Wink. "Reckon Massuh sold Mooey?" Many of the men bedded with Flurry, and some said she had a powerful conjure bag that put a spell on a man. But Wink thought she was ignorant, even for a negro. Her numerous children, all of them of random fathers, went about dirty and barely fed. Worse than that, she had another baby every other year.

Wink returned to the stables to see about the horses. While he was in a stall filing down a horse's tooth, the master and his cousins rode in. A few of the men removed the saddles and halters and turned their steeds into the paddock, while others stood about talking. Wink begrudged caring for the visiting horses while the coachmen lazed about the quarters.

The master strolled to the big house and spoke with the stranger who, in a matter of moments, led his horse and wagon to the carriage house. As the Goodwyn men drifted toward the big house, the stranger approached the stable.

"You got a fire in your place?"

Wink threw a saddle on a rack. "Don't know your business, Boss, but do it somewheres else."

"Goodwyn says for me to wait in your quarter."

"That what he said?" said Wink.

The man nodded. "I don't take to no nigger quarter, but that be warmer than the wagon."

"What you waiting around here for?" Wink unsaddled a roan.

"Just waiting. That your place?" He tipped his head.

Wink walked ahead of the man and stopped before his cabin door. "Firewood's over there." He pointed to the wall where the wood was stacked out of sight. The stranger pushed in the door. "Got any hooch?"

Wink sold him a couple gills and profited as if it were a pint. He hoped this buckra wasn't going to stay the night.

CHAPTER 10

DANGER AS A FEELING

DECEMBER 1857

Mooey noticed the many carriages arriving at the big house with white people. The visiting servants put up in cots left empty when some of the hands had disappeared. That Lacy had left hadn't surprised Mooey, for her friend had already stayed longer than ever before.

In the quarters, the women fixed up their best dresses. Some of them brought in wild bullis vines, which they bent to shape their skirts and make them stand out. People walked in glints of motion. The air flickered with expectation.

Mooey chased a lamb that had escaped into the yard but stopped at the kitchen house to watch a stranger drive his wagon to the back lot. His brute eyes and steady hands were those of a dangerous person. Apparently unwelcome even by the whites, he pulled his marsh tacky horse to a stop at the carriage house. He took wiry steps. His coat drooped like it was made for a bigger man.

The lamb had stopped as well, and Mooey picked it up and carried it back to the pasture. The distant sun was withdrawing, readying for its departure. Though the sky was clear and cold, a shadow fell on Mooey. She felt it as circles inside her head, spirits churning with a message for her. By the time she finished her tasks, their haunting anxiety affected her vision. If they got into her throat, she'd disturb the whole place, including Auntie. She hurried to a good-natured oak tree where she could fathom what the spirits were trying to tell her. By now she intuited a warning of danger. When she saw the stranger as the cause, her head cleared.

From her perch in the joint of branches, she saw Early and the hands stream out of the gin house to the quarters. His thunder gait made her nervous. His arms gesticulated, his shoulder nudged his ear, the brim of his hat shaded his eyes. Some time ago she gained the knowledge that he bossed everybody. Above all, he presided over the whip.

A cold breeze flushed down from the leaves and so chilled Mooey's breath it squeezed her chest. She scrambled from the tree and slipped into her cabin where the smell of wood and smoke comforted her. Auntie dropped heavily into her chair and took off her head rag and rubbed dust from her short white hair. The tilt of her head and slump of her back spoke of weariness. Mooey crouched at the bristling log in the fireplace and rocked on her heels.

Magic opened the door, came to the fire, and put a tow sack on the hearth. After she inspected sores on Auntie's neck, she took a vial from the sack and dabbed the sores with oil and then patched one with a poultice.

The presence of the two women and their tranquil movements provided Mooey with some confidence. The arrival of the stranger was only the latest in a series of disturbances. Lacy had left the plantation with a smile on her face and a happy farewell, to Mooey's distress. Just the previous night, Sunny and Lovey hadn't come to their cabin, and Mooey worried herself to a frazzle about the baby. In the middle of the night, she had found him in Mammy's cabin. Lovey had slept with a young man who lived with Mooey's brother.

Magic brushed ashes aside and removed an ashcake. She slapped on it a piece of greasy bacon and offered it to Mooey, who ignored her. Food worsened Mooey's growing sense of dread. Magic gave it to Auntie and sat on a stool in a naturally graceful way, for she carried her goodly size with ease.

From their enlivened faces, busy lips, and glances, Mooey could see a connection between Auntie and Magic. She realized this connection broke down when it came to herself. Auntie's kindly wrinkles became worried. Magic removed another ashcake, pinched off a bite, ate it, and offered what remained to Mooey, who turned away from her and toward the fire.

The very air in the room felt peculiar. The white stranger's ordinary roundabout told Mooey he was not a man of the master's station. Moreover, he had arrived, not riding a horse, but driving a wagon. And he went to the back door instead of the front, all of which meant he would likely haul off goods, stock, or some other valuable. Mooey's breath came and went like waves in a stormy sea. She mumbled and rocked herself back and forth as she squatted at the fire. Magic broke off another piece of ashcake and put it to Mooey's lips. Mooey took the food and chewed on it at length. Magic tried to give her another bite, but Mooey's throat hurt. She had difficulty swallowing. Her hands whirled in her face.

Magic rubbed Mooey's shoulders and the room seemed safe again. Auntie stretched into the back of her chair and closed her eyes. Magic stood and put Mooey's uneaten food in the iron spider on the hearth. She helped Auntie out of her linsey woolsey dress and into her cot. When Magic left, Mooey lay on her cot and gazed into the smoldering fire. The flames crackled and licked at her. She missed Lacy. She awaited the baby boy.

Lovey, with Sunny drooping in her arm, groped her way in the door and slumped into her cot on top of Sunny. Mooey got up and pulled the baby from under Lovey. Waves of distress wrinkled his face. Mooey cuddled and rocked him in her arms as she paced before the fire. When he calmed, she placed him in the cot with her.

Winter hedged in through chinks in the cabin and sent an icy whiff up her spine. The restless air seized her as if the spirit of the sky gave it breath. Bad smoke wormed its way into the room. Mooey could hardly breathe. Nearly paralyzed with terror, she felt the presence of an evil spirit. She placed Sunny in his basket, wrapped herself in a blanket, and hurried outside where she felt safer in the limbs of the live oak near the sick house.

CHAPTER 11

SEARCH FOR MOOEY

DECEMBER 1857

Wink glanced inside the stables and saw Farley currying his horse Skeeter. The stranger sat nearby on a stool smoking a clay pipe. His flat grey eyes shifted from Wink to Farley and back to Wink.

Wink picked up a broom and swept the common passageway. People in the quarters who had noticed the visitor's wagon had to worry about why it had been stowed in the carriage house. Worse yet, why hadn't the man been given the goods he'd come after and been sent on his way? Wink knew how to act normal, even if rain turned to blood. It was something a person learned before he got out of shirttails. He leaned the broom against the wall and came to Skeeter's gate.

After a spell he said to Farley, "Where bouts you buy Skeeter?"

"What you asking for?"

"I been thinking bout getting a horse."

"Horses cost a passel of money." Farley picked burrs out of his horse's forelocks.

"You got a bill of sale to show you own Skeeter?"

Farley stopped brushing Skeeter's mane and looked over the horse. "Onliest place I own Skeeter is on this here plantation. Papers don't mean shit to niggers like us. Whatsomever we have is owned by the massuh."

"And iffen you is in the village and some white buckra rides off on Skeeter?"

Farley dug the scissors out of the gear box and trimmed his horse's mane. "Massuh might could git him back."

"Iffen you be sold, can you take Skeeter?"

"Dat depend on the massuh." Farley rubbed oil in the wiry hair.

"What you buy Skeeter for?"

"So's I don't have to call on the massuh ever time I want to ride around. So's I don't have to think about paying massuh iffen by some accident I break his horse's leg. So's I don't have to ride any of his spiteful horses."

Polly came skipping up to Farley. "Massuh be wanting you," she said.

"Yessum," Farley said. She turned and skipped back toward the big house. "Skeeter needs a hoof packing," he said to Wink as he handed over a bag of tobacco meant as payment. Before Wink could protest the manner or amount, Farley marched toward the big house.

Because Wink was left in the company of the stranger, he could hardly stand still. Only one explanation why the master would put him up over the night. Somebody had been sold. Wink didn't think it was himself, but he hadn't thought his mother would have been sold. Nor his wife.

The stranger knew who it was. And Farley was about to find out. Wink lit his lantern before beginning on Skeeter's hoof.

When Farley returned and pulled Wink out of the stranger's range, his words still surprised Wink. "Mooey done been sold. Massuh says for us to catch her in the night. Eat your supper and come to my place."

Of all the people Wink suspected, he least expected it to be Mooey. She was hardly a quarter-task slave. "Dis ain't my task. I be the stableman."

"Massuh don't have no time to git a patroller. He said to git you to help and he'll pay you wid a shoat."

"I don't want no shoat."

"I don't reckon I wants the task neither, but you, me, we not going to keep dis girl at Westfall."

"Dat don't mean we oughta help dat white bastard off wid her."

"All you can do is git yourself lashed or toted off wid her."

"Git Iverson to help. I gots a belly ache from eating too many oysters." Wink had a belly ache all right, but it was for Mooey. Her new master might well be a trader, and those bastards were mean as snakes. How would she survive? The girl could hardly do simple tasks with the help of Doll, Puddin, and the others. She was a spiritual creature who lived in greater harmony with trees than with people.

"Massuh be strict about you. He don't want one of the fieldhands blabbing the business about the quarters. Worrying everbody."

"What the hell? You think they not worrying?"

"They drinking hooch and having a big time." Farley motioned toward the quarters where laughter and the stringy notes of whistles could be heard.

Wink listened but what he heard was the racket of people getting shaky in their joints.

"We'll wait for her to bed down and git her while she's sleeping."

"No, suh! I gots the shivers all over on account of them oysters. I ain't in no shape to be hauling nobody nowhere."

Farley seemed to sigh. "You going to get the shivers from Massuh iffen you don't git your ass to the quarters and help me haul Mooey to this here man's wagon." Farley nodded toward the stranger. "He be waiting for her after the niggers settles down." Farley strutted toward the quarters.

Wink ate supper with Thor and dallied about the quarters, which were unusually noisy. Cheerful voices scattered from one shanty to another. If he happened upon Mooey, he wanted to signal her about the danger, but where would she go? Somebody blew off a rocket in the yard, which set off squeals of delight. Claude and the fiddler played for what was becoming a hoedown until Farley stalked into the street with an angry whip and drove everybody into their cabins. Only when the moon was well above the pines did the laughter and commotion trail off into the night.

Wink drank more whiskey than usual and sat in the dark on Farley's porch rather than wait inside with the man.

"What you doing here?" said Flurry, who came up the steps and knocked on the door.

"I'se waiting on the count." Wink, who could hardly see Flurry though the moon was bright, realized his eyes weren't working well. When he stood, he discovered his legs weren't either.

"What you want wid the count?" Flurry pulled her shawl over her head.

Farley opened the door. "Everbody accounted for?"

"There's so many cullud folks sleeping here and yon I can't make heads nor tails of who's sleeping where. How can I keep count wid half the hands stepping off the place and all these different niggers sleeping in the cots?"

"You seen Mooey?"

Wink finished off the last of his whiskey as he leaned against the wall.

"I reckon Mooey be somewheres, but I didn't see her," said Flurry.

"You see anybody roaming around like a stray dog?"

"Everbody's off the street."

"Git yourself abed." Farley picked up leather cords and stuffed some into his coat pocket. When Flurry disappeared into the dark, he gave a couple cords to Wink. "We'll tie her hands and feet wid these. Come on." He grabbed the lantern and headed down the street. At Mooey's cabin, he pushed on the door gently, but the hinges squeaked all the more. When Wink dallied outside, Farley pulled him in by the ear. Auntie Nell slept in one cot, Lovey in another, and her baby in the basket. A stranger slept in the cot usually occupied by Kedzie, who had left for Charleston to visit her mother. Mooey's cot was empty.

"What you doing here?" Auntie mumbled. The light from the fireplace gave Farley a giant shadow.

"Where be Mooey?"

Auntie Nell raised up. "Who you coming after?"

"I'se making the count. Where be Mooey?" Farley looked under the cots and in the rafters.

Lovey slept even as the baby opened his eyes, squirmed, and kicked his cover off.

Auntie Nell lay back and spoke to the wall. "She must be scusing herself."

Farley pulled Wink outside. "Look in the shit house." He handed over the lantern.

Wink walked down the path to the slaves' privy, but it was empty. If she was in the woods attending to the necessities of nature, he hoped she'd stay there. He returned to Auntie Nell's cabin. Farley said, "You wait around back. I'll wait inside. She's bound to come back, cold as it is."

Dogs barked in the distance. Wink stood until his legs tired and he squatted. He removed a leather lash from his pocket and pulled it through his fingers. What was he doing helping Farley? Even with the soothing effects of the whiskey, Wink hated himself for what he was doing. The girl had done nothing to warrant being sold.

When the baby cried, Farley stepped outside, and the two of them walked the street looking for Mooey while Flurry entered the cabin and suckled the baby. When Flurry left, they returned. Farley kicked Auntie Nell's cot. "Git up and find Mooey!" She was the only person who might know Mooey's whereabouts.

Lovey moaned and turned over. Auntie Nell didn't move.

What the hell was Farley doing? Auntie wouldn't look for Mooey unless her own life was threatened. Wink didn't know what he'd do if Farley made such a threat to Auntie Nell. Wink needed more whiskey.

Farley walked over and shook Auntie's shoulder. "Git up! Git out here and find Mooey!"

Auntie turned over and sat up. "Is dat stranger looking to take Mooey?" Her voice was pitched high. Farley slapped his leather lash against his thigh and stomped out.

From Auntie's place they opened the door to every other cabin in the quarters, but Mooey was nowhere to be found. They searched the yard, the barn, the tool shed, and other outbuildings. Farley knocked on Puddin's door and demanded that she open up. They searched the stables and carriage house. The stranger sat wrapped in a blanket in the wagon, waiting in the yard. His horse blew cold clouds from its nostrils. In the deepening cold of early morning, Farley gave up the search.

Wink was so tired he threw himself into his cot with his clothes and brogans on. Before daylight, the stranger came into his cabin, added a log to the fire, and lay on the floor at the hearth. Wink, who had no heart for sleeping in the room with the man, grabbed his blanket and went to the quarters where he bedded down on Thor's floor.

CHAPTER 12

CHRISTMAS EVE MORNING

DECEMBER 1857

At daybreak the morning of Christmas Eve, the bell that usually signaled the hands to the fields was silent. Though he couldn't actually hear Tootie neighing, Wink knew she was calling for breakfast. He awoke cold, for Thor's fire had flickered down to smoke. He rolled over, got up from his pallet on the floor, and hawked into the fireplace.

A piece of wood had rolled onto the hearth, and smoke drifted into the room. Wink grabbed the iron poker and shuffled the fire. He added some heartwood and sat in a comfortable silence while Thor and Limbo slept on their cots. Then he left for the stables.

In the back lot, several men sloshed the carcasses of a couple of hogs in steaming barrels buried butt-end in the ground. In the other direction toward the carriage house, Wink saw the stranger's wagon.

Gideon was impatient to get out of his stall. One of the visiting mares neighed so shrilly she scared off the cats, which usually slept on the backs of the horses. Regardless of what Wink did, his horses liked him. Tootie had eased his mind more than once and he stroked her flank. A sense of calm, if not pleasure, shifted from the horse's hair to the palm of Wink's hand. As he curried the croup, tail, and mane, he freehanded her bodily. She blew kindly with her nose and nickered in a consoling way.

After tending to the horses, he walked to the kitchen and sat in the warmth of Puddin's fire. The room smelled of yeast and baking breads. Puddin swung a crane with a pot of apples from the fire to the hearth as if she could think of nothing but her cooking. The scent of cinnamon arose from the pot as she sprinkled the spice onto the sauce. She gave the apples more attention than they required.

Wink touched her arm but she withdrew. At the table she began to peel boiled shrimp with one eye on the cooking pots.

Wink sensed her nervousness. Looked back at her. "Anything I can do?"

She wiped her palms on her apron. "They say he's a slave trader."

Anner, who entered wanting more jam for the table, smiled at Wink. "What you get me for Christmas, Wink?"

"Billy done took extra jars of jam to the big house. Look in the pantry," said Puddin.

"Next snapping turtle I catch be yours," Wink said to Anner.

Anner laughed. "I'se going to the quarters after supper tonight." The look she gave Wink was an invitation to meet her there.

"You going to the quarters, Puddin?" Wink said.

Lettie brought in several empty bowls. "Billy be looking for you," she said to Anner. She glanced at Puddin as if they had a mutual worry and returned to the big house.

Anner puffed up at Wink and left.

Puddin took a spider from the fire, pushed it to the hearth, and removed the iron lid to reveal two dozen brown biscuits. Steam from the biscuits smelled good enough to call forth the dead. "Flurry said he's after Lovey. Limbo said he come for Kedzie ... didn't know she was in Charleston. Lettie wants me to hide her boy under my cot." Her voice gave way.

Wink wanted to end Puddin's distress, but even if he told her it was Mooey, it wouldn't put her mind at ease. Anyway, he couldn't reveal what he knew without admitting to helping Farley look for Mooey. There was nothing he could say or do to change anything. "He's more likely after a field hand," he said.

With a spatula, she offered him a biscuit. "Better put this in your pocket before somebody else comes in here."

It was so hot he put it on the table to cool.

"Where is it writ dat I got no feelings? Dat I got no mind?" She threw shrimp peels in a slop bucket. Tears were in her eyes.

Wink tried to hold her in his arms, but she pushed him away. "When is white people going to notice a nigger's not the same as a hog or a cow?"

Billy came to the door but stopped when he saw Puddin.

"How can God let this happen?" She knocked the bowl of shrimp so hard it teetered on the edge of the table. Wink caught and settled it, then grabbed her in his arms to calm her. He kissed tears that trickled onto her cheek.

"How many times is this going to happen ...." Some words about how God hated negros were lost in his collar.

"Shhhh. Maybe this buckra come after seed corn. How you know he come after somebody?" He raised her chin and smooched her face.

She kept her eyes closed. "I don't want to live like this."

"We going to live any way we got to, baby." Wink held her close.

Billy practically tiptoed inside. "Wink, you de person I needs. Tell Farley we is short lamp oil."

Puddin wiped her face, turned to the fireplace, and shuffled the coals with the iron poker.

Wink left to find Farley, who had the key to the storehouse. Most everybody took it hard when a slave was sold, but some people made like it didn't matter. Didn't grieve or anything. Said it was just the way of things. Puddin worried more than most, but she had never cried before or talked about it. This was a particular wearying time for her, cooking for a house full of white people. When he returned with the oil, Billy was in the kitchen. Wink left his biscuit rather than reveal that Puddin had given him food from the master's kitchen.

Back at his shanty, Wink found the stranger sitting at the fire. He headed back out the door. In the lot, Iverson and several hands dragged the carcass of a porker from the back of a wagon and rolled it into the steaming water of one of the barrels partially sunk into the ground. Nearby other men scraped the hair from a previously scalded hog. Two other men were skinning a wild ox hanging by its tendons from a crossbeam. Wink stopped long enough to ask, "Anybody seen Mooey?" The men shook their heads and continued working. "She come amiss last night."

"She's got more sense than the rest of us," said one of the men. A knowing look passed between them. Everybody knew the stranger was still there.

In the quarters, barefoot children chased around on the street. The chimneys churned with smoke as parents revived fires and mothers cooked ashcakes and fathers poured cups of clabber for the children.

Wink sat at Thor's fire and warmed his hands and feet. Lovey came in with two cups and woke Thor, who opened an eye. He sat on the side of his cot, his head in his hands.

She gave a cup to Thor. "This'll perk you up."

Thor held his ears as if her voice had damaged his eardrums.

"Where'd you get dat coffee?" said Wink.

Lovey rubbed Thor's wool. "Bought it. But Nitsy don't have no more."

Limbo's snoring snagged. He mumbled and rolled over.

Once he had warmed up, Wink wandered down the street and approached the sound of voices at Flurry's cabin. Children clamored about the hearth, jostling one other. Several people took turns warming by her fire. Flurry made more ashcakes as first one then another took the cooked ones from the fire. Wink managed to get part of one for himself and a cup of coffee made with parched meal, a far cry from Puddin's coffee.

"I seen that buckra dis morning. Still in the carriage house," said Flurry. Though she was known as a blabbermouth given to sounding the worst of any story, people had begun to pay attention to her. Her talk seemed to give the others permission to worry.

"What's he doing here anyway?"

"Reckon the massuh giving him a wagonload of cotton?"

"Don't take all night to load a bale of cotton."

"Maybe he come after a porker."

"You can't haul no live porker in that wagon."

"Is he a pattyroller?"

"They don't come up in no wagon."

"What's he doing wid a wagon?"

Wink could hardly swallow his ashcake. By now, they had to know the man had come for one of them or perhaps two or three. But to admit the man's obvious purpose, they'd have to consider who had been sold, and that wasn't something they could talk about. Husbands didn't want to worry for their wives or wives their husbands. Nobody wanted to think they'd lose a mother. Son. Brother.

Wink could at least let them know that only one person had been sold. He sipped the charred wheat taste of what passed for coffee. He would say nothing. If he told them it was Mooey, they might be so relieved for their own families they'd help Farley find her.

Hardly had Wink swallowed his food when Claude stuck his head in the door to say a jug of hooch had turned up. Down at his cabin. One of the visiting coachmen had brought it. The cabin emptied out quickly enough as most everybody took out after Claude. Wink walked the street and was passed by Limbo and Lovey. The merriment increased as many a person just stepped in at Claude's place. Others, especially the children, wandered into the yard to watch the butchers cut off the hogs' heads and split the carcasses.

Claude plucked the strings of his banjo, then paused and listened as the visiting fiddler tuned his instrument. The musicians gradually came together in a song with so much drag it might have been a conjuration. Several people kept time with tin lids. Others clapped their hands. Wink whistled. The voices gradually raised the spirit of the musicians and filled the room with harmony. It didn't take long for them to feel the rhythm and sway and stomp, getting winter out of their fingers and feet. Getting worry off their shoulders.

Standing near the door, Wink moved over to make room for several children pushing their way inside. As he did so, he bumped into Rosa, a fieldhand known for such showy clothes she attracted more attention than the preacher. Her red eyes were awash with tears.

She blew her nose and wiped her eyes, but Wink turned quickly to avoid coming face to face with her. He didn't want the task of comforting her should she have some premonition that the stranger had come after her. Somebody handed Wink the jug that was making its way around the room. He took a hefty draft and passed it to Claude, who was talking to Rosa.

When Wink overheard Claude say, "You know who's been sold?" he paid attention to them.

Rosa sniffled and shook her head.

"Do our chording lather tears?" Claude tipped his face to hers.

In fact, Wink thought Flurry sang too loud with "Juba this and Juba that," and the whole shebang needed Puddin to keep on key.

Rosa perked up and smiled at Claude. The long and short of the tears was that she had washed her good dress and the colors streaked and she was ashamed to be seen in it. The worst of it was she had nothing nice to wear for Christmas.

Claude looked at her with sympathetic eyes. "Honey, don't you worry. You can borrow Nitsy's Sunday dress."

Lovey said, "Come on, Claude! Git to the music. How we going to warm up for the big house widout no banjo!" She patted her feet in a dance that everybody felt in one way or another.

Claude hit the strings with a whomp that thrilled the bodies warming up. Several couples rearing to go tore into a shuffle toe. The laughter that swelled from the lot of them could fool any white person into thinking nobody had noticed the wagon.

Flurry's youngest boy, barely old enough to stand, wobbled about in the crowded room where grown-ups stomped and joggled. He was patting his little foot at another boy's foot, his napkin draped down with a well-soiled look and a worse smell. There was danger to one so little, but Flurry didn't notice.

Though he had awakened with a pounding head, Wink was feeling better until he overheard the visiting coachman ask about Puddin, if she was married, if she was spoke for, if she messed around, such questions as that.

To put distance between himself and the coachman Wink made his way outside only to encounter Anner. She handed him an envelope. "Massuh says to take this here to a man named Edmund. He lives in the village."

"Dat be a pattyroller. Is you heard who's been sold?" Several children screamed down the street.

"Sold? Honey, Massuh wouldn't sell a body at Christmas!" Anner licked her lips like she wanted a kiss. From the frolicking shanty a fine voice was singing "Chilly Nights."

"You reckon Massuh is inviting a pattyroller to Christmas dinner?"

"Maybe he done sold you. And you'se going to the village to get yourself put in shackles." Anner turned her sympathetic eyes on him.

"Maybe. Or maybe dis here pattyroller is going to load you in dat wagon and send you to the cane fields in Alabama." Wink moved aside for a pack of yelping dogs and stepped toward the yard.

"Maybe he take dat no-count devil Billy." She brightened. "He's going to wish he was in Alabama come Christmas Day." Several more children raced after the dogs.

"What you up to now?" Wink wandered to where the street led into the yard.

She smiled gleefuly. "Lordy! The front door is going to put Billy in his place. Dat's all I'se going to say."

"You must be drinking too much eggnog."

She pulled him closer. "I is drinking. And my lips tastes just like eggnog."

Wink, who didn't care much for himself lately, wanted somebody to care for him. He kissed Anner until Limbo came by and bumped into them.

Wink saddled up and rode to St. Helenaville and the boarding house where Edmund lived. The man didn't answer his knock on the door. Wink asked after him at the blacksmith and Salina's without getting intelligence about the patroller's whereabouts. He took a second turn to the boarding house, pushed the letter under the door, and returned to Westfall.

CHAPTER 13

AROUND THE COOKING POT

DECEMBER 1857

Though Wink did his best to keep out of Farley's sight, the overseer sent Matilda for him. "Search in the woods hereabouts for Mooey. She's probably in a tree. Bring her to my place."

Wink tarried in the woods as if searching, though he had decided he'd hide Mooey in the stables should he accidentally encounter her. But he didn't see her. In the yard, older folks milled around Iverson and his crew as they butchered the hogs and wild ox. The dogs stole about, ready to gobble up any driblet or to lick up spilled blood.

Women added wood to the fires burning under four big pots sitting on chunky legs. As they cleaned the offal, they added it to the pots and fetched spices from the quarters. One of the butchers brought over a hog's head and looked at Flurry. "You ready for dis?"

"Put it in the pot." She pointed and the man put the head inside.

With whole heads and half-heads safely cooking, Flurry added enough water to cover them. Just looking on so much meat put Wink in a good mood.

Doll said, "Flurry, you look spare-made. You stopped eating?"

"I been looking to get more cow's milk from the Massuh. Seems like my bosoms is drying up," said Flurry.

"How old is your baby?" said Mammy Livy.

"Bout three years old," said Flurry. "But I spect I'll be in a family way if Thor keeps at me like he's been doing." She smiled across the cooking pot to Thor.

The men surrounding Thor grinned and slapped him on the back.

Thor shrugged them off. "What you say that for, Flurry! You know I ain't been in your cot."

Lovey came from the quarters in time to hear. "Thor, is you messing wid Flurry?" She tossed her head back like a purebred.

"Flurry don't mean nothing." Thor looked at Lovey.

"Wasn't nothing I felt last time I was in your cabin," said Flurry.

"Shut up, Flurry! You ain't been in my cabin," said Thor.

"Flurry sneaks in my cot in the middle of the night," said one of the men, "and she shore do warm up the place."

"I don't sneak nowhere!" With a paddle, Flurry pushed a hog head down into the broth.

"You oughta find one man and make a home for your chillun." Iverson brought a hog heart for the stew.

"You is plum careless about who humps you," said Lovey.

Limbo, with a slightly off-balance gait, strolled over. "Flurry, I got a hump. Come on. Let's find a cot." He reached an arm around her. She shrugged him off.

In one pot, the cooks boiled blood mixed with seasonings, which thickened into pudding for the children. In another, they made rice liver pudding from the liver, lights, and haslets. While the puddings cooked, they made a stew of hog heart, kidney, and head including the tongue, snout, and ears, enough food for everybody to eat plenty. The butchers took care to keep the dogs from getting at the meat, with somebody always guarding the carcasses.

The pots bubbled and cooked and scented the yard with the smell of onion and sage. Shirttail boys, those not yet big enough for pants, played ball with a bladder Iverson had blown up. Children rushed about the yard, impatient to get a taste. When the cooks spooned blood pudding into the children's piggins, everybody else began to converge on the pots. Wink brought his bowl, for this was the one time he could eat his fill. During Christmas Eve and Christmas Day, there would be food all day long.

Flurry, who portioned out stew to anybody and everybody, said, "Somebody ask dat buckra in the carriage house what he's doing still here."

The longer the stranger stayed the more people tried to ignore him, and the more they worried about somebody's leaving. Only Wink noticed when Farley sent a field hand to tend the stock, but even at that, he made no mention of Mooey's situation.

"It shore be a puzzlement," said Limbo.

Limbo's mild "puzzlement" signaled his confidence that the trader hadn't come for him. Wink sat on a stump near the cooking fires and ate his stew as Claude and the musicians from the quarters came and went. When Auntie Nell plodded up for dinner, he gave her his seat.

"He be watching us." Lovey scooped out liver pudding until the cast iron pot was practically empty and laid the paddle across the top. Matilda picked it up and licked off particles that stuck to the wood.

Auntie Nell said, "He be after Mooey." A cloud crossed the sun, and silence fell on the yard.

Wink looked across the iron pot to Auntie. Since she gave him no accusatory glances, he was led to believe she hadn't seen him with Farley the previous night.

"He gots Mooey?" said Iverson.

"Farley waited all night for her, but she done flew the coop," said Auntie Nell.

Lovey laughed out loud and poured water into an empty pot.

As the fire died down, everybody hovered closer. Thor shoved several sticks of wood underneath the pots still simmering.

Flurry said to Limbo, "Dat buckra wid the wagon come for your sister."

Limbo overcame a coughing spell and said, "Good. Maybe he be taking her to Mississippi!"

"That be a provoking thing to say!" said Iverson. "Mooey don't know how to survive in a coffle."

Lovey said, "That's the reason Farley be in a pucker this morning!"

Thor said, "Where be Mooey?"

Auntie Nell said, "She run off."

On leaving, Wink passed near Auntie, giving her every opportunity to accuse him of betraying Mooey, but she didn't.

As the fires under the pots died out, they built new ones in a trench they dug for the barbecue. In the afternoon when a group of men brought a basket of oysters from Station Creek, they bedded them on grates over the barbecue pit. Storytellers and gossipers lingered about the fire.

Children shrieked with excitement and ran around the men, tugging at their pants legs. Wink was among the men the boys steered to the fire where they pointed to cracks in oysters cooking over the coals. Wink brought clinchers from the tool shed to retrieve them while Thor and others made do with sticks or tin dippers. In no time, a bigger crowd gathered. As they split open the shells, Wink showed several youngsters how to cup the juicy oyster in the deeper half, add salt and pepper, and suck it dry.

When Farley came to the fire, the hands tucked away their whiskey bottles and put a lid on their mouths. Everybody had been talking about Farley's snooping in the quarters, obviously looking for Mooey. They devised stories to tell him, making whatever effort they could to hamper his search. Thor said he'd seen Mooey in the loft of the carriage house. Lovey claimed she was hiding in the corncrib. Flurry declared Mooey had been sneaking around the kitchen looking for bread.

Farley listened to their accounts and warmed his hands at embers drawn by the breeze.

Several shirttail boys scrambled so close to the fire Iverson said, "Stop dat running round the fire!"

Flurry grabbed one of the shirttails to slow down a boy.

"Is you asked the massuh bout a school for the chillun?" said Iverson. Several men wandered toward the quarters when Claude's banjo struck a note.

Farley looked into the fire as if it had spelled him. "No."

"Why not?"

"He done give his word on dat."

"Reckon his word change iffen we pester him?"

Everybody knew it preyed on Iverson's mind that the negros couldn't read the Bible.

"I'se not going to worry the man." Farley hawked and spit. "Schooling don't make them pick more cotton."

Wink spoke up. "Leastways, they oughta learn to cipher." A negro who couldn't count had to get somebody else to do his trading, even for liquor.

"Don't need no ciphering to handle a hoe," Farley said.

"Niggers can't even find the road to Charleston widout a white man to read the sign posts," said Iverson.

"Niggers don't go nowhere 'cept the field. They don't need no sign to git there."

"I got hopes my boys will get outen the field." Iverson rubbed the back of his hand across his mouth.

Wink looked over at Iverson's face, glistening in spite of the cold. Those words, which might be taken as resistance, were borderline dangerous. Farley, who didn't seem to notice, looked at the cooking meat. "Niggers what reads and writes causes nothing but trouble for the rest of us. They gits to thinking they good as white folks. Dat what you want for your boys?" he said.

"Brother Milton gits us niggers to thinking dat God cares as much for our black hides as He do the whites."

Wink had heard this from Iverson before, and he recognized where it was going. Iverson had religion on his brain, and he wanted to read the Bible like the Brother.

Farley looked from the fire to Iverson. "I don't partialize wid dat man. Nothing ever hatched of his shouts but trembling and shaking. And you git the same thing for better reason wid ague." He put several oysters in his hat and sat on his steps to eat them.

Iverson had charge of barbecuing meat the master provided for Christmas Day dinners, a wild ox for the white folks and hogs for the negros. The butchering came to an end as the women cleaned the intestines and removed the inner lining before soaking them in salt water. Planks set across trestles provided tables at the shed they called the wash house where several field hands sawed the carcasses in half. Others carved them into quarters and rubbed them with vinegar and salt.

Iverson and the butchers hauled the hunks of meat to the racks and spread them over embers smouldering in the trenches. Wink and several young bucks sneaked a bottle from one to the other while Iverson adjusted the meaty hindquarters to best advantage on the racks. The bulk of the work was now done. The remaining effort was merely watchfulness to assure the coals stayed hot but not too hot and the meat didn't burn.

As the day waned, the slaves gathered close to keep warm and watch the meat cook. Iverson added hickory sticks to the fire, which flavored the meat and scented the air. The smell reminded Wink of a time with his mother—he remembered it as his mother, though he was never sure—who held his hand while they stood watching an alligator barbecue. Now Wink stared at the bristling embers. Since Farley hadn't solicited his help, he figured the search for Mooey had ended, but the stranger's continued presence bothered him. The men's conversation dropped off to one person talking. Then a burst of laughter.

Were it not for the buckra waiting with the wagon in the carriage house, Wink could have relaxed. Mooey had to be hereabouts, but they weren't going to find her without help. It was unlikely the master would bring out the dogs or call on the band of patrollers with his house full of visitors.

Mooey was making a mockery of Farley, and though it amused Wink and the others, she would pay. Farley wasn't one to forget an insult. Mooey might well be up in some tree looking at them that very minute. Wink looked up. A cold breeze shuffled the leaves. Mooey's breath would be about that cold if she stayed another night in the woods.

In preparation to drive the Goodwyns to a shindig that night, Wink went to his quarter and put on the new fancy coat and vest the master had given him. He slipped to the kitchen to see Puddin. It was obvious from the help and the array of food in varying degrees of preparation, that Christmas Eve was another night of labor for her. "Puddin, what you doing in them rags on Christmas Eve?"

Mamba glanced up at him. "The shine from them buttons is enough to blind a body."

Puddin pulled the spider out of the fire and flapped a cloth against her apron, raising a cloud of flour. One look at Wink and she said, "You must be the most dudish nigger on the place." She wiped sweat from her forehead.

"Sweetie, I gots them horses trained to take theirselves home tonight!" He took a bottle from an inside pocket, drank, and caught his breath. "Whew! Dis is good stuff!" He offered it to Puddin. "Here, you needs dis more'n me."

Puddin scoffed at him. "I needs to be cooking, not socializing wid you."

Wink tweaked his head and cut his eyes at her. "Come-on. A toast to Christmas Eve." He urged the bottle near her nose.

A twinkle of delight lit her eyes.

He touched her lips with the bottle. She accepted a sip and pushed him away with an amused look that gave Wink a glow of confidence.

Anner came in the kitchen with the foot warmer in her hand. "You going on a spree?"

He put his bottle in his pocket. "Yessum! Old Man Goodwyn's not the onliest one going to carouse tonight."

"Come here." Anner pulled him out the door. "You is high-toned. You better save your loving for me." She looked as if she might kiss him.

Wink gave himself some leeway by pulling out his bottle for another sip.

From inside the kitchen Puddin said, "Anner, come here and git this foot warmer out the way."

Anner returned and scooped embers from the fireplace into the tin cavity. As she left, she gave Wink a smile that served as a warning.

Wink leaned on the doorframe. Puddin was wiping her dewy eyes.

"Don't you cry none bout me." Wink began to regret his high spirits.

Puddin stopped slicing onions and stood back from them. She took a drink of what looked like coffee. "It's these onions ..."

Mamba said, "You better watch yourself, Wink. Anner's got fingers like crab claws."

Wink couldn't resist sparking off to Puddin. "I know you be worried about me ... off having a good time widout you."

"Darling, that stuff you drinking is messing wid your head," said Puddin, but her eyes suggested she might mess with more than his head.

"Wink!" called a coachman from the carriage house.

Wink caught Puddin's eye. "I'se going to come looking for you tonight!" She gave him a look suggestive of her capabilities to take care of whatever he needed. He hurried to the stables, so light-footed his feet hardly touched the ground.

He and the visiting coachmen hitched horses to carriages and lined them up at the portico in preparation to drive the white families to an uncle's plantation.

The mistress, in a velvet mantle and silk gown, descended the steps on the arm of the master, who wore a frock coat and top hat. Missy Margarita's dress floated over hoops so wide no boy could get within kissing distance. Wink stood at the open door of the carriage, taking part in what seemed like a hifalutin parade. As he opened the carriage door and helped them in, he was extravagantly accommodating, in part because of the Christmas cheer he had already sampled. As they departed, another family came to the portico, all dressed in silks and long tails.

Wink knew the women and children in the quarters gazed at them, their eyes wide at the sight of so many shiny dresses and top hats.

Wink and the visiting coachmen drove the Goodwyn families to a plantation located on the island some six miles north of Westfall. While the white families celebrated inside the big house, the coachmen spent the evening eating, dancing, and drinking in the quarters with other Goodwyn slaves they hardly knew. Several men stuck torches in the ground to provide light for a dance. The women wore colorful head scarves and their best dresses, which set the tone for a party no less than their laughter and cooing.

Wink went to the kitchen for a light, knowing full well his cigar was the envy of most of the men.

The children finished eating their supper and scurried to the sound of a fiddle, dancing in riotous circles. Youngsters tapped their tin plates in rhythm. Several women played bones; somebody drummed on a pan. Young couples moved about as if warming up their feet. "Come on, hotten up wid me," a young woman said to Wink who did a walk-around with her. He even gave her a drag on his stub. Everybody's feet were jumping and jiving.

"You know whereabouts I can git some hooch?" one of the field hands asked Wink, who could have sold a cask if he'd had it. He kept what remained of a bottle in his coat pocket, for he needed that for himself. As the common supply dwindled, one of the coachmen went to the kitchen and managed to sweet-talk a house slave into giving him what was left of a bottle from the master's table.

When the houseboy arrived with orders to make the coaches ready to leave, Wink rounded up the others. They revived their horses and went in train to the front door to load up the white families for the ride back to Westfall. With only the rustle of the harnesses to keep him awake, Wink fought to stay alert on the silent and frigid road. Even the whites inside the coach spoke in subdued voices. Upon meeting a horseman, Wink hardly controlled his team and almost fell from his seat, which brought him out of a stupor. He took off his hat and coat. The smack of cold air shocked him awake.

It was well after midnight when the carriages finally rolled into Westfall's yard. They queued at the door to unload the Goodwyns and their relations, after which the coachmen unhitched the horses and stored the carriages.

Wink walked across the yard to the kitchen and Puddin's quarter. The light of her fire framed the shutters. If the master sold Puddin ... Wink couldn't think about that.

He knocked privately on her door, knowing it was locked.
"Who dat?" Puddin said.
"It be me, Wink."

"What's wrong?"

"It be Christmas Eve."

No answer.

"And I needs my woman." Wink leaned on the door to steady himself. He had not only finished his bottle but had indulged in the jug passed about the shindig.

"I'm not your woman," came the rather sleepy reply.

"Just one little kiss. A Christmas kiss."

"Go kiss Anner."

"I don't want Anner."

No answer.

"Puddin? You be my woman?"

No answer.

"Just tonight? Just for Christmas?"

"Go to bed."

"I'll go to bed iffen you gives me one kiss."

"I'll think about a kiss iffen you go to bed."

Wink considered that. It sounded like he was making progress. "Iffen I go to bed, you owes me a kiss, dat's the fact!"

"I'll think about it," came from Puddin.

"Little filly, you jes think on dis. Your man's going to give you some loving and I'm ready right now, but iffen you wants to wait, I kin wait, but not for long."

"Go to sleep, Wink."

"You my woman, Puddin." Wink shuffled off, intent on going back to his shanty at the stables, but joyful noises came from the quarters.

The street had turned into an old time breakdown that had spread to the back lot. Children had fallen asleep on the ground. Several men and women sat on Farley's steps and leaned on each other, too corned to go to their cabins. Claude's well-oiled banjo led the fiddler into "Cutting Pigeon Wings." Some dancers did the clog and some the pigeon, swinging their partners. At one time or another, every man had his eyes on Flurry. Her breasts jounced roundly, threatening to peek out from behind her banyan. The wanton way she pushed and shoved her hips gave rhythm a bad name.

Farley appeared with his whip. "This frolic is over. Git back to your quarters!"

"Go to the big house, where you belong," somebody shouted.

"De meat cutter is loose wid his whip!" another said.

"Goodwyn's guinea!"

Farley lashed leather against the side of a cabin. "Git going!"

Slowly the revelers spread out, some of them still dancing and singing. Claude plinked a final few peeps on the banjo as they wandered toward their cabins. A couple of men, fighting over Flurry's attention, knocked in the shutters on Doll's cabin and fell inside on the floor, breaking a chair.

Wink moseyed from the quarters over to where Iverson was watching the barbecue and pulled off a piece of meat. "You seen Mooey?"

"Nah. Farley don't neither. Dat man so worried his hair won't stand still."

When Wink opened the door to his quarter, to his surprise the stranger wasn't there. He found the man with his wagon parked behind the gin house, waiting. Whether or not Farley had found Mooey, somebody was leaving Westfall that night.

PART II
POOR MILK FOR A SUCKLING BABY

CHAPTER 14

IN THE DARK OF MORNING

CHRISTMAS, DECEMBER 1857

"Wink, git up!" Farley shook his shoulder.

Wink emerged from a stupor and rolled out of his cot, fully dressed. He found he hadn't even removed his brogans. He came to his unsteady feet. His mouth felt like a flour bin, and he dipped water to drink.

"Come wid me." Farley threw Wink's coat at him and walked out the door carrying his lantern with him.

Wink flipped open the cover of his pocket watch and held the face to the glimmer of coals in his hearth. Because he was only one of two slaves with a timepiece, he guarded his against thievery, especially at night. Almost four o'clock in the morning. He stumbled over his fireside stool and cursed so loudly Tootie snorted and bumped her stall. In no hurry to keep up with Farley, he limped along, hardly able to keep his balance.

As he crossed the back lot, embers glowed in the barbecue pits, casting light on two men, though Wink couldn't tell who they were nor if they were awake. One of them was likely Iverson, who had supervised the butchering. It fell to him to stay awake all night to turn and tend the meat, though he had helpers who came and went.

When Wink arrived at the quarters, he no longer saw Farley who had disappeared down the street. Beside a cabin door, he sat on a stool made of a tree trunk. Farley returned and gave him a clumsy slap with his whip. "Come on, you pesky varmint. We got work to do."

Wink staggered to his feet and walked behind Farley. He tripped over a man passed out on the ground. Several others slumped in a doorway.

"Listen here," said Farley. "Lovey be of a size to cause trouble. She might run for the woods or fight or tear up the cabin."

"We going for Lovey?" Wink's alcoholic haze didn't protect him from dismay. Mooey had evaded capture, but now he had the dirty job of catching Lovey. He should refuse, return to his cabin. "I'se not in no shape to handle her." He stopped walking.

"You going to be in worser shape iffen you don't git your ass in gear."

Wink turned back anyway. Hardly had he taken five steps when a sizzling pain cut into the side of his neck and ear. Another lash from Farley's whip hit the top of his head and knocked off his hat.

"By the time you git back to your shanty, I'll be at the massuh's back door. Won't be me telling you nothing onct the massuh come to the door."

Wink couldn't think properly, but he knew what Farley meant. The master crushed anything that hinted of rebellion, which meant that Wink might well accompany Lovey. He had two bad choices. Would he follow his conscience and risk the auction block or would he hate himself and follow Farley's orders? Whatever his feelings, Lovey was leaving Westfall whether or not Wink helped. He put on his hat, pulled up his collar, and turned back to Farley.

He felt sorry for Lovey. She was defenseless and had been badly used by the master. She was a reminder that doing a good job didn't keep a slave from being sold. Her lip knew no respect, but Wink didn't fault her for that. It was her way of being proud.

They went to the shanty where Lovey and her baby lived, but she wasn't there, though the cots were full up. Of all the people sleeping, only Auntie Nell lived there. Making their way down the street, Farley opened doors and looked inside. Claude was asleep on his floor along with numerous others. In other cabins, men, women, and children slept in the spare light of the dwindling fires. As in Auntie Nell's cabin, a number of slaves weren't where they'd been assigned. Farley said, as if explaining to himself, "Niggers going to stray at Christmas."

At Thor's place Farley shoved open the door while Wink stood in the street. Lovey slept on the cot at Thor's side. Limbo lay in his cot like a frozen lizard.

"Wake up!" Farley shook Lovey's shoulder.

Thor lifted his head and squinted his eyes.

Lovey rolled to her feet and coughed. She held her hands to the dying fire.

"Where be your sprout?" Farley fingered the leather cord in his belt.

"He's wid Mammy Livy. What you want wid him?"

Thor got up, took the poker and shuffled the log until a flicker turned into a low flame. When he looked at Farley, Wink backed into the dark street. "What you doing here?"

Farley paced closer to the fire as if to warm himself.

Wink, getting colder by the minute, held his breath. If Thor turned this into a ruckus, Wink wasn't sure he could enter the fray to defend Farley. He was feeling sickly.

"There's a wild shoat down by the cedar brake." Farley reached over and shook Limbo. "Boy! Git up here!" Limbo didn't move.

"You seen a shoat in the dark?" Thor mumbled.

"Go down there afore it gits gone and drive it up to the hog pen."

"It be the middle of the night," Thor said as if he couldn't believe Farley.

"Limbo! Boy! Wake up!" Farley rattled Limbo's cot. "This boy's dead to the world. Git one of the hands to go wid you."

"It's too damn cold."

Farley shrugged his shoulders and turned toward the door. "Dat what you want me to say to Massuh?"

Was it possible a hog was near the cedar trees? Earlier in the day, one of the hands had said something about a wild shoat. On second thought, Wink figured out what Farley was doing. Thor had no idea he was being sent on a wild goose chase and that Lovey would be gone when he returned.

Thor sighed. "I must be dreaming." He looked at the floor. "Shit, my feet's going to freeze." He couldn't find his shoes.

"Your feet ain't nothing to Massuh, not lak a hog." Lovey tipped her chin in her scornful way.

"As for you, your little feller belong wid you at night," Farley said.

"Mammy Livy don't mind him staying wid her," said Lovey. She hadn't done much tending to her baby, which had raised criticism in the quarters.

"Massuh mind where he be staying," Farley said.

Lovey scoffed. "The Massuh got a good mind for minding."

Thor took Limbo's brogans off his feet, dug out ragged wool cloth from a basket, and wrapped his shoes in several pieces. As he approached the door, Wink disappeared behind the cabin. After Thor left, Wink watched the light of his torch fade in the direction of the cedars down near the creek.

Farley said, "Git in here, you cowardly wart." He gripped a leather cord, stretched his backbone, and said to Lovey, "Git your duffle and come wid me."

Wink stood barely inside the door, trying to be invisible.

"What for?" Lovey's lips were spouts where words steamed out. She glanced from Wink to Farley's leather rope.

"Massuh sending you to the main," said Farley.

"To the main? Where?" Lovey's eyes betrayed mean fear. Whatever her attitude, she hadn't been defiant before, but she hadn't been sold before. Wink dreaded the thought that she might fight.

"He don't say." Farley motioned her toward the door with his head.

Lovey hesitated. "He going to drown me in the river?" Anger and terror flashed in the light of her eyes.

"Nah. He done gone and sold you."

Lovey's face took on a callow look, like one lost. When the master had moved her out of the big house and back to the quarters, it had put her on notice, as if she'd failed in her task. His displeasure with her had given rise to rumors about her uncertain future. "I had to do to suit him and I done it." She held her head up and looked at Farley with accusatory eyes.

"Nobody said dat would keep a nigger off the block." When Farley went to the open door, Wink stepped into the street. Even if she got away from Farley, she couldn't get off the island before the patrollers tracked her with the hounds.

"He sell me to a trader?" Lovey's voice was hoarse. She licked her lips and swallowed.

"Don't know." Farley's voice was pitched with reason, but his fingers gripped the leather rope. "Now git your duffle if you gonna."

Lovey didn't move.

If she bucked, they would have to take her to the ground and haul her to the wagon. Such was Wink's distress he walked to the shadows between the cabins and heaved his supper.

"You going to git your duffle, or is you going widout?" Farley stepped outside the door.

"What about the baby?" Her voice froze up.

"Mammy Livy'll take care of the little fellow." Farley walked back inside.

"What'll become of him?" Lovey said.

Farley stood near Lovey but didn't touch her. "Come on."

Wink understood what she was asking, for her son had the extra burden of being a mulatto. Even negros shunned yellow babies.

"I wants to take him wid me." Lovey's voice was strong but agitated.

"Just your duffle." Farley grew edgy and he handed Wink the lantern.

Wink said, "I'll watch out for the little feller." That Lovey's baby would never remember his mother ached in his chest.

"The devil in me blamed the baby for his daddy." Lovey's eyes glistened and filled with tears.

"This ain't no time for such truck! Come on," Farley said gruffly.

Her gaze lingered on Wink. "Take better care of him than I did." She stalked out and they followed close behind as she went to her cabin.

Wink's feet stumbled as much from his agitation as the dark. He swallowed to keep from choking on the bitter sup of self hate.

Without waking Auntie Nell or the other women, Lovey stashed her few belongings in her blanket and wadded it in her arms. She headed toward the chillun house, but Farley jerked her back toward the yard.

"I want to say goodbye to the baby."

"Don't make no difference to him." Farley forced her ahead of him.

Tears glistened on Lovey's cheeks. "It makes a difference to me!"

"Don't make no difference nohow. Now git to the yard." Farley shoved again.

Lovey stumbled ahead to keep from being pushed down. As they quit the quarters, Farley grabbed her arm and steered her away from the barbecue fires and toward the wagon where the stranger sat in the dark waiting. Lovey jerked free and ran at the big house, yelling, "Goodwyn! you low-down dirty, no-count devil!" Her voice screeched.

Farley gave chase. Wink's heart went to his shoes. He moved clumsily, staggered. He hated Farley. He hated old man Goodwyn. He hated every white person in the big house.

Lovey was screaming. "You sire your own slaves, you yellow-bellied son-of-a ..." Farley wrestled her to the ground and punched a rag into her mouth. She was kicking him and rolling away. "Git her!" growled Farley.

Wink put down the lantern, grabbed Lovey's arms, and pinned them to the ground. His tears dropped on Lovey as he held her arms. Farley tied a gag on her mouth, swaddled her in her duffle, and secured it with a rope. Her few possessions—a hand mirror, dress, stockings, bright yellow head rag—were scattered in the yard. Though she jerked and mumbled, Farley and the stranger dragged her to the wagon and hoisted her into the back. The stranger wrapped another rope around her and knotted it to each side of the seat frame. Farley hung the light on the lantern hook.

"Giddiup!" The buckra slapped the lines on the horse's back, and the wheels began to roll. Lovey's legs thumped against the flatbed.

"Pick up her stuff," Farley said to Wink, who wiped his nose and walked away without a word. Lovey wasn't the only slave to know the loneliness of a leaf falling in the woods leaving no mark or witness. Wink's mother was a memory that made him so sad he avoided thinking of her. To fend off such misery, he put himself to thinking of his future and Puddin. He wanted her to be his family.

The night seemed darker near his shanty. He opened the door to the room where he had lived alone for too long. The place had no heart. Though of limited space, it seemed cavernous, wide, empty. Even the owl that sometimes perched in the ceiling beams had left. He could only imagine what it would be like to open the door and see Puddin asleep in his cot. But how could he in good conscience ask her to be his wife without telling her that he couldn't give her a child?

He threw wood on embers going to ashes. On the floor near the hearth was a piece of the calendar on which he had first recorded the tides, back when he'd learned how. Where it usually hung on the wall was a bare nail. "Damned bog trotter!" he muttered. The buckra had obviously used his calendar to revive the fire.

It had hung on his wall for well over ten years. He threw the last shred of it into the fire. Up in flames went the keepsake that had reminded him of how he had learned to calculate high and low tides. But the flames couldn't erase Wink's memory of the previous stableman, who during the days of his dying, taught Wink how to figure the tides.

He went direct to his trunk to see that the stranger hadn't disturbed his current calendars. Without them, he couldn't advise the master about the ferry schedule. It was a relief to see the rolled papers, though he hadn't yet begun to figure out the tides for the new year.

CHAPTER 15

THE WATCHER

DECEMBER 1857

Mooey favored live oaks, for they kept their leaves in hot and cold weather. The limbs as well as trunks grew to great girth, which lessened the risk of falling if she nodded. The one she chose spread out in low-lying limbs, some of which propped against the ground. She climbed up to where she could wedge between a limb and the trunk and got some sleep.

Early morning came in cold. With her paltry blanket she could wrap only half of herself, and she alternately warmed her legs and her shoulders. She was hungry and climbed down. In a tree near the springhouse, she waited until the cook stored the crocks before drinking her fill.

She moved to a tall live oak where she could see into the yard. Though near the quarters, the tree was so difficult to climb nobody would look for her in it. Its lowest limb was as high as the roof of the big house's portico. Mooey had cleverly poked holes in the trunk in such a way that she was able to climb it. After wrapping herself in the blanket, she reclined on a thick limb and spent the day watching what went on in the yard.

Though she became hungry and thirsty, she didn't dare climb down because of the many people milling around. They were butchering hogs and cooking in the back lot while children ran around everywhere, the negro children in the back and white children in the front yard. About sundown the groomsmen, wearing black suits, drove carriages to the portico where the white people, dressed to death, swept down the step. With high-spirited movements and lively bearing they stepped into shiny carriages, which left, one after the other, down the carriageway.

To Mooey's disappointment, the slaves stirred about the yards even after moon-up. She sat and entertained herself by watching everybody come and go about the fire that obviously cooked the meat she smelled. By the light of torches stuck in the yard they wrestled, danced, hugged, and carried on awful.

A cold darkness filtered into her tree. Mooey felt sleepy. She was beginning to wonder if she'd be up there all night. A midnight moon shone in a sky of ever-shifting clouds. The carriages returned with the white people, and not until the lights in the big house dimmed did she look about to see if it was safe to come down. In the back lot, the torches waned and went out. The slaves disappeared into the cabins. Mooey was preparing to climb down when the moon suddenly went behind clouds accompanied by a strong horse scent. A cold breeze chilled her blood. In the utter darkness that came on like danger, a pinlight moved across the yard, a light separate from the pit fires.

The flow of air changed about Mooey and bewitched her breath. When the moon reappeared, she sat up and stared. The pinlight rooted to one spot while a shock of movement surrounded it. Her eyes burned as she tried to figure out what was happening at such a late hour. The ruction below seemed to startle the very clouds and cause moonlight to score the yard like large animal tracks.

A woman who appeared to be Lovey ran at the big house raging. A person—Mooey guessed it was Early—knocked her over and another man held her down. The flutter of light revealed the stranger's horse and wagon standing in the yard like evil ghosts waiting to transport somebody to a region of no return. Mooey clasped her hand over her mouth, for her throat twitched fearfully.

The moon disappeared. A darkness crawled into the tree, on to Mooey's skin, and into her eyes. She wrapped into her blanket to protect herself.

She peeked out but an odd grazing sensation scrubbed her face. She blew her breath into the crusty spirit until she could face the air.

The moon spit through the clouds forcefully and lit the yard where it was still, as if nothing had happened.

She climbed down.

In the quarters, men had fallen asleep in the street. People lay on the floors of the cabins. Mooey sneaked inside her shanty and warmed by flinty flames. Auntie slept in her cot. One of the field hands was in Mooey's cot. A strange woman occupied Lacy's. Lovey wasn't there. Nor was Sunny or the basket.

Mooey drank a dipper of water and ate collards with her fingers. Two sugar yams rested on the hearth. She ate one and put the other in her pocket. As she looked for wool stockings, the drawer rubbed its housing and became stuck before opening, and one of the women sat up. Mooey crouched and froze. Long moments passed and the woman lay back down. Mooey confined her movements and searched until she found the wool pieces but didn't dare shove in the drawer. She sneaked out and wrapped her legs.

Where was Sunny? Her feet brushed the cold dirt without a sound as she appproached and slipped inside Mammy's cabin. Three shirttail boys slept in a cot. A stranger in another. Mammy turned in hers and rustled her covers. Mooey's heart raced when she saw the basket. Inside, Sunny slept peacefully. She sighed with joy and as she picked him up several marbles rolled from his blanket. The children had no doubt put them in his basket. He opened his eyes and put his fist into his mouth. Mooey warmed her nose and cheeks with his. She sat in a chair before the fire and gazed at him. He beamed at her with eyes illuminated with wonder. His little arm lashed about. He kicked his legs. His face wrinkled up, his quivering mouth opened so wide his eyes closed. She returned him to his basket and tiptoed to the woods.

While she watched the cabin from a distance, the cold of night ached in her feet and legs. The still air seemed to be frozen. The longer the wait the angrier Mooey became. The baby needed milk and the woman with breasts was nowhere to be seen. Mooey's stomach ached because the baby hadn't been fed. She became edgy and discontented. It seemed unfair that the woman who had milk cared so little about whether the baby got what he needed.

Mooey couldn't stand many more nights outside in such weather. If only there was some way she could command the heat of the chimney to drift over to where she crouched. She nodded off but awoke at a whispery sense of motion. The woman with big breasts went into the baby's cabin and Mooey sighed. Poor Sunny. He had been obliged to wait for his milk until a pale notice of morning changed the sky.

She recovered her blanket. Upon climbing back into the tall tree, she noticed the stranger and his wagon were gone. His departure released her from a cloudy uncertainty that had kept her alert and irritable. She felt depleted, as if she had barely escaped a grave danger.

One thing was certain—it was too cold to sleep in the woods another night. Nobody would look for her on Auntie's roof, and she could sleep better near the heat of the chimney. Already she felt better.

After a time, slaves began wandering from the quarters into the yard and stood on the ground before the portico, so many Mooey realized something special was happening. As white people came outside and watched, she recognized a ritual that brought forth distant pictures of a celebration with plentiful food and happy people and more importantly many visitors. At once Mooey felt satisfied, for the plantation's many white callers didn't tug at her any more. She could sense that this happening in the yard was the reason they had come.

She looked about the crowd, gratified to see familiar faces until she spotted Early. When she didn't see Lovey, the moonlit picture of the yard came to mind.

CHAPTER 16

CHRISTMAS REVELRY

DECEMBER 1857

Christmas morning, the sky looked rocky and cold. In spite of crushing aches from every direction, Wink roused early to tend the horses. He leaned on the stall and watched a visiting mare he had stabled apart from the others for pawing. Since it had no additional signs of colic, he released it into the paddock with the others. His feet felt like they'd been shod with iron shoes. As he was filling the troughs with oats, a couple of coachmen tottered up. "Where be the curry comb?" They strew combs and brushes on the ground before setting about to curry the horses' coats, manes, and tails.

Wink gave a turnip to the master's horse, which had taken a dislike to one of the visiting stallions. Even in separate paddocks, the two of them snorted at each other. Doll stopped at the gate to complain about having too much work since Mooey had run off. Even when he was wide awake, Wink hardly listened to her complaints.

Back in his cabin, he poured hot water from the iron kettle into his cup of tea leaves and looked at the fire, trying to ignore a headache. Puddin would probably hate him if she knew he had helped to catch Lovey.

Pulling on his coat, he walked across the back lot where the barbecue scented the air with the smell of charred meat and vinegary spices. He stopped at the fire long enough to warm his hands and feet. Iverson sat nearby in a chair, dozing. Whatever Iverson had heard while tending the meat the previous night, he couldn't have seen much in the dark. Wink hoped the blame about Lovey would fall to Farley alone.

He headed to the quarters. Since he wasn't sure where Lovey's baby would be, he moseyed toward Auntie Nell's cabin where Lovey had stayed. The baby boy wasn't there.

"He be wid Livy." Auntie Nell trembled as she tried to cut a broken thumbnail with a paring knife.

Wink took out his pocket knife and reached for her hand. "Let me cut dat." He sliced the nail where it was broken and lifted off the damaged piece. Blood dropped to the floor.

Auntie Nell winced and stuck her hand into the washpan. "Massuh done come by. Said he be moving dat boy in the chillun house. Reckon he's going to sell Lovey?"

Wink forced a weak look of concern. "Don't know. Maybe Mammy Livy be lonesome."

"Maybe so. She be by herself of a night since the massuh sold dat girl what married the Jenkins boy." Auntie pulled a cloth out of her rag basket and ripped off a bandage, which Wink tied around her finger. "But I 'spect she favors a quiet place of a night after tending all them chillun."

Approaching the chillun house, he paused at a most keen baby's cry. It was of such urgency Wink weakened at the thought that the baby had found out his mother had been sold. Inside, Mammy Livy hovered over the boy as he jerked his arms and legs with energy comparable to his voice. "What you doing here, Wink?"

Wink could hardly hear anything but the screaming baby. "Lovey asked me to look in on her boy," he said loudly.

"She oughta look in on him herself. Dat baby ain't seen his mammy in two days, and it Christmas."

The baby's crying trembled. He knew something was wrong.

Wink could say Lovey wasn't ever going to look in on him again, but he'd let Mammy find that out for herself. "What's wrong wid dat boy's bottom?" said Wink on seeing his fiery red skin.

"Lovey don't keep this baby clean." Mammy rubbed what looked like hog grease on the rash.

The baby twisted and jolted with such energy he lurched to the side of the table. Wink grabbed him before he fell. "You is hurting him ...." Wink could hardly stand it.

"Hand me dat clean napkin." She pointed to a cot.

Wink picked up a ragged piece of cloth. "This here?"

She nodded and he passed it to her and watched as she tied on the napkin.

"Hush, baby! Stop dat crying." Mammy turned and said to Wink, "Reckon you can get some liniment from Mamba?"

The baby's crying pained Wink. He went direct to Mamba's cabin and brought back liniment.

"I'se too old to be tending younguns." Mammy sat in a chair while the baby in his basket cried so hard his breath came in shuddering snuffles.

Wink saw that she said the truth. He had hardly touched a baby since Raynell's girl was born, but he picked up the boy and jostled him. "Don't you cry, little feller. Don't you cry." He walked back and to. The little hands were cold. Wink coursed near the fire. "What you call him?"

"Boy. He don't have no name I know of."

"This little feller needs a good name."

"Needs more'n a name."

"Boy, you like your name?" said Wink, but the baby didn't seem to like anything. *"Sonny,* how bout dat?"

"Give him a titty rag." Mammy pointed to a knotted rag. "Dip that in the molasses."

"Shhhh! Baby Sonny. I'se fixing something good for you." Wink balanced the baby in one arm to open the molasses crock. The baby stopped crying and sucked on the rag.

"Flurry be here in a while to feed him."

Farley could be heard on the street. "Git up, you stinking tomcats!"

Wink put the baby back in his cold basket on the cold floor and left reluctantly.

About the quarters, doors squeaked and slammed. "Smells like a stillery in here." Farley's whiplash hissed and snapped. Feet thumped the ground. "Git out here and look spry." Moans, groans, and children's voices drifted on the street.

A ragged bunch of men, women, and children tramped toward the big house and congregated in the front yard before the portico. The morning seemed all the colder because of the clouds. Wink, who was familiar with the Christmas tradition, straggled behind them. Claude, with a wan face and trembling fingers, started a familiar melody on the banjo and singers chimed in. "Up that oak and down that river, Two overseers and one little nigger ..." The longer they repeated the chorus, the clearer the voices. Lettie played the quill. Gussie played bones, and children kept time beating their spoons on their piggins.

More and more Goodwyn cousins ambled out the door of the big house to the portico. The white children sneaked about the grown-ups, hiding and giggling. Wink looked on as Billy moved about the portico with a tray of eggnog and cake for the white people.

By the time the master and mistress appeared, the negro children were dancing and everybody sang full force with harmonies exalted by the spirit of Christmas. A mist crept into the yard and the voices dampened. Eventually their eyes glanced at Farley, signaling him that they'd grown tired and wanted to stop. Farley nodded to Claude, who struck up the chords of a song they had sung on other Christmases: "Cradled on his bed of hay, Jesus Christ was born today. Let a merry Christmas be, Massa, both to me and thee!"

Billy and Anner came down the steps with several jugs of eggnog, one of which went to Farley, who took an exceptional draft, and passed it along to the field hand standing nearby. They doled the rest out to others who drank from the jugs and handed them on. When a jug came to Wink, he swallowed in gulps, for the master provided more when the jugs came empty.

Then Goodwyn spoke. Anybody just meeting the master would think he cared about his slaves, the way he thanked them for their hard work. He had presents of kerchiefs for the women, tobacco for the men, and oranges for the children, with special handouts to workers who did exceptional work. Wink, who had already received his new livery clothes, also took one of the small sacks of tobacco. When Wink slipped into thinking the man might have some regard for the slaves, he thought about Mooey and Lovey.

As a mist grew thicker and wetter, the master continued to speak from the shelter of the portico while wintery water dripped from the hats and scarves of the negros in the yard. Children hovered under their parents' coats.

Thor, who inched about the group as if he couldn't stand still, came close to Wink, whose nerves cramped up. After a moment of anxiety, he decided Thor couldn't have seen him helping haul off Lovey. But he couldn't be sure. He felt a tremble in his chest. He was near desperate for a drink of whiskey or something stronger to see him through what was going to be tribulation for Thor.

"You seen Lovey?" Thor whispered as Master Goodwyn told the slaves he was supplying a Christmas barbecue for them, as if they didn't know the hogs they had been cooking came from his drove.

Wink pretended he didn't hear, but Thor nudged him on the shoulder and murmured, "Wink! You seen Lovey?" Wink shook his head.

Billy and Anner brought out a cask of whiskey and handed it to Master Goodwyn, who rested it on the rail and said, "You nigras and pickaninnies are the heart of Westfall." Were it not for the whiskey on the portico just waiting to be drunk, Wink couldn't have stood the master's shame-faced pretense at crediting the negros' hard work.

"My family and myself appreciate your efforts."

A man could better tolerate being a slave if he didn't have to pretend to be respected by the master. By the time Master Goodwyn finished, the hands were murmuring and restless. "That be a white man for you. Can't see it be raining," grumbled Flurry.

"Old man Goodwyn thinks you is a flower and this rain is going to make you grow," whispered Limbo.

Somebody else mumbled, "Let's pee in his yard." Wink looked at Farley. What would he do? Yell at them in front of the high-class white women on the portico? Wink moved behind a sizeable woman and peed, as did several other men. The children giggled and some of them pointed. Flurry doubled over with sniggers.

When the master handed the cask to Farley, the slaves cheered through the drizzle. They would have tapped it and drunk to the master's health in the yard but for the weather. Farley took the cask to the shelter of the woodshed where Limbo stood up front as everybody bunched up and waited for their dram, except for the children and those who didn't drink, like Iverson, Auntie Nell, and Mammy. When Wink stuck his cup under the stopcock for the third time, Farley said, "Git back till everybody gits some!"

"Just a dram!" Wink, who didn't move, shook his empty cup.

Farley opened the cock and whiskey splashed into the cup. "Now git outa the way."

Wink usually didn't drink this much, but he needed to mollify his conscience. He kept up with Limbo, who was not only Wink's cover but his best customer. Farley even gave Matilda whiskey when she came with a cup.

"Matilda, give me that cup!" said Wink. "You not old enough for hooch." Before he could get the cup, she ran toward the quarters. "Farley, you an asshole, giving hooch to dat girl."

"She be old enough to breed in a year. Dat's old enough to drink."

Even after everybody had drunk what they wanted, there was plenty of whiskey left for the rest of the day. Earlier in the morning Iverson and several men had moved the barbecued hogs from the grates to washtubs which rested on trestle tables they had set up under the woodshed. A happy crowd squeezed under the open covering. Women twittered and men laughed. Children screamed and pushed everybody together as Gussie and Iverson piled meat on their plates.

Polly, whose hair was wrapped with red ribbon, skidded to the shed with the message that the master needed two tall men at the kitchen to hold umbrellas as the servants carried food to the big house.

"Thor! Git up to the kitchen. Limbo, go wid him!" Farley said.

"Where be Lovey?" The tone of Thor's voice put a chill on the good spirits. Wink could feel a ruckus coming on.

Farley usually stood apart from the others in a dispute, but the shelter was crowded, and Thor stood so close Farley had to look up at him. Gussie and Iverson stopped dishing up barbecue. Other men and women looked around as if searching the faces for Lovey. Even the children gazed about.

"She been sold," Farley said.

The crowd shifted and Wink was pushed from under the shelter. Even though he was in whiskey up to his eyebrows, the words hurt.

"Damn! Damn the Massuh to hell!" Thor said. He knocked a plate on the ground and said to Farley, "You lying nigger. There wasn't no shoat in the canebrake." Thor's face was in Farley's.

"Go on, boy! Massuh be waiting." Farley, who gave his backbone a stretch, showed no sign of retreat.

Thor delivered a blow in the chest that knocked Farley over and jostled the crowd. "You not even a nigger. You be a hog yourself." Thor pounced at Farley, but Iverson intercepted him, and the three of them tumbled, landing against a stack of wood.

Iverson recovered his balance and used his elbows to keep the men separate. He said, "Iffen you wants the person sending Lovey to the block, go over to the big house and wrassle wid the massuh."

"Come on," Limbo said, pulling at Thor's arm, but he was shrugged off. Limbo trudged out into the rain in the direction of the kitchen house.

Thor backed down and said to Iverson, "The massuh use us like hogs and we keeps on grunting." His stern eyes drilled Farley with hatred. "I ain't holding no umbrella for no white man." He strolled toward the quarters as if he didn't feel the rain.

Farley sent another field hand to help Limbo.

"Massuh sell the baby?" Iverson filled the plate that a slave had been holding out.

"Nah. He just sold Lovey," Farley said.

Gussie looked at Iverson. "Where be her baby?"

"Mammy Livy's taking care of him," said Farley.

Wink tried to ignore Gussie's frown, Flurry's blink, and Iverson's look of dismay. He told himself that it wasn't his fault Lovey had been sold and sent away. It wasn't his fault the baby had no mother.

"How come he sell her?" Iverson spilled barbecue on the dress of a field hand.

"Lawdy! You ruint my Sunday dress!" The woman pushed people aside going to the quarters to wash it off. The crowd parted for her and came back together, and though they looked expectantly at Farley for an answer, he growled at Iverson, "Give these people barbecue!"

The woodshed cleared out as the hands carried their filled plates to the nearest cabins where they sat by a fire and ate in groups. A pall spread from the news of Lovey, but it lifted as Farley continued to bring more whiskey.

The drizzle finally tapered off and stopped. Hardly had Wink rested his head on his cot for a nap when word came from the big house that the ladies wanted to go for a ride. "How many womens riding?" Wink sent Polly back to the big house. Obviously the message came from the mistress, for the master would have told him the number. When Polly returned, Wink employed another coachman, and they hitched up two carriages. Wink worked hard to sit tall and drive the women several miles down the village causeway as far as Station Creek swamp. He had hitched Lad and Freckles, two spirited horses, to the carriage and made a point of hitting every hole in the road. If there was a puddle, he hastened the horses through it to splash as much as possible. He jerked the horses from a canter to a trot. Upon returning, he opened the door for the ladies, all of whom awarded him an uppity look, which gave him no end of satisfaction. He went to his quarter for a nap. Claude was snoring on his cot so he nodded off on the floor but was awakened sometime later when Limbo stuck his head in the door. "Claude, you fit to play your banjo?" He grabbed Claude's foot. "Come on. All creation's at your cabin."

After Claude left, Wink couldn't rest easy. He sauntered to the quarters. So many people gathered at Claude's place they overflowed into the street, which was still damp. Wink and several young men brought hay to cover an area to dance. The girls and women dressed with colorful decorations in their hair and Sunday-go-to-meeting dresses. Polly, Mamba's daughter, wore a wreath of ribbons in her hair.

A cold afternoon sun came out, but the hands warmed up with the music. Rhythm shook the walls of Claude's shanty, so packed with bodies everybody felt the same moves. The entire place was singing and patting juba. Their feet tapped the floor in rhythm so coordinated it sounded like a bass drum. They sang in rounds: "Juba this and juba that, Juba killed a yaller cat, Juba this and juba that, Hold your partner where you at." The banjo, fiddle, bones, quill, voices, and Wink's whistling produced a frenzy of harmonies that spread to nearby cabins.

In one of them, young girls danced with a glass of water on their heads. Onlookers bet on who could dance the longest without spilling a drop. Matilda, who often won such contests, was one of the first to sit down, though she just laughed about it.

Wink strolled about the noisy frolicking, a vast improvement over the silence that had marked his barbecue dinner. At one cabin he overheard Flurry telling several hands about the master's Christmas dinner, which had been spoiled when the dogs ran into the house and tracked mud into the fancy rugs. Laughter rang out. Wink paid little attention to who was doing what until he came upon Thor in a tussle with a field hand and dragged his friend off.

Now that the stranger had taken Lovey, finding Mooey was no longer urgent. Wink could only wonder how she'd found out that the master had intended to sell her. Only Kedzie made any attempt to understand Mooey. Like other slaves who occasionally ran off to avoid punishment or work, Mooey couldn't stay in the winter woods for long without food or warmth. He realized she was probably hungry at that moment. At Mamba's cabin he peeked inside and, seeing nobody, shuffled the ashes until he found an ashcake for Mooey.

Back in the street, he noticed rustling and groans coming from Thor's place and, on looking inside, saw him fighting with Limbo who was so liquored up he couldn't defend himself. When Wink tried to separate them, Thor jumped him, and they tumbled out the door into the street. Wink, who felt he deserved a licking, didn't fight back. Iverson came to his rescue and shoved Thor back into his cabin and put him in his cot.

The ashcake in Wink's pocket had practically turned to crumbs. He hadn't seen Puddin all morning. He went to the kitchen. Inside the door he nodded to Mamba and said to Puddin, "You got a tow sack for me?"

"I don't know. What you got for me?" She looked at him with hooded eyelashes.

"I gots everything you wants and more." Wink made a miraculous recovery.

"Puddin, I can't wait all day." Mamba held a coarse cloth over a big bowl.

Puddin removed an iron pot from the fireplace and hoisted it up.

"Let me help wid that." Wink grabbed a couple of dish rags and helped Puddin. They poured the contents into the cloth Mamba held. Saturated bones collected on the cloth as the broth drained through, raising steam and a meaty smell. "What would you do widout me?" Wink said to Puddin. Her lips, so plump and tempting, smiled.

Mamba gathered the corners and squeezed the bones inside the cloth and whatever remained of the broth into the bowl. She shook the bones into a slop bucket, picked it up, and offered it to Wink. "Wink, take this to the hog pen."

"Puddin needs me here," Wink said, though in reality he needed her. He needed her affection, for he had none for himself.

Puddin poured the strained broth back into the iron pot, and Wink returned it to the hearth.

"Scuse my ignorance. I didn't know you was Puddin's guinea nigger." Mamba gave him a playful look as she went out the door.

Puddin took a tow sack from a stack on a shelf. "What you want wid a tow sack?"

"I'se going to put this ashcake out for Mooey." He took what was left of it from his pocket.

"Where you going to put it?" said Puddin.

"Mooey likes the tree by the sick house."

"Here, put this in there too." She gave him a biscuit and a link of sausage.

He put his hand on her shoulder and stroked down her back to the rosy round of her hip. The feel of her body aroused in him an insane desire. At that moment, he felt that if he couldn't have her, he might as well throw himself into the Beaufort River and drown. He pulled a breath.

She removed a wide wood bowl from the top of the safe and placed it on the table.

"You owes me a Christmas kiss," he said.

"I said I'd think about it." She mixed together flour and lard.

"The fact of de business is, you promised me." The moment she stood in one place long enough, he nuzzled her neck.

When she turned to answer, he kissed her, harder than he meant. "Puddin, you be the ruination of my character."

"Didn't notice your pious character to start wid." She took a jar from the pie safe and added a concoction of hops to the dough.

Anner came in the door with a bedroom pitcher. "Puddin, massuh said to wash this out. Somebody put molasses in the water." She smiled at Wink as if she owned him.

"That be your task," Puddin said.

"What's I going to do? Tell Massuh you don't do what he says?" Anner's lip curled in a smirk.

"I'll tell him myself." Puddin headed for the door.

"No! I'll tell him!" Anner stood in the doorway.

"Tell him what?" Puddin, who was taller than Anner, looked down at her.

"He said I was too slow. Said you'd clean them quicker, but I'se going to clean them." Anner looked at Wink as if he should help her out.

Wink mumbled something about getting back to the horses and left in spite of Anner's beseeching look. The last thing he wanted was for Puddin to think he favored Anner.

CHAPTER 17

WINK VISITS SONNY

CHRISTMAS, DECEMBER 1857

The morning after Christmas, Wink could hardly say good morning even to Tootie. He felt like he had been thrown and trampled by a bucking bronco. He fed and watered the horses and turned them to pasture before going to Mamba for feverroot to make tea for his head. Farley stuck his nose in Mamba's cabin to call on her to doctor the numerous cuts and scrapes. "Git every one of these piddling niggers in shape to do their tasks."

Though the master excused the hands from the field, they were by no means given the day off. Wink as well was expected to whitewash the cabin walls, clean his hearth, store up firewood and make repairs that were needed. He paid Mamba to help him with what were the women's tasks—scrub pots, spread white ashes on the floor, freshen ticks, and such. Whatever tools the slaves had borrowed from the tool shed had to be accounted for and returned. In the afternoon when Farley and the master inspected the quarters, anything amiss or not in good working order had to be explained.

After Wink's place—smaller than most—was clean, he strolled to the chillun house. Mammy Livy wasn't there. Lovey's boy lay in his basket on the floor. Wink knelt on one knee for a closer look. So much wool made his head the size of an August citron. The baby gave Wink an unrestrained gaze of wonder. A body couldn't help but smile at him.

But Sonny didn't smile back. He stared, watched, and when Wink's hand neared his face, he kicked his feet, punched his arms, and lurched as if trying to get himself going. His eyes showed what must have been puzzlement at not getting anywhere.

Wink realized his rough fingers might scratch skin so soft. He wrapped the boy in his blanket, picked him up, and almost dropped him when he reared back forcefully. "Hold on there, Sonny!" Wink laughed. "You is little but you is strengthy." With a firmer grasp on the baby, he walked him to the fire where the two of them warmed. "Your little butt do git cold down there on the floor."

Sonny squirmed and made a face as if he didn't like the company he was keeping. Before Wink could put him back in his basket, he sputtered and whimpered, threatening a full-blown bawl. "What you getting so wrathy about? I'se the best friend you got."

Mammy Livy came in with an armload of firewood. No point trying to help her with it at this point, she was already in the door. She threw the wood on top of the twigs and bark on the floor by the hearth.

In spite of the crying, Wink returned the baby to his basket. "Sonny's getting big for that basket. Reckon you got room for a cradle in here?"

Mammy didn't object to the idea as she added wood to the fire.

In the following days the white families gradually departed Westfall. Wink looked forward to seeing the visiting coachmen and their horses leave. A couple of them had lazily attended their animals, which had bumped their stalls at night. The men so disorganized the equipage room Wink had had to search for simple things like halters, bits, and stirrups.

Two Goodwyn families left on the same day, and Wink finished cleaning a stall where one of their horses had been stabled after biting Freckles. It was late by the time he watered, fed, and curried the horses. The quarters had settled down for the night.

In the dark, he headed to the kitchen hoping to get food for Mooey. Whatever he put in the live oak tree disappeared from the towsack. Upon nearing the kitchen, he halted when he saw the visiting fiddler walking Puddin from the kitchen to the door of her quarter. This cut Wink in the heart. He tarried long enough to see if Puddin allowed the coachman inside her place. Though she didn't exactly participate in his kiss, she didn't act offended. When the visitor tried to wedge himself in the door, she raised her voice. "I don't believe in such goings on." Had the man protested or tried to force himself on her, Wink would have gladly come to the rescue. However, he spoke in affectionate tones, words Wink couldn't make out.

Wink wandered to the quarters, angry and hurt at Puddin's socializing with the coachman. Something like a pall had overtaken Auntie Nell's cabin without the presence of Kedzie, Mooey, Lovey, or baby Sonny. He visited her long enough to wangle an ashcake for Mooey's tow sack.

At the chillun house, Sonny cried like he didn't have a friend. In spite of his noise, Mammy Livy lay on her cot asleep. Wink rocked Sonny before the fire late into the night. Eventually the baby's howling turned to sniveling, turned to whimpering, turned to noisy breathing. Wink watched the flames and decided to steal the coachman's coat and give it to Mooey. The baby's peaceful face knew no sign of the life he had lost, the life he'd have to live without a mother. He slept in Wink's arms as if somebody loved him.

Wink pilfered the coat from the sleeping coachman on his way back to his quarter. Hardly had he fallen to sleep when he heard scrubbing in the stables. He put on the big coat, lit the lantern, and headed outside.

"What you doing here?" Wink said when he knew positive it was Farley climbing down from the hay loft.

"Mooey be herebouts. Dat gal can't scrap along in the woods dis kind of weather."

"I'd know iffen she be in here." Wink realized the edge he was on.

Farley told him boldface. "Dat's what massuh be thinking."

At the risk of getting himself into deeper shit, Wink couldn't let the accusation stand. "Massuh be addled by a cup too much. Nothing in my stables but horses."

"Gimme a pitchfork."

"Git it yourself."

Farley carried up the pitchfork. Wink heard him forking the hay. Wink went back to his cot. He had to get the coat to Mooey before Farley started a search for it.

* * *

At first Mooey credited Auntie with providing her food, but by watching the oak tree, she saw the stableman hang up the sack. She wished he'd leave a candy with the victuals. As she rushed back to the woods, she chewed off a piece of dried fish and sniffed the ashcake.

The following night the wind blew hard, but she didn't dare venture into the quarters or climb any roof as long as people stirred about. She sought shelter underneath the big house near the base of a chimney, but the dogs were so rowdy they ran her away. She climbed into the hayloft, but one of the horses thumped the walls. When she saw the stableman appear at the top of the ladder, she was afraid in spite of his supplying her food, for he might trick her. After all, he had been kind to the foal he had killed. She buried herself under the hay until he disappeared and then sneaked back to the live oak.

She wrapped in her blanket and dozed. When the sky took on a luster, she adjusted on a different branch and settled in for a day of sitting and watching. With increasing dismay, she realized a visitation of the scourge. It wasn't necessary to see the blood in her bloomers, for her body was giving notice—her fleshy fingers and achy belly, the devils in her head. As if she didn't have enough to worry about, this situation raised the risk of attracting animals, wildcats and boars.

To clean herself with well water, she'd have to wait until night. Instead, she made her way to the stream where the slaves washed their clothes. In water cold enough to pain her hands, she scrubbed the stains from her underwear. A strip torn from her blanket, folded and tied to her saddle, shielded her dress from blood until she got bloomers and rags from Auntie's shanty.

Her stomach rumbled with hunger. She waited impatiently near the oak for cover of darkness. After sundown, she checked the tree. Empty sack. She returned later and it was still empty. The cold of night seemed colder. The dark darker. The wind gave her crisp breath. Her nose ran. Her eyes watered. The shivers kept her awake.

The next night she watched the oak tree. As soon as the stableman came and went, she hurried to the tow sack, heedless of danger, and bit into a biscuit before she noticed a big phantom looming in the dark. As it approached, it became a big coat, and closer, the stableman wearing it. She choked and ran. Before she could escape, he wrestled her to the ground. The comforting smell of leather, horses, and tobacco didn't get the better of her fear of him. When he released her, she took off again, but he caught her again. He grabbed her hand and held on while taking off the coat, which he handed to her.

Mooey was so cold the pictures in her head froze. In the shadowy light of the moon, she stared at him.

He put her arm into one sleeve, the other into the other sleeve. It was so big the front lapped double. The warmth gave Mooey breath. Her eyes were smarting with tears. She swallowed hard.

The stableman took out his bottle and offered it to her. She was thirsty and took a big drink, but the strong burn shocked her.

His dimples showed clear in the milky light. In spite of everything, Mooey smiled. She declined another drink, but he took a gulp, turned and left. She searched the ground until she found what was left of the biscuit and went back to see if the tow sack had any other edibles.

***

The following morning, the coatless coachman, looking cold in the frosty dawn, hitched up his team and drove the carriage to the portico where he waited for his mistress, a widow lady with a daughter and two grandchildren. Wink was so glad to see him go he helped load the trunks. The master and mistress accompanied the departing family to the portico, giving and receiving farewells. Anner came to the carriage with a picnic basket Puddin had packed for the white people. She delivered it to them with a secretive smile to Wink.

After they left, Wink stopped at the kitchen on his way back to the stables. Puddin was washing a ham in a barrel bucket.

"I shore is glad dat fiddler is gone." Wink leaned on the door facing.

"I'se glad the whole shebang is going," she said.

"Dat fiddler honeyed around the women folks."

She took the ham out and changed the water. "He did know how to honey around."

"I reckon you going to miss him." Wink struggled to keep aggravation out of his voice.

She looked up. "Somebody poke his finger in your eye dis morning?"

When the last of the horses and carriages left, Wink returned the wagons, buggies, and carts to their usual places. The master saddled up Gideon, who had hardly been ridden in a week, and rode out. The stallion returned in better temper. Knowing the master usually went to Charleston for the January slave auction, Wink awaited word about whether he would be required to go, a requirement he'd gladly fulfill.

When he opened the door to his quarter Anner stood and wagged her finger at him. "What you doing wid dis cask?"

Wink had stolen one of the master's Christmas casks. He needed it for whiskey. "What you doing plundering through my stuff?"

"Don't get mad! I just about stumbled over it."

"Under my cot?"

Her lower lip puffed up like a setting hen. "Now you mad wid me …"

Wink put the cask back in a blanket and shoved it under his cot. "What you doing here anyway?"

Tears came to her eyes. "I was all het up and ready to tell you something special. And all you say is 'What you doing here?'"

Wink's hard feelings gave way to curiosity. Anner knew more about the big house than anybody except Billy, who didn't run on at the mouth. "I hear tell you got more secrets than a graveyard. What you going to tell me?" He sprinkled dry leaves into his cup and followed them with water he poured from the kettle and offered it to her.

She sipped tea. "This be celebrating time." She twinkled with merriment and dug into her pocket. "This here cigar is for you."

Wink took in its tempting old sod smell. "What you done now?" The girl's sparkle was contagious.

"You should of seen the dogs in the massuh's house Christmas dinner."

"I reckon." Wink turned the cigar in his fingers before lighting up with a splinter. He could celebrate dogs in the big house, but there seemed to be more to the story than what he'd heard.

"I bout died laughing. They couldn't git in the house fast enough onct they got the meat scent." She looked up from her cup with eyes suggestive of dark secrets.

Wink poured tea for himself in a tin cup, puffing his cigar.

Anner moved close to him and removed his cigar. Wink, looking for an escape, backed into his chair and sat down.

She put the cigar in her mouth, drew on it, coughed, and said, "You see, I throwed off suspicion by telling the massuh about the open door." Placing the cigar in his lips, she almost laughed as she looked down at him.

Wink, who didn't like his lowly stance, stood and pulled his other chair near the fire. Before he could offer it to her, she nuzzled his lips. Her breath entered his mouth. Her arm pulled him into her heartbeat. Her breasts swelled into his body, and he kissed her like he loved her. And maybe he wanted to. Maybe he'd never win Puddin's heart. He could feel that Anner was all woman.

Anner drew back. "I'se going to settle wid dat lying, sneaking Billy." She picked up her cup and sipped.

Wink, who'd gotten edgy for the feel of skin, anybody's skin, had lost interest in the conversation. His clothes felt tight. His hands pressed on her spare hips. A glowing bulb arose in border territory and rubbed into her saddle. Did it matter that she wasn't Puddin? A man couldn't wait forever. He walked her backward toward his cot.

"Wink, you not listening to one thing I'se saying!" She spilled her tea on his pants.

The flow of warm liquid caused an instant discharge. "Shit, you done wet me." Wink wiped his pants with a dry rag.

She put down the empty cup and tried to help him clean himself, but he stood facing the fire to dry himself. "I was listening. How you going to settle wid Billy?"

"Massuh is going to give dat man a lashing for letting the dogs in." Anner picked up and sipped on what remained of Wink's tea.

"How you know Billy let the dogs in?"

Anner gave him a look that made him feel like he'd regressed to shirttail rank.

"He didn't. But the door be cracked open, and Billy be pouring the massuh's whiskey, and in comes the dogs, looking for them bones I been giving them." She shook her head. "Them dogs be settling accounts wid Billy for sending me to the whipping tree." Her eyes flashed.

Wink hadn't credited Anner with such cleverness, not to mention spite. "You baited them dogs to come in the big house so Billy'd get a whipping?"

"What you think I wanted wid them meat bones you give me?" Anner twitched her head in a self-satisfied way.

Wink felt like he did when he accidentally stepped into a pile of horse dung. He'd helped Anner set up Billy. What was he going to do next if he kept company with this woman?

"Soon as Massuh sends Billy for a thrashing, I'se prepared to say him and me is even." Anner smiled and drank what remained of the tea.

Except for Kedzie, those slaves who had gone to other plantations to visit relatives gradually returned to Westfall, most of them exhausted and in poor condition for work. Because Kedzie hadn't returned from Charleston, it was rumored that she had been sold. Auntie Nell believed she was going to hitch a ride back to St. Helena Island with the master's mother. Wink suspected the master would bring her back, along with any slaves he bought in the January auction, the biggest sale of the year, which was held in Charleston.

Thor had been in such a bad mood over Lovey that Wink bought oysters off a Pritchard slave he passed on the causeway and took them to Thor's cabin to roast. As they sat waiting for the shells to crack, Flurry came by and in no time they had a couple more visitors "just stepping by." When Mamba came in she brought a pot of shrimp a Jervy slave had given her. Everybody knew the Jervy man carried on after her, but Mamba only admitted to interest in his presents. If Wink had had liquor to sell, they would have had an after-Christmas shindig.

"Mamba, how your mammy doing?" Lettie said.

No communication about Mamba's mother had come down the mainland of late. Most people knew Mamba had learned about potions from her mammy, a root worker respected around Walterboro for her healing powers. Though Mamba had hardly been out of shirttails when she was sold from her mother, she had already learned about herbs and tonics.

"When you see your mammy last?" Flurry said.

"This year be five years gone. Wink, you remember ... I called on Mammy while you and Massuh traded seed corn at dat plantation on the river."

Wink remembered.

"Last I heard, mammy be down in the cot," said Mamba. "I shorely do wish I could see her."

Wink, thinking ahead to the Charleston slave auction, said, "Massuh be going to the main in January. Ask him for a ride far as Jacksonboro."

"I coulda gone wid the white preacher right after Christmas but Massuh wouldn't write me no pass."

"Preacher Chaffee?" said Wink and when Mamba nodded, he said, "I passed him on the village road Christmas Eve."

Limbo came in loud and too cheerful; he'd clearly been drinking. "How come I don't git no notice about oysters?"

"Where you get hooch?" said Wink.

Limbo slumped on his cot beside Mamba. "A white nigger over on Lands End Road."

"What white nigger?" Wink wondered if Limbo had discovered his supplier, but Limbo leaned back on the wall, his eyes closed.

Farley stuck his head in the door. "Any you niggers seen Iverson?" Nobody answered and he left.

"Iverson's going to ask the preacher to teach him to read," said Flurry.

"All Iverson's going to git is a sermon dat the good Lord only favors white peoples wid reading," said Mamba.

Iverson opened the door. "Mamba, come wid me."

"What for?" She had just prized open an oyster.

"Claude's down in the cot. You better come see."

Everybody hauled to the street behind Iverson and Mamba. Before they could get inside the sick house, Farley came to the door and pushed them outside. "Git on back to your cabins!"

After Wink returned to his quarter at the stables, Polly came with a message that the master wanted him to go for the doctor. Though she didn't say it was Claude, that's what Wink thought. Despite the danger to a negro to call on a white at night, Wink carried his empty cask and stopped at the shack of a buckra who sold whiskey. The man, who had a taste for his own brew, fired his pistol in the air before Wink could make himself known. Wink was so shaky after buying that he took a healthy gulp to calm his nerves before riding to Dr. Drayton's plantation, which was accustomed to callers at all hours. On their way to Westfall, Wink followed the doctor who remained overnight to treat Claude, who showed no improvement by the time the doctor was called away in the early morning hours.

CHAPTER 18

TREATMENT FOR A HEAD WOUND

DECEMBER 1857

Even if hardly anybody knocked before entering a cabin, Wink expected Anner to. He would have ushered her outside but for the frantic look on her face.

"Something's the matter wid Nitsy!" She sat down to catch her breath. "Matilda come to the big house and said Nitsy be in a frantic."

"Matilda done messed up. Claude is sick. The doctor come for Claude." Wink wondered what this had to do with him.

Anner started crying. "Nitsy be plumb out of her head."

Wink poured a cup of hot water and added a peppermint ball he'd been saving for Mooey. "Here, drink some of this."

"Come wid me to the sick house." Her dark eyes pleaded with him.

"Git Iverson. I can't make no mends of no kind."

"Iverson don't take care of me like you do." Anner sipped and sipped, and Wink hoped she'd leave some for him.

"I don't take care of you, and you knows it," he said.

She burst into such a fit of bawling that the horses beat on their stalls loud enough to rouse the master.

"Sweetie, let's git on down to the sick house and see about Nitsy." He roped his arm around her and swept her out the door, carrying the hysterics away from the stables.

Anner seemed hardly able to walk as they crossed the yard. Doll and Flurry and the shirttail children stopped what they were doing to watch them, for Anner carried on like somebody had died.

Before they even entered the sick house, Wink could hear somebody murmuring. The floor, recently strewn with lime, looked unnaturally bright. Claude lay on a cot apparently sleeping. Nitsy perched in a chair and slumped on the side of his cot. She raised up her head and moaned. Her slimy nose wet her lips. Auntie Nell occupied a chair by the fire. Matilda rested on the hearth. Wink looked for but didn't see Mamba.

"Dat boy's dead to the world. Can't nobody wake him up," said Auntie.

"Nitsy, is you rightly yourself?" Anner touched her sister on the arm.

Nobody knew for certain what had brought on his condition. Some people said he was possessed by a jinn, some said his spirit was bewitched by a hag. Some people even said Nitsy crossed him. Others wondered if a conjurer had been among the Christmas visitors.

Mamba opened the door and stepped inside. She removed her shawl, placed a tow sack on the hearth, and warmed her hands at the fire.

"Nitsy, go on home. It be nigh time you feed your little chaps," Auntie said.

Nitsy didn't budge nor acknowledge Auntie. Her glassy eyes gazed at Claude with mindless intensity.

"Lordy! Nitsy's plumb lost her mind!" Anner sat on Claude's leg and shook her sister. "Nitsy! Girl! You is in the worstest shape I ever seen!"

Auntie Nell pushed herself up from the chair and limped as if one leg was longer than the other. She nodded toward Nitsy. "Leastways she quit whipping herself."

"What the doctor say about Claude?" said Wink.

"Lordy, that doctor taken out a drill and was going to bore a hole in Claude's head, but Nitsy pitched a fit," Auntie Nell said.

Wink noticed the lump on Claude's head. He had heard of such treatment to rid the head of evil spirits. "How he git dat knot on his head?"

Mamba inspected the swelling and touched it with her finger. "Nitsy."

Wink looked at Nitsy, who was sucking wind and trembling, and said, "Nitsy?"

Nitsy mumbled and snorted, said something like "Hebby Jedus! Mek mo'bettuh."

Wink stared at Mamba. "Nitsy?" Claude and Nitsy had had fights before, some of them heard from one end of the quarters to the other.

"Hit him on de head wid one of them iron pots."

Nitsy moaned and rocked and worked herself up to a howl. "Mussy fuh Claude, come back ..."

Anner reached her arms around her sister but was dragged to the floor when Nitsy went down and rolled back and forth, her arms hugging herself. "One done-um. Lord, pray Jedus!"

Anner stood up. "Nitsy, git up off the floor! You is rolling round like a pig in a wallow."

"Girl, git a hold of yourself." Mamba sprinkled several drops of water on Nitsy. "Your man is going to be afeared to come back here wid your racket."

Wink could hardly stand their fawning over Nitsy. "You trifling, snot-nosed nigger!" Hadn't anybody noticed that Claude was near death on account of her? "Git out of here!" He picked up Nitsy and shoved her across the room.

Anner started screaming.

Wink pushed Nitsy toward the door, but she landed against the wall. He said, "What kind a fool is you?"

"For the love of God!" said Auntie.

Wink kicked at Nitsy, who shriveled into a knot on the floor.

"Wink, stop it!" Anner hovered to protect Nitsy.

"Wink!" Mamba grabbed his arm and pulled him back. "This ain't helping Claude one bit!"

Wink wiped his mouth on his coat sleeve. The woman deserved a thrashing. Why didn't Farley haul her to the whipping tree?

"Come on, Nitsy. Let's see bout your chillun." Auntie pulled on Nitsy to help her up.

Nitsy's bawling turned to moaning. "No! No. Lordy, no ..." She teetered to her feet and was helped back to the stool. Anner gave Wink a look like he might end up with a knot on his head.

Auntie Nell extended a rag to Nitsy. "Wipe your face." Nitsy ignored the rag, which Anner took and wiped her own face.

Wink headed out the door. Behind him, Mamba called, "Wink, come back. I needs help." He halted. With Nitsy in the room, Claude wasn't safe. But with Wink in the room Nitsy wasn't safe. When he thought of it that way, he returned.

Mamba said, "Help me git dry clothes on him and the bed."

"Git her out of here." He nodded at Nitsy.

Nitsy shuddered as if she was on the verge of another fit.

Auntie tried to coax her out the door, but Nitsy sat on the floor and screamed. Anner sat and cried. Mamba persuaded Anner to fetch Nitsy's children. With an audience of children and numerous field hands, Nitsy left, even more aggrieved than under Wink's foot.

Mamba said to Anner, "Take care of this here powder. I don't have no more bezoar stones."

"I don't truck wid no doctoring!" Anner, trembling from head to toe, dropped the vial.

Wink caught it before it hit the floor and placed it on the mantlepiece. Anner gave him a woeful look, her eyes brimming with angry tears. He was at a loss. Nitsy hit Claude for no good reason, laid him out half dead, and she got everybody's sympathy. Wink's head throbbed. Claude might be dying on account of Nitsy. But here was Anner, doing everything but accusing Wink of ill treatment.

With a withering scowl she stomped out and slammed the door, which sprung open a crack.

Wink did the lifting and turning, and Mamba changed Claude into clean clothes and bedding.

Mamba sighed and pulled out a collard leaf that obviously enclosed something else. "Claude's got bad blood in his brain. This here poultice is going to purge the hurtful pips." With a strip rag, she tied the collard leaf on Claude's head. She looked at Wink.

Even Mamba's glare accused Wink of wrong, which bothered him even more. Mamba had her wits about her, unlike Anner who didn't make much sense on a good day. In spite of that, he felt Nitsy deserved worse than what he'd delivered.

"Stand over there and help me." Mamba pointed to the other side of Claude's cot and handed him the vial. "The powder's going to make his brain strengthy."

With Wink on one side of the cot and Mamba on the other, they bent to Claude's placid face. "Hold this eye open." She pulled apart his eyelids. Wink rested the vial on Claude's arm and used both hands to expose the eyeball. Mamba shook powder into a spoon and blew some across Claude's eye. She repeated this in the other eye. The powder that was left Mamba put back into the vial.

"That is going to free his head from a jinn, but if it's a devilish jinn we hafta do this again tomorrow morning." Mamba sat in a chair by Claude and recited: "When I passed by you and seed you polluted in your own blood, I said to you when you was in your blood, Live; yes, I said to you when you was in your blood, Live." She repeated the verse without pause.

"How long you going to say them words?" Wink stared at Claude's face, expectant but not sure of what.

Mamba caressed Claude's cheek and paused long enough to say, "Till Claude wakes up."

Auntie chanted the words with Mamba. Wink sensed in Mamba a strong spirituality and in that was hope for Claude. He chanted.

Between the roosters' crowing and the break of day Claude opened his eyes. Auntie went to Nitsy with the intelligence, and her scream was so loud everybody in the quarters heard. By dinnertime, Claude said he was hungry. Later in the day, the story of Claude's injury was street talk—that Nitsy got into such a frantic over his loaning her best dress to another gal she hit him with an iron pan. Whether or not the pan had been jinxed, Claude had awakened from a deep sleep that had lasted two days.

Anner didn't hold a grudge against Wink about Nitsy. To Wink's surprise, even Claude didn't hold a grudge against his wife. Anner brought Wink a biscuit and bacon from the kitchen and sat at his fire, worrying. "Billy stayed in the massuh's room the longest time. I couldn't hear a word of what Massuh said." She picked at broken skin on her chapped lip.

Wink couldn't very well ignore her while he ate food she had brought. "How you git this biscuit from Puddin?" He'd already had one earlier from Puddin herself.

"I done pilfered it on account of you." Anner's look notified him that he owed her gratitude if not more.

"You going to git Puddin in trouble wid the massuh." Wink dragged his stool near the hearth and sat.

"You worried more about Puddin than me! Why do everbody worry about Puddin?" Anner flung herself out of the chair. Her voice veered to a higher tone.

"Who's everbody?"

"Billy goes all white-eyed iffen anybody find fault wid Puddin."

That Billy favored Puddin startled Wink. She had charmed the fiddle player at Christmas, and Wink had suffered the man's obvious flirtation with her. But Billy...Wink wanted to know if the butler's interest was of a kindly or romantic sort, but he didn't dare ask, given the dark clouds around Anner. Billy was more of a loner than Wink. In fact, Wink felt sympathy for Billy. If any man on the place needed a wife more than Wink, it was Billy, who had never married.

"Iffen Massuh blamed Billy bout the dogs, I'd a heard it widout my ear to the door." She paced to the table and stuck her wet finger into a small gourd containing sugar and licked it off.

"Maybe Massuh don't think Billy is dumb enough to let dogs in the house," said Wink.

"How could he ward off blame? He be the onliest one allowed to answer the front door." Anner returned to Wink and rubbed her hand over his wool.

Wink got up for a dipper of water. "Maybe Billy told Massuh you put them meat scraps on the portico."

Anner could hardly speak, as if her breath had stuck in her throat. "Billy don't know anything about them scraps. You tell him?"

"Naw, honey. You think I'm a downright fool?" It was too early to think about taking a dram, but Anner gave him a thirst. "What did Billy say when he come out?"

"Billy be so impudent he blamed the dogs on the white boys. Said it musta been chillun leaving the door unlatched."

"Massuh's going to fetch you in his room to account for not watching them white boys."

"Massuh's boys showed theirselves over Christmas." Anner's stormy eyes flashed. "I done told Missus I can't watch them boys and serve the table." When Wink sat down, Anner climbed into his lap. "The massuh is going to scare me into saying the wrongest thing!" She nuzzled his face and sighed. "Lordy! I'se going to end up in them cane fields in Alabama. I just know I will."

Wink didn't resist Anner's warm and pillowy lips. Nor did he pull away when she fondled his nobby. The way things looked, it seemed necessary to content himself with her.

On a Sunday morning after he'd tended to the horses, Wink said to Thor and Limbo, "Come on. Let's get some rabbits." They called up the master's hunting dogs and headed to the woods, followed by several more men.

They picked up one rabbit from their trap. Taz and Peaches went on a spree after another one, barking like a wild pack. Their hullabaloo bounced back and forth on the trail. After a wild frolic in the bushes, the hunters had not one but two more rabbits in their sack.

Thor noticed the human footprints first, prints about the size of Mooey's. The two of them headed the other men away from the tracks. Wink whistled for the dogs. Hardly had the men cleared the footprints when the hounds picked up the trail and went after it. Wink grabbed the sack from Thor, stumbled deliberately, and released one of the rabbits.

"Git that rabbit!" yelled one of the hunters.

Wink whistled the dogs, which leaped and yapped and took after the rabbit. Wink looked up into the oak and saw Mooey, hugging a stout limb at the top of the tree. He motioned with his head to Thor, who looked up. They took off after the dogs.

The dogs killed the rabbit before the arrival of the hunters, who grabbed the carcass. Wink claimed he knew of a rabbit den in the direction of the creek and whistled the dogs to follow him. To make sure they did, he furtively dropped pieces of the dead rabbit's fur on the ground.

When they returned to the quarters, the men wanted to give the mangled rabbit to the master, but Wink knew Puddin wouldn't cook it, which might cause trouble. He dressed a whole rabbit and took it to the kitchen. He told Puddin about Mooey. "It's just a matter of time til the massuh goes after her wid the dogs."

"Them dogs will chew her feets off," said Puddin, for every slave had heard the story of the runaway who lost his feet to the dogs.

"I'se not going to put out no more food. She's got to come in."

That night he put a small vial of whiskey in the tow sack. Maybe Mooey could figure out that she needed to brace herself.

CHAPTER 19

BROUGHT IN AND BRUSHED DOWN

JANUARY 1858

As the Master's visitors took leave and the number of horses and carriages returned to normal, Mooey began to suspect that whatever bad spirits had come to the place were leaving with the white people. Their departure calmed the wind that stole her breath, but she still felt the gritty rub of a warning, traceable to Early's whip. So real was the picture of him lashing the nursemaid it ached her cold back.

On a night when the stars shivered in the sky, she sneaked into the street and stroked Auntie's closed shutter searching for a toe hold. She dug her toes into the crack under the shutter and stretched her fingers to the upper reaches of the frame where a shifty board allowed space enough for her to grip it. She hoisted herself to the top of the windowsill and from there to the roof where she sat with her back to the warm chimney. The ashcake in her pocket had been crushed. Her fingers, no longer achy and quivering, picked out every crumb. Near morning frost covered the roof. As she climbed down, her foot slipped on ice and she slid to the ground. Most of the day she spent in a dry ditch wrapped in her coat and under a blanket of leaves.

The following night the white doctor came to the quarters, and Mooey stayed in the woods. Were it not so cold she wouldn't have felt so alone. Even the trees seemed to be uncaring creatures. Such a lack of kinship drove her to Mammy's cabin and Sunny, whatever the danger. She pulled his basket close to the lazy coals, sat on the hearth, and gazed on his sleeping face. She loved even his foul odor, though she was apparently the only one who did. The children had taken to taunting him and his scent. More than once she had found him naked, shivering, and wet. He was growing so his feet touched the end of the basket. Under his legs was a sand stone the size of a crab. Shiny crystals showed in the rubbed surface. Though it was doubtless the treasure of some child who stayed with Mammy during the day, Mooey removed it. Sonny's basket was no place for the children to hide things. She kissed his toes. Her hands grew warm at the touch of him.

As the light of dawn threatened, she considered remaining where she was and facing Early and hoping she could escape the whip. She was tired of going hungry and spending nights in the cold. Her throat ached all the way to her belly. She was thirsty, itchy, and achy. She wanted to stay with Sunny and wash his little bottom and put on a clean napkin and keep him safe from the other children. Sunny jumped as if he had been stuck with a pin. He was telling her it was time to run.

Mooey scurried to the woods. She sat cradled in the limbs of an unfamiliar oak as morning light gradually reached across the sky. While she nodded, the master's dogs raved from the underbrush to the trunk of her tree, excitedly jumping and pouncing. She held her breath as a hunter came through the bushes and looked up into the branches. It was the stableman. He saw her but turned back and was gone. The dogs bounded after him. In a muddle of indecision, she waited, unsure of whether she'd see him again. The stonelike presence of nearby palmettos and hickory trees gave notice of the forest's solitude. Still, she waited. Barren twigs gripped the silence. She climbed down.

At night, when the lamplights gradually went out from the windows of the big house, she crept to the kitchen window and peeked in. The smell of loaf bread and oranges rushed into her nose, and the sight of fried bacon on the table brought her to a standstill. The cook rolled a ball of dough in her hand, plopped it on a pan, and pulled off another ball of dough. The butler entered. Then the nursemaid. Mooey could eat raw dough, but she couldn't up and run into the kitchen for it.

She sneaked to the wash shed side and sat under the table, rooted like a tree, as if she couldn't move. Her head felt empty. She had no plan, only hunger. If the cook locked the door, Mooey would have to break a window to get in and everybody would know. She understood that she had to get into the kitchen before the cook went to her quarter.

While Mooey waited, the cook went to the well with the water bucket. Mooey scrambled to the window. The room was empty. She rushed inside, grabbed bacon and a ball of dough, and ran out to myrtle bushes at the edge of the woods and ate the bacon and dough. The cook closed and locked the kitchen.

Candles went out. The ground told Mooey the slaves had settled into their cots, but she bade her time, for the woman with breasts visited every cabin late of a night. Mooey had learned that if this woman found her cot empty, she looked for her and chased her back to Auntie's cabin. If Mooey waited until after she visited to leave her cot, nobody bothered her. The woman's torch inched from one cabin to another and went out at Early's house.

Mooey sneaked to her quarter and climbed up on the roof. She crouched at the chimney, the pleasure of its warmth coursing into her. The moon's light gnawed at the roof, but she didn't notice. She missed Auntie's company. She longed to be with Sunny. She even regarded kindly the Lot Boss, despite the whacks she had given Mooey.

Smoke from the chimney twisted over on top of her. Red sparks blistered the sky, but she was too tired to pay attention. A whiff of a white person passed in a sudden gust, but she was so tired the fear of being caught faded away and she fell asleep.

She woke up to an itch that tormented her back. The chimney crawled with what looked like bugs, which she recognized as a warning of danger. She jumped away, went on her hands and knees to the edge of the roof, and climbed down, realizing something or somebody pursued her. Barely on the ground, she ran as fast as her feet would go, a creature at her heels. Somebody tugged on her coat, and she couldn't get loose. Before she knew it, she was pinned to the ground.

Several men hauled her to the smoke house, thrust her inside, threw her coat on the ground, shut and locked the door. In a shallow pit in the center of the one-room building, low embers bristled and gave off gasps of wan light and thick smoke.

At least this wasn't as cold as a tree. A strong stench arose from dirt so dark it might be cow manure. The brown walls looked to be smeared with the stuff. When the men butchered a hog or beef, they took meat from the slaughtered animals to this house. Only the cook removed meat. Scattered on the ground were pieces of animal flesh and bones. Mooey sat against a wall, her eyes wide open and burning from the smoke. She coughed to get breath. It had been a mystery to her why the meat turned black inside this house, but now she understood and worried that she herself would turn even blacker.

With some effort, she slowed her breathing. After a time she became aware of shadowy lumps hovering above her like evil spirits. She stared and waited for the meat to move. She waited and watched. A big one grew bigger. Mooey suspected that amongst the chunks were haints with eyes watching her. From the smoldering fire curled smoke that was taking her breath. Her chest ached for air. She draped her coat over her head for protection. Haints pinched at her for hours. Mooey worried that if she lost her breath, she might die as ashes rather than burst into the sky as a star.

The pounding of the ground spirit on her butt woke her up. The door opened and Early motioned her outside. She escaped into a morning so fresh the air iced her lungs. Her triumph at living in spite of the shadows quickly melted away when Early shoved her to the whipping tree. She ran but he caught her and tied a rope around her neck. Any tension on the rope choked her. She became momentarily senseless from fighting as Early removed her clothes. Somebody tied her to the tree.

The pain, swift and searing, caused her throat spirit to jump up and down. One stinging smack of the leather lash followed another. And another. Her throat spirit's fury trembled into her mouth. From the sky came a stony force that thrust a feeling inside her head. When she paused to breathe, the sky's force stopped altogether. As the whip singed into her skin again, the spirit muttered from her throat, which sent another jab into her head, not unlike the sky's warning when it flashed with lights and rained. In spite of the pain, Mooey realized that the sky's jabs into her head occurred when her throat spirit struggled the hardest. In a moment of clarity she understood that the spirit in her throat had the power to put a signal into her head. She realized why lips moved. It was possible for one person to summon the mind of another. Her back seized up with the blows. She became dizzy, sagged into the tree, and slumped to her knees.

In the sick house, she awoke on her stomach with Magic dabbing oil to her back. Auntie brought her food, but she had lost her appetite. Her misery involved more than the lashes of the whip. Mooey wanted to see Sunny. He'd make her better.

CHAPTER 20

ANNER'S WRATH

JANUARY 1858

Near tears, Anner barged in on Wink who was washing his hair in his water bucket. "Lordy, I is all over in a shiver." She tottered as if her knees might go down.

Wink raised up and wiped his wet head with a cloth. "Girl, sit down before you fall." He motioned to a chair.

Anner collapsed on the chair and took a deep breath. "Massuh near bout scared me to death."

Wink cleaned out his ears. Anner was going to narrate.

"I knowed soon as I heard his voice he was going to fly into me. 'Anner, come in here!' he says. He done sounded out Lettie and Mamba about them dogs. And nobody been blamed. I be the last nigger he drug in his room."

"Did he blame you?" Wink wouldn't put it past the master to figure out who enticed the dogs into the house. By rights, Anner should bear the blame, but Wink hated to think of her getting another whipping.

"First thing he says is, 'Is there some reason why you left the front door cracked open?' That mighty near broke me."

"He knowed you did it?" Wink sat near the fire and held his wet head to the heat.

"That old snake said that just to scare the daylights out of me." Anner blinked as she put forth the story.

"Then he didn't fault you wid the dogs ..." Wink, sensing Anner's needy nature, put in a chaw of tobacco.

"He tried to make like he knew it was me, but I told him it was Billy. I done told him before Christmas the door been left open. Iffen he disremembers, it's not my fault. And I told him so." Anner's voice conveyed pride, as if she had taken a stand against the master.

"You told him it was Billy?" In his heart, Wink hoped he'd misunderstood.

"Massuh says, 'You see Lettie at the front door?' Like he was thinking she done it." Anner's fingers twitched as she adjusted her head rag. "Honey, iffen he blames Lettie, she's going to the block. I couldn't let dat happen." Most people knew Lettie had lost her front teeth years ago when some womanizer hit her with a fire poker. The master tried to sell her then but couldn't get what he wanted and kept her. "I told Massuh Lettie wasn't in charge the door, Billy was. And Billy be particular about his tasks."

Wink realized anew that Anner's soul had mud holes and sooner or later, he was going to slip into one of them, just like Billy had. "Massuh just messing wid you. Don't know what you so riled up about." He stood and put on his hat in spite of his damp hair. He had listened to her bile about Billy too long without objecting. He didn't want her to count on him as if he was part of her dealing.

"I'll get over these nerves most fine wid a little help." She approached and wrapped an arm around Wink.

He spit into the fireplace. "Darling, my nerves is acting up too. Dat's why I got this chaw in my mouth."

She smiled but her eyes were serious. "I got something bettern that chaw."

Wink couldn't make spit, even with his cud. "Come back tonight, baby. I be aching good by then."

He left and so did Anner. She didn't show up later, but if she had, she'd have interrupted Wink's poker game in which the bidding was with chits for drafts of whiskey. Limbo, who was winning, passed out on the cot and the game broke up.

When it got right down to the grit, Wink was entertained by Anner's attention, but he didn't trust her. Her visits to the stable brought quality victuals she'd stolen from the master's kitchen as well as cigars she sneaked from the big house. She kept her ears open and told Wink intelligence about the master and his family. At the same time, she had a temper, held grudges, and could be spiteful. For many reasons, she was a person to keep close, but not too close.

During January the fieldhands began to prepare the ground for spring planting. In the freezing hours of daybreak, they plodded to the fields to list, plow, and trench the acres of land. Though Wink didn't work in the field, he hitched up the wagon and hauled loads of fertilizer in the form of sedge, crushed cottonseed, or marl, which the field hands spread with their hoes.

Driving the wagon to and from the fields wasn't nearly as interesting as a trip to the main. Wink didn't think about sedge as he pitched it on the wagon. Rather, he speculated about the trip that might be some days coming. If the master took a carriage to the Charleston slave auction in expectation of buying more hands, Wink would make the trip, an opportunity for him to stock up on whiskey.

Polly came to the stables with orders from the master for a task Wink disliked above all others. It was time to muck the cow lot and stables and haul the manure to the fields. Next morning about daybreak, he hitched up the cart and drove it into the cow lot. Instead of Doll, he met Billy, dressed in a roundabout fit for a fieldhand. "What you doing out here?"

"I'se going to muck the cow stalls."

"Where's Doll?" Wink tied the mule's lines on a stall post.

Billy shrugged and began to shovel manure into the cart.

"Massuh done throwed you out the big house?"

"Reckon so."

"What you do?" Wink, in spite of his cynicism, suspected the master had a personal attachment to Billy. That the man was shoveling manure gave reason to doubt that he had any more security than the rest of the slaves.

"I shoulda kept the dogs out the house Christmas."

"Is Missus going to let you in your quarter tonight wid cow flop stuck to your shoes?"

"I'se going to bed down wid Thor and Limbo."

Another bad sign. Wink took his shovel, and the two of them worked from one stall to another. Billy rode on the cart with him to the field where they shoveled off the manure in a pile and returned to the lot.

Doll arrived with her shovel and mucked for about an hour before dinner, knocked off, and didn't return. At the end of the day, Billy's inexperience showed in the way he smelled, which was worse than Wink and Doll put together. With no gloves, manure caked under his fingernails. And he had no special shoes, the consequence of which his shoes carried a smell however much he washed up.

When Wink saw him sitting outside in the cold eating his supper, he asked Billy in to his fire. Thor and Limbo claimed Billy smelled too bad and wouldn't let him sleep on their floor until Farley made them.

In the two weeks Billy worked about the stables and cow lot, he became as good as Wink at judging the wind's direction and its effect on airborn muck. At least he learned to throw manure with, instead of against, the wind.

The hands in the quarters didn't socialize with him, and he made little effort to carry on a conversation. By the time he returned to the big house, his eyes looked red and droopy, as if he hadn't slept in a month.

Negro strangers didn't cause near the fright a buckra did, but nobody wanted to see their kind as stock to be traded. The two men who arrived with Jervy stayed after the white neighbor left. Farley showed them to the quarters.

While Wink was trimming fetlocks, Farley came to the stall with the new men and said, "I needs two horses saddled up, and get along smartly."

"I'se busy wid this here mare." Wink took his time with the shears.

"Git up here and saddle horses for these niggers Massuh done hired off Riverben." Farley leaned over the stall divider.

Wink didn't bother to straighten up or look at Farley. "Your highfalutin orders don't mean chicken shit in here."

"Boss, which horse can I ride?" said the younger of the men. "I'll saddle up myself."

Wink glanced up at steady eyes, a stony face, and hair in spirals unlike any other's. A person of reckless intelligence. Wink walked to the paddock, and led Nicky out. "This be a good horse, long as you go easy on the bit." He showed the man where he kept the equipage.

The older negro, name of Lamar, complained that he didn't ride, but Farley said he could handle a mule. Wink took measure of Lamar and decided that for the mule's well-being he'd better saddle it himself. As he flung on the leather mantle used when the children rode, he watched the younger man with Nicky and, to Wink's relief, the man knew what he was doing. The two men rode into the pasture along with Farley, on the horse he owned.

Wink thought again that if Farley could buy a horse, it didn't seem so far-fetched that Wink could. The beautiful bay filly for sale in the village came to mind. More than merely a dream, the horse could be his if he had more whiskey to sell.

In less than an hour, Lamar, the older of the two hirelings, stomped through the stables and without a word went to the quarters. Wink walked down to the pasture and met the mule coming in. He scratched the mule's ears and patted it on the haunches. "What that black-necked sluggard do?" He led it back to the paddock, swearing to himself about ratty-nosed people who didn't know how to treat an animal.

He was raking out old litter and putting down clean straw when Farley and the young man returned. Wink was ready to cross words with Farley. "That mule is gonna go mean on account of you."

But Farley didn't argue. He pulled his horse into a cleaned stall and unsaddled him. "Dress down Skeeter and feed him," he said to Wink in an imperious tone on his way out.

"Noooowww, Massuh Farley." Wink, who took care of Skeeter as long as Farley made it worth his while, figured he had more than worked off the payment of a brass buckle Farley had given him. "I reckon it be time to settle up."

"What you want now?" Farley backtracked to the doorway. The young man, who had unsaddled Nicky, curried the horse.

Wink had become impatient to go to Beaufort. The problem with trading in whiskey was that he didn't go to the main often enough to keep up his supply. Farley might give the master a reason for a trip. "Maybe you need a barrel of tar or some blue pills or something from the main."

Wink didn't have to spell out what he wanted. Farley, though he had no respect for his own people, wasn't stupid. He didn't hesitate, just agreed to ask something of the master and left.

As Wink and the young man took the horses to the trough for water, Wink learned his name was Rio and the two new men were carpenters. Wink put his foot up on the side of the trough and leaned on his leg as the horses drank. "What the massuh hire you for?"

"He's building on the big house, but I reckon we going to mend fences first," Rio said. "Is dat nigger the overseer?"

"We don't hardly know what he is. But he lives in the overseer's house." Wink started back to the stables.

"Why you want to go to Beaufort?" Rio walked beside Wink.

"I got affairs." Wink, who knew too many negros eager for intelligence to pass along to Farley, kept particulars to himself.

"Maybe I need a adz or drawknife or a sharpening stone from the main. The tool house bound to be short something," said Rio.

Wink smiled to himself. He might like the boy.

CHAPTER 21

IN A CHARLESTON ALLEY

JANUARY 1858

Whether Wink would accompany the master to the slave auction in Charleston kept him in suspense until the master sent him to borrow a Goodwyn cousin's coach. That the master called for the coach, which was larger than the carriage, in all likelihood meant he expected to return with more negros. It was a foregone conclusion that the master wouldn't drive the coach. Wink whistled all the way back to Westfall.

In the afternoon he hustled to the chillun house to see Sonny before his trip. Wink looked in the new cradle he had bought from Salina's. Sonny studied something like a fluff stuck to his thumb. A baby in a basket on the floor sputtered and gasped as a hound licked its face. A youngun crawling nearby sucked on a dirty corncob. Children in shirttails ran in and out the door, yelling as they chased one other.

"Mammy, how is Sonny?" The baby, who smelled no better than the stables, looked up from his finger. "Sonny, you been chewing on dat blanket?" The cloth was not just frayed but pitted with holes and looked all the more worn in the new cradle. The baby twisted as if he needed to get up.

"He do chew on it on account of Flurry making him wait."

That bothered Wink. "She don't suckle this boy like she should?" Sonny gave his legs a purposeful kick.

"Menfolks about to drive dat woman crazy and she don't have far to go." Mammy pushed aside the children and spooned peas from a pot on the fire into a bowl she gave to a little harelip girl. "Me next!"

"Me next!" Voices squealed as she once again dipped the spoon into the pot.

Wink stuck out his finger and Sonny grabbed it. "You is going to scare off the chickens wid that smell, little feller." Before Wink could clean Sonny, he had to go to the well, for the water bucket was empty.

"You little stinker!" He picked up Sonny, gathering the blanket with him, laid him on the table, cleaned his bottom, and changed his napkin. Mammy dropped the dirty one into others in a basket in the corner.

He took Sonny to the fire and crouched among the children. Sonny gazed from the children to the blazes, entranced. In that moment, Wink had no need of liquor or horses or money or anything else to be happy.

As he left the cabin, he looked beside the door to see that the firewood he had brought for Mammy was still stacked there. If stealing firewood was a crime, most of the negros would be in jail, but it was especially low-down to steal from Mammy who couldn't hear well and had no man to help her.

Early the following morning, Wink hitched up the coach and drove the causeway to the ferry landing on the Beaufort River. He was trailed by the master on Gideon. Because high tide came early on that day, the ferry delivered them in Beaufort before the merchants opened their stores. The road from Beaufort to Charleston went far inland before turning north, for there were few if any ferries to take them across the many lowland creeks and tidal inlets. At nightfall, they stopped at Cane Brake Lodge to spend the night.

The next day as they neared Charleston, Master Goodwyn took the Johns Island road while Wink continued to the city. For the final miles of the trip, Wink, as a lone negro in possession of a coach and fine horses, drove with greater attention, always on the lookout for other travelers. The paper pass the master had written for him only served to protect him from duly employed patrollers and rich whites. If a buckra needed a coach and several fine horses, that pass would land in the ditch with Wink. The closer he came to the city the more relaxed he became. It was dark by the time he drove into Missus Lambeth's yard that night.

The master's mother had a reputation among older Westfall slaves as a fickle woman not fond of Saint Helena Island. While married to the master's father, she had remained in Charleston much of the time while her husband managed Westfall. Wink wondered if she'd ever known that another woman took her place when she was absent from Westfall.

He parked the coach in the carriage house, unhitched the horses, and settled them at the livery. Then he went looking for Kedzie, but one of the women told him she stayed with her mother in a separate cabin considered the sewing room, a first-class place with a wood floor and weatherboarded walls. Wink could only assume Kedzie's mother Dina was faring better with Missus Lambeth than she had at Westfall.

He was so tired, the loud laughter and babble of the slaves hardly disturbed him as he bedded down in the quarters, which were unlike those at Westfall. Two families lived under one roof, the single-pen homes joined by a chimney wall.

The following morning the master, who'd arrived separately, sent word to hitch up Missus Lambeth's wagon to go to the slave auction. It squeaked as if its girding had never been oiled. Wink drove to the slave shed on Market Street where he parked in a nearby alley and waited. Master Goodwyn arrived, dismounted, and handed over the reins of his horse. While the master traded at the slave auction, Wink watched the wagon and horses. He knew it would be a long wait, but nothing to compare to the slave auction the previous March in Savannah. Over four hundred slaves, all owned by a planter name of Butler, had been sold. Despite the gossip at the Victoria Hotel about abolitionists, as long as men like Butler lived, talk of freedom only raised false hopes. From the doorman, Wink got word that Brother Milton had been allowed a pass to travel to St. Helena Island in January, a communication Iverson would be glad to hear.

Before settling down, Wink drove over to the carriage shop and greased the axles and running gear. When he asked where he could find hooch, a man's big walled eyes glazed over. Another shook his head. They looked dumbstruck, as if they never touched the stuff. On his way back to the auction, he searched out a dry goods store to buy a scarf for Puddin and a blanket for Sonny. In one, the clerk chased him out. "Niggers git to the back door!" Wink left and looked for a store like Salina's, where blacks were allowed to make purchases as long as they didn't hang around inside or try to buy something like a knife or rifle or rat poison. Eventually he found a street cart and bought a red headscarf from a buckra. The man said he could get a baby blanket by the next day, but Wink had no way to return.

Back at the alley, he parked the wagon and waited in the cold shade of the buildings with several other wagons, most of them unattended. The elderly man he approached about whiskey answered, "Boy, dat hooch be powerful evil. Dat's the God's truth. You put it in your mouth and it's going to eat up your soul." He carried on about Jesus and seeking the word, and Wink could hardly get away fast enough.

Back at the wagon, he threw on a blanket and tried to doze off. By the afternoon he'd become so bored he drove up the street to the public water trough and watered the horses. Returning to the alley, he ambled around to keep himself warm, and as he sidled out to the street, a cold whiff of river air brushed him back. Down an alley on the opposing side of the street he spotted a small open fire. Several men crouched close to it. Wink joined them and opened his palms to the warmth. He recognized one of them as the liveryman at a plantation on Bull Island.

The man nodded. "Yessah. Freeze your ass off out here no damn how."

"My fingers is about to break off." Wink squatted around the fire with the men who accepted him since he had been recognized.

After a silence, their conversation continued. "Why'd he throw a pot of hot soup on her?" said a wall-eyed man with a head the size of Puddin's kettle.

"He said the soup was bad."

"She a bad cook?"

"Donno. She's a dead cook now."

"That man deserves to die."

"He's not the onliest one. Every one-a us knows a white man what deserves to die."

"He's not going to die by hisself."

"What we going to do? Buy some guns wid nothing but chaw tobacco?"

"Naaa. We going to scare him to death!"

"I'se going to sneak in his chamber and cut his throat."

"Yessuh, and white folks from here to Savannah going to hang ever nigger on the plantation."

Wink kept quiet. A woman was apparently dead. He thought of Puddin. What would he do if the master killed Puddin because of bad soup? His heart thumped in his chest. A powerful helplessness climbed on his shoulders. He could do with a drink. The man with whiskey in Beaufort came to mind. Wink had kept the connection alive, but it was time to be trading.

One of the men stirred the fire.

"She was unlucky."

"More niggers than whites in these hereabouts."

"First shot fired and the niggers'll run for the woods."

"You think we going to fight wid bare hands?"

"Iffen you kill one white man, ten niggers gets killed, what's the good a that?"

"Gotta kill every damn one of the whites."

They all stared into the fire, their silence acknowledging the truth of what had been said. The only way to punish one white man was a massive slaughter of every one of them.

Wink returned to the wagon. Other wagons and drivers gradually departed. The lamplighter came around with his pole and lit the street lamps. When the master appeared, he had bought two slaves, one a skinny boy named Primus, the other a man name of Joe. Wink gave them water from his jug and helped Primus, his wrists and ankles bound, into the back of the wagon. Joe stood like a stubborn bull and wouldn't move until the master conked him on the head with the butt of his shotgun.

Wink threw the blanket over them and whistled as he flapped the lines on the horse's haunches. "Giddiup here, girl. Come on now! Giddiup!" His whistle nearly froze his teeth. The wagon wheels turned, and they headed out of the alley, the master on Gideon just behind him.

At Mistress Lambeth's house on Tradd Street. Wink and the younger slave ate a supper of hominy in the quarters. Joe, who had thrown a servant's shoe in the fireplace, had been taken to the cellar and tied up.

Primus gulped his food and looked at Wink. "One time Old Miss had my mammy flogged for letting flies get in the milk." The boy swallowed as if he had a fly in his throat. "The overseer tied her up to the rail where they hung the hogs."

"Missus Goodwyn don't have no rail." Wink, who could see worry in the boy's eyes, didn't mention Westfall's whipping tree.

"Your massuh whip niggers?" Primus shifted on his stool.

It wasn't a good time to confess the flogging Mooey had taken. "He don't strop us no more'n any other massuh."

"My old massuh give my brother a thrashing." Primus gulped down the last of his hominy. "He couldn't find the duck what fell in the river." His eyes went watery. "He hollered a-plenty. Hollered all night. Them cuts turned to boils." The boy's hands trembled. He looked in the fire.

Wink listened without saying much. Word about whippings would only scare the boy more. He washed out his bowl in the dishpan and set it to dry on the table.

"Massuh got mad and whipped like the mischief." Primus talked on about his master's rawhide whip and the cobbing paddle. Even after he lay on the floor, he told of a slave who had been pegged to the ground and whipped. Primus was just out of shirttails. Nobody to care about him. The boy twitched in his sleep.

Wink arose before the others and struck a light for the coach lantern. The smell, sharp as ammonia, hung about the cabin as he drank coffee made of parched meal. He took breakfast from a pot of hominy on the hearth and left to hitch up the horses. Before he drove the coach to the front yard, a burly slave shoved Primus, his wrists once again tied by a rope, inside. Joe, the bigger one, reared back, and though he kicked against the wheel hub, he was thrown in with Primus and the door slammed.

Wink walked to the sewing house, stuck his head in the door, and said, "Come on, Kedzie. It's time to go." Back at the coach he listened to Master Goodwyn's directions about where the two of them would meet up. Because the master wasn't accompanying the coach until they arrived at the Parker's Ferry road crossing, Wink was accountable for the two new slaves and Kedzie, who climbed up to the driver's seat. He could handle horses, but slaves were a different matter altogether.

"I'll be there dinnertime or thereabouts," the master said as he adjusted his hat.

Wink whistled, slapped the lines on the horses' rumps, and called, "Giddiup, there. Come on! Giddiup!"

Kedzie busied herself sewing a hem into a piece of cloth about big enough for a head rag. In the course of their conversation, Wink was reminded of Kedzie's bright spirit. The previous summer when she'd returned to Westfall, she had earned his admiration by speaking up for Mooey and protecting her. People said she was stuck-up, but that was because she talked smart like a book.

She asked him to teach her to whistle. He showed her how to pucker, and she puckered and blew through her lips. The harder she tried the thinner her whistle but she wouldn't give up. He touched her once, but warned himself away from her. She was like a china doll, too perfect to mess with.

After hours of riding, they stopped at a brook that washed across the road to water the horses and refill their flagon. While Wink relieved himself in the woods, he heard Kedzie call out, "Where you going?"

He hustled to the road in time to see Joe shamble into the brook, his hands free but his feet still hobbled. "Come back here, nigger!" Wink ran, easily overtook the man, and grabbed his muscular arm. Before Wink knew it, he was sprawled in the bushes while Joe sloshed away.

Wink went after him again, but the bigger man threw him into briars. "Shit!" Wink pulled out thorns stuck in his shoulder. What business did he have chasing a negro? Joe wasn't his slave. As Wink headed back to the coach, Kedzie dodged him and ran into the brook. "I'm going too!"

The girl was more innocent and foolish than Wink had realized. "Kedzie! You going to freeze in the woods!" As she disappeared from sight, he yelled, "Massuh is going to say your mammy put you up to this!" He had known Dina when she was Westfall's nurse, and he knew how much Kedzie meant to her.

Wink picked burrs out of his shirt and brushed off his pants. Water had leaked into his brogans, and his feet were cold. He heard splashing water before he saw Kedzie. She plodded back to the coach, her lips blue and shivering.

"Get inside out the wind," said Wink.

He held the lines and Tootie and Skittles forded to the far side of the stream. After they came to a stop, he opened the door. "Here, wrap this round your feets before you lose your toes to frostbite." He handed Kedzie the blanket, and she curled up in it.

Wink crouched on the driver's seat and tucked a chew into his jaw. The brook gurgled. The breeze picked up sharp edges from frozen twigs and cut into his coat. He huddled in his blanket, blew into his gloves, and tried to ignore the raw ache in his feet. What he dreaded was the master's temper when he found out about Joe.

The approach of a white buckra on the lonely road revived Wink's diligence. No negro carried a gun, and no white went without one. From the tent of his blanket, he cautiously watched the stranger drive his bony mule and wagon toward them, slow down, and continue past. Wink was able to relax after they could no longer be seen or heard.

The distant clop-clop of a horse echoed from behind them. Wink took a cold breath and climbed down from the seat as the master came into view. Joe was gone and Wink had to explain. He adjusted his chew, spit in the road, and cleared his throat.

As it turned out, Joe got the worst of the master's wrath. Master Goodwyn rode after him and returned, dragging the man in the brook behind his horse. While the master gave Joe a good, sound thrashing, Primus gazed away and mumbled to himself. Wink put on his mask of indifference. They dragged Joe into the cab, and Wink whistled the horses back to life.

Following an overnight at the public house in Jacksonboro, they rolled south through Beaufort without a stop, took the ferry, and continued into the yard at Westfall. Light from the windows of the big house streaked into the perpetual darkness. Light rimmed the shutters of the shanties. Farley arrived with a lantern and took the slaves to the quarters. Kedzie jumped down and followed in the afterglow of Farley's lantern.

A misty cold cloud chilled Wink from inside out as he unhitched the horses by the light of a lantern. Charleston confirmed Wink's awareness that though Westfall was no safe place for a negro, neither was any other place. And every white man was a danger to every black. At the same time, he knew he was lucky to get a view of a world beyond the plantation. There were hands at Westfall who had never seen the village, much less Beaufort or Charleston. He folded the headscarf he'd bought for Puddin. He wished he had a blanket for Sonny. The thought of Puddin and Sonny made him glad to be back at Westfall, for if he had a home, this was it.

The following day Wink mucked stalls and put away equipment to restore the stables and horses to their usual clean, well-groomed appearance. Thor, given the task of tending the horses when Wink traveled, did little more than feed them. While Wink curried first one then another, he half expected the master to show up at any minute to question him about Joe's escape. What would he say if the master, in his calm manner, asked him how Joe had ended up in the woods? Wink knew the master well enough to understand that a bucketful of shit began with what appeared to be a simple question.

Wink mulled everything over. It would have been foolhardy of him to leave the horses, coach, and other slaves alone on the roadway to take off after the man. What if a deer or a fox spooked the horses? What if they bolted with the negros inside the coach? What if some buckra came along and stole the coach, horses, and negros? Though any such event was a long shot, none of them could be denied.

In spite of all this logic, Wink knew Farley might appear with his cat-o-nine tails looped on his belt. Wink had never been whipped. He found his whiskey bottle in a sack of oyster shells and drank. He didn't think he could stand for a whipping.

* * *

Mooey sat up carefully. At times she stretched the scabs on her back and caused them to snap apart and bleed. Her unsteady feet wobbled to the dwindling fire where its meager heat glowed into her skin like liniment. Auntie, who usually kept up the fire, was in the field with the other hands. Mooey threw on a blanket and went outside, but where they stacked wood by the door she found only twigs and slabs of bark. The cabin, as well as the street, ebbed with hardly any motion, a stillness like midnight.

She meandered down to the chillun house. Some youngsters moved about in blustery fashion, some fought over marbles. Some sat listlessly by the fire. Others lay on the earthen floor. Mammy Livy was wiping a wet cloth on the face of a little girl all stiff and jittery on a cot, her eyes rolling, her teeth grinding. Mooey made her way to the fire and squeezed in among the children and warmed, back and front.

Two baskets contained babies Mooey didn't recognize, one even smaller than Sunny, whose basket was missing. Pushed into the corner was a new cradle. To her surprise, that was where Sunny lay, his face all twisted into a painful look. His lips shuddered with an overflow of unhappy spirit. With her hand she caressed his cheeks and neck, both burning to the touch. A haint was burning his little body. Poor baby.

Mooey sensed her legs losing strength, the coming-on of a fall if she didn't sit. She tottered over to Mammy's rocking chair and slumped on the boy sitting in it. He wiggled out from under her and crawled on the floor.

As soon as her legs recovered enough to stand, Mooey picked up Sunny and sat back in the rocker. His little body, thick and hot with misery, fought his blanket. His arms, legs, and body lurched stiffly. Mooey rocked him and rubbed his tight nubs of hair.

Mammy came to the fire with the pan and added steaming water from the kettle. Her troubled face gave Mooey to know how difficult was the day. She moved her lips. She wiped her own forehead with the wet rag. Upon looking at Sunny, she put well water in a piggin and showed Mooey how to wet a cold rag and hold it to his hot forehead. She returned to the little girl having a fit.

Sunny grew tired and his gestures turned limp. His eyes closed. His entire body sighed with breathing. Mooey took him to the cot beside the sick girl, laid him down, and as Mammy bathed the girl in warm water, Mooey bathed Sunny in cold. She squeezed water from the rag into his mouth.

The rigid body of Mammy's little girl gradually relaxed; her legs and arms slackened. Her jaw unclenched. She appeared to be asleep. Mammy moved her to the back side of the cot and covered her with a blanket. As soon as there was space, another little girl, sucking her thumb, climbed into the cot with the sick child and put her arm around her.

Mammy placed her palm on Sunny's forehead and motioned to Mooey to continue with the cold washing. Mooey sat on the side of the cot, so tired she could hardly sit, but she couldn't rest as long as Sunny needed her.

Because so many were in the room, children often bumped into her or knocked Sunny's head or stumbled over her feet. After she had rested long enough to stand, she carried Sunny to her cabin. Mammy, stirring batter in a big wood bowl, seemed not to notice.

In her cabin, Mooey laid Sunny on her cot and lay beside him. She constantly refreshed the wet cloth with cold water and swabbed his little body. When he began to shiver, she wrapped him in blankets and drew him close to herself.

For two days and nights Mooey slept with Sunny and took care of him. She warmed him when he was cold and cooled him when he was hot. Auntie made victuals for her, changed and washed Sunny's napkins. Magic brought a poultice for his chest. The suckling nurse tried to get him to take her breast, but he was too sick. When he was aroused enough that he didn't choke, Mooey fed him water with a wet rag. She drizzled goat milk into his mouth from hers.

On the third day, Sunny awoke and looked around. Though his eyes were hollow, his face no longer flared with heat. He stretched and twisted. When Mooey put her face to his, he sucked on her cheek. He sucked her nose, her chin. She beamed at him and he stared at her. When the woman with breasts came, he suckled. When she left, he gazed at his fingers. He hiked his feet into the air.

Mammy appeared that night and visited with Auntie. It was obvious from their glances in the direction of the cot that they signaled each other about either Mooey or Sunny or both. Mooey held the baby and loved him with her kisses. She felt her breath hovering outside her body, as if she was about to lose something.

Mammy approached and reached for Sunny. Mooey clasped him to herself. Auntie came to their cot. The stern faces of the two women only meant one thing, Mooey had to let Sunny return to Mammy's cabin. Tears flooded Mooey's cheeks.

After they left, Auntie sat beside Mooey and stroked her wool. She dabbed liniment on the scabs of her back with a kindly touch.

The next day, Mooey hauled out of her cot and went to the chillun house. She stayed and rocked Sunny by the fire until she was too tired to carry on. After dinner and a nap, she returned to hold Sunny. The gleam came back to his eyes. His feisty little feet kicked. He farted and grunted and made a big poop in his napkin. By the time she cleaned him up, Mooey was exhausted. She went back to her cabin and took a nap.

She awoke to the weight of somebody sitting on her cot. She turned and to her surprise Lacy gazed down at her. Mooey could hardly contain her joy. Lacy's hug so hurt her back she recoiled. With greater care for Mooey's back, they gave and got hugs and kisses.

The touch of Lacy's fingers tracing the lash marks calmed the galloping spirits inside Mooey, drove away the loneliness and gave her a peaceable feeling, like somebody shared the calamity that had befallen her. She sat up and put on the headscarf Lacy gave her. With her friend back in their cabin that night, things seemed to be returning to normal.

CHAPTER 22

FROZEN PEACOCK

JANUARY 1858

The bucket with oyster shells was full, and Wink carried it to a lime heap near the creek. Earlier in the week, Farley had burned and crushed the previous heap of shells the slaves had collected. Wink and Primus had shoveled the white fresh-burned lime, as soft as flour with hardly a lump in it, into calabash containers where it was kept until time to whitewash the cabins again.

When Wink arrived in the kitchen, Puddin's headscarf in his pocket, his hands were dusted with the white lime powder.

Puddin hardly ever left the kitchen, and she complained of having no occasions to get away. She liked to talk recipes, but with no other cooks about, she had little opportunity. With a bent for adventure, she created new dishes on her own from time to time. If they were less than successful, Wink knew about it first-hand, for her nerves rattled loose. She had good reason to worry if any amount of meat, sugar, flour or such had been wasted, for the master kept account of how much went into the kitchen. If he suspected less came to the table in the big house, Puddin had to explain. Every slave on the place knew the master wasn't fond of explanations.

Puddin, who was making yeast, mashed white potatoes she had boiled with hops and returned it to the pot. Billy shooed a duck off the lean-to as he came inside with firewood.

"Massuh got you tending the kitchen fire?" said Wink.

"Dat new boy supposed to." Billy dumped a couple of cut logs on the fire.

Puddin rearranged them with a poker. "Dis ain't no oak wood."

"How's I supposed to know oak wood?" said Billy.

"I can't cook wid just any wood. Massuh's bread's going to be crusty instead of puffy wid dis pine wood. It burns up in a minute and goes cold the next."

"Wink, go git dat boy! Tell him Puddin needs wood," said Billy.

"I'se not dat boy's boss man. I can't rightly tell him to do nothing lessen the massuh sends me."

"I don't care a scrap who's the boss. I'se going to get dat boy in here." Billy left.

Puddin stirred the pot of mush and removed it from a cross pole. As she reached for a pot, Wink helped her. "Iffen you tells me you loves me, I gots a present for you."

Her glance clipped his with a sassy look. "You tell me first." She guided the pot as they poured the contents into a sieve.

"I loves you, baby ... And I'se ready for some loving too."

Her eyelids edged down and she looked up. "What you got for me?"

"Say it!"

Her rosy lips resisted a smile. If he had been closer, he would have taken those lips to his and tasted their sweet, moist, warmth.

She let go of the pot and Wink was holding it.

She turned her face away and mumbled, "I love you," and began to press out liquid on which she sprinkled brown sugar.

"What dat you say?" He replaced the pot at the fireplace.

"You heard me." She was rubbing flour into a little of the hops liquid.

A door slammed. Wink pulled out the red headscarf.

Puddin's eyes went from brown to bright. "Dat's the prettiest color!" She shook out the folds.

"Don't I git a kiss?"

Primus and Billy were talking outside the door.

Puddin smiled at Wink as the two men came inside followed by Mamba, who went to the fire and held her hands close. "Lord–

a-mercy, it be too cold to be washing clothes. Dat water's about to freeze up."

Wink wanted another saucy look from Puddin, but she was storing the yeast pan on a shelf, a cloth over the top.

As days passed and the master's questions didn't come, Wink began to believe he had escaped the whipping tree. Though the master hadn't punished him as such, he had kept Wink on a short leash. No errands to the village. No messages to the neighbors. No deliveries. No mail. No whiskey.

As darkness fell, what had started as drizzle sheeted as ice on the trees. Once the field hands came in, they kept close to their hearths. Chimneys chugged smoke and cinders. Wink walked the unnaturally quiet street on his way to see Sonny. Rarely had there been such intolerable cold weather. Families huddled together. Fathers stoked their fires. Mothers warmed blankets by the blaze and wrapped the children up.

In the chillun house, only Sonny stayed with Mammy. The other babies had been taken to their parents' cabins. Wink gazed at his peaceful face as he slept in the cradle under two threadbare blankets, hardly enough to keep a cat warm. He touched the baby's foot and Sonny stirred.

"His foots be cold. Where's another blanket for this boy?"

Mammy nodded in a rocking chair by the fire.

"Look in dat basket of rags under the cot." She hardly roused. "Don't have but one thickness twixt myself and daylight."

There were three cots, all of them undergirded with baskets and crates. Wink located the rag basket and dragged out several scraps, none of them big enough to make a bird's nest. "This here all you got for a blanket for this boy?" Wink held up one of the rags.

She sighed and looked and nodded.

"Damnit! This baby's going to freeze to death." He returned to his quarter and cut a piece off one of his blankets for Sonny. He toted wood from his pile to Mammy's cabin and stacked some beside the hearth and the rest outside by the door.

With the coming of night, the sheets of ice thickened. To keep the stables as warm as possible, Wink heaved shut the paddock gate, which he seldom used, and stacked bundles of hay against it as well as the entry gate. He added straw to the stalls.

In the middle of the night, Wink's toes were cold, but he had the satisfaction of knowing Sonny had a blanket. The yard creaked in sounds so mysterious even Wink wondered if a jinn had moved into the trees. The master's hunting dogs, Peaches and Taz, whined at his door until he let them in. He got up twice to add wood to the fire.

A solitary rooster crowed to proclaim a cold sunrise. Wink's foot felt the icy ground in spite of his wool stockings. His dipper bounced on ice so thick he had to pour water from the kettle into the bucket to get a drink. Wearing just about all the clothes he owned, he went out to see to the horses. The water trough had frozen, and he returned to his cabin for the kettle.

Promises of light showed beyond the east horizon, but no bell tolled to signal the hands to the field. The live oaks squeaked with shifts in the weight of ice. The ground crackled under Wink's brogans as he crossed the yard to get well water. Farley was knocking at the back door of the big house. Even with his gloves, Wink's knuckles went numb drawing water.

A limb had cracked off the whipping tree and perched on a lower branch. Ice glistened on the roofs of the wood shed, barn, tool shed, and every other building except the kitchen. With a full bucket of water back in his quarter, Wink made tea and ate several spoonsful of molasses.

People stayed inside. Nobody ginned or packed cotton, dug out ditches, or went to the field with the grubbing hoes. Children sat at the hearth and played. Women shelled dried peas, darned holes in stockings, and mended ticks. Men whittled, sharpened knives, repaired tin pans. Many slept. The eaves of the buildings eventually dripped with icicles.

As Wink headed to the carriage house, the master approached with the lifeless peacock in his hand. Wink braced himself. Who killed the peacock?

"Take this." The master offered the peacock. "It's good meat. Froze last night."

Wink took hold of the legs. Hard as it was to believe, the master was giving it to him. The young master Ellison whined, kicked the ground, and protested that the peacock belonged to him because he'd found it.

"Much oblige, Massuh." Wink took the fowl and turned back to his cabin, leaving Ellison's loud complaints behind him. The feathers alone could fetch enough specie to buy a pillow, which he needed since somebody had peed on his over Christmas. Safely inside his quarter, he put the fowl on his table and plucked the long green feathers.

Anner came in, shut the door, and backed up to the fire. "I come to see the peacock."

"How you know I got it?" Wink was laying the long feathers in a neat row.

"That white boy done pitched a conniption fit. And his little dirty mouth was cussing you."

"I best sell these feathers afore he goes on the warpath." He wet a feather that was gummed with what looked like mud but didn't smell like it.

"Honey, he is done there already." She touched two feathers to Wink's face. "These is uncommon pretty. Lookit that color." He took them and placed them back on the table.

Anner leaned over near his face and smiled. "How many can I have?"

Wink should have been prepared. She hadn't shown up for no reason. "Here. You can have this one." He handed her a feather.

She looked at it but didn't take it. "Dat one ain't big enough to fit in my trunk."

Assuming he had misunderstood her, Wink offered a smaller one.

Anner ignored his feather and inspected the others on the table. She picked up the one she had before. "Sugar, this one is mighty fine. And here's one to match." She held them up together, looked at them and at him.

Wink shrugged and went back to plucking. Anner chose another one and compared the three. She picked and compared until Wink had plucked every feather. By then, Anner couldn't make up her mind and wondered aloud if she could have three. They were so pretty. Could she have four? Wink collected the feathers, including those she had in her hand.

"Give this one to Puddin on your way back to the big house." He handed her one of the biggest with shimmering colors and a perfectly formed eye.

"You can have these." He offered her two—a perfect match but smaller. He shoved the remaining feathers under his cot and ushered her to the door. "Honey, I gots business to tend to ..."

Anner took the feathers, swished them across his nose, and left, a sly squint to her eyes.

Wink knew how to make tea. He had been roasting oysters for years. His recipe for stew changed every time he and Thor cooked. But a fowl baffled him. Notwithstanding that, he washed the carcass, gutted it, and put it into a pot that hadn't been used since Raynell left. He went to the kitchen for hog grease, salt, and pepper. A peacock feather, not the big one he'd told Anner to give to Puddin, was stuck in a crock on the table and wafted with Puddin's coming and going. "Don't I get no sweet lip for dis here feather I sent you?"

"You? Anner said you give her three feathers." The tone of Puddin's voice accused him of some deficiency. "Said she was partializing wid me."

"Anner is wrong-headed." Wink wasn't surprised. She had given him the right to hold a grudge against her.

Puddin looked at him with amused disbelief when he announced he was going to cook the peacock. She mixed a concoction of spices, brandy, chicken broth, and vinegar and handed it to him. "Soak your bird in this for a couple hours before you set it to the fire."

"You going to come to my shanty and help me eat it?"

She spooned hog fat from a barrel into a small crockery pot. "Is I going to sit at your table on your onliest chair and eat by myself?"

"We both sit at the table."

"On what?"

"I gots a stool."

She said she'd think about it.

After supper she tapped on his door. "How is your fowl?" Wink took pleasure in showing her the cooking pot. The smell of spicy meat escaped from the opened lid. She looked inside and poked the bird with a long handled fork Wink had borrowed from Mamba. "Long as you keep broth in there, you can't cook it too much." The light of the fire glowed in her face.

He dipped broth with a wooden spoon Iverson had made and offered it to her lips. Puddin's presence reminded Wink of the time when his small room had been a home. He had hardly realized when it had changed into a place to sleep.

She blew on it. He blew on it. He was about to spill it when she took hold the handle and tasted the broth. She nodded when he said, "It be ready to eat?"

Wink took down his tin plates.

After Puddin lifted her shawl and draped it on the rickety chair, she spooned meat from the pot onto the two plates.

His poor quality chair shamed him. Soon as he made enough money, he was going to buy a first class chair, maybe a stuffed one like those in the big house. Wink pushed the small square table against the cot and shoved the chair to the opposite side. He made two cups of tea and placed them on the table.

He sat on the cot, which was only marginally higher than his stool, and Puddin on the chair. He had to look up to her, but it didn't bother him. He tried not to eat more than his share. "Where you eat most the time?" He had never seen Puddin take a meal, all that food around her all the time.

"I don't never sit and eat like this. I just tastes what I be cooking."

"Billy and Anner eat in the kitchen?"

"They come in after the massuh's meal, not both at the same time."

"You is having high class fare now." Wink was more than a little proud of his cooking.

Puddin laughed. "You done yourself credit."

"Would you come visit me iffen I had a flowery chair stuffed wid horse hair?"

Puddin sipped her tea. "Maybe."

"Iffen I had a foot warmer?" He wanted her to feel the way he did, the two of them together, like the creek in the balance of the incoming and outgoing tides.

"Would you cook venison and hams iffen I bought them?"

"Bought them wid what?" Puddin leaned back in the chair and quickly caught herself when the chairback shifted.

"Would you eat supper wid me iffen I had crockery plates from London?"

She blew through her lips.

"I'se going to have money, wait and see."

When they finished eating, he fetched a bucket of water. She washed the plates. He put them away.

"Would you sleep in my cot iffen I had a feather mattress?"

She reached for her shawl. "I be going."

Her lips were thick-bodied and seductive, firm rolling hills on top of a plump, perfectly formed rim. Wink kissed her lips and cheeks.

"There's money in hooch." Wink knew he should keep his mouth shut about whiskey, but he couldn't help himself.

"Hooch? Is you trading in hooch?" Puddin's eyes were so honest she had at one time fooled Wink into thinking she was innocent.

"Baby, I'se going to have as much specie as leaves on the ground."

She kissed him. He didn't want her to leave but she did. He gave her three of the prettiest peacock feathers.

When he went to the quarters to see Sonny, a gang of children stampeded him with a chorus of supplications. He could hardly move. "Please!" "Just one!" In the chillun house, Mooey sat in the rocker with Sonny in her arms. He took a look at the sleeping baby and smiled at Mooey. Wink had never thought of her as being mother-like, but from the way she looked at the baby her affection was obvious. He regretted having given away the best feathers, but he gave her several from the ones he had left.

As it turned out, every child in the quarters got a feather, but by the next day, most of them had disappeared. They showed up in the women's hats and as fans, hair bows, and jewelry.

On the second day, the ice melted, and the children sneaked outside, followed, eventually, by the parents. Farley rang the bell, rallied the hands, and they gathered to go to the field.

The master came to the stables one afternoon to tell Wink they'd go to Beaufort the following morning to pick up slaves loaned to Westfall by Mistress Lambeth. Wink rode over to the master's uncle's plantation and borrowed his coach to bring them back. That night before going to bed he stored his empty cask in the trunk of the coach. He could hardly sleep. He had enough money saved, and he intended to buy an entire cask of whiskey.

Before sunrise, he put the mojo bag Mamba had made for him into his pocket. He felt a need for protection from the bad spirits that had been pestering him. Lately, he'd come within a hair's breadth of disaster dealing with Limbo and Thor. Had it not been for a crock of oil, he would have been tongue-tied in front of the master. It had begun with Limbo's idea. Because of breaks in the pasture fence, Limbo and Thor were able to steal one of the master's beefs and tether it to a certain sycamore tree near the causeway. Wink was supposed to collect it. When the master went to the village for muster, Wink made like he needed lamp oil to get Missus's permission to go to Salina's. Instead of the store, he stopped off at the sycamore tree and led the beef to a poor white farmer who bought it.

As Wink returned to Westfall, the master rode up earlier than expected, pulled Gideon to a walk beside the wagon, and asked where Wink had been. He'd had the good sense to put a crock of oil in his wagon on leaving, which had saved his butt. He had come through without a lash and with money to show for his trouble, but the narrow escape had made him skittish.

He hitched the horses to the coach; the master had sent word that he didn't need Gideon saddled, which meant he would ride inside. Wink fingered his mojo bag to make a decision. Despite the added risk of having the master present in the coach, Wink was too committed to his plan to give it up.

They took to the road, Wink's pouch of bills fidgety in his pocket. He prodded the horses along the causeway to the ferry, devising a pretense for getting to Artis's leather shop. Upon reaching the jail where the slaves were being housed, Wink tensed the reins to stop the horses. As the master stepped down to the ground, Wink followed and inspected the front wheel, jostling it with his hand. "Massuh, it feels like we got a loose wheel."

On his way to the office door, the master paused long enough to glance back. "Take it down to the wheelwright on Carteret Street. He's not far from the town stables. You know where I'm talking about?"

"Yessuh," said Wink.

Wink found Artis and bought whiskey for his cask, which he returned to the chest under the coach seat and covered with a loosely filled sack of lime. He stopped at the Victoria Hotel. A ten minute talk with the doorman and Wink heard about what was going on up and down the coast, from the mainland to the islands, who'd died, escaped, had been sold, whipped, or was sick. But there was no unusual drama respecting people Wink knew. no word from Walterboro about Mamba's mother.

A local man paused at the door and appealed to any person who happened to be present to help him find a buyer for himself. "Massuh give me one more day ..." The man moaned between his words. "... to git somebody hereabouts to buy me. And dat be it. I be sold to dat godawful trader DeSaussure." Wink winced—such a pittance of mercy from the man's owner to allow the slave to try to find a local buyer who might save him from being carted off to parts unknown.

Wink made an appearance at the wheelwright's, but as he expected, the man could find nothing amiss. However, Wink explained to the master that a piece of shell had lodged between the rim and the wheel. Nobody could prove him wrong. On their way back to Westfall, the master sat on the bench beside Wink, his feet just inches away from the stash of forbidden spirits. Wink's nerves were trigger quick, but when he told Puddin about it, he laughed out loud.

PART III
AN ODDS-ON PAPPY

CHAPTER 23

THE BROODY HEN

JANUARY 1858

Before Mooey saw Early, she knew it was him by the way the door swung open. He motioned her outside. Lacy stood up to him, but his mouth snarled like a possum's. If Mooey had done something wrong, she couldn't picture what it was. She sat on the cot, afraid to move. Early grabbed her arm, picked up her bedding, and pushed her out of her cabin and down the street to the dilapidated place at the end of the row. Nobody had lived there until the new men arrived. So many new men worried Mooey, for the master hadn't brought new women to stay with them. Early shoved her inside, threw her tick on the floor, and shut the door. She noticed with surprise that the cabin had a door. The hole beneath the roof had been repaired. And the fire in the fireplace burned better than Auntie's.

On the cot lay one of the new negros, the one with rings of hair. His back was to her and he didn't stir. His long hair was like black sunlight. Thick veins mapped his neck and hands. When he walked, he took solid but stealthy steps. He wore clean clothes.

Mooey edged into the room. Her back felt as if a snake crawled on it. She halted, ready to escape out the door in case the man turned and tried to jump her. He was spare-made and strong, and because she suspected he was not only deep but swift, she summoned up "River" when he came into her head.

A man she had been put with before had climbed on top of her and tried to push her dress up to her neck and her bloomers down. She had found she could get rid of him if she bit his ear long enough.

The playful flutter of the fire summoned her. She kept her eye on River as her feet took her closer to the fire. His bodily spirit purred with unchanging motion. She warmed herself, made a pallet of her tick, and sat on it. Night shadows crept into her eyelids and closed them in spite of the man's presence.

To Mooey's great relief, River didn't try to force her clothes off. In fact, he ignored her and she was able to sleep at night, though at times she awoke in order to visit Sunny in the chillun house. And she returned to her cabin for her peacock feathers and often ate meals with Lacy and Auntie.

* * *

Wink woke up cold. If he didn't find another blanket soon, he'd have to give up sleeping. After rustling up the fire and warming himself, he lit the lantern and went to the stables to see to the horses. The yard dog barked excitedly. He took the light outside, listened, and followed the sound toward the master's yard.

Puddin stood wrapped in her shawl at her door, apparently listening to the dog as well. Her neat hair was plaited in rows. It was like seeing her underwear, for Puddin always wore a head rag. She had the clear eyes and dewy skin of a woman fresh from dreams. Wink imagined the pleasure of waking with her at his side. The pleasure of watching her put on her dress made of white plains.

"What's got into that dog?" he said. It was the young master's pet dog.

"Bout time it wakes up the missus, she's going to be mad as a March hare." Puddin walked with him to the front yard where the dog yelped and paced around the trunk of the bullbay, looking up.

"Go on! Git outa here!" Wink kicked sand at the dog. It scampered to a distance and whined. He threw a stick at it and it retreated further.

"Something's in the tree," said Puddin.

Wink squinted to see into the upper limbs. The heavy green leaves might well hide a coon, or worse, a wild cat. "I don't see nothin."

"That dog's not barking at nothin. I'll climb up and see."

"Hold on, now. I'se going to see what's up there." Wink grabbed a limb and pulled his feet up to it and from there advanced by branches. "What the hell?" A dead chicken, tied by its feet, was hanging over a limb.

"What you see?" Puddin said from below.

"This ain't no coon. No wild cat neither." He climbed down.

"Is dat what it looks like?" said Puddin when he handed her the chicken.

"If it ain't a chicken, I needs a dram worser than ever."

"Whiskey's not going to turn this into no coon." The cast of her eyes turned playful.

Wink felt her flares of light tugging at him. "Where'd dat chicken come from?"

"This looks just like the massuh's Leghorn hen what lays white eggs." She gazed at Wink as if he had an explanation. "How'd this get up there in the tree?"

"I speck it fell out the sky."

"Somebody throwed it up there."

"God knowed we was hungry and sent it direct from dat big white throne of Hisn."

"Somebody stole it out the chicken coop."

"Something good to eat is God's blessing. Just ask Iverson."

"This here hen be jinxed," said Puddin.

"Shit no, baby. It's a miracle."

"Somebody's going to come back for it."

"That's not no worry-ation for us." He took the chicken and started toward the back lot.

"My turn to cook. Give it to me."

* * *

Early in the morning Mooey hauled oats to the troughs while the cows were milked. A new person, more of a boy than a man, came to help with the hay and the milking. Once the milk was stored in the springhouse and the cows turned to pasture, she tended the chickens. As long as they had food and water, they stayed about the yard and coop, though several roosted in a tree no matter how often she shooed them out.

Mooey retrieved her basket and entered the coop to gather eggs. Straw nests, some built in old crates, dotted the broad boards framed up at differing heights and running the length of the coop. She picked up an egg from each nest, sometimes two. Deeper into the coop, she slowed as she approached the broody hen's nest.

The hen had a new clutch of eggs and was fiercely protective. Mooey, who had tried to shoo her off the nest before, had met with a show of ruffled feathers. Even when the hen wasn't brooding, she had an ornery disposition, her mutilated wattle evidence of a fight that had nearly ripped it off. The poor chicken didn't act right, brooding in winter. But as Mooey neared the corner, she realized the brooder's bare eggs lay exposed to cold air.

Something was wrong. The hen wouldn't voluntarily abandon her nest. Mooey inched up and as she reached over to touch an egg, a rooster roused from the dark of the coop. He churred, ruffled up, and flew at her, clawing her hands and face in a flurry of feathers. She escaped from the coop with the rooster flapping and pecking the back of her head. She swirled her hands at it, ran into the yard, her throat spirit roaring into her mouth.

As she neared the boy, he rose up ferociously, hit it with a stick, and shocked the bird into retreating. The rooster pranced in a circle and stretched its claws and boldly stepped back to the door of the coop.

Mooey wiped her face and withdrew a bloody hand. She rubbed her wool and found more blood. The boy looked at her closely as if to inspect her wounds, which worried her. Blood dripped into one eye. Her upper lip was swelling.

The boy moved his mouth in a manner Mooey understood as his way of giving her orders. He motioned her toward the kitchen, but her blood smelled powerful and pain gnashed her face. He tried to grab her arm, but Mooey jerked away. Her throat gave forth a spirit she didn't care to control. From the sky a spirit sent a notice in response, reminding her of the link she'd discovered between her throat and the sky's warning. To test her new finding, she willed her throat to tremble and when the sky shot a sensation into her head, a feeling of mastery overcame her. But that wouldn't help her cuts and bleeding. At a safe distance from the coop she crouched.

The boy changed to softer motions as he took shy steps toward her. When he reached for her arm, Mooey shook her head. He extended a handkerchief, but she was too confused to take it. She wiped her face with the hem of her dress.

The scratches and punctures were stinging, but something else pained her even more. The fact that the brooder was missing. The same brooder that had refused to get off the nest. It wouldn't waddle away and leave to a cold death the baby chicks inside the shells. In fact, even when the hen didn't brood, it seldom went any further from the coop than the feeder in the pen.

As the boy left the chicken yard, Mooey's terror grew that he was going after Early. She took a stick for protection and searched about the coop, pen, and yard, but the hen had seemingly disappeared. She couldn't explain it and nobody else would be expected to, since she alone went into the coop.

Her head ached, but it didn't keep her from seeing in her mind's eye the master's cold blue eyes. He owned the chickens ... his cows, his hogs, his ducks, all his. The brooder. The negros, all his. Early didn't fool Mooey. She knew the white man was the real boss. He was the one who had ordered her to be whipped when the white stranger with an evil spirit scared her.

The master's brooder had disappeared, and somebody would be punished. She couldn't stand another lashing. In a panic, she ran out of the yard and headed for the woods. Sitting in a cradle of boughs, she calmed herself.

When night fell, she sneaked into the old and seldom used carriage, wrapped in her coat, and covered herself with the blanket she had found in her favorite tree by the sick house. She curled up on the padded seat and slept until roused by a sense of movement. A torch appeared in the dark yard and threw light on the stableman. He approached the carriage house and strode from the wagons to the buggy to the cart and carriages. Mooey crouched on the footboard under her blanket, hardly breathing while the light paused at her carriage.

After he left, her senses told her to find another hiding place, but slumber cast a spell and her eyes closed.

A light seemed to come from a great distance and make its way through her lids. She opened her eyes, surprised that they had been closed. Notions stirred in her head like a wind blowing pictures here and yon. As the wind calmed, she realized where she was. She saw the source of light, and as it moved closer, her blood went shaky, for in its glow she recognized the man wasn't the stableman. It was Early, and he was looking in the conveyances.

Even if she sneaked out of the carriage, she couldn't get past Early without being seen. No escape presented itself. To calm her spirits, she swallowed hard and waited for the dreaded moment. The stableman marched in, and he and Early gestured forcefully. Mooey slipped out of the carriage and crept under a wagon. As if a kindly spirit protected her, the men continued to wrangle. She crawled behind the vehicles and out of the carriage house.

Her long and lean legs took her back to the woods where she spent the remainder of the night trying to rest against the trunk of a fallen tree. Winter crept from the ground into her legs. Her back ached from the unyielding trunk. She shivered. An unfriendly dark surrounded her. She remembered how cold and hungry had been her previous stay in the woods. There was no safe hideout near the plantation.

Come morning, she wandered the woods and came upon a familiar footpath that trailed so far she hadn't discovered where it went. Just when she considered turning around, the path opened into a field where she could see another big house in the distance with huts. She watched the place only to discover that the whites lived in the big house and the blacks in the shanties. This disappointed her. Mooey would like to find the place where Lacy got her high style dresses and leather shoes, but this obviously wasn't it. Notwithstanding that, she approached the yard, but activity around the kitchen house kept her at a distance until dark. When she attempted to sneak closer, three dogs rushed at her. Though she took flight, one ripped her sleeve and cut a skin-deep gash in her arm before she reached a tree she could climb.

Sitting on a limb, she realized the smell of blood from her arm would attract every sort of wild animal. She unwrapped a section of the long strap of cloth used for her stocking and ripped off a piece with her teeth. After she bandaged the wound she rewrapped the strap around her leg, tighter this time. The dogs continued to jump at the trunk of the tree until Mooey sighed in despair. It was only a matter of time until somebody found her. She waited for the white men to get her.

To her amazement, the dogs suddenly bounded away, as if a goodly spirit had herded them toward the yard of the unfamiliar plantation. As soon as they disappeared, she climbed down and ran for the wooded path and only slowed down to get her breath.

She returned to her home plantation and spent the night in the oak tree at the sick house. Though a cheerful morning light streamed through the bare limbs, it was cold. A sadness descended on Mooey as she realized she couldn't survive in the woods, and she refused to stand for another lashing. What was she to do? She cried. The only course of action was to leave the plantation. Her tears choked her. She could hardly face parting from Sunny, from Lacy, from Auntie. Mooey could only hope that somewhere beyond the plantation were other people who might befriend her.

The hands left for the field. Mooey watched the chillun house and imagined Sunny inside, sucking on his fist. She reckoned a goodbye to the baby. In Auntie's cabin, she put on shoes and grabbed the ashcakes in the fire. On leaving, she was so unhappy she forgot her blanket.

She wandered in the woods far from the plantation and encountered only trees, shrubs, briars, and vines. In search of some other settlement, one without dogs, she forged into deeper undergrowth. A sprinkle of cold rain chilled her to the bone. Winter-hardened twigs nicked her coat and pricked her skin.

She kept going beyond the range of familiar trees to low ground that wet the floppy soles of her shoes. She forged a path through tangles of dried vines. Bay bushes stood in her way. A naked limb picked up her headrag. She grabbed it back. At a place of dense and swampy undergrowth, she pushed woody stems aside only to step into ice-cold water too deep to ford. There was only one way to go, back.

As she trudged to higher ground, desperation broke out in an agitation arising in her throat and fluttering to her tongue and lips. Its rebounding sensation no longer interested her. No path crossed her journey. Switches whipped her face. Her nose bled. A twig poked into her eye. She stopped and rubbed it, but a pain shot into her head and she patted the closed lid. She knew scores of trees around the plantation, but she didn't know these. As the sun sank toward the horizon and Mooey continued to be lost, she realized she needed to find a protected place away from the wind before dark. Worse than the wind were starving animals.

After the sun flamed into the west in deceiving colors of warmth, the woods ebbed into its nightly gray stillness. Mooey had spent many an evening watching the sky as the light died, transforming clear images into murky shadows. The dark of every night, subject to the moon's phases and clouds, was different. On this night, shadowy figures moved through the woods with Mooey, some of them just out of sight, behind the skeletal trees.

Her arms wildly flayed at the savage branches and thick briars. Without realizing it, she stepped into a rill deep enough to wet her ankles and forded to the other side. Her woolen leggings fell loose and drifted down to her knees. The cold of night shrank her blood and a shortage came to her breath. Her legs ached, but she didn't have the wherewithal to tighten her leggings. Her fingers felt clumsy and numb. The spirit in her throat cried out for help. She gulped cold air, knowing it chilled the thumping inside her chest, a thumping that, if it froze, would mean she was dead.

What had been a brittle, unforgiving darkness turned spacious. Trees stood aside. Bushes retreated. The familiar smell of sedge and mud flats. Her head could feel an open expanse above her.

Her feet came alive to the feel of pebbles. She had found a roadway. Her shoes were so heavy she tried walking without them, but the crusty ground cut her soles. The wind carried sea moisture, and she detected a body of water.

Her knees folded. She stood up but they folded again, and she crawled. Sharp edges of broken oyster shells cut her palms and tore holes in her coat and leggings. The ground spirit revived her with a pulsing message that entered her hands and knees. She climbed to her feet, putting all her hopes in a traveler, approaching as surely as the clop-clop in the earth.

Her eyes teared from the strain of staring into the dark. A barely discernable spark appeared in the distance and jiggled. Mooey waved her arms. Her untamed spirit rushed from her throat. The light came upon her. A horse's muzzle blew hot air on her. The monstrous animal stampeded her, the ground heaved. What felt like an orbiting log brushed her backwards. She dropped to the road as the fuzzy freedom of darkness overtook her. Even as the earth slapped against her head, she hardly felt it.

CHAPTER 24

BRUSH ARBOR

JANUARY 1858

Wink had discovered that Mooey was amiss before Farley did. She hadn't showed up at the lot to tend the cows. Kedzie had taken her place.

"Where be Mooey?" he asked Kedzie.

"She's scared to go in the coop. That mean old rooster flew on her like a haint and scratched her up."

"She's not running away again, is she?" Wink asked, for Mooey looked pitiful thin from the whipping she'd gotten after Christmas.

"Lord, no! Farley might kill her iffen he gets after her again."

When night came, Wink noticed that Mooey didn't take the milk to the springhouse. He wandered to the quarters but wasn't able to find her.

"You seen Mooey?" Wink asked Rio.

"What you want wid her?" Rio didn't look up from the large needle he threaded through netting fixed to a wire hoop.

"I got a ribbon for her." Wink faked a reason, noticing the net. "What you going to do wid that net?"

"Haul in shrimp." Rio cut a line with his pocket knife and knotted it.

Wink knew the master allowed Rio use of a mule and cart every Saturday afternoon. The cart returned at night smelling of mud and marshes. "Where you selling them?"

"In the village." When Rio stood, the netting drooped full length from the wire ring.

"What you do when dat net comes in empty?" Wink had taken notice of Rio's business like manner.

"Sell whatsoever I gets. Oysters, clams ... fish." Rio nodded toward Mooey's cot where a cat was sleeping. "Leave her stuff on her cot. She comes in bout midnight."

Wink walked to the stables and rubbed down Tootie, knowing it'd take more than a haint for the girl to hide in a tree in such cold weather.

That night he awoke to Gideon's snorting, the kind of snort that meant something wasn't right. When Wink had scouted about the carriage house, he saw footprints in the dust near the old carriage. Undoubtedly Mooey had put up inside the cab for the night. When Farley had showed up to make a midnight search, Wink waylaid him long enough for Mooey to slip out of the carriage.

A day passed and another and nobody mentioned that Mooey had come amiss. Wink stopped at the kitchen to see Puddin about their chicken dinner, but neither she nor Billy said a word about Mooey. In the quarters, even Flurry had no particulars to give about the girl.

Wink had to wonder whether it was the missing hen or Mooey that caused the master to call on Farley. The two of them had been talking in the yard for a goodly time. If anybody dared go near, the master tipped his head to warn them away. Whatever their communication, Farley returned to the field.

When the hands came in for dinner, Wink heard Kedzie singing "Hog Eye! Old Hog Eye!" the signal for an arbor meeting. Since neither Anner nor Puddin would know what went on in the quarters, Wink went to Thor's cabin. Thor and Limbo were eating collard greens Flurry had taken from Farley's pot. Wink ate ashcake smeared with hog grease and salt.

"Mooey is come amiss, dat's what I heard," said Thor.

"You seen your sister?" Wink said to Limbo.

"Hell no."

Low but excited voices sounded in the street. Wink went outside where several people separated and drifted away. He followed Doll and caught up with her. "What's the meeting about?"

"Some shit from the massuh."

"Dat's not no reason for Iverson to call a meeting."

When Wink arrived at Iverson's place, several people stood around the open door. Gussie was telling them something about a stolen hen, Mooey being missing.

As evening came on, Wink brought the horses into the stable and, while they fed, he brushed and groomed them. Skittles pawed the ground until he came into her stall and talked to her. With the horses settled, he headed toward the quarters. Except for shreds of light emerging around the shutters and doors, the cabins melded into darkness. One child's cough incited a host of coughing. He stopped in the chillun house long enough to see Sonny, bounce him in his arms, and warm him at the fire. Beyond the quarters he entered the woods on his way to the secret gathering place. At the glade where they met, he halted at the rear of the crowd.

As he had hoped, he had arrived late enough to miss most of Iverson's sermon. Unlike most preachers, Iverson kept his sermons short, but even at that, not short enough for Wink. Iverson repeated the message Farley had given them from the big house. Because of Mooey and the hen, the master had cancelled the praise meeting. People mumbled and shuffled about. Some of them accused Mooey of bringing grievance on all of them.

"Mooey don't cause nobody no grievance. Old Man Goodwyn be grievance." Wink spoke louder than he intended, for the negros had everything ass-backwards.

"If she'd a took one of the other chickens, nobody would a noticed," said Primus.

"Don't matter. Iffen Mooey freezes to death over a chicken, dat be the massuh's fault." Wink said, which brought on a silence.

Nobody seemed to know Mooey's whereabouts. Or have any intelligence about the master's missing hen. Wink had no intention of mentioning that he'd found one in the bullbay since he hadn't killed it. He searched for Puddin, and when he spotted her, he watched until she met his eyes. She blinked with a hint of a smile.

Wink heard Iverson call his name. "Get word to Brother Milton about the cancelled meeting."

As the people wandered back to the quarters, Wink wended his way to Puddin. She said, "This was so big, I give some of it to Thor and several others." She slipped a sack into his pocket. "You don't mind, do you?"

The sizable heft of the sack gave him no reason for complaint. He took her hand. "Come to my place. Let's eat our fill."

She glanced at him and withdrew her hand. "It be late for chicken."

"I got more'n chicken."

"Dat's what I be afeared of."

"What?" He held up his hands to protest innocence.

She gave him a mischievous glance.

Iverson appeared beside them, and Puddin smiled at him, saying, "You get massuh's permission for schooling for the chillun?"

"Nah. The man's gloatin in our ignorance."

Wink dropped away from the conversation and watched Puddin walk ahead as if she hadn't been intimate with him. Soon as he could save up the money, he had to buy a fine chair for his place, just for her.

When word arrived of the death of the master's cousin's wife, the big house became solemn and Mooey was all but forgotten. Wink noticed good victuals piling up in the kitchen, for Anner took heaping plates to the big house and returned to the kitchen with them. Billy hinted that the master was looking through a glass instead of eating. For several days, Puddin sneaked victuals the master's family hadn't eaten to Wink, which provided him with first-rate fare.

The funeral of Rachel Goodwyn, who had been considered a genteel lady, was observed thoughout the island. Wink drove the mistress to meet the master at the village church. On their way, they met carriages carrying the Chaplins and Spires, the bridles fitted with black plumes. Such a crowd of people attended, the men had to stand in the churchyard. The coffin coach arrived drawn by four black, blaze-face horses, carrying their heads and tails high. Wink had never seen such a beautiful four.

Visitors paid their respects at Westfall for several days. When the master began to appear in the fields and about the outbuildings again, people worried anew about Mooey's fate. They watched the sky for swirls of turkey buzzards.

One morning Wink saddled up Gideon and the master rode off with Rio and the slave hunting dogs. Wink curried Puff, cleaned her hoofs and cut away dead frog. The mare had taken up the bad habit of swishing her tail since foaling in the fall. He clucked at her when she swished. Because she understood but paid him no mind, he trimmed her tail to a nub. As he put her back to pasture he brought in Cricket to inspect her shoes.

If Mooey wasn't already dead, she might wish she was if the master found her. Kedzie had mustered some of the negros to search for her. Auntie Nell worried everybody. Iverson stopped by the stables.

"How can dat girl stay alive in this kind of weather?" Iverson said.

Wink had no answer as he oiled Cricket's mane and tail.

The master and Rio returned empty-handed. The patrollers showed up with their dogs, and they couldn't find her. By now, most people supposed they were looking for Mooey's body.

Wink drove the master with his trunk to the Beaufort wharf to catch the packet boat to Charleston for the races. That the mistress didn't accompany him caused Wink to wonder. She had always attended except when her confinement had been close at hand. If she was in the family way, her belly didn't show it.

The previous time Wink had driven the master and mistress he hardly closed his eyes for fear of missing something spectacular. He had never seen such finery. Horses groomed to the hilt, with docked tails and glistening manes, and trained to walk, canter, or trot with beauty and ease. Silver harness rings and tooled leather saddles. White people rigged out to beat the band. And Mistress Goodwyn kept up with the best of them with hoops, beads, lace, gold chains, and feathered bonnets. Every outfit of velvet or silk, even the men's topcoats.

Wink loaded the trunk on the steamer and returned to the wharf. Master Goodwyn said, "Be back on Monday. I'll have Mistress Margarita with me. We'll take her to Walterboro before going home."

Wink waited as the motor roared, the smokestack churned with clouds of black smoke, and the whistle sounded a dull blast that could be heard as far as Coosaw Island. The steamer lumbered out midstream and headed down-current toward Port Royal Sound and the Atlantic Ocean.

Wink drove the carriage into town to buy a blanket, socks, and napkins for baby Sonny before heading to the leather shop for whiskey. It was dark by the time he was on the St. Helena Island causeway and the patrollers stopped him.

"Boy, who's your master?" said a man Wink had seen before in the village. His hair looked as if somebody had taken a butcher knife to it.

"Massuh Tilmon Goodwyn." Wink offered the pass the master had written.

The patroller didn't look at it. Wink put it back in his pocket. Lad, the young gelding, started blowing, and Wink took it as a sign of more than usual trouble.

"Git down off dere."

The whiskey cask under his seat put a great reluctance in Wink to move. He was tempted to lash the horses into a run and get out of there. Lad was fast.

"Boy!" One of the patrollers leveled a rifle barrel at Wink.

On the other hand, Wink wasn't anywhere near ready to die. He climbed down and held on to Lad's lines.

The youngest of the patrollers mounted the coach and looked under Wink's blanket. He pulled up the lid of the trunk and dragged out the second blanket. "Benny, you was right!" He laughed as he pulled out the cask and held it up for the others to see.

"Told you."

"Where you git your red-eye, nigger?"

The boy hauled the cask over to one of the men sitting horseback and continued to look about the driver's seat.

"Dat be the massuh's cask," said Wink, with little hope the men would believe him.

They laughed. "Goodwyn wouldn't trust you wid a gill of red-eye, you stinking son of a bitch."

"Look inside the cab," the head patroller said to one of the men. After they searched the back end, bottom, inside and out, they headed down the causeway.

Some people called the patrollers night riders. When it came to delivering whiskey, Wink needed to get it done in daylight—more respectable white people on the road. Less chance of meeting patrollers.

CHAPTER 25

ANNER AT THE STABLE

FEBRUARY 1858

When the Pritchard negros sent for Claude to play for a hoedown, word spread throughout the quarters. Wink, like the others, didn't bother about a pass, for even if the patrollers knew of the path through the woods, they were unlikely to put their horses through the narrow passage.

"You going to Pritchard's hoedown?" Wink stopped by the kitchen to ask Puddin.

"You think Old Man Pritchard give leave to carouse on his place?"

"Claude's going to play."

"Them poor people gets one shindig a year, and dat be corn shucking." She skimmed cream off a pan of milk.

"Come on, baby. Let's shuck some corn."

She laughed. "Is they shucking for shore?"

"Must be," said Wink, though Claude had said nothing about shucking anything.

"Go on. Them Pritchards is poor quality white people."

Billy came into the kitchen.

"Billy, you going to the hoedown at Pritchard's place?" Wink suspected Billy had never been to a dance in his life.

Billy put an empty glass on the table and smiled. "I be too scared of gitting lost in the woods."

"Go wid me. I knows the path." Wink had heard that Billy had gotten lost from a coffle as a boy and had wandered in the woods until he nearly starved to death.

"Lordy, I wouldn't know what to do wid myself. My feets don't do no shuffle toe."

"I got a hooch cure. Fixes your feets so they dance like nobody's business."

Puddin poured cream into a churn. "That hooch don't fix nothin but your head. Makes you think you doing the shuffle toe when by facts, you making a fool of yourself."

Billy's smile threatened to become a laugh. "You going?" he said as he looked on Puddin with too much appreciation for Wink's comfort.

Puddin glanced at him with her don't-be-an-idiot face, a look that charmed Wink. He wished Billy would return to the big house. He turned his ear to the door. "Billy, is dat Anner calling you?"

"Anner done got a pass from Massuh and headed out. Won't be back till the morrow." Billy looked at Puddin. "You know where she be going?"

"Said she was seeing about her mammy." Puddin fit the dasher into the churn and sat near the fire.

"Dat so? How come she headed out on the big road instead of the back road?" Billy said.

"Nitsy go too?" Wink hadn't seen Anner leave, but if she went to the public road she wasn't going to Saxby, where her mother lived.

"Nitsy didn't ask Massuh for no pass. Leastways, she didn't come to the big house for none." Billy pulled a stool nearer the fire.

Outside, the noise of Claude and several others could be heard in the back lot. Puddin was churning butter. Billy held his hands to the fire. The sight of the two of them, too much like a couple, gave Wink a thirst for hooch. As soon as he stepped into the yard, he took the bottle from his pocket. A long draft and he felt better.

People from the quarters followed the path in the woods, laughing and carousing as they rambled past winter vines and bushes. Limbo, who knew the way best, led them into the field and, though the moon was below a quarter, they found the old barn where several people were tuning up for a song. Pritchard's slaves had worse conditions than Westfall's, and maybe that was why they played harder and did so in spite of the old man's mean streak.

The Pritchard hands sneaked across the field singly to gather at the dilapidated barn, built near the edge of the woods and at some distance from the big house. It was used to store fodder, most of which Pritchard's men had moved to a wagon. The remainder they pushed to the walls, which served to damper the noise. Wink asked about a look-out. A brawny negro so black he disappeared in the dark named a Pritchard hand and sent him to keep watch.

As soon as Claude and the Westfall group arrived, the music took life, and dancers reeled with rhythm. People caroused in and out the wide doorway. Claude's banjo played along with a fiddle, cowhide drums, quill, and various combinations of spoons and tin bowls. "Ladies, sashay left." The caller stood on a barrel. Men and women pushed and shoved their hips, tromped their feet, swirled, jammed up, and rubbed down.

Wink rarely danced, but he liked to watch. Claude had improved to the point people called on him to play for hoedowns. When music got into Wink's blood, life was good, so good everyday injustices disappeared. His heart glowed with affection for his fellow slaves. Women kissed him and he kissed them in return, but he wanted Puddin.

Whiskey passed from hand to hand. The crowd got so loud Wink got edgy. Because field hands seldom left the plantation, they were less acquainted with patrollers than Wink, who knew how fast the devil's legion could ride up. Although cushioned with hooch, he turned nervously to the sound of a distant dog's bark, the rustle of a breeze in dry leaves, the grate of a freezing wind in the trees. He went to check on the lookout. The man entertained a woman friend with such enthusiasm Wink walked up on him without the lookout taking notice.

"Boy! Iffen I was a pattyroller, you'd be in shackles!" Wink interrupted the tumble and mumble of their amorous relations.

The girl stood up, but the boy pulled her back to the croker sack and said to Wink, "I heard you coming, boss."

"Shit, you did! Your ears don't work good as your mouth." It was obvious to Wink that the lookout had more important things to do than keep watch.

Since the Westfall slaves didn't have passes, Wink couldn't rest easy. He moved to the woodline, sat, and leaned against the trunk of an old stump. The music drifted pleasantly on the cold air, blending with it a sense of warmth. Hardly had he settled when the "Good time's a-coming" song picked up a note that brought Wink to his feet—snorts, the sound of a horse blowing. His eyes stared into the darkness, and where the distant field gave way to woods he saw a motion that shouldn't have been there. He ran to the barn.

"Pattyrollers!" He didn't have to shout. Negros jumped out of the loft, climbed over each other, bounded out the open bay. Wink headed away from the barn on a run and worked his way into a thicket. Those people slow to get out of the field were quickly caught and locked in leg irons.

To keep from getting lost, Wink made his way to the path. When he found it, he walked parallel to it but at a goodly distance and saw a Westfall field hand scurry by on the path. The man was followed by two white men.

Wink made it back to Westfall before daylight. He fell asleep in his quarter as soon as he lay on his cot but hardly had time to get comfortable when the horses called for breakfast. He rolled out of his cot, rubbed his short nubs of hair, and made himself a cup of tea with water from his kettle.

His horses nuzzled him. They befriended him regardless of his gloomy face. And they didn't complain about his sluggish steps, the slow delivery of hay, or the dreary way he unlocked the gates.

Wink perked up when the master came to the stables. Trying to look innocent, sober, and alert, Wink said "Yessuh" to whatever the master said. It didn't take long to realize why the master was in a worse mood than Wink. Four of Westfall's field hands had been caught by the patrollers, and Wink's task was to go to the village with the wagon to fetch them from the jailhouse. As he hitched Tootie to the wagon, his gloom disappeared. He stashed his empty cask in the seat locker and whistled to the horse. "Come on, girl. We is going to town!" His whistle, like silver sparks, put Tootie in good form. She held her head high, her hindquarters moving like a pendulum from one side to the other, as if she knew they'd return with a full cask as well as the field hands.

The Sunday afternoon sun was bright and promising of better weather. Hardly anybody stirred in the yard. Even the children took naps. Wink nodded on the stable stool and caught himself. His sharp knife fell to the floor. He set aside the leather strips he had cut and put the cutting board on the ground. Freckles had come into the paddock from the pasture. Wink rose and stroked the horse's neck. He picked burrs from the mane and went for the curry comb.

"Wink!" Anner stood outside the gate, an eager look on her face. Because Wink had been thinking about how to discourage her attention, he stood inside.

"Come here!" She motioned him to her.

"I'm busy. You come here." He tipped his head his way.

"I'll git my shoes dirty."

He looked from her fine leather shoes to the straw on the ground. "It's not dirty in here."

She gazed at him, but he ignored her look.

"How's your mammy?" said Wink. Because he knew how conniving Anner could be, he was curious about where she had gone.

She gave him a surprised look. "What you asking bout her for?"

"I thought you went to see her."

"Who said dat?" Anner's eyebrows pressed for an answer.

"Saturday past. I seen you heading down the carriageway." Wink lied to avoid an interrogation about where he got his intelligence.

Her head took a playful twist, by which Wink figured she had been up to no good.

"Is you afeard I been out sparking?" Her voice teased him.

"Come on over here. I can't carry on wid you over there."

"Guess who's moved in the big house to take Lovey's place." Anner's smile twinkled.

Wink carried on anyway. "Who?"

"Come here."

"I'm going to curry Freckles. Come on through here to the paddock." He motioned her his way and walked away from her to the far gate, opened it, and went into the open air.

Anner hesitated. As if dodging horse plops, she tiptoed to the second gate and climbed on the lower slat.

Wink raised dust brushing Freckles's mane.

"Guess!" She leaned against the boards.

"Somebody he bought off de block?"

"Noooo. You knows her."

"Mammy Livy."

"You in a pucker?"

"Why don't you just tell me."

"Guess." She swayed the gate.

Wink was thinking. Lovey had got herself with child in the master's house. Master was an old tomcat. He'd find some woman put up good. "Nitsy."

"No, Nitsy's older than the new servant."

"You going to git the gate crank-sided." He pointed the brush at her.

"Guess!"

"Puddin."

"Puddin? He's not going to take her out the kitchen." She screwed up her nose as if his guess made a bad smell.

"Puddin's bout the best looking woman on the place."

"Not better looking than the new girl. Anyway, Puddin's older too."

Wink named young field hands he hardly knew, even after he had figured out who it was. Kedzie hadn't occurred to him, for she was hardly old enough. On consideration, however, she was sassy enough.

"You should of heard them. Missus was wrathy widout raising her voice." Anner swayed off balance and caught herself. "Massuh, now he got all fired up."

Wink clenched his teeth. He took out his tobacco sack and planted a cud. That white sonofabitch had Kedzie in his claws. He brushed Freckles's coat powerfully to keep himself peaceable. Nicky came in the paddock.

"Missus been complaining bout not having enough people to wait the table. Now she's complaining bout the new servant. Can't please dat woman."

"Nothing ever hatched of what she said." Wink cleaned around Freckles's ears, aware that Nicky paced to and from the palings and swished his tail as if to say he needed currying.

"Massuh sent the chillun to bed. Sent me out the room. Ever time the missus said something, the massuh called Billy for more liquor."

"Missus didn't want Kedzie in the house?"

"Missus wants Mamba. That be what started the hellacious argument."

Nicky edged closer and closer and nibbled at Wink's hat.

"Massuh rared up, cursed at missus. 'What you gots against the girl?' he said."

Wink figured any fool, even old man Goodwyn, had sense enough to know why his wife didn't want somebody pretty as Kedzie in the house. "So you don't have to serve the table no more?"

"Don't have to be in the room wid Billy. And I'm plenty glad to go."

When Wink turned his curry comb to Nicky, Freckles barged between them.

"What I can't figure out is why Billy didn't get lashes over the dogs in the house."

"Mucking the cow stalls works on him like a bullwhip." Wink stood between the horses and brushed first one then the other.

"He must've talked his way out of a whipping." Anner's voice left no doubt that she wasn't satisfied with the situation.

"You ever tried mucking de stalls?"

"You ever had a whipping? Billy don't get a single scar and I gots a back full of them. I'm going to settle wid him."

Wink took a tin from the equipage room and oiled Nicky's tail. He didn't want to hear about Anner's scars.

"You is going to the main tomorrow," Anner said. Nicky nosed into her, and she jerked back as if touched by a hag.

"How you know?"

"Massuh told Missus dis morning. Said you going to get his plow." Anner dug into her apron pocket and showed him currency. "Is this enough to buy shoes?"

Wink looked at the specie. "Where you get dat?"

She smiled. "Can you get me shoes?"

"You is wearing the best shoes on the place. What you want wid more shoes?"

"I wants shoes like Missus."

"There be shoes at Salina's ... like you wearing."

"I wants silk shoes wid a silver buckle. Wid a knot of ribbons."

"I speck your money is bout enough to buy a ribbon."

Anner put on a glum face. "How much more do I need?"

Wink, who'd have to find out the price for such shoes, promised to let her know.

When Wink returned from the main after picking up the master's new double moldboard plow, the Marcus Goodwyn buggy was parked at the front of the big house. Wink unloaded the plow in the tool shed and hid his cask of whiskey in the hayloft. When he finished unhitching the horse and storing the wagon, he went to the kitchen and warmed his hands and feet at the fire.

The room smelled of vinegar. Puddin was stirring a brine that boiled in the cook pot, and Mamba sat at the table shelling and cleaning shrimp.

"Where you been?" Puddin turned aside to ask.

"The main." Wink watched Mamba strip out a gut and cut off a head and drop the meaty part of the shrimp into the pan of ice water.

Kedzie entered, refilled the teapot, and returned to the big house.

All things considered, Wink would rather not be the messenger of bad news. If he didn't tell Mamba, she would be content cleaning those shrimp. She'd go to bed after supper and get a good night's sleep.

Mamba said, "What you want to say, Wink?"

"It's about your mammy." He swallowed to clear his throat.

She rested her small knife on the rim of the pan and gazed at him, her amber eyes glistening.

He turned away, to face the fire, and stretched his hands to the heat. "She done passed."

Mamba bit her lower lip and looked at her hands. "That's why the wind blowed these three days widout rest." Her voice was deep in her throat.

Wink said, "They say she went peaceable." He watched the flames dart about the log with glowing energy.

Puddin approached the table. "Leave them shrimps be. I'll get Kedzie to help. Go on to the quarters."

"No. I'll finish this here what I started ..." Mamba's voice trembled. Tears rolled down her cheeks. "Who helped Mammy across?" She wiped her face with the dishcloth.

"Your mammy stood good wid heaps of niggers. They took her in charge," Wink said.

Puddin handed Mamba a fresh cloth and began to pack a crock with cleaned shrimp and slices of onions.

Mamba wiped her nose.

"Where's the brandy? Mamba needs a snort." Wink needed one himself.

Puddin unlocked the cabinet, took out the bottle, uncorked it, and poured a drink. Mamba downed it and handed back the cup. Puddin poured Wink a dram.

Mamba's shoulders shook and she cried. When she regained a voice, she said, "Who funeralized her?"

"I don't know. Morgan's nigger just said to git word to you that your mammy passed and it be peaceable."

Mamba split a shell and peeled another shrimp. She moaned. "Oh, Mammy, I done let you down. Left you to pass over widout so much as a kind word."

"Now hush that talk. The Good Lord don't need no help bringing em in." Puddin handed her another draft of brandy.

Mamba blew her nose and looked at the cup. "I did want to see Mammy one more time." She shook her head to the brandy, and Puddin passed it to Wink. "Mamba, if I can do anything ..." Wink's voice trailed off.

"Much oblige for getting the word," said Mamba.

Wink pulled a stool close to the fire and sat.

Puddin peeled and cleaned shrimp with Mamba until the pan was empty. As Puddin poured hot brine to the top of the crock and set it on the window shelf, Mamba stood and wrapped herself in her shawl. Puddin gave her a hug, and Mamba started to cry again.

Wink felt useless. He knew how long Mamba had waited to visit her mammy. She'd started asking at Christmas. After Mamba left, Wink stood and took Puddin in his arms. He caressed her back, removed her head rag, and stroked her hair. He rubbed her tears into his cheek. "We don't have no time to mess around." His heart ached for losses beyond a mother and he wanted comfort. He wanted Puddin in spite of his weakness. "You going to marry me?"

Puddin didn't answer.

Was it dishonest to let her believe they would have children? He knew he should tell her. But she hadn't answered. Her breath came in staggers. Her eyes glistened. She trembled. He closed her body into his and held on.

The back door of the big house slammed. She didn't move away from him but remained in his arms as Billy came in. That in itself encouraged Wink, for she seemed ready to openly admit their attachment to each other.

"What's wrong wid Puddin?" Billy's voice came across as kind-hearted.

"Mamba's mammy passed."

Billy patted Puddin on the shoulder. "Don't cry, Puddin." He waited, an empty bottle in his hand, until Puddin stopped shaking. "I'll git the wine," he said as he left.

Puddin pulled herself up.

"You going to be alright?" Wink wiped his own eyes. He wanted her to answer his proposal. He was ready to tell her that he couldn't father children. But she simply nodded that she'd be alright. When she turned to the fire, he touched her shoulder by way of leaving.

At his shanty he picked up the baby gown and cap he'd bought and went to the chillun house. Without the other children, the cabin walls seemed stark. The fire gave off lonely light. Mammy Livy slept. Sonny slept as well and hardly moved when Wink put the cap on his head. He put the gown over the baby's feet. It made Wink sad to watch Sonny, sad for the life this little boy would have to live.

CHAPTER 26

MOOEY WAKES UP

FEBRUARY 1858

Mooey rubbed her fingers on the tick, feeling for the crumple of corn shucks. Instead, her hand glided over something so silky she decided a spirit had taken her into the clouds. Perhaps she had begun the journey to become a star. This idea began to fade away as a smell like a sweet bay tree drifted in.

Her hand swept from the smooth surface to her face. Something wasn't right. One eye didn't open. She felt a patch on it, and an aspect of Magic floated into her mind's view. A pain shot through her head. As she turned, she discovered a cover of white cloth and over that a thick quilt of red and yellow colors. Where was her gray blanket? Though measly and scratchy, it was what made sense of a morning. Another thing that didn't make sense—she was warm, even her feet.

Mooey moved herself across the expanse of bedding, easily big enough for three or four people, and looked over the side. The floor, made of even boards, was covered with a rug of mysterious pictures. The walls were framed up without chinks. Rather than sticks and mud, the chimney was made of bricks. Light streaming into the room came through glazed panes. Glazed panes! She had either gotten into a white person's house or a place where negros lived high style. Was this where Lacy went?

She sat up, but her head went swimmy, and she fell back into a pillow. The marvel of a pillow faded as she returned to the subterranean rivers of sleep.

The smell of white people roused her, but not enough to wake her. Her restful darkness brushed away fear and she drifted off.

When something warm touched her forehead, she jerked upright. A white man stepped back as Mooey scrambled to the far side of the bed and shrank to the edge; the wall was so close she could almost lean against it. She gasped, felt a weakness in her belly, and feared she didn't have the strength to defend herself.

She dared to look at him long enough to determine that his well-rounded earlobes allowed grip enough for her teeth. He was familiar, and it took but a moment for her to remember the man who came to the plantation's back lot on occasion. Though Mooey could see little of interest in the man's show of many motions, the others, in particular Auntie, sat and watched him as if he was important.

He moved to come closer. If she had to run, the room had two doors, one opening to the outside and one likely to another room. And if worse came to worst, there were windows. In her terror she shut her eyes. Her throat spirit thrummed forcefully. Her lips rippled.

She peeked through her one good eye. He backed away, bowing to her as if he was her servant. She made him disappear by pulling the cover over her head. In her dark chamber, she waited with dread for a hand to touch the cloth. She slumped down under the quilt's thick warmth. Her eyelids drooped.

She woke up needing to pee. Shadows in the room described the sun as far away and on its journey to night. The fire flickered lazily. Nobody sat in the leather-bottomed chair. Her eye ached. When she turned to put her feet outside the cot, she had to stretch downward to reach the floor and scoot off the bed. Her legs caved under her. When she tried to get up, even her feet felt loose.

The cold floor seemed all the colder because she wore only her shimmy and flannel underdrawers. Where was her coat? Her linsey woolsey dress and quilted underskirt? Her wool leggins? The man? Because she only knew him as the outsider who came to the plantation on occasion, she identified him as "Comer." Had he taken off her dress? Her leggins? She pushed aside her underdrawers and felt her privates. If his pecker had been in there, he hadn't left a mess. She crawled toward the outside door.

Comer came into the room through the other doorway. Mooey squeezed herself against the wall and shut her eyes behind the barrier of her fingers. Her throat spirit quivered. When she looked, he had disappeared.

Outside, the familiar sky returned her to her normal senses. She moved from the double-stride porch to the steps and relieved herself in the drip line, still wet where water had spilled from the roof when it rained.

She sat on the plank steps and rested. Hunger pinched her stomach. Beyond the yard was a stand of stones she recognized as markers where bodies were planted in the ground, a burial place larger than at the plantation. The master's dead babies had been marked with stones carved like sleeping lambs. People like herself were buried under wood stobs. Colored babies didn't get anything. Because she had seen people after they lost their spirit, even babies, she reckoned that everybody met the spirit of no return sooner or later.

A much bigger building with strange windows and a spear-like tower stood beyond the stones. She slumped on the steps and in spite of the wintery boards, fell asleep.

She awoke to the room again. Both her eyes opened and because the pain was gone, she took off the patch. Comer vanished through the door and returned with a tin bowl. He stood at the edge of the bedstead and held out a spoon of broth. She scowled and turned her head, but the steamy scent of chicken, onions, and sage forced her nose in the direction of the spoon. Her mouth watered. She closed her eyes and took a bite. Against her best judgment, she ate, her eyes squeezed shut, until the spoon disappeared. To her surprise, she neither sickened nor died but began to feel better.

The room smelled brittle clean. With the ground covered by boards, the usual earthy smell of Auntie's place was missing. Near the fire, Mooey's dress and underskirt were draped over a chair. So were the narrow wool cloths she'd wrapped around her legs and fastened with string. Her clothes looked as if they had just been washed.

From the window beside the bed she saw a stable house, but no chickens, cows, hogs, or dogs, no fences or barns. There were no fields, no other negros. Hardly any movement stirred in the yard. The several big old trees seemed stone-like and lonely, as if no spirits had ever wagged the leaves. This hardly seemed to be a place where any negro would draw breath, much less Lacy.

When the man tended the fire, she watched him through her lashes. His roundly body had spent more time at a table than in a field. The skin of his clean, shaved cheeks and chin had a pink glow. The grooming he had given his moustache failed to mask its skimpy nature.

As soon as her legs held steady, she sneaked to the door and spied on him. He sat at a table hunched over a book. There was no other bedstead. She became aware that he lived in the whole of the place by himself. When he happened to see her peeking at him, he motioned her into his room. Mooey gyrated with alarm and stumbled back into what had become her room.

He stayed inside more than any person she knew. How he could be content without spending some time with trees, the ground, and sky puzzled her. When he hitched up his buggy and left, Mooey wondered about the room where he stayed. In his absence she examined the house and found out there were but two rooms, the bed chamber and parlor. The small kitchen house out back served to hardly any effect. Though the cupboard shelves contained loaf bread, jelly, ham, a crock of butter, and other victuals, the fireplace was plumb cold. She pinched off bits of ham and crumbs of bread in such a way that Comer wouldn't notice.

Days went by and he didn't return her to the master's plantation. She explored outside around the stable and shed where the buggy was parked. Further from the house she found the privy. The big white building in the distance gave her bad feelings. She suspected harmful spirits.

Between the big building and the man's house was the field of headstones. Seashells with ripples or swirls covered several graves like small gardens of flowering sand. It didn't seem fair that most graves were bare of such beauty. Mooey moved shells around so that all the graves had about the same.

Because Comer distanced himself from Mooey, her fear turned to curiosity. She ate whatever he offered—for his victuals were better by far than any she had ever had: hog meat, chicken, white bread, and fish, more than she could eat. Of a night, she sneaked into the parlor where he slept on a pallet near the fire and looked at him.

One day, he brought in from the stable a tub big enough to cook a shoat. He set it in the kitchen house where he had built a fire and filled it with warm water. When he offered her a piece of soap and motioned at the tub, she suspected a trick. For certain, she didn't want to be without her clothes when he was anywhere about. She backed out the door, ran to the woods, and stayed away until he returned the empty pot to the stable.

As she sneaked back inside the house, she noticed a strong smell of lye soap and sweet bayleaf. The man's chubby cheeks shone in the lamplight, and his hair was combed and pomaded.

She sniffed under her arm and didn't like what she smelled. Between her toes ran tracks of dirt. If ever a body needed washing, hers did, and she had been foolish enough to refuse the warm water of his tub. Eventually, at a time when he was away, she cleaned herself using the basin. She changed the water two times before washing her hair. Afterward, she began to feel like herself again.

One morning she noticed his gaze glanced off her. He licked his lip. His movements sharpened. When she made for the door, he held her elbow, which moved Mooey in more ways than one. He hadn't touched her before. She turned and, for the first time in her life, looked into a white man's eyes. They opened wide with fear. She touched his cheek. He stumbled backwards and Mooey caught his hand to keep him from falling. He drew away. He was scared of her. He backed out the door and, with his hands pumping the air, closed her inside.

A carriage of white people drove by the house and parked in the yard of the big building. Carriage followed carriage. Men, women, and children made their way inside the building, more white people than Mooey had ever seen. After a time, they returned to the yard and stood about in groups. Eventually they filed back into the carriages and left.

The next time the white people came, Mooey was less surprised. Eventually she discovered that white people and a few blacks regularly called at the big building, and Comer always stayed with them. On those days, he departed after they did and returned at candle time, usually with baskets of food.

Their meals were simple but up to the notch, suppers usually whatever remained of dinner. If nothing remained, he toasted loaf bread by the fire and crumbled it in milk. His hands had obviously never touched a cow's teats or a hoe. His clean fingernails had never dug dirt. At sundown, he prepared two plates or bowls and placed them on the small table in the parlor.

As she accepted his food, she looked at him with affection not only to put his mind at ease about her but to show that she was thankful. But for him, she would have been cold and alone in the woods, if not worse. However, the extra chair at the table remained empty, for she took her food to the bedchamber hearth rather than sit with him. Even if he was the kindest man she had ever known, she couldn't swallow around a white person.

After supper she climbed into the cottony bedstead with an increasing sense of guilt as the preacher bedded down on a pallet on the parlor floor. It didn't seem right to take his bedstead. She began to sneak into the parlor in the middle of the night and lie beside him. The firelight darted on his face and body. With the stealth of a cat, she raised his blanket and looked at his feet, white feet. After several nights of uncovering and peeking at his body she found his knobby. It was asleep and she wasn't afraid.

She hovered in his face and felt his wisps of breath. His tousled hair revealed more clearly how thin it was. A tenderness for him swelled her heart. Even in sleep, his kindness showed. She lowered her lips ever closer to his until they touched.

He awoke, his eyes icy, his breath frozen. He pushed her away and went outside in spite of a bleak and wintry wind.

Mooey could hardly accept that she had made such a mistake as to send him out of the house. She lay on the pallet. She should have worried about him and what she had done, but she fell asleep.

When she awoke, the man was drinking coffee. She stood and asked, in a way he had learned to understand, for a cup of coffee. He poured one without looking at her. His eyes avoided her the entire day. At bedtime, when he lay on his pallet, she lay with him. He got up and left the house. Mooey bodily missed him. Because he treated her so kindly, she wanted, in whatever way she could, to claim him for herself.

The yard grew shiny as the moon got bigger, and Mooey wrapped in a blanket to walk about in a night glittering with spirits. The air urged briny scents on her. The grim stones in the field cast shadows so solid Mooey was afraid to step on them.
 Though the night was calm, the old oak with enormous elbows shivered in the moonlight. Knot holes in its bark showed signs of rough contact with spirits. Its roots dug into the dirt so deep that its secrets would stay buried when it died. Mooey rested in a cradle of its boughs and felt it become calm inside, down to the pith. The tree let her know that the white man was afraid of what he needed most, and that was to be loved.

One day, Comer seemed especially nervous. His lips shaped to some purpose she couldn't divine. He hustled her to the large white building that was empty most of the time. She suspicioned the presence of dangerous white spirits inside, a feeling that worsened when she saw the enormous room inside with a ceiling high enough to capture clouds.
 He showed her to a bench and put his finger to his lips in a motion that Mooey took to mean she shouldn't eat anything, which was strange because there was no sign of food anywhere. As he left, she followed, but he motioned her back to the bench, and when she didn't move, he took hold of her hand. His was a gentle and persuasive touch. His hands said he would never hurt her.
 Her hand, though rough in comparison, held his in hers. His face flushed. He pulled free and left her sitting on the bench. She sneaked after him, and as soon as he pulled the door closed behind him, she turned the knob. It opened easily. The man was just

outside, as if he waited for her. He cradled her elbow and guided her back and gestured in a way that pleaded with her. In spite of the cold and eerie room, she sat, for she wanted to please him.

The roomy overhead gave her ideas of a powerful tall person. Perhaps the white people called on spirits that stretched them just so high. At the far end of the room was a cove with two padded chairs and a table and a tall stand obviously made for performers like Comer when he visited the plantation. Her mind's eye caught glimpses of the brush arbor meetings. What was it about those meetings that held the attention of the slaves? And did the whites in like manner get together? Pictures came to her, met and mingled, and particular ones blended together. Mooey was coming to recognize meetings as places where throat spirits quivered to the lips and sent signals into people's heads.

She inspected the shaped and colored pieces of glass framed in ways to make pictures in the windows. Sunlight changed into colors as it streamed through them. Such beauty fascinated Mooey, and she touched first one and then another, ran her fingers on the icy surface and trailed the metal. Through a pale colored piece, she could see the man's house. A horse and buggy pulled up and stopped in the yard. A negro driver helped a white woman tote several baskets to the porch. Was this the preacher's wife? Mooey gazed through the pane as he carried on with the woman, but not in the manner of a husband.

Why did he keep her a secret from other people? He behaved as if she meant something evil or shamefaced but gave up his bedstead to her. He fed her from his own food but hid her when the woman brought the baskets. Though he had saved her life, he didn't put her to work as his slave. Obviously he didn't know how to treat negros.

The strangers left, and the man strode toward her building. As Mooey watched him, she supposed that he was unwilling to have her as a slave. When he opened the door and motioned her outside, she ran for the woods. She needed to sort out the many images swirling in her head. If she wasn't his slave, what was she? While balanced in a tree, she watched the forest lights for answers.

The smell of cooked apples and ham coaxed her closer to the house. A pressing hunger overtook her at the sight of a dish of potatoes and a pan of fried ham on the parlor table. The preacher sat at the fire, his back to her, peeling an orange. The tangy citrus scent drew beads of saliva to her mouth. Another orange was on the table. She took it and slipped back outside.

As her strength returned to normal, Mooey wandered restlessly in the woods. Markers kept her from getting lost—a cluster of cedars, a sandy bottom, a yoke of hickories. What she longed to find was a settlement of cabins where slaves lived, for though the white man treated her well, his kindness left her lonely. No matter how good his food or how soft his tick or how warm his fire, he had little warmth for her. She hadn't seen a smiling face since she awoke in his cabin. She would sooner have the cheerful companionship of Sunny, Auntie, and Lacy than his kindly but guarded company.

Going barefoot posed no problem, for her soles had tough hide. When the preacher appeared with a pair of leather brogans, Mooey gave up trying to figure out what she meant to him. She discovered that the shoes didn't fit both feet equally well, like all other shoes she'd ever owned. After he showed her a couple of times, she could figure out which shoe matched which foot. Though a smidgen big, they kept her feet so warm she hardly felt her toes. Had the bed clothes not been so clean and fine, she would have worn them all night.

She learned that the man's nervousness meant strangers. On such a day, she hid outside without being ordered to do so. She knew that he wanted no other person to see her. Two women of her kind arrived on a wagon. They washed his bedclothes, underwear, and shirts and hung them to dry on a line. They swept his floor, shoveled ashes, restocked firewood, put the parlor in order, and left. He hardly spoke to them.

At times, he performed rituals more mysterious than any she'd seen before. He got on his knees and, with his palms together and his chin tucked in, swayed with his eyes closed. Other times, he held his hands up. Mooey looked up but could see nothing unusual, except that this ceiling had a wood barrier to the beams and shingles she could see in the quarters.

She had to wonder if the book he read so often brought about his strange behavior. On an occasion when he left the house without the book, Mooey touched the pages, ran her fingers over the black images. These symbols reminded her of the ones on the stone markers outside. She yanked her finger away. Perhaps they had magic power over the preacher. Did they take away his laughter, friends, and work? Though he devoted most of his time to the book, he profited from it in no way she could see.

One afternoon he returned with a calico dress, which he held up to his shoulders. Mooey shuffled her feet nervously. Obviously he didn't wear a dress. If she was supposed to fix something about it, she wasn't like the plantation sewing woman. Her fingers couldn't hold on to a tiny needle, and she could hardly see thread. When he shoved the dress at her, she put her hands behind her back, and in a storm of confusion, turned to the doorway and ran.

The following day, he brought the dress to her again. Only after enduring a torrent of his gestures did Mooey allow him to place it in her hands. Her frets mounted. She could no longer deny that he was giving her the dress. Had it been as fine as Lacy's dresses, Mooey would have been of more clashing views. As it was, the timing of the gift worried her. Cold weather had been around too long for the winter allotment, and it wasn't warm enough for new summer clothes. Only once had she seen the master give a woman an exceptional dress. She had also been given white loaf bread and hog meat for days. Early showed her how to look smart by greasing her skin with lard. And then a man came with a wagon and carried her away.

Mooey couldn't trust Comer to be like Lacy's benefactor. She refused to put on his dress. In the woods, she draped it over the bare twigs of a scrub oak and sat underneath to unscramble the pictures in her head. She had to escape from this house, some way other than to take to the woods.

He was sleeping in his bedstead when she returned, and he had laid out the pallet for her before the fire in the parlor. A sadness struck at Mooey's heart about being turned out of the bed. Whatever the meaning of her downgraded rank, she had clean clothes, had been well-fed, and had slept in the finest bedstead of her life. He had treated her like a white person. Yet in spite of everything, she wanted his affection. She lay on the bedstead beside him and waited for him to wake up. When he didn't, she gazed at him, trying to decide if she was going to touch him.

However much she tried to ignore her doubts about him, they returned each time more strongly. Perhaps he witchcrafted people to provide his necessities. He didn't hit a lick of work, not to grow peas nor peach trees nor pecan trees. Nor did he milk a cow or butcher a hog. He didn't hunt rabbits or possums or coons. He didn't bring home fish to cook. The hay he fed his horse came from other white people. He seemed to help nobody, not even himself. He didn't till the land. He didn't own a plow or a hoe or an ox cart. He didn't fix anything, use anything, or improve anything.

Mooey slipped out of the bedstead in spite of her physical longing for him. Haints and evil spirits were too real and the man too unnatural.

Early in the morning, Comer concerned himself with his shirt. He brushed his shoes and dressed in his best clothes. With gestures, he gave her to understand she should stay in the house. Obviously a drove of white people was coming to the big building, and Mooey would be stuck inside for the longest time. As soon as the preacher disappeared, she sneaked out the door and hid behind the trunk of a live oak.

Carriages and buggies rode to the big building where white men tied horses to the hitching posts. People bustled from the yard into the building.

A gust of wind swirled dry leaves up where they bobbed in play like grainy clouds. Sunlight glanced over them. Mooey tossed up more leaves, which floated in the sky, traveling across the yard until, like magic, they drifted down and landed as easy as snowflakes. Before she knew it, she was near the white building.

She hunkered down behind a large tombstone and rested in the sun, surrounded by markers, some of them carved into arches or urns. The rough-hewn surface of some stones looked like creek water chipped by the wind. A nearby figure of a winged person was so tall Mooey hadn't been able to reach its face. The graves with slab covers made good places to sit, especially if the sun was bright.

Mooey realized the carvings meant something to other people, but no matter how long she looked, their secrets stayed hidden. She took a twig and traced the lettering in the mealy sand. Though she made the figures clearer by drawing them twice their size, she understood them no better.

Sitting grew achy to her back. A few steps away was another stone marker, not as big but big enough. She crawled to its cover. From there to another and another, she reached the border of fewer stones near bushy palmettos and lit out for the woods where creatures such as hawks, crows, and herons befriended her.

CHAPTER 27

UNCERTAIN RETURN

MARCH 1858

A drizzle, glistening like corn silk, came down in the yard, a sign to Mooey that a change was coming. In Comer's eyes was none of the usual uncertainty. He had actually given her a nervous smile. In spite of the weather, he hitched his horse to the buggy and parked by the door. He hardly looked at her. She could feel a disturbance in his head. He shook water from his umbrella and stood at the hearth to warm by the dying fire.

As he motioned her to the door, he looked into her eyes but glanced away. He wanted her to leave and that hurt. Tears came into her eyes, for whatever his mystery and regardless of the loneliness, she had lived the best days of her life with him. She took her handkerchief from her pocket and wiped her eyes. He took it, looked at the grapes, and dabbed it on her cheeks.

To her surprise, he put his arm around her. Her forehead felt wet and she looked up and saw tears in his eyes. He put his lips on hers and took her breath with flesh so deep, warm, and powerful she responded in kind. His arms clinched around her. He snuggled her so close she could hardly breathe. When he released her, he looked into her eyes and with the least movement, shook his head. He returned her handkerchief, backed away, and opened the door.

Mooey's heart ached. Only a man of strengthy feelings could have held her with such forceful tenderness. He cared for her. He loved her. But he was sending her away. She went with him to the buggy, climbed in, and crouched under a blanket on the floor as he directed.

The buggy sloshed along the roadway for some time before Mooey stuck her face out to see where they were going. The drizzle had stopped and to her surprise she recognized a cedar with a broken limb. Thereafter they passed a familiar barren of pines. The misery in her spirit eased off. She was nearing her plantation home. She pushed back the blanket and wadded it into a ball. The man signaled "no" to her signs to halt the buggy. His motions argued with her. When they came to a washout in the road, he slowed the buggy. She clutched her blanket and jumped out.

She lost a shoe in the muddy bank of the drainage ditch and turned back to get it. The squishy, cold ground smeared onto her knees and skirt as she fished it out. Comer stood on the opposing bank and gestured to her to come back.

She shook her head, turned from him, and ran. The sharp sticks of winter bushes poked into her clothes. Her wet headrag stuck to her hair. Through soggy myrtles and around bogs she made her way back to her plantation. Like a sign for good fortune, the clouds scudded to sea and the sun came out.

Her heart raced with expectation as she crept closer to the yard watching for the dogs, in particular the mean one. Nearer and nearer. No dogs. She took off her slippery shoes to climb to the top of a live oak so near the quarters she could smell bacon cooking. Between the master's yard and the quarters a new stake and pole fence, built since she left, penned in the dogs. They chased and capered inside the fence while one followed them on the outside, the one the white boy claimed.

She gazed past the dog pen and garden plots to the quarters. With the sun low and sinking, she felt more keenly the wet gloom of the swamps that chilled her clothes. She pulled the blanket around her shoulders. In the yard, the carpenters carried their tools to the shed. The boy who had helped her tend the stock trudged under the weight of a bucket, and at the dog pen he hoisted it on the fence and dumped grub into a trough. Magic plodded across the yard carrying a pail. Cows chewed on hay in the lot, some in the milking stalls.

The field hands lumbered into the back lot and headed to the shanties. When Auntie, who was among the last of them, shuffled in, Mooey's chest beat ferociously. Tears came to her eyes. In a moment of weakness, she began to climb down to be with Auntie whatever the consequences, but she stopped when she remembered the whelps on her back.

Back up at a height, she watched mothers go into the chillun house and come out with their babies and children. She imagined Sunny in his basket, his woolly hair. She could feel his feet kicking, see in his eyes the out-and-out trust he had in her. She spotted Lacy chopping wood at the wood shed. Mooey clapped her hands over her mouth to stifle the quiver arising from her throat, so happy was she to see her friend.

When the rim of the sun sank, she waited for full-out darkness to climb down. As she passed the dogs, they bounced up and down behind the fence. She sneaked along the lower end of the garden plots to the side of the quarters distant from the big house and, when the families settled down to sleep, edged up to Sunny's cabin where she rested her back on the outside wall. An agitation ruffled her skin, warning her to hold back. Splints of light glanced from cracks in the closed shutters. The night grew colder and Mooey waited. Eventually, a calm settled into the wall, and Mooey peeked in the door. Mammy was asleep on her cot. The baby slept in a cradle. Mooey watched him and when she could no longer resist, touched him, kissed his hand.

She warmed herself, front to back, at the slowly burning fire and helped herself to cornbread mush. When Mammy twitched and turned over, Mooey stopped breathing until she sank back into sleep.

She tiptoed back to the cradle. The baby's peaceful eyelids and pudgy lips enthralled her. When he jumped in his sleep, she stroked his chubby cheek. He opened his eyes, looked around, saw her, and stared, kicked his feet, and boxed his fists. As she reached her arms around him to hug his whole little body, her feet felt a rolling in the ground. She let go of him and hurried outside.

On her hands and knees she crawled past rows of potato seedlings, onion sets, and cabbage plants. The ground gave forth a powerful smell, like the decaying side of packed leaves, though there was no upturned litter. A cold streak ran down her back. She gazed into the woods, watchful for an animal. At the live oak she climbed up, retrieved her blanket, and leaned against the trunk. Rain from earlier in the day lingered as moisture in the bark. Though damp and cold, she was so tired she could hardly stay awake in spite of her worry-ation about a wild cat or a rabid fox. When she dozed, her head churned with frightening images—a bear with human eyes climbing at her, blood dripping on her from a limb above.

Murky cold air got into her clothes and regardless of how she turned and twisted, her hips and legs ached. The night turned bluish. The tree swayed, though no breeze passed by. A full measure of misery sent her in search of a better place. She crept back through the garden plots, past the quarters, slipped around the gin house and the milking lot to the shelter where the sheep lay. They didn't resent her approach. She lay next to a mammy sheep and fell asleep to the smell of litter and wool.

CHAPTER 28

WINK'S DEALINGS

MARCH 1858

Anner appeared and leaned on the paddock gate as Wink walked so close to a colt that, when it threw its hoofs outward, they touched him. If the colt kept its hoofs in line, he patted its withers and gave it corn kernels from his pocket.

"Come here," Anner said.

He turned the horse and walked back toward Anner.

"Closer!"

"Baby, this here colt needs help keeping his feets straight."

"I gots word from the massuh."

Wink halted and waited.

She smiled like she needed something. "You is too far away. Come closer."

He turned the colt loose and opened the paddock gate, which was at the back opening of the stables. "Is dat the word of the massuh?"

"You be plenty glad wid what I gots to say." She stood her ground until Wink approached. She pulled him closer. "Massuh sends word to go to the village for more sulphur."

"Dat be the word I been waiting for." Wink, who had been avoiding Anner in the hope of warding off her advances, realized full well she hadn't taken the hint when her hand slid inside his shirt. His tongue got a case of paralysis, but he managed to say, "Baby, I best git on the road."

"Where you been keeping yourself?" Her tongue tempted his lips. She kissed him delicately at first, came in for a closer touch. "I come here plenty times and you be gone."

"I got business... I do more'n tend these horses. Serious business."

"You don't have more business than me." Her eyes sparked as if her double-dealing little mind was working on a recipe for trouble.

"Where you got business?" He knew he was going down a dicey path.

"Wid dat conjure doctor what lives in a shack over on Haigh Creek."

The impurity of her glance gave Wink a powerful yearning for something physical. "The cooper's slave? Dat hoodoo doctor?"

A mysterious shadow haunted her eyes. "Cost me all the specie I had. A cigar too."

"And what you git for specie and a cigar?" He began to think Puddin was neglecting him. She hadn't said "yes" to marriage. She hadn't said "no." She just hadn't said. Anyway, would she care if he trifled with Anner? Wink's train of thought was wandering in the direction of a satisfaction he hadn't had in a long time. He edged her across the stable passageway.

"Plenty worry-ation for Billy."

Her cruel smile landed on Wink with all the ardor of a savage kiss. He wanted more. He put her arm around himself and stopped at the stable gate for some strokes.

Anner's voice was low. "When the hearth be so hard I can't sleep on account of my back, I thinks about Billy and how he don't git no whipping on account of de dogs in the house." She roughed up Wink's knobby as if her anger was rising.

Wink couldn't think about Billy or worry-ation. He was tight in his drawers.

"And I steps out the dining room long enough to blow my nose, and I gits a lashing. He's going to be sorry for treating me the way he did."

Wink recovered his senses enough to suspect a reason for the conjure doctor. "You git dat doctor to jinx Billy?"

She drew away and shushed him.

Wink tried to pull her back, but she twisted away from him. He swallowed a knot of yearning for a woman's body, any woman.

She turned and headed toward the big house, saying, "Massuh said somebody herebouts is feeding Mooey. He been watching you."

Wink had taken an interest in Rio. To the man's credit, he didn't smell of fear in the presence of Farley or the master. It was rumored that he could hear a fly crawling on the wall. The boy was moody and had an unfriendly look, but that didn't bother Wink. Matter of fact, he needed somebody bull-headed, somebody gutsy enough to take chances.

In the stable, Wink worked on Gideon's mane, smoothing it with oil after combing out stumps of winter hair. Farley curried Skeeter in another stall.

The master strode in. His habit of late was to look in on the stables frequently. Wink worried that the man might turn up his liquor supply looking for Mooey.

The master took over with the curry comb and groomed Gideon. Wink attended to a nearby horse. Farley came forward and asked the master about Mooey's cot, which had been empty, asked whether one of the new hands could be moved in there on account of crowding in another quarter.

Wink stopped examining an older horse's loose tooth when he heard mention of Mooey. Farley obviously didn't understand the master's frame of mind regarding the girl.

"Leave it be," the master said. His tone erased any doubt about whether he had forgotten about Mooey's disappearance.

"Yessuh." Farley strolled into the yard toward his house.

Wink fumbled in the gear box and brought out pliers. The horse's tooth, which had made the animal nervous for over a day, had to come out, but it wasn't as loose as he'd thought. The pliers slipped. The horse's high-pitched neigh felt painful to Wink.

"Dammit! Give that to me!" The master snatched the pliers. Wink did what he could to settle the horse while the master, with more profanities than cots had bedbugs, pulled out the tooth.

Whether the master set aside Mooey's cot out of a belief that she was still alive Wink couldn't tell. Such a belief took for granted that she had help, for even a capable runaway would have frozen or starved in this time. Goodwyn might well suspect his own stable of sheltering her, but Wink was as puzzled as anybody about what had happened to her.

Early of a morning, Master Goodwyn arrived at the stables before breakfast. "Wink, count the cowhides and load them in the wagon. Hitch up the team."

Wink knew this trip was coming, for the hides, saved when butchering a beef, had grown into a pile high enough to make the trip worthwhile. "Yessuh, Massuh, but Tootie be nervous dis morning, laying down and getting up."

The master handed his saddlebag to Wink. "She eating her food?" He went to Tootie's stall and clicked his tongue. The horse stood up. After a look in her ears, eyes, and mouth he said, "See anything on her hoof?"

"No, suh. Don't see nothing."

"Better hitch up Cricket with Skittles." The master patted the horse on the rump. "You'll follow me with the wagon. And get Gideon ready to go. I don't want to miss the ferry." The master was already on his way across the yard toward the quarters.

It was the moment Wink had been waiting for. He hurried to find Rio, who was at the back of the big house with Lamar, putting in a foundation for a covered passageway from the kitchen to the big house. "Rio, Massuh send for you."

"What he want?" Lamar grumbled.

"I don't ask. Iffen you gotta know, ask the Massuh yourself." Wink motioned Rio to the stables with a tilt of his head. Inside, he took a chance and told Rio about his plan for trading in whiskey. As Wink suspected, Rio was something of a daredevil. He agreed not only to pay half on the whiskey, but to trade it in the village. Wink would buy whiskey by the cask in Beaufort, and Rio would sell it by the bottle from his fish cart on weekends after dark.

The carriage was already fitted with a trunk of a size to store a small cask under the driver's seat. With the master's permission, Wink had added such a box under the wagon seat, also in anticipation of his trading business. Now that Rio had agreed, the prospect of adding something to the buggy wasn't out of the question.

Without lighting on a better hiding place, they settled on the stable loft under hay. As Rio left to get his specie to buy into the deal, Wink felt in his trousers to a pocket Lettie had sewn in. She had added a yarn string to close it tight. The crunch of currency in his palm quickened his heartbeat. He wasn't sure how much a cask would cost.

CHAPTER 29

SLEEP IN THE PASTURE

MARCH 1858

In the morning Mooey awoke, and the sheep, already standing, stirred around. Much to her dismay, the boy stock tender was waving them out to pasture. She crawled practically under a sheep to get away. The near exposure frightened her from the sheep shed and forced her to look elsewhere for shelter.

She sneaked from place to place, hiding behind the corncrib or resting on the sway of a branch. The animals didn't notice her nor did the slaves. Well after the fall of night, peeps of light appeared in the quarters as doors opened and closed. Currents moved in the night air and told of passages, of bushes bending, sand shuffling, pebbles rolling. She made out one body going from a cabin to the woods, then another and another.

Mooey took a wooded route near the path that led to the brush arbor. A fire blazed in the midst of the slaves gathered there. Though she stayed out of sight and had no idea what the meeting was about, her emotions brimmed with fondness for these people, her family. For the first time in weeks she felt at home. Her eyes grew teary looking at Auntie and Lacy. After they left, she added splints to the embers and revived the ashes. She kept a fire alive and stayed warm until the rain came.

A miserable, cold puddle sprang up around her. Utterly drenched, she sneaked to the quarters and hid under Early's house near the chimney. By the time it stopped raining, the field hands stirred about, and she couldn't leave because of so many people. Chilled through and through and trapped under the house throughout the day, she smelled bacon, collards, and peas cooking and dreamed of a dinner with Auntie.

After the slaves bedded down, she threw caution to the wind and sneaked to Mammy's cabin where she waited outside for the stillness of Mammy's sleep before entering to warm by the fire. She drank clabber, ate an ashcake and bacon.

Sunny slept in his cradle. She watched the gentle wafts of breath moving his chest. When her dress was mostly dry, she took him in her arms where he wiggled so much she placed him beside her as she lay near the hearth. In no time he twisted over onto his stomach and looked around. Mooey rubbed his back.

She hardly needed to feel the footfall of the woman with breasts, for her smell of magnolia and sweat worked up the air. Mooey quickly put Sunny back in his cradle, sneaked out the door, and skittered to the woods. Alone in the dark and cold, she wrapped in her blanket and propped against the trunk of a tree further removed from the quarters. In an effort to get out of a raw wind, she moved from one side of the trunk to the other. The warmth of the chimneys tempted her to return to Auntie's house and climb up on the roof, if only for a short time, just long enough to warm her painful back.

When morning came, she explored further afield until she came to the master's graveyard. One grave with a housing of bricks and marble provided a place to lie down, though a hard one, and she fell asleep atop it.

On waking, she noticed that the slab cover was long enough that her feet didn't extend off the end and wide enough for her shoulders. The chamber was big enough that, were it opened, she could fit inside with room to spare. At the head was a tall stone carved with the usual markings as well as roses. Mooey saw water drops on the flowers and brushed one with her hand. Her fingers came back wet. Tears. Mooey stroked the roses and dried their tears.

She wandered the graveyard and took notice of the stones in shapes of vases, crosses, crescents, and angels, all carved with markings—flowers or lambs or stars—but the big grave built like a box called her back. She might well stay this far away from the quarters. She prodded bricks with a stick, going from one side of the casing to the other, but not one budged. A sharp stone did no better. She threw it on the ground and wandered about looking for something that might work.

She paused under the limbs of a motherly ash tree. On tiptoe, she reached up and hoisted herself to a lower limb. As she climbed from one branch to another, the tree carried her up. Deep trails in its bark notified Mooey of rough nights if she had nowhere to sleep. Near the top, her weight bent the delicate branches. She stretched so far she sighted yard trees at the plantation and the top of the big house.

Because the cold nights kept her awake, she took naps during the day at different places. She looked for sunny spots away from the wind. On a day of blinding brilliance she wrapped in her blanket and lay in a dip near the cows in the pasture and fell into a deep sleep.

A whisper of movement woke her, but the sunlight was so friendly it called her back to sleep. Again, something brushed by her. Even before she opened her eyes she knew the smell. It was River. Or his spiritual messenger. Her eyelids fluttered open. The sun behind the dark figure streamed out like horns of gold.

She closed her eyes to make him go away, but he didn't. She peeked through her thick lashes, reached out her hand, and touched what was solid human. He didn't move as her finger raked his knee.

Her feet charged the ground, but before she could make off, a cedar tree got in her way. Fear, loneliness, hunger, a snotty nose, ragged stockings—it all came upon her and she felt as if she'd fallen into a well. She rolled over and cried.

After a good cry, she felt better. River handed over his pocket rag. She took this to mean he wasn't going to blab on her. His face, naturally wrathy, had none of the meaness she often saw in others. She calmed down because he didn't try to touch her.

She took a breath and launched into motions with a terrible hope grinding in her chest. She wanted something to eat. She wanted him to get something for her. River's manner wasn't naturally friendly, but he made her feel worthy of his attention. He seemed to understand her need for food.

Later in the night, she was gratified to find a tow sack with an ashcake tied to a branch in a nearby pine. She took the ashcake and left the tow sack. The next night she found another ashcake.

Mooey's confidence in River grew. One day she watched the tow sack and when he appeared with the ashcake, she persuaded him to follow her to the graveyard. Beside the big grave, she gestured for a door at the foot panel, which was a solid piece of plaster.

Mooey had never seen a playful face on River, much less an open-mouthed smile. Merriment, as she had experienced it, often sprang from trickery or ill will. She ran. Her feet intuitively found secure footing as she climbed a water oak.

River neither tried to stop her nor give chase. Instead, he paced around the tomb and seemed to study it.

While she sat on a limb, a flow of tree moss in the breeze heartened Mooey, and the thumping she had felt in her chest calmed. She looked down at River, crouched at the end of the big grave and inspecting something she couldn't see. He had understood her so quickly she wondered if he had a way of getting inside her head. He walked from the master's family graves to the slaves' graves and kicked the dirt. When he scooped up a handful, carried it to the white grave, and sprinkled it around the edges, Mooey puzzled over whether he was possessed of the ground spirit. This didn't worry her. To the contrary, she revered the ground spirit and any connection River might have to it.

When he left, Mooey came out of the tree and inspected the grave, but the foot panel looked as solid as ever.

She awoke in the middle of the night unsure of why or what disturbed her. The darkness stirred. And a scent traveled with the motion ... River. A pin light appeared before he did. She sat up on the grave housing, expectant and unsure of what his presence would bring, until she saw the tool in his hand. He put the lantern beside her and began to poke at the foot panel with a chisel he had brought. When he left, a weakness affected the stars. A wind arose and channeled through her like a stream of cold water.

Mooey sat on the grave eating ashcake and waiting. The sky was bright with a gibbous moon that had grown bolder every night. When River didn't come, she realized how much she looked forward to his arrival and the sense of safety he provided.

A menacing scent grew stronger in the darkness. Because it was invisible and in the air she breathed, she hardly knew how to protect herself. Whether it was an evil spirit or a wild animal, she felt vulnerable. Like the animals, she had marked with her urine the area of the grave where she slept, but danger seemed so close she climbed to a water oak's branches. Even there, a strange presence worried her, and she sneaked down by the pasture fence. When, in the morning sun, the cows ambled nearby and chewed their cuds, she fell asleep.

Under a late moon, River arrived. Because he did unusual things, she watched him closely. Before he began to work, he paced around the tomb. He looked into the dark woods as if he could see the owl she knew was in the oak tree but couldn't see herself. He rubbed a silver stone hanging on a leather cord around his neck before setting his chisel to the trench he was making around the foot panel. When he left, spirits in the trees gave breath to the darkness.

Mooey lay down with her blanket on what was to become her roof only to doze fitfully. Unblinking eyes stared at her from behind a scrawny myrtle bush. She couldn't tell if she was awake or asleep. The smell of an animal seemed real. She opened her eyes and gazed at the tree-lined border of the graveyard. The eyes had disappeared. Her feet and legs ached. She stood, undecided about whether it was safer to remain like a gravestone or run. A wind rustled the treetops but barely brushed the ground.

She padded lightly toward her usual refuge, the ash tree, quicksilver in her veins as she stared into the dark, hunting for the agitation that meant an attack. A cat creature could climb a tree faster than she could. She lit out across the strip of woods to the open field and raced to the plantation.

She got away from what felt to be the presence of a wild animal by staying with the sheep. She lay between two of them and dozed off. A tremor passed into her hips, and she jolted awake to full daylight. Several horses pounded through the stable gate into the paddock. Mooey crawled to the edge of the shed, across the pasture, and past the wagon trail to the distant woods before she noticed her knees were scratched and bruised.

She returned to the graveyard with dread as night approached. To her relief, River arrived and began to work. When he prodded the panel open, he fell back as if a host of haints had whooshed out of the grave. The dead man's bones had rested for years in the chamber he didn't need nearly as much as Mooey did. She would have dragged out the bones and the rotted boards but for River, who pushed the panel back into place.

Well before he took leave, Mooey recognized in his hammer a weapon. At the risk of annoying him, she took it, and in spite of his anger, kept it. She sat up the rest of the night and watched dry twigs and switches for signs of motion, the hammer ready in case the animal attacked.

On the night when they cleared the tomb of splinters, bones, and the dusty remains of ragged cloth, Mooey looked inside and saw safety. No more terror over the wild cat. No more sitting under a live oak in a cold rain. No more wet clothes and cold feet.

Before she and River finished, Mooey realized she needed boards for a floor. She searched for and found a pile of slabs at the gin house. By placing several of the shorter ones on her blanket, she dragged them from the plantation to the graveyard, being careful to rub away tracks the boards made in the sand. When the last of the coffin had been removed from the tomb, she tugged each board inside and by trial and error fit them together to make a floor.

As she worked inside, she realized there was a problem with closing the foot panel the final few inches. Not only was it heavy, but the smooth inside surface made it impossible to get a grip. She worried that River considered the hideout finished and wouldn't come back.

It was a relief when she recognized the shadow of his stealthy body approaching in the moonlight. He had not only returned but brought a handle he attached to the inside of the panel. Upon leaving, he gave her a goodwill nod and shut her inside her hideout.

She crawled on her blanket and for the first time in days fell asleep without worry about her safety. When she awoke, breathing seemed burdensome. She swallowed what felt like thick air. The heaviness passed outside when she shoved open the door. Her fortification was too solid. With sturdy sticks, she eventually managed to chisel small spaces between the top layer of bricks and the stone cover.

It made more sense to stay in her hideout during daylight when people might happen upon her, but Mooey found she could tolerate the closeness of the walls best when she was sleeping. Though she tried to get into the habit of sleeping during the day, her natural rhythm resisted change and she found herself drowsy all the time. One night when she nodded and almost fell from a tree, she gave in and slept when she felt like it.

The smell of dirt inside the chamber was so strong Mooey could hardly smell anything else, but there seemed no correction for that. What bothered her more was the heaviness of the stone cover, so unlike shingles or the sky. Its solid, dense weight gave her bad dreams in which a millstone fell on her. She worried that, if she died in the tomb, her spirit couldn't escape to become a star.

By stealing from the plantation, she improved her hideout. Cotton wrapped in a blanket softened the planks she slept on. With two bottles, she didn't have to find drinking water every day. The cook's lye soap kept her cleaner.

The most precious thing she stole was a sock from Sunny, which she kept in her pocket. At times when it was too unsafe to visit him, she could smell his little foot. She rubbed the soft material to her cheek. The finely crafted sock was of a quality few slaves could afford, and she had fretted over taking it. At the same time, it meant more to her than anything else she owned.

With River's hammer, she began to loosen a brick to provide a window. By wedging a hard stick into the mortar and hammering it, she gradually crumbled away the dried grains of tabby. She was inside hammering when she felt the ground spirit speak. Though she knew something approached, without a window she couldn't tell if it was a person or an animal. If a person, her instinct was to flee to the trees. Otherwise, if the hideout should be detected, she'd be trapped. The longer she lay with her stomach to the ground, the clearer the message that it was a person, not one but two. She couldn't tell if it was day or night. There was nothing to do but wait.

PART IV
A QUALITY CARRIAGE TO DEAD GONE

CHAPTER 30

FIRST SHIPMENT

MARCH 1858

Wink loaded cowhides into the wagon for a trip to Beaufort and then saddled up Gideon. Before he and the master departed, he placed his empty cask in the seat locker and piled on top of it a rag blanket and leather lines used with harnesses.

As it so happened the master negotiated the sale of his cowhides at the very shop where the buckra with a distillery worked. Artis motioned Wink on the sly, and the two of them gestured and whispered barely out of earshot of the master. Though Wink had money to buy whiskey enough for two casks, he only had one cask. Artis loaned him one but Wink had to commit a supply of tobacco as security. The master finished his trading before Artis had time to load the casks into the wagon locker. With the master's footsteps echoing in his ears, Wink hurriedly settled with Artis to return to pick up the casks at midnight.

They went to the bank and while the master tended to money matters, Wink got permission to do his trading, though he had spent all his money. He visited the doorman at the Victoria Hotel, who kept the slave populace informed about everybody and everything. He was so agitated by a United States court case that his account of it hardly made sense. Wink supposed Dred Scott was an abolitionist who'd gotten into trouble with the law. Otherwise, he learned nothing he hadn't already heard about personages of his acquaintance.

By the time the master finished at the bank and they headed to the Fortier mansion to overnight, the town lamp lighter was making his rounds.

In the middle of the night, Wink borrowed the Fortier's wheelbarrow, collected his casks of whiskey from the leather shop, and packed them into the wagon locker.

The following morning after Wink fetched the horses from the livery stable, the master came to the carriage house while Wink hitched Cricket and Skittles to the wagon. The master said, "Mistress Fortier said she saw somebody wheelbarrowing through the yard last night."

Wink consciously breathed regular and held steady. "She say who it be?"

"You see anything?" The master raised the bridle to Gideon's head, pulled through the horse's ears, and adjusted the bit.

"No, suh." Wink threaded the lines through the rings and laid them on the wagon's dashboard. He didn't look to see if Goodwyn's eyes were questioning him.

"She's doing poorly." The master said as if to himself as he threw on Gideon's saddle and tightened the cinch.

That the master seemed to dismiss Mistress Fortier's report because of her health cleared Wink of suspicion. His breath came normal.

The master returned to the Fortier manse and in but a short time brought his saddlebags and mounted Gideon.

Wink followed him to the wharf well before the ferry's departure in order to load the wagon with sacks of seed cotton, sent from a Georgetown planter to the master by packet boat. Missy Margarita unexpectedly appeared at the landing in a buggy driven by a man Wink recognized as a planter on Coosaw Island. Wink shuffled sacks to make secure a place for Missy's trunk. They boarded the ferry, crossed the river, and arrived at Westfall in the afternoon.

After depositing Missy and her trunk at the portico, Wink drove the wagon first to the granary house where he unloaded the bags of seed. At the carriage house, he unhitched the horses and turned them to the paddock. After nightfall, he carried his whiskey from the wagon to the loft and stashed it under hay.

Wink showed Rio their supply after dark. "No more'n I goes to the main, we needs two casks. And iffen I don't take this one back, dat buckra's not going to trade wid us."

"I can make another cask," said Rio, who took measure of the wagon locker.

Wink and Rio worked out a plan. Sometime during the week, Wink hid a full cask off the causeway behind low growing myrtle bushes. Saturday following, when Rio passed by with the cart on the way to sell his fish, he picked up the cask and hid it in the bottom of the fish basket under whatever catch he had to sell in the village.

One Friday night when he returned from sneaking to the causeway to stow a cask for Rio, Wink paused in the back lot, for in the moonlight he saw a shadow moving about one of the gin houses. Too big for a cat or possum, though the cats seemed to be circling around whatever was happening there. Wink went to his shanty for his lantern, but by the time he returned to the yard even the cats were gone. A board had been pulled from underneath a barn and lay on the ground as if a haint had left notice of his appearance. Wink held the lantern high and looked in all directions.

Back in the stables, the horses slept. The owl in the eves looked down at him with disinterest. Nothing seemed amiss. The following morning the board was gone. So were several others that had been stored under the barn. Wink told his story to Tootie, but she eyed him sideways and flicked her ears. He didn't mention it to anybody else, but he thought about it. For a reason he didn't understand, Mooey came to mind. Had she died and become a spirit? But what did a spirit need with boards?

After three weekends, Rio had sold their supply of hooch, bringing in cash every Saturday night. But just when Wink was getting bigheaded about making so much money, Rio came in early one night with a swollen eye, ripped shirt, bloody face, and raw knuckles. No money and no whiskey.

Wink unhitched the cart and the two of them walked the mule to the stables where Rio sat on a pile of hay, his head in his hands. "There was four or five of them. I'se not going to get myself killed over whiskey."

When Wink found out it was Jervy's boys who had beat up Rio, he was ready to sneak over to Riverben and tear into them. At the very least he wanted to fire back a warning, but Rio wasn't in shape for much of anything. "We can't close down trading on account of them," Wink said with more enthusiasm than confidence, for they were already closed for the time being.

As Wink returned from hauling the last cartload of muck to the fields, he noticed the bob-tailed high-stepping pair that pulled a shiny coach into the front yard. Two men, one pot-bellied and both dressed better than the preacher, climbed out, followed by a woman in hoops.

Wink drove to the stables, tied the mule to the hitching post, and began to spread a pile of fresh straw into a cleaned stall. In no time, Anner arrived. She looked at him with sober eyes. "Billy wants help. Them peoples got a trunk the size of a barrel."

Wink threw down his pitchfork and started out. Anner waylaid him, allowing him to step into her arms. "Sweetie, I gots something for you!"

Wink stretched his back. "What you got?"

"What you want?" She tilted her head to eyeball him. Her apron pocket bulged.

"Let me see what's in dat pocket."

Her little eyes shone with excitement. "What you got for me?"

Wink sighed. The woman had to be paid. As he gave her a kiss, he felt into her pocket and removed a twisted sweet cake wrapped in a handkerchief. "Whoooo! This looks good!"

"It be a cruller. Puddin's been cooking for them white folks what be visiting."

Wink had never seen, much less tasted a cruller before, but between its syrupy crust and soft dough it went head to head with Christmas eggnog.

"How you get this out the kitchen widout Fuddin taking notice?" There were times when Wink couldn't help but admire the girl's daring.

"She been worrying over Billy."

Wink's momentary lapse into Anner's charms passed. "What you saying?" He handed her the empty handkerchief.

"He's been hobbling round all morning." She came close to a laugh. "He's got fancy shoes, but they be bothering him I spect." She flapped her handkerchief on her knee.

"Something the matter wid his shoes?" It was a stupid question, but Wink could only blunder blindly until she said something that made sense.

She twirled the handkerchief. "He done gone wobbly in the knees." She dabbed her upper lip.

"Billy be sick?" He grew suspicious.

"Iffen he be feeling poorly, I spect he be paid in full for tormenting me."

"Girl, what you done?" Wink had to wonder about Anner. Sometimes she was a tornado posing as a summer breeze.

"I only done what was called for. After dat sneaking weasel brung a whipping on me."

She was talking devil talk. "How you figure what was called for?" Wink said. The more he knew of Anner, the more obvious it became that what she thought was called for in any given circumstance was a far cry from what Wink expected.

She laughed. "Billy sits round rubbing his head, not strengthy enough to scare a mosquito."

"And you is gloating over it, I reckon." Wink gave her a stern look and spit. Just enough indignation to frustrate her but not enough to anger her. The last thing he wanted was Anner for an enemy. He stalked to the big house, but Billy had managed to get the visitors' hampers inside without help.

Though the stables were clean, Wink dared not allow the Westfall stock to appear less groomed than the visiting horses, which he'd latched into separate stalls with fresh straw. The high-blooded mares were of pedigree equal to Gideon. So stylish was the visitors' carriage Rio and Iverson stopped by to take a look at it. Wink had seen velvet seats before, but they hadn't. They all agreed the visitors' well-to-do style meant they weren't slave traders.

Wink had curried Tootie by the light of his lantern and was smoothing out and trimming Gideon's fetlocks when a glint of light shone in the darkness. Balls of light were occasionally seen bouncing in swamps among the cypresses, but this light had just disappeared around the side of the stable. He went outside in the dark, his chest tense and his mind not altogether clear of the idea that a haint had just passed by.

He was relieved but puzzled to recognize Kedzie by the light of her torch. Whatever she was doing, she didn't need to be close on to his horses. Her explanation—that she was looking for Billy—caused Wink to eyeball her. Billy hardly ever left the big house and even if he did, he wouldn't do it at night, and even if he did at night, he wouldn't be fooling around the stables.

"Will you come with me to look in the necessary?" Kedzie said in a voice that could have been strained with fright. Or maybe it was a hag's voice. He had heard about hags possessing people of a night, riding them in the dark. He could think of a hundred things he had to do. What he wouldn't do was go to the white people's privy and stir up some of their devils. He returned to the stable.

Just when he'd put away the hoofpick, file, and brushes, Gideon started acting up, bumping his stall, his ears twitching. One of the visiting mares started pawing the ground.

"What you scared of?" Wink patted the horse on the hind. A scruffy pitch of night noises erupted with a piercing rill. A screech owl, followed by a woman's yelp. Leaves rustled in a dead-still night. "Ho, boy ... calm yourself. Nothing's going to get inside this here stable." He murmured reassurances as much to himself as Gideon.

Hardly had the horses calmed down when Mamba appeared at the stable with a torch. "Come wid me. There's a noise coming from the necessary and I spect it be Billy."

"Billy? In the shit house?"

"Come on. I don't have time to stand here jawing all night."

"Git somebody else. These horses is riled up," said Wink.

"Who else? Farley? He'd as soon Billy die in the necessary."

"Die? Is Billy sick?"

"He's not out there carousing while the massuh be calling for him."

Wink followed Mamba to the path to the small privy. The night air dribbled thin beads of water on his face that froze the short hairs of his trim mustache.

Mamba jarred the door. "Billy, we come to help you!"

"Let's get the Massuh down here. This ain't no place for niggers!" Wink backed up.

"Don't you get squirrelly on me!" Mamba said with the authority of a massuh in homespun.

"Billy is about as likely to be on the other side of dat door as raw head and bloody bones."

"Hold this." Mamba handed over the torch and jiggled the door. A noise emerged from inside, Billy's voice but the words were impossible to follow. Wink had to do what he could to help Billy. He stepped in front of Mamba, grabbed the edge of the door, and yanked it with full force. A second time. Mamba stobbed the torch in the ground, and the two of them jerked the door off its hinges. Billy lay scrolled up on the floor holding his gut, his pants barely covering his back side. Wink pulled him up to a sitting position. "You able to git on your feets?"

Billy's eyes rolled. His arms and legs flailed.

Wink nudged him out the doorway and to the ground where there was room enough for them to help him up. Shoulder to shoulder the two of them tugged Billy back to the kitchen house and Puddin's quarter where they laid him on her cot.

"Billy! What's the matter wid you?" Puddin wiped his face with her apron rag. Her look of shock and sadness caused Wink to wonder anew if she felt more than friendship for the butler. "I'll git the brandy," she said, leaving.

"What the hell is Billy doing in the white folks' shithouse?" said Wink.

"Where's he going to go? He don't want all them white folks about and him sick."

Puddin brought him brandy. When Billy regained his senses, he said, "It musta been that sassafras tea I drunk this afternoon. My constitution ain't made for that stuff."

When Kedzie reported that the master and his guests had withdrawn from the dining room to the front parlor, Wink and Mamba helped Billy to his cot inside the big house.

Early the following morning Wink hitched up the visiting horses to the shiny carriage, drove it to the front door, and waited. When the master and the two men came down the steps, they stood and admired the horses before seating themselves. The master took the reins and they drove away.

Wink stopped at the kitchen. Puddin skimmed cream off milk. Billy sat on a stool, his back leaning against the wall. Puddin looked up, glints of worry in her eyes. He wanted to ask her why she was worried, but it might have to do with Billy. He glanced at Billy. "Is Puddin feeding you the Massuh's ham?"

Billy squirmed like bedbugs had moved into his drawers. His hand swatted at something before his face. "I done told you, the massuh got rid of dat girl. Sold her!"

"What girl is dat?" Wink said.

"It was her looks. Like striking fire. Massuh gots fire."

"Is you talking bout Lovey?" Wink wondered if he'd heard what he thought he had.

"She give him a angel and he sent her to hell." Billy wiped his face with his hand.

"Don't worry yourself bout dat. I hear tell she been having a good time over on the main." Wink said what he believed would ease Billy's mind.

Billy wiped his nose on his sleeve and shuffled his feet. "Where dese bugs come from?" He flicked dust from his shirt.

Wink looked at Puddin.

She looked back with moist eyes and subtly shook her head.

Billy leaned his head back to the wall and closed his eyes. "He be selling his baby like a mule."

"Massuh said he was selling dat boy?" Wink spoke up.

Billy seemed to be dozing.

When Puddin tried to pour cream into the churn, her hands trembled and the cream dripped outside. Wink took over and poured it. Puddin anchored the lid and put in the dasher.

"Billy, you heard the massuh say he's going to put his baby in his pocket?" Wink couldn't credit what Billy was saying, but he couldn't ignore that piece of intelligence.

"He be burning up the place. The whole damn place." Billy mumbled, his eyes closed.

Wink had never heard Billy curse before. "What's wrong wid him?" he whispered.

"Anner says some Africa spirit be troubling him."

"Anner? What kind of Africa spirit?"

"I don't know, but it must be in his shoes ... the way Anner says his feets be feeling wrathy by now."

Wink looked at Billy. "Billy, your shoes needs shining. Give them here. I'll fix them."

Billy raised a foot but didn't seem to know what to do with it. Wink removed one shoe and then the other. Inside one he found a flat cloth sack. "What you got dis in your shoe for?" He held the shoe up for Billy to see inside.

Billy rested his head on the wall, his eyes shut, his lips moving as if he talked.

Puddin took the sack in hand.

"Dat be a mojo bag," said Wink, who'd just as soon not touch it.

"No wonder Billy been limping around." When Puddin threw it into the fire, a rush of flames flared into the room.

"Shit! Must be gunpowder," said Wink, as the two of them hustled away from the fireplace. He splashed water on a flaming dish cloth and sprinkled more on the floor around the hearth.

Puddin put Billy's shoes back on, though he hardly moved. "Leastways you can walk better now," she said. He kept his eyes closed.

Wink's mouth watered at the sliced ham on the table. "Dat hog meat shore do look good." He put his hand to Puddin's back.

She pinched off a piece and offered it to his lips. Her eyes showed the affection he needed so much to see. He kissed her fingertips.

She inhaled deeply. Her eyes glistened. Wink couldn't be sure whether her emotion was tenderness for him or worry for Billy. She turned back to the cooking fire where one of the pots boiled over and broth sputtered on the hearth.

Though a wagonload of work waited for him at the stables, Wink diverted to the chillun house to see Sonny. Mammy was hanging clean napkins on a rope stretched between two trees. Babies sat on the ground outside. Inside, children played on the cots. At the cradle, a big smile greeted him. Sonny twisted and squirmed and turned over on his stomach, raised his head and looked up at Wink with expectant eyes, as if he had accomplished something monumental.

He picked the baby up and nuzzled him with his short beard, which turned the little fellow into a jabbering, wiggly creature. Sonny grabbed Wink's nose and squeezed it. "Hold on here, boy. Dat belong to me." He pulled away. Sonny reached Wink's hat, gripped the brim, and pulled it down over Wink's eyes. "Now see what you done." Wink moved his head about to rearrange the hat so he could see. The baby gazed at him, his eyes wide, as if he'd seen a miracle. Wink put the hat on Sonny's head where it fell down to his chin. The baby's fingers grasped the brim and instead of lifting the hat, he tugged it from side to side. He jostled it enough to uncover his eyes and managed to topple it to the floor. He stared after it with curious eyes. He stretched his arms reaching for it, which put a strain on Wink. The little fellow kicked his legs as if to get himself down.

The baby needed a parent. Wink, who'd begun to think like Sonny's father, needed a family and he had a plan for getting one. The first step was to convince Puddin to marry him, then get the master's permission, which was practically certain since the two of them lived at Westfall. Then he'd offer to take over the care of Sonny, move him into their cabin.

He tootled his breath onto Sonny's neck. The baby squealed excitedly. It was so easy to make Sonny laugh. Surely the master wouldn't sell such a fine, healthy baby. Surely he'd keep the boy close, even if it was in the field.

CHAPTER 31

FUNERAL

MARCH 1858

Wink pulled the cart to the well, drew water, and washed off muck leavings. He pushed it back to the carriage house. Anner rushed in so winded she leaned against the wall. Wink was having none of her tricks. A scent of whiskey wafted from her. With a carefully aimed spit of tobacco in her direction, not too close but close enough, he allowed her some leeway. But for the whiskey, he would have found some excuse to leave her with the carriages.

He rocked the cart back and forth to wedge it into its corner.

She burst into a moan, sank down the wall, and crouched, her handkerchief over her face. Her breath sounded like a stampede of wild horses.

"Dammit, Anner! Stop that!" Wink looked around to see if anybody else had heard her.

"Ooooohhhh! This is the most terrible of all!" She coughed and sputtered.

"I don't want to hear about it. Go tell Billy!" Wink, who expected her to follow him to his cabin, headed away from his place and toward the quarters. Behind him, she whispered, "Billy be dying."

He stopped in his tracks. No use pretending he hadn't heard, for his ears were ringing and he could hardly swallow. He threw his cud on the ground and cleared his throat. "How you know?"

"Puddin said for you to git the massuh. Billy be terrible sick." She looked at him with swollen, red eyes. "It wasn't what you think! I didn't fix Billy! I didn't!"

"Then who put a mojo bag in his shoe?"

"Mojo bag? I don't know nothing bout no mojo bag. Billy had a boil on his foot. He ask me to git a poultice for him."

"Dat wasn't no poultice."

"I swear! Dat's all I done. And I done it for Billy. I got a poultice from the doctor."

"Dat be the hoodoo doctor you went to see over on Haigh Creek?"

She jumped nearer and pleaded. "Billy said he didn't want no white doctor!"

"You spect me to believe you? After all you said about getting even wid Billy?"

She pulled him to face her. "I just said that so's you'd tell Puddin and she'd give Billy worry-ation." She grabbed Wink around the neck. "You believe me, don't you?"

He wanted to say she was a good match for the devil, but if he got on the wrong side of her, no telling what might happen. Wink tugged to loosen her arms.

She clutched him mightily. "Nothing ever hatched of hoodoo!" She latched her hands on his face. "I swear to God almighty!"

In her frenzy, Anner was so strong Wink wondered if he could get himself loose. "Anner, settle down and let go of me."

"Say you believes me!" She yelled so loudly Puddin came into the yard up by the big house and looked their way.

"Shit, Anner! Why you so wrathy wid me? Git a hold of yourself!"

She kissed him hard on the lips, a sloppy, wet, salty kiss. Wink suspected she did it because Puddin had appeared, even if in the distance. She released him. "You is the onliest one I told," she said in a tone that dared him to tell anybody, whether it was a poultice or a mojo bag. She turned and walked away.

Wink looked in the direction of the kitchen. Puddin wasn't in the yard. He saddled up Freckles and headed out to fetch the master.

If Wink had been thinking clearly, he would have saddled two horses and taken Gideon along, for the master had ridden out in the carriage with his visitors. As it was, he had but his feet to get him home while the master rode Freckles. To his good fortune, Jervy's houseboy rode by and Wink doubled up on his horse.

He went straight to the kitchen to see Puddin and find out what had happened to Billy. Upon seeing Iverson outside the door where a sad group of people had congregated, Wink knew the worst had happened. He stood with Lettie, Gussie, and other slaves who were attached to Billy. They asked what had been wrong with him. Had he suffered? Poor Billy. Wink's head felt numb. He watched and listened as if he was a chink in the wall.

Puddin and Kedzie and Mamba explained as they could, but Anner, so overcome with anguish, sat on a stool and hardly acknowledged their presence. Wink came out of a stupor but wished himself back in one. Anner's hoodoo had messed with Billy, sure as cream rose on milk. How else to explain his death? Leastways she wasn't acting like an outright haint. He went back to his quarter, dug his whiskey bottle out of a fishing basket, and drank a long swill.

When the visitors returned to the big house to pack their belongings, Wink watered the horses and drove the carriage to the front of the house and waited. When the master signaled him inside, he fetched their carpetbags and loaded them. Upon departing the visitors talked at length with the master, so long that Wink was allowed to take leave.

He gladly withdrew. The presence of people bothered him. What he'd have liked to do was to saddle up Nicky and ride in the pasture alone where he could think better. Make some sense of the bedlam about Billy. Gone. Nothing more than a bellyache. He could hardly believe it. Harder to believe was that Anner would hoodoo the man. Hardest to believe was that hoodoo could have such upshot.

On his way back to the stables he realized it was Friday, and Rio needed the cask of whiskey the following afternoon. That night, the funeral trail would follow the carriageway to the causeway, and their hideaway alongside the road was so close, a misstep by a field hand might accidentally expose their liquor.

By the time he found Rio, the field hands were coming in and the carpenters had knocked off for the day. "We best hide the cask somewheres else. Somebody walking wid the funeral might stumble off the road."

Rio agreed that the Lands End side of the carriageway was safer, for the funeral train would turn in the opposite direction. After haggling about which tree was where, they decided on a location.

Everything seemed in a muddle. Men and women milled around the street in grim quietude. The children walked instead of running. Even the chickens set underfoot, seemingly deep in thought. Wink began to wonder how he'd get the whiskey to its hideout in time. He had never waited until a Saturday morning when any possible mix-up might prevent him from getting it in place.

Just as the sun was going down and he made plans to wheelbarrow it after the funeral, the white preacher arrived in his buggy. Wink claimed that a wheel looked as if the rim was loose and talked the preacher into letting him take the buggy down the carriageway to put it to the test. He stashed the cask beside the road and reported to the reverend that the wheel seemed serviceable after all, but he should have the hub checked.

On his way to his quarter to change his coat for the funeral, Wink stopped by the chillun house to see Sonny. The cabin was empty. He strolled the street hoping to find the babies, for if Mammy went to the funeral somebody else kept them.

Limbo intercepted him. "These niggers be wanting hooch like nobody's business."

The two of them doubled back to the stable where Wink dug under oats in a barrel, brought out a cask, and filled three bottles.

At the sick house, Iverson said a prayer over Billy's body. Women wore their Sunday dresses, colorful shawls, and bright head rags. Everybody moved aside to let Joe enter. The man talked plenty angry, gestured like his nerves might break through his skin. Said white people was killing them. His smell shocked them as much as his shoddy clothes, which only confirmed their belief that the man was crazy as a loon.

Wink took Iverson's hint and coaxed Joe out of the room and to the carriage house where they pulled out the wagon. He brought Puff from the stable and gave her a sip of whiskey. She wanted more but Wink kissed her flubbery lips by way of saying no. He offered a dram to Joe, who shook his head.

"Us niggers is stupid," Joe said, his voice dangerously calm. He pulled the lines through the wrong rings. "I had my freedom papers. Then like a fool I eat loaf bread a nigger give me."

Wink began to pay attention. Joe's voice sounded normal, like other people.

"Fell down wid sleep and woke up a slave." Joe swallowed as if bread was caught in his throat. "Walked a hundred miles or more ..."

Wink rounded the horse and undid the mess Joe had made.

With his neck stretched upward, Joe seemed to be listening to something. "Them slavers left the chillun that fell to the side."

Wink didn't want to hear another sad story. He wanted to see Sonny's smile. To touch the tiny hands and toes. Rub his woolly head and make him sneeze.

"I lost Fanny." Joe wandered out of the carriage house. "And her seven months gone wid our second one. Lost my boy ..."

Wink left Joe drifting in the dark, presumably going to his cabin, and drove the wagon to the sick house where they loaded Billy's coffin in the back. The white preacher sat beside him as they headed for the graveyard, followed by the slaves carrying torches.

Puddin began to sing a mournful song. Mamba joined in and by the time they reached the public road, everybody sang with such sorrow the darkness sighed. From the public road they took the wagon path into the woods to the graveyard. In the distance behind them rode the master on Gideon. Most slaves paid no attention to him, but Wink did. He was aware that the man carried a shotgun.

The white preacher and Iverson funeralized Billy, but Wink heard not a word they spoke. Anner wept loudly, lashed her shawl, and fell on the ground, but Wink hardly noticed. He listened to

Puddin's humming, and when the music picked up to become song, he could tell her voice from all the others.

When Puddin grabbed a handful of sand and tossed it on the coffin, she held the bright red scarf he had given her to her nose and stifled her sobs. Tears came to his own eyes. He loved her more than ever. He needed her. Sonny needed her. She would accept their having no children if they had Sonny.

Mamba began to clap her hands and step time with "Walking Egypt." Other mourners did likewise. Cheerful songs followed, as if death had been conquered. Wink had his doubts. And he felt sure Billy would have felt the same.

CHAPTER 32

THE EARTH MOVES

MARCH 1858

Mooey woke up to the earth spirit drumming on her back as she lay in her hideout. She had grown used to the heavy darkness, gritty dirt, and close roots. She didn't dare open the hideout door. It seemed a long time until calm returned, and even then she pushed open the door nervously. In the full light of afternoon, the damp smell of the ground's underside reached into the air.

In the slave graveyard was a fresh and empty hole. Somebody in the quarters had died. In an instant she realized she had to get away before sundown, before the drove of people came with their torches. And she dared not take the trace along the side of the field in daylight.

Though the way was longer, she kept in the cover of the woods as she headed for the plantation. She rounded the pasture, the barns, and came up on the far side of the quarters. From one of her trees she looked down on the sick house where people milled about. The dead person was there, in the sick house. She began to single out people she knew as a way of putting her mind to rest about who had died. Surely not Lacy, but what if it was Auntie? Tears arose at the possibility.

In the yard at the big house stood a black carriage with enough shine to blind the birds. The master talked with other white people, and by watching, Mooey understood that the strangers were not arriving but leaving. She climbed higher and had hardly settled on a branch when she saw the master had left the yard and was now hastening back to the carriage with a bundle in his arms. This would have been of little interest except that he came from the direction of the quarters. Mooey stretched her head and strained her eyes as the bundle went into the carriage.

Though it was a still day, a sudden wind brushed her like a wiry currycomb, as if notifying her to be on her guard. Without understanding why, she felt trembly. She shimmied down the tree and, staying to the woods but within view of the yard, ran with the carriage down the carriageway. Its disappearance on the causeway worried her.

She returned to the woods near the quarters and waited, though she knew not what for. Dark descended as a group of field hands gathered and drifted in and out of the sick house. By turns, she located Lacy, Auntie, Magic, the cook, the stableman, and River. The seamstress. Ivy led the crowd. Nobody seemed amiss. The dead person was a mystery.

From the safety of a high limb she regarded the funeral train leaving the yard. Once the last torchlight disappeared from sight, she climbed down and sneaked into the quarters, which were practically deserted. A grain of hope stirred that she might find a supper for herself. Before she could eat, she had to see Sunny.

Outside the chillun house she paused and felt a stillness deep enough to be safe. In the darkness, she slipped inside but could hardly see the form of the cradle. The room was strangely dull without any babies or children. Even the cot where Mammy slept was empty. With most everybody at the funeral, Mooey had to wonder who was keeping the babies and children. At the cradle, her hand swept about the inside and felt only coarse cloth. She pulled everything out, down to the wood bottom.

Mooey supposed he was in another cabin and slipped from one to another and peeked through holes in the planks whenever possible. An occasional cot was occupied by a sleeping field hand. At Ivy's cabin, few holes were big enough to allow a good look inside. The door swung so easily that instead of opening a cranny it gave way full tilt. Mooey stumbled inside, crouched, and waited.

A field hand, not Mammy nor Ivy's wife, lay dozing on one of the cots, the curtain tied back. Babies slept in baskets and those of crawling age on pallets. Mooey looked into each basket, and if she was unsure about whether it was Sonny, she carried it to the street where she could see better. She searched the two cots in the loft, but he was nowhere to be found. The woman minding the children rested peacefully as if no baby was missing.

Mooey, getting more sorrowful by the moment, scoured the other quarters.

Had she actually seen the master take a bundle the size of a baby to the carriage? Perhaps it had been a goat or a dog or a basket of collards. She prowled the yard in the dark trying to recognize a certainty from the turmoil in her head. Could the bundle have been taken into the big house when she wasn't looking? Her worry grew. No black children stayed in the big house. In her nervousness she searched highly unlikely places—under the steps and on the portico. She looked high and low in the yard and lots, the outbuildings, and stables.

The ground grumbled in her soles, and she had to leave the whereabouts of Sunny for another time. Fearful tears twinged her eyes. Torchlights like a flow of gold approached the plantation by way of the trace beside the field. She took to the woods and waited, undecided about what to do. She couldn't make herself return to her hideout without looking once again at the baskets. She crept back and watched as mothers went in Ivy's door and came out with babies or children in their arms. Mammy didn't fetch Sunny. Had he been put in the care of somebody else? Doors closed. Torches went out. Darkness returned.

Mooey sneaked back to Ivy's cabin and sidled inside. There was no baby. Back at Mammy's cabin, the usual chillun house, Sunny's cradle remained empty, and Mammy slept as if nothing was wrong. Another woman rustled heavily in one of the other cots. Mooey looked under the cots, chairs, and table. The need to see her baby was so great she sat on the hearth where she had held him many times. She couldn't leave. Not without seeing Sunny. Had one of the mothers taken him to a different cabin? Was the big-breasted woman suckling him at her place?

The strange woman twisted and turned in the darkness. Mooey felt clouds enter her breath; danger crept into her clothes. She slipped outside to the safety of her tree. The torches of the funeral mourners blazed a glowing trail from the pasture toward the quarters. Her heart seemed solid, as if its thumping had stopped. With no other place to go, she headed to her hideout.

In the graveyard, the smell of people lingered. Footprints tousled the sand. The hole had been filled and on top were shadows she discovered to be seashells, pieces of earthenware, beads. She picked up a shard that glistened in the faint light of the moon. She stared at it long enough to understand that the bundle had been her baby. The master had put Sunny in the carriage.

Mooey dropped to her knees beside the new grave. She couldn't help the convulsion that threw her off balance. Her mouth yawned open for air. Her eyes rolled back. Her baby was gone. Breath twisted the rundles of her throat and strained her tongue. She fell to the ground and made no effort to control her throat spirit, which possessed her more powerfully than ever before. At the same time it landed a jolt in her head. Instinctively she put her hands on her ears, and the shock in her head drifted away. She had come to believe that her throat spirit controlled the sensation in her head, but even as the spirit wrestled with her lips, she had stopped the sensation in her head by covering her ears. She removed her hands and it returned. Her throat made something that only her ears could sense. In the midst of her sorrow, she realized her ears worked to some purpose.

But what did it matter? Her Sunny was gone. Even if the horrific commotion was hers, she didn't care. Her throat said her pain with enough force to frighten the stars. She kicked the ground until dirt sprayed over her. Her arms flailed. She covered herself with fresh dirt. A cry spiraled from her for as long as she had breath.

In a sudden calm she looked at the stars and realized how dreadfully tired she was. She would just as soon turn into a star this night. She closed her eyes. Something like a bug kept touching her back. Even the ground spirit felt weary. If a wild cat approached, she didn't care. She lay perfectly still, willing to be trapped by either an animal or man.

Nobody came but the ground kept whispering. She rolled over and placed her cheek to the dirt. Nothing. Then another signal. She stretched out her arms and legs to sense a direction. She forced her hand under the new dirt. Her body shook with misgivings. Something under there was moving.

Tired as she was, Mooey scooped dirt from the grave with her hands. When the spirit of the underground settled to its powerful darkness, she waited for a flinch. It came, and she dug again. Sunlight threaded through the treetops, and she was still digging.

CHAPTER 33

THE SOUND OF GRIEF

MARCH 1858

Dawn was still hours away when Wink, aroused by a noise, sat up in his cot and listened. He could hear first one then another horse whinny and scrub the stalls. He lay back motionless, waiting, listening. His mother had so feared haints she wore a conjure bag around her neck for protection from evil spirits. It was hanging on his doorknob, and he didn't discount its magic. Billy's lonely life had slipped away quickly, but that didn't mean his spirit had made its departure. Many a person believed that dying lasted for five years during which time the spirit was present to help or harm those still alive. Night was a natural haunt for the discontented dead. The stars gave forth just light enough to suggest the mystery of domains beyond what the eye could see.

After a few moments, another savage outcry chilled the night. Wink could identify every neigh and bray on the plantation, but none of them sounded like this. The utterance was too unearthly to be the screech of an owl or the cry of a wild dog. Wink shivered. Many a dying man heard the wheels of the chariot coming for him. He jumped out of his cot and into his trousers, wrapped in his coat, and went outside.

When it came to the horses, whether it was a spook or thief, he protected them. He turned up the flame of the oil lantern and slipped into the stables, his eyes and ears alert. The horses blew their noses and snorted. Several pawed the floor. Gideon flicked his head. "Ho, boy ... ho. Easy does it."

"Whoa now, Lad. Freckles ... easy," he said, looking into the stalls as he walked the central passageway calling them by name. "What be disturbing my horses?" He soothed them with a quiet voice, but his heart beat loudly. He stroked their manes, scratched their ears, nuzzled their muzzles, giving extra attention to Gideon, whose wild eyes flashed in the lantern light. "Everything be all right, boy. Now settle yourself." No horses were missing. He held the lantern up. Nothing. He searched every stall and surveyed the back of the stables. Except for the animals' nervousness, nothing seemed amiss. He sat down in a batch of hay beside the stable's arched opening, watched, and waited.

A door squeaked open and shut. A clink of metal, latch of a key. A light traveled across the yard. As he closed in on it, the torch lit up Flurry. "You minding the smokehouse?" he said, for somebody tended the embers all hours when meat was curing.

"What you doing out here at dis hour?" Flurry held her torch toward Wink and pulled her headscarf up.

"You hear a noise out here?" Wink said.

Flurry cocked her head and listened. "I reckon it be a shivering owl." She turned her back to a breeze that came out of the darkness. "Farley says some poor whites been prowling round, stealing hams and such."

"Iffen this be poor whites, they going to scare the niggers off the place."

"Mind you don't git yourself stole." Flurry tightened her wrap, turned, and continued toward the quarters. Rumors spread occasionally about shady-dealing traders spotted at this or that crossroads. It was said they came through and stole slaves, took them to places like Alabama and Mississippi.

The following morning, Farley said to Wink, "Dat musta been a helluva wild cat we heard last night."

Wink realized that Flurry's big mouth had told Farley of their nighttime meeting. "Got the horses in a frantic."

"Flurry's scaring the niggers. Says Billy's haint done got in the hogs. Got them to squealing sudden like in the night."

"Wasn't nothing I ever heard in my born days," said Wink.

"I heard a hunting horn once. Them things sounds about as bad as Mooey."

"Mooey?" Wink hadn't thought of her. "It wasn't no human sound."

"Mooey ain't but half human herself." Farley said.

Wink's brown spit came out like derision. "She ain't the onliest one missing some kindling."

With a voice of superiority, as if he was the final authority, Farley said, "She don't have the presence of mind to go anywheres. Iffen she be alive, she's hiding in the trees. She specks the Massuh forgets about her."

The unexplained cry had ripened night, and, like an old pear, rotted to worse the next day when Wink went to the well for water. Rio told him the master had sold his baby boy. Sold Sonny to one of the men in the black carriage.

Wink was so shocked he was unable to speak and Rio wasn't much for talk. The pulley chain gave off a miserable squeak. Only once before had Wink felt so aggrieved—when his mother was sold. The misery of her goodbye had made his mumps all the worse, and he had been sick for a week. When she came to the sick house to say goodbye, the trader dragged her away, but he heard her say, "Be good, Wink, and take care of Granny." His grandmother had died several months later, so he didn't think he'd taken very good care of her.

The water he poured into his bucket splashed into his brogans. Rio said something about their liquor, but Wink didn't pay attention. He returned to his stables. That he wouldn't have a son after all hurt almost as much as thinking of Sonny, alone with nobody to watch out for him. He had failed Lovey. He hadn't been able to take care of the baby as he had promised. In spite of the quantity of liquor he drank, he couldn't keep away the tears.

In the stables he groomed Tootie and wiped his nose on his sleeve. A numb-mindedness oversaw his hands as he saddled the horse and took to the pasture. The sun's glow met the grassland's winter stubble with genial warmth. He nudged Tootie to a gallop to get raw air into his face, nose, and lungs. Deep breaths. Sonny. Billy. Lovey, Mooey. He spurred Tootie to a rack run. As far from the plantation grounds as he could get. The horse's hoofs splayed new grass poking shoots above the ground. Tootie's panting reeled him in from the escape he had needed in order to compose himself. He gave her loose rein to allow her to freely gallop. They rode to the far pasture and took a path into the sparse growth of trees and scrubs.

If there was one thing he could count on, it was a future of more losses. Why had he let himself ease into something akin to contentment? As if every ordinary day prescribed the next? He had to have a hard head. His hopes had to level with the bottom of the Beaufort River—things he had forgotten in the daily run of minding the horses.

What could he have done differently had he known old man Goodwyn was going to get rid of the baby? He could have stolen the boy ... for which he'd need the cooperation, if not help, of people in the quarters. Lovey had been no different. He couldn't save them alone. And who could he count on to help? His fellow negros feared the block with such passion they lived like chickens in a cage, waiting for somebody else to get the hatchet. He hated them all. But he was no better. Most of all he hated himself for his own cowardice. If he was a man of courage, he'd shoot Goodwyn and take the lynching. But that wouldn't help Sonny. A force of tears stung his throat. He couldn't think about the baby's situation ... the baby's fate.

Wink wanted to believe, as the others did, in God's justice, that one day the black man would see the whites in chains. But on days like this, only Goodwyn's justice mattered. The man could squeeze every Westfall negro into a dried pit and that would be justice.

He pulled from his pocket the stub of a cigar and chewed on it. Fact was, Goodwyn got rid of a slave faster than a horse. Tootie shook her head harness and took a deep sigh. "You know dat's true," said Wink. Tootie's gentle snort sympathized. "Bout time old man Goodwyn needs cash for something he can't afford, he be looking at his niggers again." Wink spit. His heart pumped mean blood. His head grew hard. Whatever he could do to damage Goodwyn he'd do, as long as he didn't destroy himself. At the same time, he knew he couldn't harm the horses. Tootie quickened to a gallop. Wink hardly noticed as his horse took them back to the stables.

* * *

The past hours had pelted Mooey with anxiety. A new grave, the funeral that followed, and the fear that somebody she loved had died. A bundle the size of a baby. Gone with the master's visitors. Her search for Sonny and not finding him. Her lost Sonny.

Just when she wanted to lose herself, the ground spirit had summoned her as she lay on the fresh dirt of the grave. A faint scrape from somewhere below. The endless nightmare had retreated. Mooey answered the ground spirit and had begun to dig.

She paused to watch as River appeared. He crouched beside the hole she was digging in the new grave. He gestured in a way that seemed important to him, but the images that came to her were confusing. When he motioned her to get out of the hole, it was clear to her but she ignored him. She tried to make him understand that something spoke to her from underneath the earth.

Whatever the cause, a bad humor got ahold of him. As he left, his footsteps raised torment on the ground.

Once Mooey felt the coffin, she pushed aside dirt and lay on it. It took a few minutes, but she felt movement against the wood on the opposite side. At first she tried to haul out the coffin, but it was too heavy and too lodged into the hole. To loosen the lid, she used River's hammer and prized up the corner. As she dragged off the lid she recognized the butler.

His eyes flinched with the light. He coughed. His fingernails bled. His lips twitched.

Mooey stepped into the coffin beside him and, after several tries, succeeded in hoisting him out of the grave and onto the pile of dirt. He swayed, threatening to roll back into the hole. She used her head to shove him over far enough that she could climb out.

She wiped his face with her underskirt and held his hand in case he was afraid or lonely. She couldn't sit there all day holding his hand, so she brought him water, which he drank but sloppily. With his full weight on her blanket, she dragged him down the path toward the plantation. From time to time the burden burned into her arms and shoulders and she rested. She left him for a while to fetch more drinking water, for he trembled to a horrible excess. Darkness descended.

Their approach to the plantation put them on the far side from the quarters. Instead of circling the outbuildings to get to the quarters, she decided to take her chances and cut across the yard. Gradually candlelights faded from around the cabin doors and windows. Lamplights disappeared from the big house windows. With careful deliberation, she dragged the man across packed dirt but stopped when the ground quivered. She lay beside the butler and waited. A light brightened the windows of Early's cabin. Because they were exposed in the open yard, she couldn't wait for any length of time. When the light disappeared, she crawled the rest of the way, dragging the butler as best she could.

Though it seemed unkind, she wrenched her blanket from under him at River's door. The butler didn't know, and she couldn't tell him, that the blanket meant the difference between her resting and shivering, sleeping and staying awake. Before skittering away, she knocked on the door. From a distance she watched until somebody opened the door.

* * *

A dreadful but helpless panic surged into Wink's heartbeat and he awoke in terror. As he became aware of his cot and room, the gray clutches of the dream came back to him. He'd accidentally dropped Sonny into the creek. The harder he tried to reach the baby, the swifter the water, and Sonny had been sucked into the tide and had disappeared.

He sighed. Since he'd let his fire go out, he had no hot water for tea. He stirred molasses into water and drank, which helped to quiet the devils in his head.

Anner barged into his shanty. "Massuh says to straighten for Dr. Drayton."

"Hold up, baby. Don't mess wid me yet." Wink's vision scattered and he closed his eyes. "I needs a dram to loosen my nerves." He poked his hand into a barrel, drew out a bottle, and took a drink.

"Billy needs a doctor powerful bad."

"Billy? Is you gone plumb senseless?" He took another drink.

"Billy's in the sick house." Anner turned in a circle.

"So who did we bury in the graveyard last night?" He replaced his bottle.

"People is saying it be witchcraft."

Wink felt better as he put on his coat. "Anybody called you plat-eye yet?"

Anner slapped Wink so hard he stumbled backward. He hesitated. If he responded in kind, he might get mojo in his shoes. He pushed her aside and left. A slap in the face was reason enough for him to have nothing more to do with her. Even Anner had to know that. By the time he reached the sick house, he no longer resented the slap. In fact, he was glad.

Because it was Sunday and the hands weren't in the fields, several people watched as Mamba tended what appeared to be Billy, lying on the cot. Wink stared for several minutes. Even with his eyes wide open, he couldn't get his mouth shut. He had drunk plenty of liquor the previous night and maybe it had been bad—so bad his brain had lost what sense he once had.

People in the room were talking about it being Billy. Wink had to wonder about witchcraft.

"Sounded like kingdom come in the middle of the night."

Iverson said, "I heard dat myself. Scared the chillun near bout to death."

"Billy didn't make dat racket, sick as he was."

"Who made it then?"

"It was the devil."

"Lord a-mercy!" "Jesus, help us!" "Come after Billy?"

Several field hands shoved past Wink and into the room. Mamba waved them outside. "Give this man some peace ... all of you." She shooed most of them out.

Wink listened long enough to realize he'd better get on the road for the doctor. Not that he expected either his hurrying or the doctor to do Billy any good. The man needed powerful medicine if not a miracle, and the white doctor had already taken his best shot. He saddled up Nicky and went for Dr. Drayton.

When Billy died the second time, Wink and several others took his body back to the graveyard where the master leaned against a big headstone in the white graveyard and watched. They lowered Billy into the coffin already in the ground. Spirits attending this burial offered only a message of silence, and that in exceeding measure. In the sky above them, stars stuck to tight spots. Without a breeze, bushes lodged under mute trees. Only the forlorn scraping of the shovels. Sand got into Wink's shoes. He tasted it in his mouth. He felt it in his blood. Billy's second burial seemed all the worse for the loneliness.

They tamped down the last clumps of dirt. The stillness was broken by the jingling of metal as Skittles shook her head harness. The sound echoed into the woods. Her ears flicked. As they finished and headed to the wagon, Wink looked up at the moon through the branches of a hickory tree where a shadow perched, bigger than a coon. It seemed to watch him.

"Dat a coon up yonder?" He said as he pointed toward it.

The other men couldn't see it.

Wink stared at the branch, but the shadow had disappeared. He climbed on the wagon seat and clucked to Skittles. His mother's conjure bag, which he wore around his neck, felt hot to his touch.

Upon returning to Westfall, he unhitched the mule and stored the wagon in the carriage house and went to the kitchen. The door was locked. He rounded to Puddin's quarter, knocked, and waited.

A sense of desolation bore down on him. Death was so near he could feel the rigor in his own joints. One day Billy had been fighting fit, and the next he was in the ground. And his hard-won escape from the grave had only been sweat and pain to no account. Didn't matter how strong a body or how ferocious the fight—death won, and Wink might be the next to go. He hoped his luck would last until he could win Puddin.

On the other side of the door, the latch scratched its casing. "What you doing, Wink?" Puddin stood in the narrow opening.

"I just wants to see you is safe in your cabin."

"Is there some reason I wouldn't be?"

"You never knows, wid the haints out on account of Billy," Wink said. The word "haints" brought on a cold breath, and he looked over his shoulder.

"You wants me to walk wid you to your quarter?" Puddin said.

"Naa. I be going." But he didn't.

"I'm not going to open this door for you." Puddin looked him in the eye.

"Then come out here wid me." He reached in and pulled her outside and into his arms. He kissed her neck and ear and whispered, "You the bestest woman I ever knowed."

"I'm not going to be your woman, Wink."

"What's I got to do?" He looked into her face but she glanced down. "You likes me a little?" Wink said.

"A little."

"You don't like these rough hands?" He held one up, the skin thick as alligator hide.

"I seed worse."

"This tooth." He pointed to a chipped front tooth. "You don't like this?"

"Don't care a scrap about that."

"I smells like the horses."

"That don't bother me."

"I don't be well-muscled?'

"You well enough."

"Then what be the reason?"

She backed off. "I done got one owner. What I want wid another one?"

Wink tugged her closer. "Baby, don't say that. Don't stand me wid Old Man Goodwyn!"

"Goodwyn's got rights to me. Got rights to every woman in the quarters. And their chillun. You know any chillun he ain't claimed?"

Wink thought of Sonny, which brought on a need for a drink. Being senseless and drunk had its advantages. He loosened his hold on Puddin, ready to find his bottle.

She pulled him closer, tipped her lips up and nibbled his chin. A misery had gotten into Wink's head, and he wanted to go to his quarter. She reached up, enfolded his neck, and kissed him. "You is a fine man, Wink. And iffen I was a free nigger, you'd be my man."

Wink rallied. He nuzzled her cheek and returned her kisses. He was convinced she had just agreed to marry him, but he didn't have the courage to tell her they would have no children.

CHAPTER 34

WHISKEY IN A SEED SACK

APRIL 1858

Wink had to either stop talking with Rio or quit trying to groom Puff. The mare stamped and swished her tail, obviously bothered by Rio's presence. Wink picked up his brushes and ambled over to Nicky's stall. "It's too risky, what wid the carpetbags and trunks… wid womenfolks to boot." Wink's trip to the Beaufort wharf the following day to fetch the master's brother and his family for a visit held promise for bringing back whiskey they needed. "I be sitting on boxes myself."

Rio brought the lantern and hung it on the hook. "Tell the massuh you picking up a sack of seed. Put the cask in the sack wid the seed."

Wink looked over Nicky's flank. "And when Massuh says, 'What's a nigger want wid a whole sackful of seed?' what's I going to say?"

"Say you selling seed to the niggers for their garden."

"Massuh's going to smell a rat." Wink could already see Goodwyn's look of disbelief.

"Dat's going to be you farting."

"Damn right. He be smelling shit in my pants." Wink went outside to spit tobacco and returned. "And next thing we know, Massuh be asking Iverson how his peas growing from them seeds he bought from Wink." Nicky twitched his ears. "Don't you be listening to us talking," Wink said to the horse's muzzle.

"We needs to figure out a way to make regular runs." Rio, who had been leaning against the stall, shuffled out into the common passageway.

"I knows we need liquor. I'm just saying iffen I hides a cask in the coach, somebody's going to uncover it, what wid unloading them white folks and God knows how many carpetbags up there at the portico."

"Them peoples going to stay wid Massuh till after Easter, sure as hell," said Rio.

"You got dat right. How much hooch is left from Saturday?"

"Less than half a cask."

"Shit! Limbo can sell that much right here on Westfall."

The following morning, the ferry delivered Wink to Beaufort with time to spare before the steamer arrived from Charleston. He headed to the leather shop and summoned Artis to the street and onward to a nearby alley. Artis didn't say it was impossible when Wink asked if casks of liquor could be packed into sacks of seed or feed and sent across the river on the ferry.

"You going to have to pay for the sacks and seed." Artis was a white man, but his hands looked like those of an Indian from working with hides.

"Yessuh. That's what I be figuring. And I'se going to get five-gallon casks myself." Wink figured he could count on Rio for casks.

"Better make dat four-gallon."

"Five gallon too big for a hundred pound bag?" Wink trusted Artis's opinion, perhaps because he smelled of leather.

"That bag's going to git so heavy it'll take two full-bodied men to load it." Artis, who was short and stocky, could probably lift more than Wink. "Is Morgan going to take it on widout somebody paying fare?"

"Iffen you deliver it to the ferry, I'se going to pay when I picks it up over on Ladies Island," said Wink, though he knew he couldn't pick up the sacks on their arrival. "This be a heap easier." His head raced with ideas. He needed Morgan's man Caleb to help off-load the sacks and store them until Wink could fetch them.

Wink didn't buy whiskey, but he had what he wanted—encouragement from Artis to build a regular delivery by way of the ferry.

Wink met the Gibbs family at the wharf and took them to Westfall. Iverson, the new butler, met them at the front door. The absence of Billy had become a sorrow Wink had grown used to, something like a wart or a sty he hardly noticed as he helped unload the trunks and carpetbags.

With guests in the big house, Wink had hardly finished one task when he was required for another—driving for outings, hitching up the cart for the children, saddling up for the master and his brother.

On Good Friday, Wink, along with Rio, delivered the master, his guests, and servants to Coffin Point Landing where the families cast off in a sloop for Hunting Island and a picnic. Wink and Rio remained behind to tend the horses until their return. After watering the animals, Wink sat on the banks of the Sound and whittled on a wood block that hadn't yet taken the form of a horse. Rio searched the woods and found a straight sapling. With a hook, line, and sinker he had brought, he rigged a fishing pole. Wink helped him catch sand crabs for bait. When Rio pulled in a bream, Wink said, "Another hundred pounds and you'll have enough for tomorrow night."

"You ever buy whiskey at the boarding house?" Rio tied the fish on a line and dropped it back in the water.

"Only when I be powerful thirsty and stone dry."

"Our bestest customers going to be bad out of heart iffen I show up widout a drop tomorrow night."

"They going to be in worser shape iffen they hafta pay for boarding house liquor."

"You bring specie?" Rio pulled a roll from his trousers.

"You going to buy from the boarding house?"

"No. You is." As Rio handed over the money, Wink saw it was enough for silk to make a dress, which Wink would have liked to get for Puddin.

"Even iffen I had this much, I wouldn't spend it on boarding house whiskey." He fingered the bills in his hand.

"Then buy it for me." Rio threw the hook back in the hole where he'd caught the bream.

"Buy your own hooch." Wink stuck the money in Rio's pocket and continued to whittle but felt the heat of Rio's eyes. He knew as well as Rio that straightforward devilment was a higher risk than devilment hidden within a tangle of confusion.

Wink stood up and peed in the water. "What's I going to get dis hooch in?"

Rio brought a crock from the driver's seat.

Wink unhitched Tootie, took the crock, and headed for the boarding house. The fact that Rio would go to such lengths to keep their customers happy impressed Wink almost as much as the amount of money his friend had. At the back door of the boarding house, Wink protested the high price and tried to negotiate, but little good it did. They were charging him more than white people, but he had two choices—either pay their price or leave empty-handed. Riding back to Coffin Point with the whiskey, he swallowed his anger and got serious about setting up a more reliable system for getting their supply.

His plan to have the whiskey ferried across in feed bags, though rife with danger and pitholes, was better than no plan. But could he depend on Artis to hide the hooch well enough so that it wouldn't be detected? He figured on bags of oats rather than seed, for the horses would eat the grain and wouldn't answer the master's questions. Would Artis deliver the bags to the ferry? Could they keep the plot secret? The answer was "maybe," and a shaky one at that.

For better or worse, Wink considered the next step—Thor's father Caleb, who worked for the ferry owner. Could Wink talk him into storing the bags in the ferry house stables until Wink picked them up? Because of his efforts the previous December to help save the ferry during the stormy crossing—efforts for which he'd almost paid with his life—Wink stood good with the ferry owner. He hoped to use this to advantage.

By the time he returned with the whiskey, Rio had caught twenty-two fish and had eaten half the lunch Puddin had packed for them. Wink sat on a log and looked into the bucket at loaf bread and bacon, as well as a fried plum pie.

"You hear about the Riverben boy what got killed in the cotton screw?" Wink's intelligence came from negros at the boarding house kitchen.

"Jervy killed him. It was the Africa woman's boy." Rio skidded his bait across the water. "Old Missus been harking on dat boy for the longest time."

"What'd he do?"

"Old Missus said he be sassing her."

"He talk saucy?"

"Couldn't hardly talk a-tall. Half the time I couldn't catch his meaning."

"Them Riverben niggers ought to burn down the big house." Wink ate his pie slowly. He could almost smell Puddin's hands on the dough.

Rio pulled in his bait and spit on it, threw it back out. "A nigger gets strung up for dat." A bream hit the line but when Rio jerked it, the fish fell away. "And knowing Jervy, it might be one of the chillun that he hangs."

"Make it look like a mishap. Pour oil on the kitchen roof and when a windstorm come along blowing into the big house, set the kitchen afire." Wink packed the cloth back in the empty bucket.

"Niggers is too scared to do something like dat."

In Wink's heart, he knew when something went wrong at the big house, some unlucky negro always paid. One would have to be bold and stupid to try such a trick. The safest way to damage Goodwyn was to aim at his cash box. Broken equipment. Mangled crops. Limbo didn't accidentally dig up good cotton seedlings. Wink castigated himself for not being more vigorous in destroying property, but he couldn't bring himself to hurt the horses.

Easter Sunday the master and his guests went to the village church and returned with the preacher. The household servants put on the fancy linens and set out a feast Puddin had cooked.

In the back lot, Wink stood around the fire pit with other slaves as Mamba cooked the lamb the master had provided for their dinner.

"Claude, go git more wood for the fire," said Mamba, but Claude was intent on fingering his banjo strings to play a chord he had already played many times. "Well, watch over dis meat til I gets back." Mamba headed off to the woods.

Claude drank and played his banjo. The meat looked crispy on the bottom side and Mamba hadn't returned. "Claude, is you in charge of this here meat?" Wink said.

Claude stood and stretched. "I'se going to git some hooch from Limbo."

"Better turn this here meat afore it burns."

"Yessuh. Go right ahead. I be back in a minute." He walked toward the quarters.

When the meat was cooked, Mamba had to raise Cain to get Claude to help serve up the food while the slaves stood by with their plates. Upon tasting the meat, Wink noticed with disappointment that Mamba and Claude's barbecue was a poor substitute for Iverson's.

While they sat about the back yard eating, a scuffle broke out at the woodshed between Rio and Thor. They rammed into each other and tusseled. Rio knocked back Thor and tried to shake him off, but Thor grabbed him from behind and the two of them slammed into a post, swirled, and collided with the grindstone, which fell to the ground with them.

"Ooouuch!" Thor moaned.

Rio got up. Thor's foot was pinned under the grindstone.

Wink hustled over to help Rio raise the grindstone far enough that Thor could free his foot. It was so scratched and bleeding Thor needed help getting to his feet. He sat on a barrel. "I don't need none of dat," he said to Mamba, who appeared with a pan of water to wash it.

"You best let Mamba take charge of dat foot," said Wink, but Thor shook his head. "Help me to my cot," he said.

In the afternoon, Farley rounded up the slaves and, in spite of their protests, herded them to the open area beyond the corncrib for Reverend Chaffee's Easter sermon. Several of the men claimed Thor had hurt himself to get out of the Reverend's sermon. Wink sat on an upturned water bucket behind most of the people, ready to waste an hour or two while the preacher urged them to serve the master faithfully.

To Wink's surprise, he began to pay notice, for the white man's Jesus showed signs of changing color. The Reverend said that Jesus came to people of all color to give them an idea of how God wanted them to live. But because God was greater than any human being, His will couldn't be explained by any one man or any one people.

Most of the hands sitting in the yard yawned, leaned on their neighbor, drew pictures in the dirt, or in other ways ignored the sermon, except Iverson, who sat, head bowed and motionless as if he latched on to every word.

The preacher finished, and instead of making tracks for the big house, he paused, shook hands with Iverson, and wandered among the slaves. Wink overheard him ask about the "slave girl that escaped, the one who couldn't talk." Several people answered with what had become a suspicion in the quarters, that Mooey was either dead or had been stolen by a trader.

Afterward as they milled about the street, flocking together at doorways, it turned out a couple of people besides Wink had noticed the preacher's mention of Mooey.

"What you reckon dat man'ud do iffen he run into Mooey?"

"He'd bring her back here, iffen he could catch her," said Mamba.

"You think he's ever seen Mooey here?" said Wink.

"Some field hands never seen her here."

Mamba laughed. "Dat preacher couldn't catch her."

"Naaa, she'd put such a scare in the man, he be the one running."

"Cold as it was when Mooey left, she be shore to catch him," said Wink.

Because of the fight and Thor's injury, the master punished Rio by sending him to work in the fields during off hours, and as it turned out, Wink had no immediate need to replenish their liquor supply, except for what Limbo could sell. On Saturdays, Rio was digging up grass in the corn instead of going to the village with their whiskey.

Upon hearing the news that the packet boat had failed to arrive in Beaufort for two days, Wink had to wonder how the visiting Gibbs family would return to Charleston. The answer came when the master sent him for a cousin's coach and directed Wink to make ready to drive the family to Charleston.

Since Wink would likely load and unload the Gibbs's hampers himself, he took a chance and stashed an empty cask under the coach seat. No sooner did he have it in the box when Kedzie entered the carriage house. He quickly closed the lid and jumped down from the seat. She handed him a letter to deliver to an address in Charleston for the mistress.

One look at it and he scratched under his itchy hat. Why didn't Mistress Goodwyn simply ask him to post the letter in the village? A close look and he recognized the name on the envelope, but he could only read simple words and thought he must be mistaken. "Deliver it to who?"

"Reverend DeMere," Kedzie said softly, as if it was a secret.

Wink almost swallowed his chew.

"He lives on Beaufain Street." Kedzie pointed her finger and showed him the word. "But she don't know the number."

The mistress knew this man, for Wink had seen them together in Beaufort the previous December. The woman was playing with fire. Should the master find out his wife communicated with an abolitionist, he'd raise revolution. Whatever the reason for the mistress to go behind the master's back to send this letter, it could only mean trouble. Maybe Kedzie didn't see the danger. "How you know I won't take this straight to the massuh?"

Kedzie's eyes glistened fearfully. "You going to take it to Massuh?"

Wink let her know he might. Why should he put himself at risk of the master's wrath on account of the mistress?

The forlorn look on Kedzie's face muddled his thinking. She wasn't worried about the mistress. Had she written the letter? Could Kedzie write? He shouldn't ask. He didn't want to know.

When she as much as admitted it was a messy business, Wink knew the story behind this letter best be left to Kedzie. It was as dangerous as a rattlesnake, but he put it in his hat.

Getting off the island and on the main took the better part of a day, but Wink made good time in spite of holes in the road and dustsheets of wind that masked his face and blinded him. On the following day, rain impeded their travel. Thunder frightened the horses. They found it hard pulling in the muddy road.

In Charleston, Wink delivered the Gibbs family to the railroad station and, to his surprise, Master Gibbs gave him two bits. He pocketed the money and found Beaufain Street. From one kitchen to another he asked about Reverend DeMere until a cook explained which house was his. "He live wid the solitary lady in the tabby house wid a porch and a green swing." Nobody answered the knock at the back door. There was no fire in the kitchen. Wink slid the letter underneath the back door.

Upon arriving back in Beaufort, he called on Artis at the leather shop. Wink bought two casks of whiskey, which they loaded in the alley where there was enough privacy to talk. Would Artis be disposed to buy a sack of oats, open it, insert a cask of whiskey, and sew it back up? For certain, Wink expected to pay. Naturally, beforehand. How much did a sack of oats cost? Send it of a Monday? Artis was of agreeable mind, at a cost.

Looking to buy something for Puddin, Wink went to a store that sold to negros. The sign outside over the door proclaimed one word, but it wasn't "negro" for Wink could read that one. The building had a narrow door, no windows, and was about big enough to house a coach. Inside, a pockmarked man leaned on a wooden counter. He asked Wink where he was from, what he was doing in Beaufort, where he'd bought his hat, so much conversation Wink grew impatient to put some distance between them, but the jewelry lying on the counter caught his eye. Most of it cost more than he had, but he spotted a ring that looked like the rim of a button, a pearly button. It took all the money he had left, but he was glad to have enough to buy it.

He left and headed to the ferry landing at Carteret Street. Though he was happy about the ring, he worried about his whiskey business. A shipment from Artis could end up costing them as much as boarding house liquor.

Thor's foot got worse following the fight. It turned red and purple and swelled so the master sent Wink for Dr. Drayton. He said Thor wouldn't live if the foot didn't come off. Wink had no heart for holding down Thor while the doctor cut off his foot, but Iverson couldn't do it alone.

Wink fortified himself with whiskey. He and Iverson together tussled with Thor, who jumped out of bed and fell on the floor when he saw the doctor's surgical knife. They roped him to the cot and the two of them, along with horse doses of opium, succeeded in keeping him flat enough for the doctor to perform surgery. Wink took opium himself when Dr. Drayton wasn't looking, which went a long way in easing the misery of smelling blood and listening to Thor's bellows. By the time the surgery ended, Wink had so indulged in his personal whiskey supply there was none left.

Wink's liquor business had stalled with Rio's problems with the master, which grew more intense when Thor's foot came off. Everybody in the quarters sneaked a look at Rio when he returned to his cabin with nubby hair and a bleeding scalp. The master had ordered and Farley had delivered a haircut, but the dogs could have chewed it off to better effect.

Limbo laughed like he was having a fit, said Rio's head looked like a cooter shell. Claude said Rio's ears got bigger, so big he could hear a spider climb the wall. Mamba said Samson had done lost his power. Flurry tried to rub her palm over his noggin, but Rio brushed her away. He acted as if he didn't know people were teasing him.

Several days later, Wink noticed that somebody had taken the scissors to Rio's hair. It was more evenly cut and shorter than Iverson's.

Once the shock passed and Rio's hair grew long enough to cover his scalp, Wink noticed that people seemed to take Rio more seriously. Without his mane, his large face and prominent mouth became even more dominant. He had the look of a man with grit.

With Cricket on a lead, Wink rode Tootie to the village blacksmith to have the two horses shoed. The blacksmith's shed attracted people whether they waited for ironwork or for some other reason.

If no white person was about, negros were allowed to sit on one of the two iron benches. While Wink sat waiting, Caleb, the negro who helped pole Morgan's ferry, came in to ask about iron stobs. As he departed, Wink followed and caught up with him. "Caleb, is you heard about Thor's foot?"

Caleb had heard. "How's Thor doing?"

"The doctor said it was going to poison him all the way round. Had to come off."

"Might as well be dead as widout a foot."

The way Caleb talked about his son hardly surprised Wink. Though he didn't know the man well, Wink probably knew him better than Thor did. Some fathers weren't worth knowing, which was poor comfort for Wink, who didn't even know who his father was. His mother just cried every time he tried to find out. Mammy Livy said she thought his father was a free mulatto who tried to set up a business in the village building small boats like bateaux and flats. He eventually gave up and moved on.

Notwithstanding the man's character, Wink needed Caleb's help. "Is you ever ferrying goods? Just goods widout a body?"

"No, suh."

Wink knew better. He had once picked up barshears sent from the main by ferry. "Iffen I makes it worth your while ..."

Caleb slowed his pace.

"To bring over bags of oats," Wink said.

Caleb stopped. "You wants me to ferry over oats?"

"Dat's the size of it. And off-load them. Put them by till I fetch them."

"Where these oats coming from?" Caleb's upper lip curved in a thin line over his glistening lower lip.

"A buckra on the main. He be loading the bags on the ferry. Couple of hundred pound bags."

"And who's going to pay the fare?"

"Sure enough, I pay on account." Caleb's look of confusion prompted Wink to say, "I be thinking about a regular run. About ever two weeks. I be willing to forward specie beforehand."

"And you going to pick it up?"

"Yessuh."

"How come you don't git oats from your massuh?" Caleb gave Wink an unmistakable look of suspicion.

"A nigger at Westfall be particular about what his horse eats." Wink did his best to sound honest, dependable.

Caleb stirred impatiently "Why don't you tell me what's going to be in dat sack wid the oats?" He had the look of a man ready to walk.

Wink was out of charm beads. He had nothing to lose. "Hooch."

Caleb's look of wholesale rejection faded. "Hooch? It be a heap easier to git dat from the doctor over on Haigh Creek."

"You talking about the two-head man?" Wink's ears sharpened.

"Three-head iffen you asks me." Caleb turned and walked slowly enough that Wink realized he hadn't ended the conversation.

Wink strolled beside him. "Where he get his from?"

"Makes it hisself. Him and his boys got a stillery down by the creek."

"He put lye in the mash?"

"Naw. He don't take no shortcut."

"Them buckra up at the boarding house adds water."

"Naw. Doc's hooch is quality."

"How you know dat man don't put jinx powder in his hooch?"

"Might do. It be powerful good."

"You buy from him?"

"When I can git a pass to fetch it."

Wink returned to the blacksmith's shed where his horses were ready. On his way back to Westfall, he crossed over to Land's End Road and from there to Haigh Creek. The cooper's shop where the hoodoo doctor worked was a one-room barn-like building with a wide, three batten door, which was propped open. A stack of logs lined one side. New barrels and buckets cluttered the ground. On the walls hung other wooden goods—a rake, hayfork, pestle, an apple butter paddle. A large barrel outside the door held staves soaking in water. The white owner stood at a table and pounded a wood strip with a mallet.

On the pretense of needing a barrel, Wink spoke to the owner. "Yessuh. I needs a barrel, but I can't rightly tell how big."

"For your massuh?" said the owner.

"No, suh. I gots the specie." Wink knew shopkeepers traded with slaves buying for their masters, but it was a different matter if the negro was the buyer.

The owner called over his helper. "Find out what this nigger wants."

Wink assumed this to be the person every slave on the island knew as the conjure doctor. "Where you git them specs?" He had never seen a negro wearing spectacles.

"Come'yuh." He motioned Wink outside. "Warruh'um wantuh?" The man's talk was so heavily African, even Wink had to follow him closely. But the man understood Wink's plain island manner of speaking when he asked about hooch. As it turned out, the doctor stilled mostly for personal use. But he paid attention to Wink's proposal. Wink bought a pint to sample and left. As he returned to Westfall, he drank as much as half the sample with growing excitement.

He didn't tell Puddin that he'd broken the dasher for the churn, so when she complained to the master that she couldn't churn butter, she had no misgivings. Wink whistled as he rode to the cooper's shop to talk business with the man called Doc and, coincidentally, to buy a dasher. As Wink soon found out, Doc's two sons made most of the whiskey, and the one he talked to was plenty interested in selling by the cask. By the time he left, Wink felt like he had just been dealt an ace high flush. It was practically a done deal. He couldn't wait to tell Rio. When the two of them got back into the whiskey line of business, they would have the ammunition to stay there.

The lamps in the big house had been outened. Wink had kept Puddin's ring in his pocket until he could catch her in the kitchen alone. He leaned on the door facing. Only the bristling of the fire interrupted the silence. Puddin covered a wood bowl with a cloth.

"You going to spend the night in the kitchen?" Wink entered the open door, lately left open on warm days.

"Missus wants rice bread for breakfast. Takes the night to rise."

He followed her to the fireplace where she shuffled the embers.

"Why come you not in your cot?" she said, banking the embers in the rear.

"I be thinking about you."

Puddin paused as she added a hickory log to the fire and turned to him. "You sweet talking me?"

"I brought you a present." He fingered the ring in his pocket, a fear arising that she'd refuse him.

She pushed the iron pots out on the hearth, turned to him, and smiled. "You talking about your empty stomach?" At the wall safe she pulled out a crock of cucumber pickles, removed a spear and offered it to him.

He held out the ring. "This here just naturally looks like it belongs on your finger."

Puddin put down the crock. Wink handed her the ring and took the pickle.

"I don't hardly know what to think." She turned it in her hand.

"This here be my marriage present to you."

She offered it back to him. "Give it to somebody else."

Wink shook his head. "Nobody else but you." He refused the ring.

"I'm not marriageable."

"Me neither. We be good together."

"I'm not going to sleep in your cot. I'm not going to be one of Massuh's breeding stock."

"I'se not breeding stock neither." He tried to wrap her in his arms, but she pushed him away.

"Take this ring. I'm not going to have it." She tucked it into his pocket.

"Give me a kiss, then. For olden times ..." Wink tugged on her arm.

She nuzzled his cheek and licked the opening of his mouth, so tempting to Wink that he pulled her into his arms. Her full-bodied kiss confused him. He reared back and looked at her. "Dat's a helluva goodbye kiss."

"I done told you. I'm not no bitch. I'm not going to birth no babies for massuh to sell."

"Then we won't have no chillun."

"What you going to do? Sleep wid the horses?"

"No, baby. As a matter of fact, my cannon done fired up." Wink felt perky. The feel of her skin. Her warm sweaty smell. He could hardly hold himself together. "Let's go to your quarter."

"And what? Play a game of cards?"

Wink's amused chuckle was deep throated. "Poker. And I mean some serious poker."

"And then I gets a baby by you, and you still thinking it's a game."

"No, honey. I don't give no chillun." He sobered up. He was telling her what he had to say.

"What you mean?"

Though he loved Puddin, he hesitated to make clear his situation. He realized he had to trust her to keep his secret. "I don't know why, but I don't get no babies, no matter what."

"Raynell had her baby girl all by herself?"

"Naw. Louisa's pappy was one of the field hands."

Puddin's frank gaze sank into his skin.

"You didn't sire Louisa?"

"It was better if everbody thought Louisa was mine."

She looked down at the bowl of dough, fiddled with the covering cloth. "You still love Raynell?"

"Naaa. She been gone so long I disremember what she looks like."

"You took wid her like a husband all them years, and she didn't come wid your baby?"

Wink shrugged. A sense of shame sneaked up on him. "I'se telling you on account of iffen we be married, you going to have to find a field hand to have chillun."

Puddin smiled. As she kissed his lips, she searched in his pocket, took out the ring and put it on her ring finger. It was too big. Wink put it on her third finger, and it fit reasonably well. She slid her hand back into his pocket and fondled his knobby. His underwear got tight in a hurry. He backed her toward a table, but she turned and led him out the door and to her quarter.

He swept off her head rag and tugged her dress up over her head. She untethered his trousers. At her touch his extremity sprang to such height he became tangled in his underwear. Her sigh spread her breath onto his skin, and when her hands faltered, he put them where they needed to be. "Rub it, baby." A peppery thrill ran from his knobby to his throat and he moaned. They shuffled into her cot, brushing skin on skin. Whatever she touched—his face, back, butt—roared with pleasure. He wanted to give her the pleasure he felt. His lips nuzzled her neck, tugged at her nipples. His hand glided on skin smooth like warm waters. Her briny smell brought thick moisture to his mouth. He could hardly taste enough of her lips, tongue, even her chin and cheeks. Driven slippery and pounded senseless, he forced his breath into her body. He relieved himself of the fear of losing her.

CHAPTER 35

IN THE BIG HOUSE

MARCH–MAY 1858

Mooey sat for hours in the sweet gum tree. It was from this tree she peeled bark and scraped off the resin for a sweet chew. Children overcame their fear of her when she offered them gum to chew. She rested in the joint of a branch and leaned against the trunk. In her pocket were two baby socks she had not looked at yet but her fingers fondled the fabric. She had told herself he might come back. Lacy always did.

The first time Lacy left, Mooey had cried so she imagined she'd never be happy again. But after a time Lacy had returned. She had always returned, and wearing first-rate dresses, pretty as white people's. Mooey imagined Lacy went to a big house where she had servants and ate off of fine plates. Had a feather bed. Real coffee. And more cake than she could eat. Somewhere even finer than Comer's house and with plenty of friendly people. She wanted to see Sunny in a similar place. Perhaps there was a big house with babies and little children and a mammy to love them.

Sunny would come back. And to convince herself, she pictured the man who had disappeared and returned regularly to visit his wife and children. She sorted the many faces in her head for others who came back. But in her heart of hearts, she knew that most people who left never returned.

Sunny had been taken away in a coach that was fancier than anything the master owned. Even the horses wore stamped and tooled leather and silver trim. The white people had dressed in the best clothes—gloves and high boots, hats and silk handkerchiefs. Maybe they had been quality people. Mooey imagined the baby lying in a cradle decorated with painted pictures of lambs frolicking in a field. He had a silk blanket by now. He wore knitted shoes and fitted shirts. His suckling nurse watched him at all times, even when he slept. As soon as he squirmed and made a bad face, she took him to her breast. And she gave him kisses when he smiled and hugs when he cried.

A pinch rippled through her stomach. Inside her hideout were two ashcakes she had stolen while in the quarters. River had left a piece of dried meat in the tow sack. She watched the disappearing sun drain the color out of the trees and fields. It was time to climb down from the hickory nut tree. But she waited. A warm darkness soothed her.

A flicker of light appeared in the distance. She watched it circle in the pasture and disappear. Though she waited, it didn't reappear. Since the night when the stableman returned to bury the butler the second time, hardly anybody came to the graveyard. The cook had brought pieces of crockery she set on the butler's grave. For the most part, Mooey had the place to herself.

A rain softly pelted her skin. The soothing drops became feisty when a wind suddenly arose. Mooey hurried to her hideout. Though she didn't like being awake inside the tomb, she occasionally found herself in such a situation. To ward off boredom, she attempted to use her voice, now that she understood that throats made sounds and ears heard them. With a stone ceiling in such close proximity, her voice bounced back at her. She discovered that she could control the pitch of sounds and make them either high or low. With her fingers she rubbed her throat to make jumpy or smooth sounds, chilly or warm, loving or angry. That there were many different sounds was a realization that tarried with her for days. She felt as if she was on the verge of the biggest discovery of her life, if she could just get her notions put together.

For the second day running, a wagonload of goods had left the big house in the morning and traveled the public road. Later in the day, the empty wagon returned. The master paced about the portico while the negros hauled tables and chairs out of the house to the flatbed wagon. This didn't surprise Mooey, for every year as soon as the nights turned warm, the white people took most of their household goods and left.

Throughout the following day she watched as Ivy and River loaded bedsteads and bureaus on the wagon and left. She watched until she saw the unguarded door. As she slipped inside, an expanse opened up to her, one with a roof to keep out the rain and walls to keep away the animals. She hid under a cot in a closet under the stairs until the men tromped through the house for the last time, leaving behind minor goods, such as rugs, small tables, some chinaware, cots, mirrors, and curtains. It was then that she emerged from her hideout, unlocked the window at the rear porch, unlatched the shutter, and slipped outside.

When the white family disappeared, there were only negros left on the plantation. But even with the big house empty, Early made them stay in their one-room shacks in the quarters. On a previous summer Mooey had sneaked inside the big house before the doors were finally locked and hid overnight. What bothered her more than the smell of white people was the space. The walls had kept her from feeling loose, as if she might spread out too much. She had made a bed in a corner with feather pillows and slept the night. When she hadn't shown up for the count, Early brushed her down with several licks, but it had been worth it.

Mooey plodded back to the graveyard and her hideout for a rest, but under the glow of the midday sun, it turned hot. Dust clogged her throat. She felt her stream of life blood drying up and had to get out.

Without a nap, she trudged through the woods, hunting something, anything, that might serve as a cooler hideout. Some place dry when it rained and safe from bobcats, snakes, wild boars and such. She could remove the boards from inside the hideout and haul them into a tree to make a roof of sorts, but rain was less worrisome than the animals. As the sun went down, she headed back to her hideout.

Upon approaching the gravestones, she was shocked to catch sight of Lacy staring at her. Mooey ran to greet her friend, who caved to her knees. Mooey grabbed her in a rhythmic hug. Tears from Lacy's face smeared into Mooey's. Lacy kissed Mooey's entire head, and the two of them wrestled to the ground with hugs.

Mooey's heart grew so big it choked her throat. In being with Lacy, she realized the loneliness of her life. The flood of smiles and embraces thrilled a part of her that had been asleep. They rolled together in each other's arms and flopped flat-out open armed. When they had rested, Mooey jumped up, motioned Lacy to follow, and climbed her favorite tree.

From the top, they surveyed far afield to the distant settlement that was the plantation. Back on the ground, Lacy darted down the wagon trace to the public road and gazed from one end to the other, as if she needed to see somebody. Mooey didn't like the prospect of meeting a traveler and tugged at her arm to urge her back to the graveyard, but Lacy stayed in the road. Mooey wandered the trace toward her hideout.

When Lacy returned, Mooey wanted to show her the hideout, but Lacy worried about the road, kept her eye on it. Her friend seemed possessed of a strange spirit. Darkness descended and Lacy didn't return to the big house. She paced and began to cry. She dropped to her knees, fell on the ground, and pitched a fit.

Mooey touched her shoulder, but her friend shrugged her off. Mooey climbed a tree to arrange the angles in her mind. Was Lacy scared? Were men looking for her? It became urgent to show her the safety of the hideaway. Mooey came out of the tree and caught up with Lacy, who was making another run to the causeway. She motioned her toward the shelter of the tomb. This aggravated her friend.

Mooey's feet felt a shudder. She desperately urged Lacy back, for who could tell what sort of white man might appear from the dark? But Lacy broke away and headed for the public road. Mooey's sense of danger increased but because she knew of nothing else to do, she took to the woods, hid, and waited.

A lantern light appeared, approached, and became a horse and buggy with two men, one white and one black. Lacy ran to them and made over them like they were long lost friends. While they turned the buggy around and headed it back toward the trace, Lacy paced the ground, waving her arms. Mooey could feel her friend tugging at her, trying to get her to come out of hiding, but because the men arrived in the cover of darkness, Mooey was afraid. The buggy light inched away. Lacy ran after them until they were out of sight.

The ground told of their grinding departure. Stillness returned and Mooey was alone in the graveyard. She was aware of the owl watching her and the woodchuck scampering in the undergrowth. She detected a scent on the wind, hunkered down, motionless, and watched as a possum lumbered along, looking for carrion the buzzards hadn't found.

Despite the mysterious men, Mooey could only guess that Lacy was returning to the place where she had spent so much time. A place where she wore fancy dresses, shiny buttons, and leather shoes. When the blue dress Lacy had worn on arrival the previous summer came to Mooey's mind, her worry turned to envy. What Mooey wouldn't give to have a dress like that.

In the middle of the night, Mooey detected a disturbance in the pasture. Upon sneaking as near as she dared, she saw in the moonlight two hunched figures advancing on a beef. A colony of bats stirred above them like an angry cloud. Before she realized what had happened, the beef dropped to the ground in a sudden slump. The shadowy creatures went from one beef to another as one after another the beefs fell, their enormous sides still and motionless. The colony of bats swirled in convulsive patterns, swooped across the sky to where she crouched, and plummeted so near she fell backwards. Mooey ran to her hideout and closed herself inside and stayed there until the heat withered the air she tried to breathe.

She stayed close to her hideout until the carcasses were removed from the pasture. In their absence, a yellow mist lay in the blades of grass near the ground. Evil spirits. Mooey didn't dare put a foot on such ground. When the air cleared, she slipped back to the woods about the plantation, which was astir with people, dogs, and patrollers.

When the last load of household goods pulled away, everything became quiet except for the quarters. The recent turmoil, not to mention the appearance of mysterious creatures in the pasture, unsettled Mooey, who became desperate to be near the other slaves. She made her way to the window she had unlatched and let herself into the big house.

Such an expanse allowed her powerful breaths of gladness at getting inside. She had the entire mansion to herself, though she discovered she had to watch out for Magic's daughter, who lazed around the back steps. Upstairs she found a room with pillows and colorful quilts and made a bed on the floor. Some nights she slept there, but most of the time she slept in the comfort of the closet cot.

In a wardrobe were hoops and dresses. She wore a different one every day, not that she paraded around the house in them. Because of the carpenters working on the portico, she walked lightly. At first she avoided the front of the house, but after sleeping and resting as much as she wanted, she became bored. Watching the carpenters entertained her, especially River. He carried nails in his mouth and climbed a ladder like a squirrel. He walked and moved with certainty. Seldom smiled. A man of great depth and unknown darkness. He had secrets that frightened Mooey, but she was drawn to him anyway.

When they began to build the roof of the portico, they worked within touching distance of the upstairs windows. One day she was shocked from the curtain when River came to the window and inspected it as if he might try to open it. Mooey flattened herself to the wall and when he left slinked out of the room.

When she wasn't watching River at the front of the house, Mooey could see much of the plantation from the other upstairs windows— the stables and carriage house from the south windows; the kitchen, woodshed, and smokehouse from the east; and from the north, Early's house and behind it and in the distance, the quarters.

Little of interest occurred at the kitchen. The cook had left with the white people, but the quarters stirred with activity. Children ran, skipped, and played about the cabins. When the field hands left at dawn, Mooey watched Auntie trail behind the others. This brought on a sadness. Mooey realized her protector was old and needed somebody to help her. Ivy placed a stool in Auntie's garden plot where she sat and rested while tending her plants. In the time Mooey had survived away from her home and people, she came to treasure Auntie more than ever.

The horses, which spent little time in the stables, romped about the pasture, and Mooey never tired of watching them. A foal was born, and the stableman nursed it with kindness. He rode in and rode out of the yard frequently. When Mooey wandered out of a night, she discovered he didn't always sleep in his quarter.

To scout for food, she left the house before daylight by way of the downstairs window that overlooked the back stoop. From outside, nobody could tell the shutters were unlatched as long as they were closed and as long as the wind didn't blow. Mooey took care that she returned if a breeze threatened to blow open the window's shutters. With foodstuffs like green beans, squash, and potatoes coming up in gardens, she would have plentiful provisions.

It gave her no end of amusement to watch Early approach the doors of the house occasionally to secure the locks. As he twisted the doorknobs, she watched from inside, pleased with her cleverness. She got even more satisfaction knowing that he didn't have a house nearly as fine as hers.

THE END

NOTE FROM THE AUTHOR

Given Mooey's limitations as a deaf mute, I have tried to write her experiences in primarily visual terms. Her memory is visual. Her hopes are pictures. Her fears and loves spring forth as images. All her knowledge is stored as sensory recall related to sight, smell, and taste.

To create her in any way approximating what's logical, I couldn't use the characters' names, since she didn't know them. Instead, her recognition of them is based on her impressions: River for Rio; Lacy for Kedzie; Early-Farley; Ivy-Iverson; Magic-Mamba; Comer-Reverend Chaffee. In some cases, she uses concept names like Mammy and Auntie, stableman (Wink), cook (Puddin), big breasts (Flurry), and Lot Boss (Doll). And thus the alternate spelling of Sonny to Sunny for those chapters in Mooey's point of view.

I hope my description of her inner life will have some validity as fiction even if I haven't entered that uncharted province where people live without verbal language.

ABOUT THE AUTHOR

Bonnie Stanard is a writer of novels, short stories, and poems with credits in numerous publications, such as *The MacGuffin, Harpur Palate, Kestrel, Eclipse,* and *Phi Kappa Phi Forum.* She has edited and/or published periodicals over the last 25 years in locations where she has lived—Brussels, Belgium; Richmond, Virginia; and Lexington County, SC. This is her third antebellum novel and she is working on a fourth. She lives in Columbia, South Carolina with her husband Douglas Stanard.

Made in the USA
Columbia, SC
09 April 2019